DEADLY
LOYALTY
COLLECTION

Other Books by Bill Myers

Forbidden Doors
Dark Power Collection
Invisible Terror Collection
Deadly Loyalty Collection
Ancient Forces Collection

Dark Side of the Supernatural

The Elijah Project
On the Run
The Enemy Closes In
Trapped by Shadows
The Chamber of Lies

FORBIDDEN DOORS

DEADLY LOYALTY
COLLECTION

The Curse

The Undead

The Scream

Written by JAMES RIORDAN

Based on the **FORBIDDEN DOORS** series
created by BILL MYERS

ZONDERVAN®

ZONDERVAN.com/
AUTHOR**TRACKER**
follow your favorite authors

ZONDERVAN

Requests for information should be addressed to:

Zondervan, *Grand Rapids, Michigan 49530*

ISBN 978-0-310-72905-1

Interior design by Christine Orejuela-Winkelman

Printed in the United States of America

12 13 14 15 16 /DCI/ 22 21 20 19 18 17 16 15 14 13 12 11 10 9 8 7 6 5 4 3 2 1

THE CURSE

Therefore I tell you, whatever you ask for in prayer, believe that you have received it, and it will be yours.

MARK 11:24

1

There was an ominous clunk under the Boeing 737. Rebecca Williams stiffened, then glanced nervously at her younger brother, Scott. He sat on her left next to the window. Although he was her "little" brother, he would pass her in height before long. He had a thin frame like Becka's.

"It's just the landing gear coming down," he said, doing his best to sound like a frequent flyer.

Becka nodded. She took a deep breath and tried to release her sweaty grip on the armrests. It didn't work. She didn't like flying. Not at all. Come to think of it, Becka didn't like the whole purpose of this trip.

Who did Z, the mysterious adviser on the Internet, think he was, anyway? What was he doing sending her and her brother off to Louisiana to help some girl caught up in voodoo? Granted, they'd had lots of experience battling the supernatural lately. First, there was the Ouija board incident at the Ascension Bookshop. Becka could never forget how Scott battled that group of satanists! They wanted revenge after Becka exposed Maxwell Hunter, the reincarnation guru. And let's not forget the so-called ghost at Hawthorne mansion, the counterfeit angel, and that last encounter with a phony UFO.

But voodoo in Louisiana? Becka didn't know a thing about voodoo. She barely knew anything about Louisiana.

Fortunately Mom had an aunt who lived in the area, so she'd insisted on coming along with them to visit her. Becka looked forward to seeing her great-aunt once more.

Becka looked to her right, where her mother rested comfortably, her eyes closed. *Poor Mom.* Maybe the trip would do her some good. Ever since Dad died she'd been fretting and working nonstop. This trip just might give her the rest she needed.

Clunk ... clunk ... brang!

Then again ...

It was the same sound, only louder. Becka looked to Scott, hoping for more reassurance. "What's that clunking?" she asked.

Scott shrugged. "I don't know, but it's the *brang* that bothers me."

So much for reassurance.

Suddenly there was an announcement. "Ladies and gentlemen, this is your captain speaking. There seems to be a problem with the landing gear ..."

The collective gasp from the passengers did little to help Becka relax.

"I've called ahead for emergency measures ..."

Becka felt her mother's hand rest on top of hers. She turned to Mom.

"Don't worry," Mom said. "We'll be all right."

Don't worry?! Yeah, right.

The pilot's voice resumed. "The ground crew is going to spray the runway with foam."

"Foam?" Scott exclaimed. "Does he mean like shaving cream?"

"I'll advise you as the situation develops," the pilot continued. "Please try to remain calm."

CLUNK-CLUNK-BRAAANG!

The sound had grown steadily louder.

Becka looked past Scott out the window. They were flying low over New Orleans and dropping fast. As the plane suddenly banked to the left, she saw the airport and immediately wished she hadn't. Several large tankers sprayed foam on the runway. Fire trucks and ambulances were everywhere.

Now it was the head flight attendant's turn for an announcement. "Please make sure your seat belts are fastened securely across your lap. Then bend over as far as you can in the seat, keeping your head down. Hold a pillow to your face with one hand, and wrap your other arm around your knees."

Becka fought the fear down as she glanced at her mother. Mom had her eyes shut. Becka wondered if she was praying. Not a bad idea.

CLUNK-CLUNK-BRAAANG!

Another attendant hurried through the aisle, passing out pillows. She tried to appear calm but failed miserably.

The plane banked back to the right. Becka laid her face down on the pillow in her lap and gave her seat belt another tug.

The speakers buzzed once more with the pilot's voice. "Ladies and gentlemen, we are about to land on the foam … Please hold on."

CLUNK-CLUNK-BRAAANG!

"Don't be alarmed," he said. "That's just the landing gear … I'll keep trying it as we come in."

Becka remained hunched over with her face on the pillow. She could feel the plane dropping, and still the landing gear was not coming down. They were going to land with no wheels!

CLUNK-CLUNK-BRAAANG!
CLUNK-CLUNK-BRAAANG!

She glanced at Scott, who stared back at her from his pillow.

He tried to force an encouraging grin, but there was no missing the look of concern on his face.

She turned to look at Mom. Her eyes were still closed. Becka hoped that she continued to pray.

CLUNK-CLUNK-BRAAANG!

CLUNK-CLUNK-BRAAANG!

Becka's thoughts shot to Ryan Riordan, her boyfriend back home. If she died, how would he handle the news? And what about her friends—Julie, Krissi, and Philip? How would they handle it? She also thought of Dad—of perhaps seeing him soon. Too soon. It was this final thought that jolted her back to the present and caused her to pray. It wasn't that she didn't want to see Dad again. She just had a few more things to do first.

CLUNK-CLUNK-BRAAANG!

CLUNK-CLUNK-BRAAANG!!

CLUNK-CLUNK-CLUNK-DAARRRRREEEEEEEE...

Something was different!

The plane veered sharply upward. Becka couldn't resist the temptation to sit up and glance out the window.

The pilot spoke once more. "Ladies and gentlemen, the landing gear has engaged. We are out of danger. I repeat. We are out of danger. We will land on a different runway in just a few moments."

"Thank you, Lord," Mom whispered. She sounded relieved as she sat up, then reached over and hugged both of her children. "Thank you ..."

Becka breathed a sigh of relief as she joined the applause of the other passengers. They were safe. At least for now. But all the same, she couldn't help wondering if this was some sort of omen—a warning of the dangers that were about to begin.

❧ ❧

The three o'clock bell at Sorrento High rang. Swarms of kids poured out of the old, weathered building. One fifteen-year-old girl slowed her pace as she headed for the bus. No one talked to her. Her clothes were more ragged than most. They were too shabby to be fashionable and too conservative to be alternative.

Sara Thomas had never fit in. She had never felt like she belonged, no matter where she was. As she approached the school bus and stepped inside, she steeled herself, waiting for the taunts.

None came. Just the usual after-school chatter.

Carefully she took a seat, stealing a glance to the rear of the bus. Ronnie Fitzgerald and John Noey were engrossed in a tattoo magazine.

Maybe they'd forget about her today.

With a swoosh and a thud, the door closed. The bus jerked forward.

Maybe today would be different.

Then again, maybe not. They had traveled less than a mile when it began ...

"Hey, Rags, you shopping at Goodwill or the Salvation Army these days?"

Sara recognized Ronnie's shrill, nasal voice.

"Hey! I'm talking to you."

She didn't turn around.

"I heard Goodwill's got a special on those cruddy, stained sweaters you like so much," John Noey said snidely.

Before she could catch herself, Sara glanced down at the brown chocolate stain on her yellow sweater.

The boys roared.

"Is that from a candy bar or did your dog do a number on it?" Ronnie shouted.

Most of the others on the bus smirked and snickered. A few laughed out loud.

Sara stared out the window as the taunts continued. As always, she tried to block out the voices. And, as always, she failed. But not for long.

Soon, she thought. *Soon they'll pay. They'll both pay.*

She reached into her purse and clutched the tiny cloth-and-straw doll. Already she was thinking about her revenge.

And already she was starting to smile.

◈ ◈

Aunt Myrna's farmhouse was simple but clean. The furniture inside was made mostly of dark wood. The chairs looked like they'd been there a hundred years ... and could easily last another hundred.

After Becka dropped her bags off in the small attic room that she would be using, she headed down to the kitchen, grabbed an apple out of the fruit basket, and strolled out to the front porch. As the screen door slammed, she vaguely heard Aunt Myrna telling Mom something about a farmhand named John Garrett who was supposed to drop by.

It was hot and humid, which reminded her of her childhood days in South America. Several months had passed since Dad's death and their move from Brazil back to California. But the humidity and the smells of the rich vegetation here in Louisiana sent her mind drifting back to the Brazilian rain forests.

Unlike California, everything in Louisiana was lush and wild. Plant life seemed to explode all around. And the water. There was water everywhere—lakes, ponds, and marshes. Although most of the area around the bayou was swamp, even the dry land never really felt dry. Still, it was beautiful.

Even surrounded by beauty, Becka felt nervous. Very nervous. Z had given them so little information. Just that a young girl named Sara Thomas lived in the area and that she was in serious trouble—caught up in some kind of voodoo. Z had also stressed that Becka and Scott were not to be afraid.

"Your training is complete," he had said. "Go in his authority."

His authority. God's authority. Becka had certainly seen God work in the past. There was no denying that. But even now as she looked around, she felt a strange sense of—what? Apprehension? Uncertainty?

During the other adventures, she had always been on her home turf. But being in a strange place, helping somebody she didn't even know … it all made her nervous. Very nervous.

The late afternoon sun shimmered on the vast sea of sugarcane before her as she sat on the steps. Wind quietly rippled through the cane, making the stalks appear like great scarecrows with arms beckoning her to come closer. Closer. Closer …

Something grabbed her hand.

Becka let out a gasp and turned to see a small goat eight inches from her face. It gobbled the last of her apple.

"Aunt Myrna!" she shrieked. "There's an animal loose out here!"

"He won't bother you none."

Becka turned, startled at hearing a voice come from the field of sugarcane. She tried to locate the source of the voice while keeping one eye on the goat in case he decided to go for a finger or two.

A young African-American man suddenly walked out of the field. Becka guessed that he was about seventeen. He was tall, lean, and handsome, in a rugged sort of way.

He nodded to the goat. "That's Lukey. He's more pet than farm animal." He entered the yard and stuffed his hands into his pockets. "Try scratching his nose. He likes that."

"Oh, that's okay," Rebecca said quickly. "I'd rather not just now." Then, rising to her feet, she said, "You must be John Garrett. Aunt Myrna said you'd be coming."

The young man nodded. "Miss Myrna said I should be showing you and your brother around the place some."

"So let's get started," Scott said, appearing suddenly in the doorway. "Wow. Cool goat. C'mere, boy." He crossed to the animal. It rubbed its head against his arm. "Hey!" Scott looked up with a broad smile. "He likes me!"

"He likes everybody," John Garrett said, already turning back toward the field. "We better get started if we're going. The foreman's called a meeting of us farmhands. It should be starting pretty soon."

Scott went to walk beside John. Becka fell in behind.

In seconds the two boys were hitting it off. Becka could only marvel. Her brother got along with everybody. In fact, when they'd moved to California, he fit in like he'd always been there. Unfortunately, it wasn't so easy for Becka to make friends. She figured that was partly why she felt so uncomfortable about this trip. She didn't like the idea of barging into a total stranger's life, even if they were supposed to help her.

But that was only part of the reason. There was something else: a feeling. It felt eerie ... like something she couldn't quite explain but couldn't shake off.

"John," she called, trying to sound casual, "do you know anything about voodoo?"

He glanced back at her and laughed. "Not much. 'Cept my grandpa used to speak Gumbo all the time."

"Gumbo?" she asked.

"It's kind of a mesh of African dialects. A lot of the people into voodoo speak it. But you really got to be careful who you talk to about voodoo around these parts."

"Why's that?" Scott asked.

"Lots of folks believe in it, and if you upset them, they'd just as soon drop a curse on you as look at you."

Becka felt a tiny shiver run across her back. "A curse? Does stuff like that really happen?"

"Oh yeah. I heard about this woman who lived down the road from my father. She made an old *mambo* mad, and the mambo put a curse on her."

"Mambo?" Scott echoed with a snort. "Sounds like some kind of dance step."

John shot him a knowing look. "They're like high priestesses. And they're nothing to mess with."

"So what happened to this woman?" Scott asked.

"I heard she suddenly died in horrible pain."

"That's awful!" Becka shuddered. "Did you ever see her?"

John shook his head. "My father's cousin said he did, though. Not only that, I also heard about an old man who refused to pay the *hungan* for helping him get back his wife." At Scott's raised eyebrows John explained. "A hungan is like the male version of a mambo—the high priest. The man who wouldn't pay carried a powerful root with him at all times so the hungan couldn't work magic on him while he was alive. The root was like a good-luck charm. But when he died and they took him to the morgue, his body started shaking all over the place. And when they cut him open, they found he was full of scorpions!"

"Come on—scorpions?" Scott scoffed.

But Becka was not scoffing. In fact she felt more uneasy by the moment. "How about him?" she asked. "Did you see him?"

John shook his head again. "No, that happened before I was born. I know it sounds crazy, but some of this curse stuff might be true."

Scott shook his head, his face filled with skepticism. "I don't know. Sounds pretty fantastic to me. Like something out of a bad horror movie."

"Maybe so," John continued. "But one thing I do know, and that's to never cross Big Sweet. I've heard his magic's powerful."

"Who's Big Sweet?" Scott asked.

"You don't know who Big Sweet is? He's Miss Myrna's foreman. He's head of the harvest crew. Been picking sugarcane all his life. That's why they call him Big Sweet."

"Why's he so dangerous?" Becka asked.

"He's the local hungan. People say his father was a disciple of Marie Leveau. She's called the Queen of Conjure. She was a powerful mambo who used to live in the French Quarter of New Orleans."

"And you're afraid of him?" Becka asked.

"Everybody's afraid of Big Sweet." John turned back to Becka. There was something about his look that caused a cold knot to form deep in her stomach. "Everybody's afraid ... and you'd better be too."

Suddenly a horn bellowed across the fields. John spun toward the sound, looking startled.

"What's that?" Scott asked.

The other boy started moving away from them toward the sound. Becka and Scott exchanged concerned glances. John was clearly very nervous. "That's Big Sweet's horn," he said. "It's his conch shell. The meeting's starting. I gotta go."

"What about showing us the farm?" Scott called as John moved away.

"I can take you into the swamp tomorrow after chores. But I gotta go now."

"Yeah, but—"

"Look, I can't be late. I gotta go." With that he disappeared into the cane.

"John!" Scott called. "Hey, John! Hold on a minute!"

But there was no answer.

Scott turned to Becka. She knew her expression held the same concern she saw in her brother's face. The horn continued to bellow. Finally Becka cleared her throat. "I ... uh ... I guess we'd better head back."

"Yeah. I can't wait to get the lowdown on all this stuff from Z tonight. I'll bet he knows about this Big Sweet guy."

"And Sara Thomas," Becka reminded him.

"Right," Scott said. "But the more we learn about Big Sweet, the faster we'll be able to blow him away."

"Blow him away?" Becka felt herself growing impatient with

her brother. "Come on, Scotty. You sound like a cheesy action movie."

"That's me!" Scott threw a few mock karate kicks. "Scott Williams, Demon Terminator."

"Scott, this isn't a joke."

"What's the matter? Afraid Big Sweet may slap a curse on you?"

"Stop it!"

"Afraid he might hatch a lizard in your ear or give you a monkey face? Hmmm, looks like somebody's already done that."

"Scotty!"

"Come on, Beck—lighten up!" Then, looking across the field, his face lit up with an idea. "Let's save ourselves a little time and take a shortcut through the cane."

Becka began to protest, but her brother had already started out. And there was one thing about Scott—when he made up his mind to do something, there was no stopping him. With a heavy sigh, she followed.

The stalks of cane towered over their heads. Becka knew that Scott was right about one thing. By taking this shortcut they'd get back to the house a lot faster. And with all the uneasiness she had been feeling out there, especially now that they were alone ... well, the sooner they got home, the better.

Unfortunately, "sooner" was way too long, now that Scott was in his teasing mode. He kept jumping around and darting between the stalks of cane like some ghoul.

Brothers. What a pain, Becka thought.

"Oogity-boogity! Me Big Sweet. Me cast a big curse on you."

"Knock it off!" Becka muttered between clenched teeth. She was going to smack him if he kept it up.

"Big Sweet turn you into little mouse if you're not careful."

"Scott, you know you're not supposed to joke around with—"

"Oogity-boogity!" He leaped even higher into the air.

"Scotty ..."

"Oogity-boogity! Oogity-boog—OW!"

Suddenly he crumpled to the ground.

Becka's heart pounded as she raced to his side. "What happened? Are you okay?"

"I twisted my ankle!" he whined. "Owwww!"

Becka knew it served him right. But since he was clearly in pain, now was not the time to bring it up. Instead, she reached out and carefully touched his ankle.

"Ouch!" he yelped. "That hurts!"

"Sorry. Here ..." She tried to help him to his feet. "Lean against me and see if you can—"

"Oww!" he cried even louder. "I can't. It hurts too much. You'll have to get somebody to—"

Suddenly there was a low, distant growl. It sounded part animal and part ... well, Becka couldn't tell. It was mixed with another sound—a silent, whooshing noise.

"What's that?" Scott said, his eyes wide and suddenly alarmed.

Becka wished she had a good answer. She didn't. "I—I don't know." She rose to her feet and searched the field. "I can't see anything but sugarcane."

The sound grew louder. Becka felt her pulse kick into high gear. Whatever it was, it was moving. And by the sound of things, it was moving toward them.

Once again, Scott tried to stand, but it was no use. As soon as he put any weight on his ankle, it gave out. He toppled back to the ground.

The noise grew closer.

"Becka ..." There was no missing the fear in her brother's voice.

Becka reached for him, fighting off the fear that swept over her. She had no idea what was coming at them, but she knew lying down, unable to move, was no way for her brother to meet it. She tried pulling him forward, but he was too heavy.

The cane several yards in front of them suddenly splintered.

"Becka!"

All at once something exploded through the stalks. It was big and red.

It headed directly for them.

"What is it?!" Scott cried.

"I don't know!"

"Becka!"

She reached under his arms, trying to pull him to the side, to get him out of the way.

And still the thing bore down on them, ripping cane just a few yards in front of them and devouring it with giant, red jaws.

"Run!" Scott shouted at her. "Get out of here!"

The afternoon sun caught a sharp, shiny blade coming directly toward them, slicing through cane only a few feet away.

"Get out of here!" Scott yelled at her.

She pulled harder, but it was no use.

"Beck—"

She finally looked up. The giant blade hovered over her and was coming down fast. She screamed and gave one last tug, moving her brother only a foot before tumbling backward. The blade came down.

"Your leg!" Becka screamed. "Your—"

Scott tucked and rolled just as the blade chomped down, missing his flesh by inches.

The threshing machine roared past them, leaving a great swath of cut sugarcane in its path.

Becka couldn't see the driver, but as the machine passed, she could read a name crudely painted on the back. It was in big black letters. Originally, it had read *BIG SWEET'S CANE KILLER*. But over the years dirt and grime had covered some of the letters. Now it read *BIG SWEET CAN KILL*.

2

Sara sat in front of the cracked dresser mirror. Carefully she outlined her lips with dark lip liner before applying a deep burgundy lipstick. So far, she could have been any teenage girl applying any makeup.

So far.

Next she picked up a medium-sized paintbrush, dipped it in blood red paint, and drew a streak across her left cheek. She did the same with the right.

Then came the blue. Jagged lines, like small lightning bolts, painted above each eye.

And finally the green. This time she covered her entire chin and the lower part of her neck. At last Sara put down the brush and admired her handiwork. She was very pleased.

👁 👁

An hour after their encounter with the threshing machine, Scott sat in his great-aunt's best easy chair with his ankle packed in ice. He quietly watched a baseball game on television and poked at some potato chips on his plate.

Becka sat nearby thinking how strange it was for her brother to be so silent. Normally he'd be milking his injury for all it was worth, getting people to wait on him hand and foot. But he'd hardly said a word.

Even Mom noticed. When Becka entered the kitchen to get a refill on her lemonade, Mom said, "Why don't you talk to your brother? He seems so blue."

"What am I supposed to say?"

"It's not so much what you say," Mom replied. "It's your attitude. Just be there for him. You're a team now. If one of you is down, the other should try to help him up."

Becka shrugged, poured her lemonade, and strolled back into the living room. "So," she said, trying to sound casual, "it's almost nine. Think we should give Z a try?"

Scott glanced at his watch. "Yeah, I guess."

"Scotty?" She plopped down on the footrest directly between him and the TV. "What's wrong?"

"Hey, you're blocking my view. Move."

"Not until you tell me what's eating you."

"Becka ..."

"Talk to me."

"Beck."

"I mean it."

He let out a sigh of exasperation.

"Is it the threshing machine with Big Sweet's name on it?"

He shook his head and glanced away. "That's only part of it." She continued to wait. After a moment, he continued. "I'm scared, Beck. This time I'm really nervous."

Becka bit her lip. It was one thing for her to be nervous. But Scott? As far as she knew, her little brother wasn't afraid of anything. Normally his faith in God gave him confidence. She'd never seen him look this discouraged.

"First, our plane almost crashes. *Then,* my ankle gets twisted. *Then,* we nearly get turned into hamburger by some crazed farm machinery. All this and we haven't even talked to the girl yet."

Becka swallowed and tried to keep her voice even. "So, you think they're all related?"

"Don't you?"

Becka slowly answered, "I think someone or something doesn't want us here—that's for sure. And I think whatever it is, is very powerful."

Scott nodded in silent agreement.

For a long moment, neither said a word. Finally, Scott reached for the laptop he'd borrowed from a friend and turned it on. Now it was just a matter of logging on and hoping to see Z in the chat window, ready to tell them more.

Neither of them knew who Z was or why he had taken such an interest in them. They didn't understand how he could know so many little things about their lives—personal things that no one else would know. Then there was his knowledge about the occult. On more than one occasion he had gotten them out of trouble with knowledge only some kind of expert would have.

Of course they'd tried to track Z down to find out who he was. But each time they tried, Z foiled their attempts somehow. Whoever this Z was, he was very clever—and very, very secretive.

"Cool," Scott said as he stared at the screen. "Z's online, waiting for us."

Becka moved in closer to look.

Good evening, Scott, Rebecca. Sorry about the scare on the airplane.

Becka fought off a shudder. It was just that type of knowledge that unnerved her about Z.

Scott was already typing his comeback:

How did you know about the plane?

Z didn't answer his question. But that was no big surprise.

He never explained how he knew what he knew. Instead, his next message popped up on the screen.

> Before you contact Sara Thomas, you should be aware of the facts on voodoo.

Scott and Becka threw each other a glance. It was typical of Z to get right to the heart of the matter.

> Like many superstitions, much of voodoo's power comes from the belief people have about it. Often too much credit is given to it. It is blamed for every bad thing that happens.

Scott typed back:

Are you telling us it's all just superstition?

Z's response came quickly:

> Not always. In many cases demonic activity can feed off the fear and superstition voodoo engenders. Regardless, it is important to remember that as Christians, the only power voodoo—or any evil—holds over you is the power you give it because of your fear. Do not forget this.

Becka stared at the screen as Scott began typing another question:

Where did voodoo come from?

> Voodoo is a combination of West African traditions and rituals from Catholic missionaries. The term comes from the West African word *vodun* and the creole French word *vaudau*, both of which mean "spirit." Ceremonies consist of singing, drumming, and praying to the dead, whom they call the *loa*.

Becka leaned over her brother. "Ask about Sara. Where is she? How do we find her?"

But before Scott could type the words, Z answered the question:

Sara Thomas works at the Sorrento library on Saturdays. Contact her there. It is a twenty-minute bus ride from your great-aunt's house. Remember, people usually become part of voodoo to try to get control of their life. They use black magic and curses to seek protection from the supernatural or to get power over others. They are usually more deluded than evil. But that doesn't mean they aren't dangerous. Be careful. Good night.

Scott immediately began typing:

Wait. Don't go yet. We need to know more.

At first they thought he'd logged off. But after a moment, the final comment appeared:

I must go. You've been trained. You have the Word, and you have your Lord. The only power voodoo has over you is the power you give it through your fear. Your tools are prayer and faith. If you remember these, you will be victorious. Should trouble arise, seek help from the local pastor. Good-bye.

Z

"Good-bye?!" Scott turned to his sister in panic. "What does he mean 'good-bye'?"

"I guess—" Becka took a deep breath. "I guess he means we're on our own."

Scott spun back to the computer. "No way! Not this time! Not here!"

Z . . . Z, are you there? Z, answer me . . .

The two waited silently for an answer. But there was none. Z had logged off.

"Great!" Scott said. "Just great! He sends us all the way out here, then just leaves us on our own!" He closed the laptop angrily.

Becka ventured a thought. "If Z says we can do it, then maybe—"

"We can't do this!" Scott interrupted. "Not on our own! You know what we've been through. We haven't even met this ... this Sara chick. We're going to need some help. Lots of it."

Becka agreed. "He said if we get into trouble we should contact a local pastor."

"A local pastor?" Scott repeated. "What local pastor? We're out here in the middle of Hicksville! What would any pastor out here know?"

"Excuse me?" It was Aunt Myrna poking her head in from the kitchen. "Did you kids say you were looking for a pastor?"

Scott and Becka exchanged glances.

"I go to the church over in Sorrento. Maybe you'd like to meet my pastor? Our church is the little one right next to a park."

"Uh, yeah, well ... thanks, Aunt Myrna," Scott said, doing his best to sound polite. "We'll sure give that some thought."

"That would be nice. I'm sure Pastor Barchett would be able to help you," she said with a smile as she disappeared back into the kitchen.

"Sorrento?" Becka repeated. "Did she say 'Sorrento'?"

"Yeah ..."

"Isn't that where Z—"

Scott finished the sentence, "—said Sara was working."

The two traded nervous looks. Was it just coincidence, or had the mysterious Z given them more information than they'd thought?

"We'll try again tomorrow night," Scott ventured. "Maybe he'll be back online."

Becka nodded, but she had her doubts. Even now she suspected this encounter was going to be different from the others. Different and far more dangerous.

❧ ❧

In the darkness, the drums pounded.

Doomba-doomba-doom. Doomba-doomba-doom.

Sara pushed her way through the branches toward the sound. For the hundredth time she wondered if she should go back home. She had a nagging feeling that this was wrong. Very wrong. But each time she thought of turning back, she remembered Ronnie Fitzgerald and John Noey. Their voices, their merciless taunts. No. It had been going on too long. It was time to stop it.

Now.

Doomba-doomba-doom. Doomba-doomba-doom.

The drums grew louder. She was getting closer.

Sara had been to voodoo ceremonies before, but only the public ones—never the secret rites. These secret ceremonies were held in secluded places and known only to members of the cult ... and to those about to be initiated.

That last phrase stuck in her mind. *Those about to be initiated.* Sara felt her heart beating harder, almost in rhythm with the drums.

Doomba-doomba-doom. Doomba-doomba-doom.

Through the leaves, she could see the glimmer of a fire. She had found them. They had not given her directions—just simply told her to follow the sound of the drums.

Doomba-doomba-doom. Doomba-doomba-doom.

She forced herself to go forward, her legs weak and trembling with fear. She knew the stories. She knew what voodoo could do to you. But she also knew what it could do *for* you. How it could protect you from the others, from the Ronnie Fitzgeralds and John Noeys of the world.

She continued through the brush.

Now she was close enough to see the people dancing about the fire. Some moved in perfect rhythm to the drums. Others darted about, convulsing and writhing like wild animals.

She reached the edge of the clearing. This was her last chance to turn back.

She took a deep, unsteady breath, clutched the small cloth doll hanging around her neck, and entered the clearing.

👁 👁

"Scott. Scotty, wake up!"

It was his sister's voice, but it sounded like it was coming from a long, long way away.

"Scotty, you're dreaming! Scotty, wake up!"

Suddenly he bolted upright. It took a moment to get his bearings, to realize he'd fallen asleep in the hammock on the porch.

"You okay?" Becka asked. "It sounded like you were having a nightmare."

Scott frowned, trying hard to remember. "Yeah ... I don't ... I think I heard screaming. In my dream, someone or something was screaming and—"

Doomba-doomba-doom.

He froze. "What's that?"

Doomba-doomba-doom. Doomba-doomba-doom.

The screen door creaked loudly. Aunt Myrna stepped onto the porch carrying two glasses of lemonade. "You kids want a cold drink?"

"Aunt Myrna, what's that noise?" Scott asked.

She paused to listen. "Oh," she said, handing out the glasses. "It's them."

"Them?" Becka asked.

"Yes. Big Sweet and his group. They have a voodoo ceremony most every night this time of year." She gave a gesture of distaste. "You'll get used to the drums after a while."

Scott and Becka exchanged glances, both knowing that they would never get used to it.

"Oh, Rebecca?" Aunt Myrna stood at the door, ready to go in. "Did Lukey—you know, my goat—did he follow you out into the cane fields today?"

"No, I don't think so," Becka answered. "Why?"

"Oh, no reason," Aunt Myrna said, running her hands through her hair. It was long and gray and beautiful. "It's just … well, I guess he's run off again. Can't seem to find him anywhere. Well—" she forced a smile and headed back into the house—"I'm sure he'll turn up."

The door slammed shut behind her, but Scott barely noticed. He was feeling very sick.

"Scotty, what's wrong?" Becka asked. "Are you okay?"

He nodded. When he spoke, his voice was strangely hoarse. "The screaming … in my dream …"

"Yeah …"

The drums grew louder now.

Doomba-doomba-doom. Doomba-doomba-doom.

"What about it?" Rebecca asked.

"It definitely wasn't a person or anything like that. I remember now. It was an animal."

"An animal?"

Scott nodded. "And it wasn't screaming—it was bleating … 'cause it was being slaughtered."

"Bleating?" Becka repeated.

"Yeah, you know … like a goat."

The great conch horn sounded, sending its haunting echo throughout the woods.

3

The morning air was so fresh and beautiful that Becka almost forgot their purpose, let alone the danger that surrounded them.

Almost.

The weather forecast promised that rain would move in later that day, but for now everything smelled warm and moist and full of life. Becka especially loved the flowers. They were her passion, her weakness. They always had been. And as she and Scott headed down Aunt Myrna's long driveway to the main road, a gentle breeze stirred and brought half a dozen different fragrances to her.

Scott's ankle was much better. He limped only slightly as they approached the mailbox and began the wait for the bus to Sorrento.

Unfortunately, when the old, broken-down vehicle finally appeared, it belched out more smoke than Mom had created the last time she tried to barbecue. The metal beast screeched to a halt before them. As they boarded and headed to the back, any fragrance of flowers was blotted out by the smell of diesel oil and exhaust fumes.

The gears ground loudly as the bus lumbered down the road. Soon they passed a large potato field, then a group of run-down shacks. Dirty-faced children in ragged clothes ran all around the yards.

"Look how they're dressed," Becka said sadly.

Scott nodded. "And check out their shoes."

Becka looked. "They don't have any."

"Exactly."

Becka nodded. "I read that voodoo is most widespread among the poor. Like Z said, it's a way for them to try to gain some control over their lives."

Scott grunted. "Doesn't look like it's working too well."

Becka watched a young mother rushing to pick up a dirt-smeared child who had fallen near the ditch. The little one didn't appear hurt, but the mother carefully soothed and cuddled him, tenderly holding him in her arms. Becka sighed, touched by the love the mother had for her child, yet sad at the same time. "It's terrible what happens to people who don't have a lot of hope."

Scott nodded.

Suddenly there was a loud explosion.

"What was that?!" Becka cried.

"A blown tire," Scott guessed. He grabbed the seat in front of him and held on.

Had the bus been a newer model, it might have held on to the road. Being old and decrepit, the bus went into a tailspin. The back end—where Becka and Scott sat—skidded toward the oncoming traffic.

The two looked out of their window just as the bus hurtled toward a tractor. The tractor driver turned hard. But the bus kept going at it, brakes screeching as the tires smoldered from the friction with the road.

At last they skidded to a stop only a few feet from the tractor. But the trouble wasn't over yet. The bus started tipping. Becka let out a scream, certain they were going over. Suddenly it stopped and righted itself with a mighty thud.

"Sorry 'bout that folks!" the driver called back. "Everyone okay?"

Other than arriving in Sorrento an hour and a half late (it took the bus driver that long to find his tools and fix the tire), Becka and Scott were fine. Well, not exactly fine. Narrowly escaping a plane crash, nearly being chopped by a thresher, and now surviving a bus accident — all within the first twenty-four hours of their arrival — had taken its toll.

"That does it!" Scott said as he stormed off the bus and over to a small park. "I'm not going anywhere the rest of the time we're here!"

"Scotty."

"Say what you want, Beck! Something's after us. Somebody's definitely put some sort of curse on us!"

Becka took a moment to quiet her own fears, then tried to explain. "Remember what Z said? Even if it is a curse, even if it is real, the only power it has over us is fear. We have to trust that God — "

But Scott was in no mood to listen to reason. "I think we should turn right around and go back to California."

She knew he had a point. Something *was* definitely going on. If whoever — or *whatever* — it was wanted to scare them, it was doing a pretty good job. Still, Z had never been wrong before.

She looked up to see Scott heading across the road. "Hey!" she called. "Where are you going?"

Scott pointed to the large building directly in front of them. "Z said this Sara chick worked at the library, right?" He motioned ahead of him. "Well, there's the library."

Becka crossed the road and joined him. "Listen," she said as they headed up the steps, "better let me do the talking." It wasn't that she wanted to be the one who spoke to Sara. Far from it. She just knew from experience that Scott was in no mood to be overly sensitive — which meant he'd probably offend everyone in his path.

They opened the library door and stepped in. Becka led the way to the circulation desk, where an older woman checked out books. "Excuse me," Becka said, "we're looking for Sara Thomas. Is she here?"

The older woman smiled and nodded toward two young girls who were shelving books.

One girl looked fairly normal. The other one had wild hair with purple highlights. She wore a black leather jacket with small chains attached to the pockets.

Becka took a deep breath. "Well, here goes."

They walked across the room straight to the purple-haired girl.

"Can I help you?" the girl asked.

"Uh, yes," Rebecca began. "This is probably going to sound a little crazy to you, but a friend of ours on the Internet, whose name is Z, asked us to visit you to . . . to try to help you through some sort of voodoo thing."

The girl made a face. "Some sort of what?"

Becka tried again. "Your voodoo thing. We have some experience with the occult and . . ."

"Voodoo?" The girl looked at Becka like she had a screw loose. "My *voodoo thing?* What are you, some kind of wacko? I don't have any voodoo thing."

"But aren't you . . . aren't you Sara Thomas?"

The girl snorted and shook her head. "No. My name is Stacy. This is Sara Thomas."

With great embarrassment, Becka turned to face the other girl — the "normal"-looking one — who now glared at her.

"Nice job, sis," Scott muttered quietly.

"I'm sorry," Becka stuttered. "I . . . I didn't mean . . ."

The purple-haired girl nodded and went back to shelving books.

Becka turned to Sara. "Hello." She smiled self-consciously. "You're Sara?"

Sara Thomas nodded. "Yes." Her voice was cold. "And you are?"

"I'm Rebecca Williams. This is my brother, Scott. We're here from California to —"

"Yes, I heard," Sara cut her off. "You're here to help me deal with my 'voodoo thing.'"

Becka tried to snicker, hoping that Sara would join in and they could laugh off the whole silly thing. But Sara wasn't laughing. She wasn't even smiling. Becka was forced to continue. "Yes, I'm sorry about that ... I, uh —"

"Listen," Sara cut her off again. "I don't know you. I don't even have a computer, so I certainly don't know anyone named Z. And what's more, I don't need your help. I don't *want* your help. And I think you'd better go now." That said, Sara turned her attention to her books.

Becka stood for a long moment staring at Sara's back, trying to think of something to say. Finally she cleared her throat. "Look, I'm very sorry. I didn't mean any harm."

Without turning to her, Sara said, "Would you just go, please?"

"Listen." Scott stepped forward. The tone of his voice was not happy. "We didn't come all the way to Louisiana just to —"

"Never mind," Becka interrupted quickly. "We've, uh, we've bothered her long enough. We should go."

"Yeah, but —"

"Let's go." She took Scott's arm and started turning him toward the door. It was only then that she caught sight of something that sent a chill through her. She hadn't noticed it before, but Sara was now fingering something hanging on a chain around her neck. A small cloth doll.

A doll that looked very similar to the ones the witch doctors used in Brazil.

❧ ❧

They were halfway down the library steps when Scott let out an exasperated sigh. "So tell me, could we have messed that up any worse?"

"We just got off on the wrong foot," Becka answered. "That's all."

"Well, she doesn't want our help. I think she made that pretty clear."

Becka nodded and was about to speak when something else caught her eye. Across the road was the small park beside which was a small church. "Isn't that the church Aunt Myrna was talking about?"

Scott followed her gaze and shrugged. "I guess. She said it was next to a park."

Becka nodded and started for it.

"Becka . . ."

"Come on. We've got an hour before the bus leaves."

A reluctant Scott followed. Although he limped a bit more, he joined his sister anyway.

They knocked on the door of the church. The pastor was not there. Instead, an elderly lady answered and directed them to the parsonage next door.

They crossed to a small house. Becka noticed that part of the porch stairs had rotted. It had also been a long time since the building had seen a paintbrush. She knocked on the door, but there was no answer. She tried again with the same result. Then one final time.

There was no answer.

As they started back down the steps, the door suddenly opened. A small, frail, elderly man appeared. "May I help you?"

"Oh—" Becka turned. "We thought no one was home."

The older man smiled. "I'm home, but I'm slow. It takes me a while to get to the door."

"We're looking for Pastor Barchett," Scott said.

The older man nodded. "That's me."

"My name is Rebecca Williams. This is my brother, Scott. We're here visiting Myrna Carmen. She's my mother's aunt."

Pastor Barchett looked confused. "Who?"

Scott shot a glance at Becka as if to say, "Here we go again."

"Myrna Carmen," Becka repeated. "She attends your church."

"She's been a member here for like a zillion years," Scott added.

"Oh … Myrna." The pastor broke into a grin. "My goodness, yes. So you're Myrna's … what did you say?"

"Great-niece and nephew," Becka said.

"Ah yes, of course."

"Anyway, we wondered if we could have a few moments of your time."

Pastor Barchett stepped back from the door and graciously waved them in. "Of course, of course."

Inside, the house was small and well kept … except for a cat box that needed to be changed.

Pretending not to notice the odor, Becka said, "What a nice house you have."

"One of the ladies from the church comes in every few days and cleans it," the pastor said as he closed the door. "All I have to do is pick up after myself and …" He trailed off, forgetting what the other thing was until he noticed Scott's upturned nose. "And change the cat litter, that's it! Sorry about the smell. I forget because the old nose ain't what she used to be. Would you two like some tea?"

Scott shook his head to Becka. She took the cue. "No thanks."

Pastor Barchett motioned for them to sit on the sofa. He took a seat across from them. "So … how can I help you?"

Becka leaned forward. "Pastor, do you know much about voodoo?"

"I should hope so." The old man's eyes sparkled with a bit of life. "With a church in the heart of Ascension Parish here on the bayou, I'd better know a thing or two."

Becka's eyes widened. "Did you say Ascension Parish?"

"Why, yes." The old man nodded. "You know Louisiana is divided into parishes. It's like counties in other states. And this parish is called Ascension."

Becka and Scott exchanged glances. They had had numerous encounters with the occult through a New Age bookstore back home called the Ascension Bookshop.

"Now tell me, what do you want to know about voodoo, child?" Pastor Barchett asked.

Becka told him everything: how Z had sent them to help Sara Thomas, about their experiences with the occult in California. She even described the necklace Sara wore.

The old pastor leaned back in his chair, closed his eyes, and thought for a long moment.

Then the moment became longer.

And longer still . . .

Finally, Scott whispered to his sister, "I think he fell asleep."

At the sound of Scott's voice, the old man's eyes popped opened. "I think I have your answer."

"You do?!" they both exclaimed at the same time. They leaned forward so as not to miss a single word of the wisdom he was about to speak.

Pastor Barchett hesitated just a moment and then answered, "Pray."

Scott and Becka blinked. They remained silent, waiting for the rest of the answer. But there was nothing else.

"Pray?" Scott said. "That's it? Just pray?"

The pastor nodded. "And believe. Pray that God will show

Sara the error of her ways, that she will repent. And believe that he has sent you for a purpose that will not be thwarted."

Scott and Becka glanced at one another in exasperation. Another dead end.

❧ ❧

Once outside, it was Becka's turn to show disgust. "Pray?" she said. "Pray?? We could've done that at Aunt Myrna's. We could have done that in *California*."

"*And* believe," Scott snorted, shaking his head. "Don't forget believe. It's just the same answer we've heard a million times before."

Becka nodded. She knew it was good advice. There was nothing wrong with praying and believing. Still, she had to agree that the pastor's advice was pretty much a formula answer and not very helpful in their particular situation.

"Hey! There she is!"

Becka looked up to see Scott pointing toward Sara Thomas. She had left the library and was heading down the street.

"Come on!" Becka said.

"What?"

Becka started forward. Before she would admit defeat, she had to try one last time. "Sara, Sara!... Wait up!"

The girl looked over in surprise—and annoyance. "What do you want?" she demanded as Becka arrived at her side.

"I, uh ... I thought maybe, you know, if you were going to lunch, maybe we could sort of treat you."

"You don't think I can afford lunch?"

Becka faltered. "No, that's not it. I just ... well, it's sort of ... you know ... to make up for getting off ...," the words were coming harder now, "on the wrong ... foot..."

For a brief second, something softened in Sara's eyes. Like she appreciated the thought. Like she really wanted to talk. But suddenly, she reached for her stomach and doubled over.

"Hey!" Scott said, moving to her side. "Are you all right?"

"Get away from me—both of you!"

Becka was taken aback. "Sara, are you sure you're—?"

"Leave me alone!" She shoved Becka away hard—so hard that Becka stumbled back and fell against a lamppost. That hurt a bit, but not enough to stop her from heading toward the girl again until—

"I'm warning you." Sara was still doubled over and gasping for breath. "If you don't stay away from me, the next time . . . the next time you'll really get hurt." Then, struggling to stand up straight, she turned and ran down the street.

"Sara!" Becka called after her. "Sara, come back!"

But she didn't stop.

Slowly Becka turned to Scott. She wondered if he was thinking the exact thing she was: *What did Sara mean by "The next time you'll really get hurt"?*

Becka knew. It was one of two things: either the bruise she'd received from the lamppost or . . .

. . . or Sara Thomas was aware of everything that had been happening to them—the near accidents . . . the near-fatal accidents. If these accidents were really someone's attempts to scare off Becka and Scott, then they'd failed so far. But would they succeed "the next time"?

The next time you'll really get hurt.

Becka could feel a chill creep over her body. All morning she had been fighting the fear, trying to keep it at bay. But now it flooded in. She didn't feel strong enough to stop it. The plane, the thresher, and the bus—these were more than coincidences. Scott was right—something was happening. Something was pursuing them—something more powerful and evil than they had ever encountered before.

And if they didn't back off, if they didn't stop now, it could destroy them.

"Beck . . . Beck, you all right?"

She met her brother's concerned gaze and tried to smile but couldn't. "Let's get out of here," she whispered. Sara's words echoed in her head: *The next time you'll really get hurt.* "Let's get out of here now."

4

The trip back to Aunt Myrna's was sad. It was one of the few times Scott and Becka had ever admitted defeat. They knew they'd lost. Not only did Sara not want their help, whatever power she was caught up in was far too powerful for them to battle. Z had overestimated their strength. They could not fight this enemy. And if they tried, they knew they would be seriously injured.

Becka wondered why it was different this time; why they felt so powerless, so overwhelmed. Maybe they were missing something. But when she tried to think it through, Sara's ominous words mocked her.

The next time you'll really get hurt.

When they arrived back at the farm, John Garrett waited to take them on the tour he had promised. But things had changed considerably in the last twenty-four hours. Neither Scott nor Becka was particularly thrilled about the idea.

Scott was able to get out of it, making some excuse about his ankle. And, as much as Becka wanted to find her own reason not to go, part of her knew the walk would do her good.

Besides, she would no longer be in danger. It was over.

They were no longer pursuing Sara. Evil had won. And now as long as they didn't bother it, it wouldn't bother them. The war was over. Peace had been declared—a peace that left Sara as its victim.

That thought bothered Becka, but there was nothing she could do now. She pushed it out of her mind as she followed John past the sugarcane and into the woods.

The place was breathtaking. River waters had molded the low, flat swamplands for thousands of years. Vegetation grew wildly, enclosing everything in dim, leafy vaulted chambers. As she followed John Garrett deeper into the foliage, she almost felt as though she had entered an inner sanctum where the sun was an intruder. Plants grew everywhere. Mosses, vines, trees, algae, ferns. Everything had life.

And the flowers smelled richer in here than anywhere else she'd ever been before.

Becka felt as though she were in a holy place, a great cathedral of nature, where speaking was forbidden. She stopped for a moment and took a deep breath. "It's ... beautiful," she whispered. "Beyond beautiful."

John sat on a nearby log. "Always is. Some people get used to it, I suppose, but not me. Every time I come here, I feel like I did the first time I saw it."

Becka nodded. In the distance she heard a rumbling. "Is that thunder?"

"Could be. Kinda feels like it." He looked at the trees. The leaves waved in the sudden breeze. "Suppose we better get you back before the storm hits. It doesn't last long, but in these parts, when it rains, it rains."

"Oh, not yet!" Becka protested. "It's so beautiful. Can't we stay just a few more minutes?"

John shrugged. "If you don't mind gettin' wet."

There was another rumble. Closer this time.

"I don't mind."

"Me neither." John grinned. "Nothing like a good shower to wash away your cares and make you feel alive."

Becka nodded. She needed that more than he knew. She looked up and breathed in deeply. Everything about this place made her feel free, alive. She couldn't help grinning.

"What?" John asked.

"Nothing."

"No, tell me."

"It's just ... all this beauty makes me ... I don't know ... more aware of ... God — of how powerful he is and how much he loves us."

John broke into an easy smile. "Me too. Guess that's why I never got too caught up in all that voodoo stuff we were talking about yesterday."

The word *voodoo* brought reality crashing back into Becka's mind. Poor Sara. She would never experience this freedom. She would never taste and enjoy this love. The image of Sara, frightened and alone, fingering the doll around her neck, would not leave Becka's thoughts.

"John?"

"Yes?"

"What does it mean when someone wears a small cloth doll around their neck?"

There was another rumble. Much closer. She looked up. The branches overhead swayed in the wind.

"Might mean nothing." John stood up and started down the path. Becka followed. "But round here, that's what an initiate does."

"An initiate?"

"Someone newly admitted into the cult."

Becka's heart sank.

A gentle tapping began as drops of water struck the leaves overhead and dripped through the canopy in little streams.

But it didn't matter. Becka had volunteered to be soaked, and soaked she would be.

The deeper they went into the woods, the thicker the vegetation became, until at one point, the swamp on each side of them was covered from bank to bank with plants. It reminded Becka of a beautiful, jade green blanket.

"Oh, look!" She pointed to a patch of vivid pink flowers. Even in the downpour they seemed to shimmer. "What are those called?"

"Got me." John shrugged. "You can find lots of 'em around back in here."

"They're so beautiful." She took a step or two toward them until John swung out and grabbed her arm. "Be careful."

She looked to him quizzically until he pointed to the green carpet she was about to step on. He stuck his toe into it to show that it was actually water. "Don't want to go in there. You'll find lots of critters you don't want to tangle with."

Becka nodded her thanks and looked back over to the flowers. Too bad. They were so beautiful.

John turned and continued leading her down the path.

Once again thoughts of Sara flooded Becka's mind until a sudden clap of thunder caused her to jump.

The rain came down even harder. Becka tilted her head back and let it pour over her face. It was refreshing.

But still, there was Sara.

"John!" she shouted over the pounding rain. "Do you know a girl named Sara Thomas?"

John shook his head. "Don't think so."

"I think she might be part of Big Sweet's—"

"Shhh!" John cut her off. Before Becka could react, he resumed speaking. "I don't know anybody named Sara! You shouldn't be talking about Big Sweet in here!" His voice was barely discernible over the pouring water.

Lightning flashed, followed by an immediate explosion of thunder that caused Becka's ears to ring.

"You see that over there?" John pointed toward the woods.

Becka peered through the rain, but the downpour was too heavy to make out anything.

But John kept his hand outstretched. She stared at the spot until she finally saw two bald cypress trees rising into the air.

"I see a couple of trees!" she shouted.

"Between them!" he yelled. "Look between them!"

Ever so faintly through the sheets of falling water, Becka caught a glimpse of something. "Is it a cabin?" she shouted.

John Garrett nodded. "That's Big Sweet's place. I never go farther than this."

Becka looked at him. There was no missing the concern in his eyes. She turned back to peer at the trees through the rain. There was another flash of lightning. For the briefest second she saw the cabin.

Suddenly she felt very cold, very wet—and very frightened.

👁 👁

Over at Sorrento the rain was just beginning to come down. But the baseball coach wasn't about to let a little water stop his boys from practicing.

It must have seemed strange to see Sara Thomas sitting by herself up in the bleachers, no umbrella, the only one sitting in the rain to watch. But Sara had important business to attend to.

Behind the backstop, John Noey swung hard at a pitch and connected. The ball sailed high over the pitcher's head and deep into center field.

"Nice hit, Noey!" Coach yelled. "Nice hit!"

On the mound the pitcher took another windup and delivered another fastball. This time John sent it into left field, even farther than the last one. At sixteen, John was bigger than most of the guys his age and easily the best hitter on Sorrento High's team.

In the stands, Sara, who was growing wetter by the second, reached into her purse and pulled out a doll. This one was also made of cloth but was much larger than the one she wore around her neck.

And it was wearing a baseball uniform.

John Noey stepped out of the batter's box, wiped his bat on a towel, then scuffed his shoes on the ground the way he'd seen the pros do. Noey was cocky, to be sure, but it was more than that. Being a star athlete in high school had given him an arrogance usually found in much older boys.

Stepping back into the box, he nodded to the pitcher.

Sara held the doll in her left hand while she dug in her purse with the other. For a second she panicked, thinking she'd lost it. But then she felt it and pulled out a large hatpin.

Noey stood confidently as the pitcher wound up to deliver another fastball.

In the stands Sara began quietly chanting something over and over. She placed the doll beside her on the bleacher. The chant grew louder. She raised the hatpin high. Then, at the peak of her chant, she jammed the pin hard into the doll's head.

The ball had left the pitcher's hand. It was coming in hard and high.

Water suddenly dribbled from John's cap. He blinked once, taking his eye off the speeding ball. But that was all it took. He didn't see it suddenly veer up and inside. He tried to duck, but he was too late. The ball crashed into his forehead at seventy-four miles an hour.

John Noey collapsed into the mud.

Players raced to him. The coaches shoved players aside to get to him. But Noey was going nowhere. He was unconscious. Maybe for good.

Sara Thomas smiled. "Home run," she whispered, feeling a

rush of power sweep over her. Revenge was sweet. But she wasn't finished.

Not by a long shot.

❧   ❧

Becka knew that she would get yelled at for staying out in the rain. Her soaked clothes and the chilly wind from the storm could make anyone sick. In fact, when she sloshed through the family room and up the stairs, even Scott rolled his eyes at her foolishness.

After a hot shower and a change into dry clothes, she joined her brother down at the computer. "Any word from Z?" she asked.

Scott shook his head. "Not a thing." He reached over, closed the laptop, and let out a long, slow sigh. "We blew it, Beck. It's over."

Becka nodded sadly.

"Whatever's been happening to us is way out of our league. We've run into stuff more powerful than we can handle. I mean, it's one thing to deal with supposed ghosts and Ouija boards. But how do we deal with something that can drop a plane out of the sky or make a bus spin like a top? And now even Z's bailing on us."

"Problems?"

At the quietly spoken question, the two glanced up and found Mom standing in the doorway of the family room. She'd just finished helping Aunt Myrna with the dishes and had come to join her children.

When neither of them answered her question, she sat on the sofa and tried again. "Scotty says this is the toughest case you've had."

"You've got that right," Becka said. "For starters, the girl we're supposed to be helping—Sara Thomas—doesn't even want our help."

Mom nodded. "That's hard. But not unusual."

"What do you mean?"

"Lots of times the people who need help are the ones who don't want it. Like Julie. Or Krissi."

Becka stared at her mother. She was right! How had she forgotten the resistance they'd met anytime they'd tried to help someone caught up in the occult?

Mom went on. "What did Z say?"

"That's another thing," Scott said. "He won't talk to us. He sends us out here all on our own and then just abandons us."

"He didn't give you any advice?"

"Just that we're suppose to pray, believe, and not give in to our fears."

"And he mentioned the pastor," Becka reminded him.

"Oh yeah." Scott's tone was filled with scorn. "The pastor. Z said the local pastor would help."

"And?"

"All he came up with was 'Pray and believe.'" Scott shook his head. "Can you believe that? Just 'pray and believe.'"

Mom frowned slightly. "Sounds like pretty solid advice."

"Well, yeah ... I mean ... I know," Scott said, blinking. "But we've only heard it a million times."

"So you've done it already, then?"

Scott blinked again. "Done it?"

Mom tilted her head. "Prayed."

Scott and Becka looked at each other, then at their mother.

"Uh, well, no ...," Scott admitted hesitantly.

"Not exactly," Becka added. "We've been ... busy." But even as she said it, she knew it was a lame excuse.

Mom nodded. "Well, I've got time now, if you're interested."

"For what?"

"Well, to pray, of course."

"Here?" Becka asked. "Now?"

"Can you think of a better time?"

The brother and sister glanced at each other a little sheepishly. Becka laughed softly. She couldn't believe it. In all their hurry and determination to be the great teen demon slayers, they had forgotten a couple of very important ingredients: to pray and believe. Pastor Barchett had reminded them about those ingredients. She grinned. Maybe he wasn't as out of it as they'd thought.

"Sure," Becka said while Scott nodded. They moved to the couch, bowed their heads, and began to pray with Mom.

👁 👁

In the dream, Sara wore a wedding veil. She looked beautiful all in white. Her face glowed with anticipation as she walked down the aisle toward her future husband. Though the groom's back was to her, she knew he would be perfect.

Everything in this dream was perfect.

There was her mother in the first pew. She was as healthy and vibrant as she had been before she got sick. And there by her side was her father—handsome and proud like he had been before he started drinking.

Everything was just the way she'd always hoped it would be . . .

Until the groom turned around.

A thick red horn protruded from his forehead, and his face was black and blistered as if it had been charred. But it was the eyes that terrified her most. Huge and black. Staring at them was like looking into deep wells. Wells that had no bottom. Only horror. Deep, dark, everlasting horror.

Sara woke up screaming.

She fell back against the pillow, her chest heaving with ragged breaths, and closed her eyes in an effort to go back to sleep. She couldn't. The dreams had been coming more and more frequently. And with them came the nausea—the same nausea she had felt when talking with the two kids from California.

There was only one way to take her mind off the nausea. And the monster. To think back to the beautiful woman she had seen in the dream. To remember how things had been when her mother was alive, before she got sick and died, before her father buried his grief in alcohol ... before her life had been ripped out from under her.

Hot tears sprang to her eyes. Thinking about the past was always like this. But that was okay. Sooner or later the crying would tire her out and she would fall asleep. That's how it worked most nights. She hoped it would tonight.

5

Sara Thomas knew that Ronnie Fitzgerald would show up at Janet Baylor's sweet-sixteen party. Janet was the most popular girl in school. Sara was surprised to have even been invited. Apparently Janet had decided to invite the entire sophomore class, even the poor outcast whom everyone ignored.

Sara spent most of the evening off by herself, secretly spying on Ronnie and watching for the right moment.

Earlier she had hollowed out a large candle and buried a lock of Ronnie's hair in the wax along with a slip of paper on which she had written "Worst Luck" and "Ronnie Fitzgerald" seven times. She then dug a small hole in a field near Ronnie's house in a place where the moonlight would shine on it. She buried the bottom half of the candle in the hole, lit the wick, and went home.

All of this was according to the instructions the hungan had given her. The hardest part had been getting the lock of hair, but even that proved easier than she had expected. All she had done was sit behind him on the bus, and when he leaned his head back, she snipped off a piece.

He never even knew.

Many of the kids at the party had started changing into their swimsuits and jumping into the Baylors' large pool. Ronnie wasn't out there yet, but Sara knew he soon would be. He wouldn't miss a chance to show off his body and his diving skills.

Sara moved closer to the patio doors so she could get a better view of the crowd around the pool. It was then that she heard someone crying. Cautiously she peered around the kitchen door and listened to an older woman talking with Mrs. Baylor.

"They say they don't know ... He might never wake up!" the older woman sobbed.

"Try not to worry, Amelia. John's in good hands," Mrs. Baylor said. "He's in the best hospital in the county."

Sara felt a pang of guilt jab into her gut. That had to be John Noey's mother. So, he was still in a coma that he might never come out of?

"I know he's not always a good boy," Mrs. Noey said, wiping her nose. "But he lost his papa when he was little, you know. He never got over it. He loved his papa so much ... He's been angry at the world ever since. But he's always helped take care of me and his little sister. He's like a daddy to little Gina. She was just a baby when Ralph died. John's tried hard to make it up to her."

Sara's head spun, and her heart filled with remorse. She'd never given a thought to John Noey's family and how they might feel. She never considered how losing him might affect their lives.

Sara drifted away from the kitchen, trying hard not to hear Mrs. Noey's sobs. Out of the corner of her eye she saw Ronnie Fitzgerald bouncing high on the diving board. Her eyes widened in horror.

Oh no! I don't want this now! Not after what happened to John. No! Don't let—!

But it happened. Ronnie—the perfect athlete, the expert diver—lost his footing on a high jump and flipped backward instead of forward. Thrown back onto the board, he struck his head with a hard thump.

The blow was so solid that Sara heard it through the patio glass. Nearly sick with guilt and horror, she watched the unconscious Ronnie roll off the board and strike his head again on the side of the pool before tumbling into the water.

People rushed to his aid. Sara heard someone say something about not moving him. A couple of girls screamed over the blood.

She couldn't look. All she could do was turn and walk away, wondering if she would ever stop feeling totally awful.

The following morning Becka was sick. The wind and rain from Saturday afternoon had taken their toll.

"You look terrible," Scott said as she arrived at the breakfast table.

She sniffed and mumbled something about his looking in a mirror once in a while himself.

"Are you feeling all right, dear?" Aunt Myrna asked as she shoved a plate of eggs, a thick slice of ham, and grits under Becka's nose.

"It's just a little cold," Becka mumbled through a sniffle. It wasn't exactly a lie, but it wasn't the truth either. Whatever she was coming down with was going to be bad. One good clue was the way her stomach was turning at the smell of the food. Or the way her head was already starting to ache.

"So, what are we going to do with our next three days off?" Scott asked as he started on his second bowl of grits.

"I think—" Becka sniffed again—"I think we should give Sara one last chance."

"Beck ..." Scott started to protest.

"I know, I know. We said it was over, but don't you think we should at least give her one more try? And this time, maybe do it the right way?"

Scott gave her a look. "You mean like the pastor said—with prayer and believing?"

Becka nodded. "That's what Z said too—remember?"

Scott gave a loud sigh. It was a sound she recognized—one that said he was really frustrated with her. But as she glanced at him, she saw the gleam in his eyes. He knew that she was right. No doubt about it.

👁 👁

There were many dancers at the ceremony, but Sara danced the wildest of all. Her movements were frenzied, driven, as though she were stomping all her troubles into the earth.

Suddenly she couldn't breathe. She choked, gasping for air. The other dancers came to a stop and stared as she gagged, pointing at her throat in a silent plea for help.

No one moved.

She dropped to her knees, motioning frantically. Everything grew fuzzy and white, then whiter and whiter until she crumpled to the ground.

A large African-American man rose from an old wicker chair that looked like some sort of throne. Sara watched hazily as he came to kneel over her, placing his fingers on her neck as though feeling for a pulse.

At last he looked up and spoke. "Sara is dead. She defied the gods. She has been struck down."

Sara wanted to argue, to disagree, but she could not seem to open her mouth or move her body.

Suddenly she felt herself being lifted up. But now she was no longer herself. Somehow she had become somebody else.

Now she was John Noey!

She lay in a hospital bed hearing her mother weep over her.

No, not *her* mother. *John Noey's* mother. She tried to move but could not. She could still hear. She could still feel. She knew all that was going on around her, but she could not move.

John Noey could not move.

Hot tears fell onto her arms as the mother began to sob and cry over her.

"I'm sorry," a doctor's voice said. "We've done all we can do."

She felt a sheet pulled over her face. Dead! John Noey had just been declared dead!

But she was alive! She had to tell them! John Noey was still alive. Only now she wasn't John Noey.

Now she was Ronnie Fitzgerald!

Wires covered her body. Tubes stuck into her nose and mouth — no, *his* nose and mouth. She was alone. All alone. Just the quiet blip of the heart monitor over her head. And the rhythmic sound of the air as it was being pushed in and out of her lungs by a respirator.

Suddenly the heart monitor started blipping irregularly. She panicked, tried to move, but there was nothing she could do. She could feel the heart inside her chest pounding like a jackhammer gone berserk. Then it stopped altogether. So did the blips on the monitor. Now there was nothing but a long, loud whine.

She tried to breathe but couldn't. She tried to scream, but no words would come. Soon she heard people racing around her and someone shouting, "He's flat-lining! We're going to lose him!"

Sara was desperate to move, to breathe. She silently choked until —

She sat bolt upright, awake and coughing.

When she caught her breath, she glanced around the classroom. More than a few students stared at her. Several smirked. She had fallen asleep in class again. This was not surprising, since she'd given up sleeping during the night in an effort to stop the dreams. But apparently that didn't matter now.

The dreams were coming during the day, whenever she closed her eyes and started to doze. Day or night, the dreams came.

Sara looked at the clock. It was almost three o'clock. She was anxious to leave. All this time she'd thought revenge on the boys would make her feel better. It didn't. It made her feel worse. The sobs of John's mother and the sound of Ronnie slamming into the board echoed in her mind.

But Sara felt more than guilt. She also felt afraid. Now she knew the power of voodoo. She knew that it could turn back on her if she wasn't careful.

At last the bell sounded. Sara let out a sigh of relief. All day long the school had been getting reports on John's and Ronnie's conditions from the hospital. It was all anyone talked about. Both were in comas in the ICU. Sara wanted to get away—to go home and cover her head.

To sleep.

These were the only thoughts running through her mind as she headed toward the bus.

"Sara! Excuse me! Sara Thomas?"

Someone called her. She turned and saw the same girl and her brother who had bothered her a couple of days before, waiting at the bottom of the steps. *Oh no!* Sara thought. *They're the last people I want to see!*

Becka stepped forward. "Sara, it's us again, Rebecca and Scott. Listen, I just want to say something. It may not be any of my business, but if you're messing around with—"

"Then leave, okay?" Sara cut her off. "If it's none of your business, then you and your creepy brother can just—"

"I just wanted to warn you," Becka interrupted. "If you're messing around with voodoo, you could be losing control of your life."

Sara's eyes grew wild. "Why are you trying to hurt me?" she demanded. Her voice sounded shrill. She knew others were listening but didn't care. "You want to take away my powers, don't you?"

Becka reached toward her. "Sara—"

"No! I'm warning you for the last time. Leave me alone!"

Now it was Scott's turn. "Listen, we're not trying to hurt you or take away any—"

"You bet you won't! 'Cause I won't let you." Sara reached inside her purse and pulled out the scissors she had used to cut Ronnie's hair. "Get out of my way!"

Becka froze. "All right, Sara, we'll leave. But couldn't we just—?"

Suddenly Sara lunged at her. "I warned you!"

Becka jerked backward, lost her footing, and fell hard onto the sidewalk. Sara swooped down at her with the scissors.

"Stop!" Scott tried to block her, but she was too fast.

But instead of stabbing Becka, Sara suddenly cut off a lock of her hair.

Rising to her feet, she shouted, "I curse you! Worst luck will befall you! *Pire* sort! *Pire* chance! *Pire* fortune!" She started backing away. "Worst luck! Worst luck! Worst luck! It will be worse for you than it was for John and Ronnie."

Sara spun around and started running. Her heart pounded in her chest. She had to get away. The magic was about to begin. She did not want to stay around and watch Rebecca suffer.

👁 👁

Scott helped his sister to her feet. "You okay?"

Becka nodded. "Yes, just sort of stunned ... that was weird! She cut my hair!"

"I know," Scott said. "Nothing like being cursed to really trash a day. C'mon. I think we'd better get home."

"But the bus to Aunt Myrna's isn't due for another hour."

"I mean *home* home," Scott replied. "Back to California."

By the time they got to the bus stop, Becka felt a lot worse. Maybe it was the emotion, or maybe it was the fever she knew had been rising steadily all morning. Whatever the case, when she reached the bus stop, Becka had to sit on a bench.

"Can I get you anything?" Scott asked. "A Coke or something?"

She could see that he was worried. "Maybe some juice," she said.

"All right. I'll check the gas station over there. Just wait here." Scott quickly headed across the street.

Becka dreaded the bus ride back to Aunt Myrna's. The jouncing of that old bus would only make her feel worse. She closed her eyes. The throbbing in her head was unbearable.

She opened her eyes and glanced at an abandoned newspaper lying beside her on the bench. It was the *Sorrento Times*. The headline read "Second Sorrento High Student in Coma."

Despite her throbbing headache, Becka forced herself to read on. Ronnie Fitzgerald had been injured on Sunday night; John Noey, the day before that. Both boys were in the hospital, barely clinging to life. Both had been the victims of strange accidents that, according to the paper, "many in the area believe were due to religious rituals."

Suddenly Sara's words came screaming back into her mind: *It will be worse for you than it was for John and Ronnie.*

Her eyes shifted back to the paper, scanning for the injured boys' names again. There they were. Ronnie Fitzgerald and John Noey.

Becka's vision blurred. The trees and people around her started to move. She felt worse than she thought. The fever, the headache, the encounter with Sara all contributed to that. And now this.

It will be worse for you.

Fear continued to grow, consuming her, fogging her thinking.

Next time you'll really be hurt.

Fear after fear had piled up since even before they had landed. She tried to focus her eyes, but it was impossible. The people, the trees, the buildings seemed to spin around her.

It will be worse.

She could feel herself growing clammy with icy perspiration.

Worst luck! Worst luck!

She was going to faint. She knew it.

I curse you! I curse you!

She was going to —

Suddenly she felt her body tilt forward. She tried to stop herself but couldn't. A moment later, she toppled onto the sidewalk.

Rebecca Williams had passed out.

6

When Becka woke up, she found herself lying on the bench with Scott and Pastor Barchett standing over her. "But you'll pray for her, won't you, Pastor?" Scott was asking.

Pastor Barchett nodded. "Of course I will. But you have the authority of prayer also. Curses and spells have no power over Christians unless we give it to them."

Becka moved and tried to sit up.

"Beck, you're awake. Are you all right?" Scott asked. "I ran over and got the pastor."

"How are you feeling, my dear?" Pastor Barchett asked.

"I feel better, I think," she said, though she was still a little woozy.

"Maybe you should see a doctor," Pastor Barchett offered.

"I'm all right," Becka said. "It's just ... well, I haven't felt real good all day. With Sara attacking me, and all that's been happening to us, and then reading in the newspaper about those two Sorrento High boys and their freak accidents ..."

Pastor Barchett nodded. "Both are classmates of Sara's, I've heard. I'm afraid it sounds like more than a coincidence to me too."

"I think I'll be all right now," Rebecca repeated. "Did we miss our bus?"

Scott shook his head. "Should be here any sec. Unless ..." He turned to the pastor. "I don't suppose you'd drive us home?"

Pastor Barchett laughed. "No, they've long since stopped letting me drive a car. My eyes are bad. But I'm sure I can find someone to take you."

"I'll be fine on the bus," Becka assured them. "It's just a short ride. But what should we do about Sara?"

"Keep praying," Pastor Barchett said, "and believing. But remember, you can't deliver someone from something if they don't want to be free. They have to want it."

"Well, she's made it pretty clear that she doesn't," Scott said. "Sounds like Z really missed the boat this time. How could God possibly want us to visit Sara when she doesn't even want to listen?"

"What about Moses and Pharaoh?" Pastor Barchett asked. "God sent Moses, didn't he? And what about the prophets? Just because the people didn't listen doesn't mean God didn't send them."

Becka leaned forward. She was still feeling a little light-headed, but she wasn't about to admit it. "I think we should give it a couple more days," she said.

"Becka ...," Scott protested.

"Two more days," she repeated.

Pastor Barchett nodded in agreement. "And in the meantime, keep praying ... and believing."

❧   ❧

By the time they returned to the farm, Scott had to argue with Becka to get her to take a nap.

"But I feel good now," Becka insisted. "In fact, I'd like to go for a walk. I want to show you these pretty flowers I saw in the swamp."

"A walk?!" Scott exclaimed. "No way! You have to lie down and rest!"

"Stop acting like Mom!" she snapped. "I feel fine!"

"All right," Scott said. "If you won't listen to me, let's talk to Mom and see what she says."

Becka panicked. "No! Don't tell Mom! She'll make me stay in bed for a week!"

"Then take a nap."

"If I take a nap, will you walk with me into the woods so we can smell those pink flowers?"

Scott made a face. "Flowers?! What do I care about flowers?"

"There's lots of other stuff too. It's really cool. Please?"

Scott hesitated.

"I'll owe you," she promised.

"All right," Scott finally agreed. "But you have to rest first."

"Will do."

But Becka couldn't sleep. She still felt a little foggy. She knew the fever hadn't left. She also knew something else: although she pretended it wasn't true, her fear of Sara and her powers was still very, very strong. Probably *too* strong.

Then there were the other thoughts — the ones that had been growing more powerful every hour. These thoughts urged her to go into the swamp and smell those incredible pink flowers.

❧　❧

On Sara Thomas's bedroom dresser was a vase full of those incredible pink flowers. Buried in the midst of them was the lock of Becka's hair. And underneath the flowers?

Underneath the flowers was a live snake.

❧　❧

An hour later, Becka and Scott set off for the woods and

swamp. Becka couldn't explain it. Even though she still felt weak, finding those flowers and seeing their beautiful color had become very important. It was like a craving, something she couldn't stop wanting.

She led the way. For a while they followed the path she had taken with John Garrett. But each time she thought she saw a glimpse of the pink flowers, she veered a little farther off until, before she knew it, they were on a path she'd never seen before—a path surrounded by thick vegetation.

They continued forward for several minutes until they spotted a large clearing in the distance.

It looked like some sort of gathering place. A dozen logs were arranged in a huge circle. The pink flowers grew all around the clearing.

"Wow! Cool place!" Scott exclaimed. "You never told me about this."

"I've never seen it before," Becka said. "I must've taken a wrong turn back there."

"What do you think this was?" Scott asked as he explored the area. "Maybe a Native American church or something? It looks ancient."

Becka barely heard him. Instead, she walked along the logs, stopping every so often to smell one of the flowers. "Aren't they beautiful?"

"What?"

"The flowers. Aren't they beautiful?"

"Yeah. Beautiful. You know, Beck, those flowers are all you've talked about since we came out here."

"They're so beautiful."

"What's the matter with you?" Before she could answer, Scott's eyes landed on something else—a large, makeshift altar made of flat gray stones. "Hey, check it out!"

They ran to it but suddenly came to a stop.

"Is that red stain what I think it is?" Scott asked.

Becka nodded, glancing around. "Don't see any flowers here."

"Beck, I'm pretty sure that's blood. And look here. There's some kind of animal hair sticking to the rock. Something was killed here recently... Somebody's using this place for animal sacrifices." Scott stepped back as the memory of his terrifying dream about the goat came rushing back.

"Let's go look for more flowers," Becka said.

Her words pulled Scott from his momentary shock. He looked at his sister long and hard. Something was up. He was feeling more uneasy by the second. "I think we'd better get you home."

This time Scott took the lead. He headed out of the clearing and searched for the path. But after about thirty feet, he stopped cold and pointed at something in a nearby ditch. "Look, Beck!"

Becka joined him. "More flowers?"

Scott didn't respond. He just stood and stared. In the pit were the remains of a slaughtered goat.

"Oh ... that's terrible!" Becka said.

"Guess we know now why Aunt Myrna's goat hasn't come home," Scott said sadly. "Big Sweet slaughtered him in one of his rituals."

"We should go."

"You're right." Scott headed toward what he hoped was Aunt Myrna's farm.

Becka stopped suddenly. "No. We should go and look for more flowers."

Scott spun around to look at Becka. Her face was flushed and her eyes looked glazed. The unease in the pit of his stomach became full-blown concern, then anger. Something had happened to Becka. And whatever was wrong with his sister was getting worse by the minute. He had to get her out of there. But as he looked around, he had a sinking feeling that they were lost. He was sure of it.

"Becka? Beck, I think we'd better pray. I think—"

But when he turned back to her, she was gone.

"Becka!" he shouted, looking around. He began to panic, running first one way, then the other. "Becka!" he shouted again. *Dear God,* he prayed, *don't let me lose her. Not in here!* "Becka!"

But she was nowhere to be found. Desperately he continued the search. Plants were everywhere. Spanish moss hung down thick in his face. Everything looked the same. He had no idea where he was or if he'd been running around in circles.

"Becka! Beck—"

Then he heard the sound of splashing. And he knew as certainly as if he'd seen it happen—Becka had jumped into the water.

"Becka!"

He raced along a log, following the sound.

"Becka! Becka!"

At last he saw her. She was up to her neck in the water a few feet from the shore.

"What are you doing?!" he demanded.

She didn't answer. Instead, she treaded water, moving *away* from him.

"Becka!!"

A moment later he had his answer. She reached out and grabbed a handful of the pink flowers.

"See?" she called. "Flowers!"

"Yes, very nice." It was all Scott could do to contain himself. "Now if you don't mind, would you hurry up and get out of there? We've got to—"

Suddenly he saw movement in the water. It looked like a log drifting across the swamp. But it was no log. His heart began pounding. It was an alligator! And it was swimming right for his sister!

"More flowers over here!" she called, starting to paddle even farther away.

"No, Beck! Come back! Get out of there! Look over your shoulder!"

Becka did, but she seemed oblivious to the approaching gator. Its two large, yellow eyes headed straight toward her.

"Look, Scotty." She pointed past the gator toward another group of flowers. "More flowers."

Scott was beside himself. "Nooo!" he screamed from the shore. "Look, Beck! I've got flowers here!" He scrambled around the shore scooping up flowers wherever he saw them. "See, Beck? I've got bigger ones — prettier ones! See? Right over here!"

Becka turned and saw Scott waving his handful of flowers. She smiled vacantly and began swimming back to him.

It was too late.

Her pace was no match for the gator, which rapidly closed the distance between them. It would be on her in seconds.

"Oh, God!" Scott cried. "Please save Beck! In the name of Jesus, please save her! Please ..."

The alligator was only a few feet from her now. Its mouth opened wide, preparing to attack, when suddenly —

BAM! BAM!

The shots cracked through the swamp like thunder.

At first Scott was unsure what had happened. Then he saw the alligator roll over onto its back. Blood soon appeared in the water. Finally, the creature sank slowly under the green carpet of water and plants.

A sudden rustle of leaves caused Scott to spin around. A huge African-American man carrying a rifle soon appeared. Perched on his head was a battered straw hat. He chewed on a piece of sugarcane.

"It's all right now, missy," he called. "You can take your time comin' back. But you best get outta there soon as possible. This area's got more gators than that old-timer."

Scott could only stare as Becka swam toward him. Once again she smiled vacantly.

When she arrived, the big man reached his hand out to help her. "Hello there, missy. Pleased to make your acquaintance. My name is Benjamin. But most folks in these parts call me Big Sweet."

7

Big Sweet continued to hold out his hand to help Becka from the swamp. She hesitated, remaining in the chest-deep water.

"Flowers?" she asked.

The big man smiled. "What?"

"She's talking about these!" Scott called. He was about thirty feet away, holding up a handful of the pink flowers for Big Sweet to see. "She's obsessed with them. That's why she dove into the water."

Big Sweet nodded as if he understood. "Sounds like she's under some kind of spell."

Confused and growing more angry by the second, Scott crossed toward the man. "Yes, and you did it ... or one of your people did!"

Big Sweet held up his hand. "Whoa, son. Easy. We can talk about all that later. But no matter what you've heard, I am still preferable to another alligator."

"What?"

"We must get this girl out of that water before we have more company."

Scott understood and quickly joined Big Sweet. He leaned

71

over the bank and held out the flowers to his sister. "Here they are, Beck. Come and get 'em."

As Becka reached for the flowers, Scott and Big Sweet took her arms and pulled her out of the water. She was soaked and dripping with slime.

"Look at your leg," Scott said. "It's bleeding!"

"She must've cut it on a briar under the water," Big Sweet said. "You better come over to my cabin and let me clean that wound for you."

"I don't know," Scott said warily. "We should be heading back. Just point the way to Myrna Carmen's house and—"

"Look, son, if I wanted to harm you, you'd already be dead. I could've let that gator eat your friend here and shot you instead. Truth is, I hate shooting gators. Ain't that many more left. And we got plenty of kids. Especially Yankee kids out messing where they don't belong."

Scott was unsure whether to be terrified or angry. But suddenly Big Sweet broke into a big, booming laugh. "Now, c'mon to my place," he said, "and let me dress that wound 'fore your friend winds up with an infection."

Scott nodded. "Okay. But don't try anything funny."

Big Sweet laughed again, then turned and made his way up a small hill. Scott followed cautiously, taking Becka by the hand and leading her carefully.

On the way to Big Sweet's cabin, Scott introduced himself and Becka. He was surprised at how much Big Sweet already seemed to know about them. He wondered if Big Sweet had asked John Garrett about them.

Big Sweet's cabin lay on the other side of the hill. It looked foreboding on the outside, but once inside, Scott was surprised to see that it was small and cozy. He was also surprised to discover that the man had a wife and two cute little girls who were four and six. In fact, the whole place looked suspiciously normal.

Becka sat quietly, playing with her handful of flowers while

Big Sweet washed the blood off her leg. "Why you keep looking around like that?" Big Sweet asked. "You expect bats to fly out of the closet?"

Scott almost smiled. "Something like that, I guess. We've never been in a ..." He stopped in midsentence, unsure of what words to use.

"In a hungan's house?" Big Sweet asked. "Is that what you mean?"

Scott swallowed.

"Well, son, a hungan is just like anyone else ... most of the time. It's only during the ceremony that the loa commune with the hungan. Otherwise he's like anyone else."

"How can you say you commune with the dead and call yourself normal?" Scott asked. He knew he was being pretty direct, but after all, this was the top man, the guy with all the answers.

Big Sweet cocked his head and looked at Scott. "What's a city kid like you know about the loa?"

Scott shrugged. "Not much. I just like studying stuff like that."

Big Sweet's thick eyebrows knitted into a frown. "Stuff like what?"

Usually words came easily to Scott, but now, with Big Sweet staring at him—looking through him actually—he wasn't sure how to answer. "I just ... like to read about ... weird stuff." Scott winced as soon as he had said the words. Calling someone's religion "weird stuff" was not too bright, especially if that someone happened to be the high priest and was two or three times your size.

Big Sweet's eyes narrowed. He looked meaner than ever ... until he suddenly broke into the biggest laugh yet. "Weird stuff." He continued laughing. "Weird stuff. That's pretty good!"

Scott gave Big Sweet half a smile, then glanced at Becka.

She did not say a word. She was too busy playing with the pink flowers.

Big Sweet reached for a bottle of alcohol and poured some onto a wad of cotton. "This might sting a bit," he warned. But as he swabbed the cut with alcohol, Becka didn't even react.

Big Sweet shook his head. "That's a powerful curse. May take some doing to break it."

"Ask Sara Thomas," Scott said. "She's the one who put the curse on her."

Big Sweet was taken aback. "Sara Thomas? How do you know—?" He stopped himself, then shook his head. "I must explain to you what is happening to Sara Thomas. You know about the loa, the dead spirits. Well, there are two kinds of loa. *Rada loas* and *petro loas.*"

Scott listened, feeling uneasy.

"Rada loas are good spirits that help a person do good. Petro loas are mean spirits that help them do evil."

"What's that got to do with Sara or my sis—?"

"Sara Thomas has been picked on all her life. She needed something to defend herself, to fight back. That's a petro loa. That's what she sought and—" he let out a sigh— "that's what she got—a spirit of revenge."

"So you put a curse on Sara, and Sara put one on my sister."

Big Sweet looked at Scott a moment, then shook his head. "I did not put a curse on Sara. She asked for help; I gave it to her. She got herself a powerful petro loa, though. A strong one. I'm afraid Sara's a loa's *cheval* now."

"A what?"

"That means horse, a horse for the spirit to ride. And there is not much she can do until it decides it wants to get off."

"What about my sister?"

Big Sweet thought a moment. "I've got a black root. It can break spells like—"

"I don't want any of that stuff!" Scott interrupted.

Big Sweet frowned, not understanding.

"She's a Christian," Scott explained. "Curses have no power over Christians."

"So I see ...," Big Sweet said, motioning to Becka, who still played with the flowers.

Scott faltered. "That is, unless we allow someone or something else to have power over us."

Big Sweet sat, waiting for more.

Scott continued. "A lot of weird stuff's been happening to us. And Becka's been getting kinda spooked. And now with the fever and all, and Sara's curse, I guess she just started to give in and believe —"

"So what are you going to do?" Big Sweet interrupted.

Scott swallowed. "I guess ... pray."

"Pray?"

"Yes."

"Pray? That's it?"

"Well ... yeah."

Big Sweet folded his arms. "Okay, let me see."

"What? Here?" Scott asked.

"I would not be taking her back into the swamp this way. But then again, if you don't think it will work ..."

Scott quickly rose to the occasion. "Oh, it will work, all right. You bet it will work!"

Big Sweet grinned. "Then, I am waiting."

With growing determination, Scott pushed aside his apprehension and reached for Becka's hand. He bowed his head and closed his eyes. "Dear Lord ..." He cleared his throat, still feeling a little self-conscious. "Dear Lord, please break the power of this curse. Please help Becka to see that she doesn't have to be under this or any spell because of what you did for us on the cross. Because you set us free and gave us an even greater power." Scott hesitated. Part of him wanted to make the prayer longer and more dramatic, maybe turn it into a mini-sermon. But he knew he said what needed to be said. That was enough. "I ask these things in the name of Jesus Christ. Amen."

Scott opened his eyes.

Big Sweet sat silent, waiting. "That was it?" he asked.

Scott nodded. "That's it."

"No root or balm or potion?"

Scott shook his head. "We don't use that stuff. We don't need it."

Big Sweet turned and stared hard at Becka, waiting.

Nothing happened.

"Missy?" Big Sweet called. "Missy, are you there?"

Ever so slowly, Becka turned her head.

Scott and Big Sweet held their breath.

At last Becka spoke. "Would you like a flower?"

Scott winced. Big Sweet smiled.

Becka continued, frowning slightly. "No? Then can I dump them somewhere? I think they're making me sick. I must be allergic to them or something." She looked around the room, blinking in confusion. "Hey, where are we?" She looked down at her soaked clothes. "And how did I get all wet?"

Scott let out a sigh of relief. Big Sweet laughed his big laugh.

"Hello, missy," the man said. "My name is Big Sweet."

Becka turned to Scott, a trace of panic in her voice. "Is he serious?"

Scott nodded. "It's okay. You were out of it for a while. Big Sweet saved your life. We came here so he could clean that gash on your leg, and … uh … well, I just prayed and broke Sara's curse."

Becka leaned back in her chair. She felt a little weak. And for good reason. It was all coming back to her now: the cravings, the wanderings, and Sara's curse. She rubbed her neck. It felt stiff and hot from the fever. "Boy, do I feel stupid."

Scott said, "Big Sweet says Sara is possessed by a violent spirit."

"A petro loa," Big Sweet added. "There are good spirits and bad spirits that can possess a person and—"

"But possession is wrong," Becka interrupted.

Big Sweet looked at her.

She continued. "If there's one thing we've learned over the months, it's that any spirit that possesses someone is not a good spirit. Those spirits always cause a person to do evil. Only the Holy Spirit comes into a person's life and causes him to do good."

Big Sweet rubbed his chin. "For a couple of kids, you sure think you know a lot about spirits."

Becka and Scott exchanged glances. If he only knew ...

Big Sweet went on. "I don't know what you got, but it is clear it has power. Breaking that curse with no roots or potions is mighty strong power."

"Our power doesn't come from some*thing*," Scott explained. "It comes from some*one*—the Holy Spirit, like Beck said."

Big Sweet eyed him. "All right, then. If you really want to help Sara Thomas, you must come to the ceremony tonight. Her petro loa is a dangerous one. I tried talking to it, but it won't listen. I've tried to get its ancestors to talk to me, but—"

"You can't talk to the dead," Becka cut in.

Big Sweet was obviously growing impatient with all the interruptions. "You cannot? Then who have I been talking to every week all these years?"

Again Scott and Becka traded looks.

After a deep breath, Scott finally answered him. "Demons. You've been talking to demons who are using you for their own purposes."

Big Sweet stood up. "You kids give me a big headache! You better head back now. Miss Myrna will be worried."

"And Sara?" Scott asked.

"If you are serious 'bout helping Sara, then you come to our ceremony tonight."

❧ ❧

Sara had spent most of the night tossing, turning, and groaning, thanks to a horrible nightmare. She woke up gasping for air, then jumped out of bed and hurried over to the dresser mirror to stare at her reflection. What she saw caused her to let out a scream.

In the mirror, snakes writhed in her hair. They vanished suddenly.

She sat on a nearby chair and stared at herself. She felt as if she had aged several years in the last few days.

Angrily she grabbed the small cloth doll still hanging around her neck and broke the chain. She threw the doll on the floor, then hurriedly dressed.

But just before she left the room, she walked back over to where the doll lay on the floor and stared at it for a long moment. Then, although it was the last thing she wanted to do, she picked it up and put it in her purse.

She had to. She no longer had a choice.

❧ ❧

Going to the ceremony was the last thing Becka and Scott wanted to do, especially given Becka's condition and all they'd been through. But they both agreed that it would be their last opportunity to help Sara. And like it or not, that was why they had been sent to Louisiana in the first place.

Before they left for the ceremony, both of them knew they needed a reminder of the power God had given them through Jesus. The events of the past days had shaken their trust and weakened their faith. There was only one way to build it back up. They grabbed their Bibles and headed for the porch.

"Hey, remember this?" Scott asked as he flipped to a well-worn page. He quickly read the verse: " 'The one who is in you is greater than the one who is in the world.' "

"Yeah," Becka sighed. "Too bad I forgot that earlier." She looked at the page her finger rested on in her Bible. "Here's another one we'd better not forget: 'These signs will accompany those who believe: In my name they will drive out demons.'"

Scott nodded. "'If you believe, you will receive whatever you ask for in prayer.'"

"Praying and believing," Becka mused. "Sounds exactly like what Z told us at the very beginning."

"And Mom *and* Aunt Myrna's pastor," Scott added.

Becka shook her head. "Funny how you can hear some stuff so much that pretty soon you don't even pay attention to it."

"Well, we're paying attention now," Scott said as he stood. "Nothing's going to make us back down tonight."

"Scotty?"

"No, sir, we're going to get in there and bust some heads …"

"Scotty?"

" … and show them they're not messing around with just any—"

"Scotty!"

"What?"

"Before we go, shouldn't we, like … you know … pray first?"

"Oh …"

For the first time she could remember, Becka actually thought she saw her brother blush.

"Yeah, of course." He cleared his throat. "I, uh, I knew that."

She gave him a grin as he sat back down. And there, together, brother and sister bowed their heads to pray for God's protection. They asked God's forgiveness for their wavering faith and pride, then asked for wisdom and faith to do whatever he wanted. Neither was sure how long the prayer lasted. But that didn't really matter. They continued praying, not wanting to stop until they were positive that the Lord had strengthened them. What was most important for them was to know whether God wanted them to go to the ceremony. At the conclusion of the prayer, both were certain.

They had to go.

👁 👁

The ceremony was in full swing when Becka and Scott arrived. A large fire burned in the center of the clearing. A dozen dancers, all dressed in colorful costumes with faces painted different colors, moved slowly around the fire to the beat of the ever present drums. Most of those gathered were barefoot.

Sara Thomas was nowhere to be seen.

Big Sweet, on the other hand, was. He wore the same battered straw hat he'd had on earlier and chewed on a piece of sugarcane. He sat in a big wicker chair that looked more like a piece of run-down patio furniture than a seat of honor. Every once in a while, he smiled and waved at Becka and Scott from across the sea of dancers.

Finally the drumming stopped.

Big Sweet stood and chanted in a language Becka didn't understand. She guessed that it was probably French or Creole. At the end of what seemed to be a prayer, the drums began beating again—much faster this time.

Big Sweet raised his arms to the sky. "I call upon you, *Bon Dieu.*" He closed his eyes and waved his arms. "Bring forth the loa now to guide the people."

As soon as he returned to his chair, the drums churned out an even faster rhythm.

"I know loa means the dead," Becka whispered to Scott, "but who is *Bon Dieu* again?"

"I think he's the most powerful of the gods," Scott whispered back. "Kind of like the supreme ruler."

Most of the dancers moved in the same undulating rhythm as they had before. Others jerked spasmodically like puppets on a string. A few threw themselves to the ground, twitching like bugs in the dirt. One man ran wildly around the circle as fast as he could, screaming hysterically until he collapsed on the ground from exhaustion.

"This is getting too weird," Scott whispered.

Becka nodded. Once again she had a sick feeling in the pit of her stomach that they were in over their heads. But the prayers and the Bible verses they had read still echoed in her heart. She knew that they were exactly where they were called to be. Not only would God protect them, but he would also show them what to do.

On the other side of the dancers, she noticed a man whose face was painted bright red. She also noticed that he glared at them. She nudged her brother. "Do you see that man? The one with the red face?"

Scott looked around. "Nope. I see a green-faced man, a guy with orange spiders on his cheek, a woman with a blue star on her forehead, and … oh, that guy. What's the matter with him?"

Becka gulped. "He's coming over here."

Scott shook his head. "No, he's not. He's just heading out to … wait. He *is* coming over here."

The red-faced man never took his eyes off Becka and Scott as he used his walking stick to clear the dancers out of his way. He towered over them. *"Sama sama tay, sama sama tay!"* he shouted, pointing at them.

A few of the dancers nearby stopped and stared at Becka and Scott.

Suddenly the red-faced man leaped high into the air and screamed, *"AIEEEEEEYA!"*

The cry sent chills through Becka. She glanced at Scott in a silent signal to hold their ground.

The drums stopped beating. Everyone quieted.

"Sama sama tay!" The red-faced man shouted, still pointing at Becka and Scott. *"Sama sama tay!"*

The whole group stared now. Becka tensed. She waited, silently praying. Others in the group joined in with the red-faced man, chanting, *"Sama sama tay! Sama sama tay!"* They crowded around Scott and Becka.

"Sama sama tay! Sama sama tay!"

More and more joined in, pushing themselves closer and closer.

"Sama sama tay! Sama sama tay!"

The red-faced man raised his walking stick high into the air.

"Sama sama tay! Sama sama tay! SAMA SAMA TAY! SAMA SAMA TAY!"

Becka wanted to bolt, to break through the crowd. She was sure the red-faced man intended to crack either Scott or her over the head with his stick. But instead of running, she closed her eyes and prayed for all she was worth. She hoped Scott did the same.

Suddenly the conch horn sounded.

Everyone froze and turned toward Big Sweet. He blew the giant shell two more times.

The red-faced man was not about to give up. He pointed at Becka and Scott and shouted, *"Sama sama tay!"*

Big Sweet angrily shook his head. "No! No *sama sama tay. Untero tay. Untero my tay!"*

The dancers seemed relieved by what they heard and turned away. But the red-faced man still pointed at Becka and Scott.

"No!" Big Sweet shouted again. *"Untero tay! My tay!"*

The red-faced man stepped back. He gave a slight bow in Big Sweet's direction and rejoined the group. The drums began again, and the dancers resumed their gyrations.

"What was *that* all about?" Scott whispered.

"That fellow thought you were intruders—spies trying to steal our secrets," Big Sweet replied. "I told him you were my guests. Potential members to join the group."

"Potential members?!" Scott shouted, incredulously. "You told him that?!"

Big Sweet laughed. "Who knows? The night is young."

Before Scott could respond, a pale girl broke through the brush and entered the ring of dancers.

"Look." Scott pointed. "It's Sara."

Though she wore nothing unusual—just jean shorts and a T-shirt—Sara stood out dramatically from the dancers. True enough, most of the others were having some kind of experience. But Sara seemed to be fighting a war. She contorted one moment, flowed with the rhythm of the drums the next, then contorted again, fighting against something with all her strength.

Slowly Big Sweet stood. This time he shouted out the names of several spirits. Some he called *rada loas*.

The drummers increased their tempo. Big Sweet walked through the dancers until he finally arrived at Sara's side. "And you, Sara? Are you ready for your final rite of initiation into our group?"

Suddenly Sara stopped moving. She glared at Big Sweet and tried to shake her head. But her whole body began to tremble.

Scott leaned over to Becka and whispered, "Look at her eyes. She's scared to death! She's trying to fight this thing."

Scott was right. The girl's eyes were wild and filled with fear as her body shook harder and harder, clearly out of control.

Becka rose to her feet. "We have to help her. We have to—"

Animal growls suddenly came from Sara's mouth. Her body twisted and contorted uncontrollably.

Big Sweet tried to embrace her, but she pushed him away and flung herself to the ground.

The crowd began to murmur, but Big Sweet raised his hands. "Sara is fighting with her *petro loa* for control of her body. She will tear herself apart unless I can quiet the spirit with the magic balm."

"No!" Becka called. She started to push her way through the crowd. "Don't—"

But her voice was drowned out as Sara began shrieking and rolling in the dirt. Big Sweet signaled two other men for help. It took all three of them to hold her.

"No!" Becka repeated. "She doesn't need potions! She needs—"

Sara's scream was unearthly, unrecognizable, as Big Sweet applied some special ointment. Then, almost instantly, she quieted. The fit subsided, and she lay perfectly still.

Scott and Becka stared.

"I guess he does have power," Scott finally ventured.

But Becka wasn't convinced. There was something wrong. She couldn't put her finger on it, but something wasn't right.

The drums began again, and the dancers resumed their actions. Big Sweet turned to Scott and smiled triumphantly. But Becka barely noticed. As she knelt beside Sara, she knew what was wrong.

Sara wasn't breathing.

Quickly Becka reached for Sara's neck, searching for a pulse. There was none.

"She's dead!" Becka cried. "Sara's dead!"

8

Immediately Becka and Scott put their CPR training to work. Scott blew air into Sara's mouth several times while Becka pumped Sara's chest.

"It's not working!" Becka shouted.

"We've gotta keep trying!" Scott yelled.

Becka continued pumping Sara's chest. But it was no use.

"Still no response!" Becka cried, feeling for Sara's pulse again. "We have to get her to the hospital."

Big Sweet offered his battered pickup truck. They quickly loaded Sara into the back. Becka and Scott crawled in with her to resume CPR as Big Sweet sped off.

"I've seen this before!" Big Sweet called through the back window. "When the *petro loa* gets violent, the magic balm sends the *loa cheval* into a deep sleep. She will wake up okay. I give you my word."

"She's dead!" Becka shouted. Her eyes burned with tears. "Don't you get it? She's dead!"

"Don't blame yourself!" Scott shouted over the wind. "We did everything we could do! Like Pastor Barchett said, you can't deliver someone if she doesn't want—"

"But she did!" Becka cried, wiping the tears out of her eyes. "She wanted to be delivered. I could see it in her eyes. She was fighting for control when that demon killed her!"

Minutes later Big Sweet skidded the pickup into the emergency entrance of Sorrento's hospital. Scott threw down the gate while Big Sweet scooped up Sara and raced inside with her.

An orderly helped him get her onto a gurney, while an admissions staff person asked questions in the background. Becka gave the admissions clerk all the information she knew as the orderly wheeled Sara into another room. Scott and Big Sweet stayed behind near the hospital entrance.

Time passed while the emergency room team worked on Sara. Becka paced in the narrow waiting area. She stopped as Scott approached. "Where's Big Sweet?" she asked.

Scott gave a slight shrug. "He had to get back to the ceremony."

"He what?!" Becka felt herself growing angry.

"Yeah, he said the people needed him and, uh …"

"And what?"

"And that … well … that Sara would be all right."

Becka couldn't believe what she heard. She slumped into a chair, feeling a sudden chill. Her fever was on the rise again. It drained what little energy she had left. She was angry, scared, and reaching the point of total exhaustion.

Scott sat beside her. "Are you gonna be okay?"

"I don't know." Once again hot tears sprang to her eyes. She tried to blink them back but couldn't. Finally she turned to Scott. "Someone died, Scotty. That's never happened to us before."

Scott nodded.

"Where's all our power? All those verses said we're supposed to have the victory."

Scott looked away. When he spoke, his voice was thick and faint. "I don't know."

"I'm scared, Scotty."

"Don't say that," he said. "Fear is a weapon of the enemy. If we believe he has the power instead of God, then he can beat us."

"He's already beaten us."

"Don't say—"

"She's dead, Scott! We lost! She's dead!"

"Excuse me?"

They both looked up to see a nurse approach. She seemed nervous. "Are you the ones who brought Sara Thomas in?"

"Yes," Becka said, already preparing herself for the worst.

"Well ..." The nurse took a breath. "She's gone."

Becka nodded. "I know. We were just hoping you could do something to—"

"No, you misunderstand me," the nurse said. "She's not gone as in dead. She's gone as in she left the hospital."

"She what?!"

"I don't know where she went. When she arrived in the ER, I checked her vital signs. One minute I couldn't detect any, and the next ... she just sat up and said she was fine."

"How's that possible?" Scott asked.

"I couldn't believe it myself. I raced to get the doctor. But when we got back to the room, she was ... gone."

Becka and Scott exchanged glances.

For several minutes Sara stood outside the hospital—the same hospital where John Noey and Ronnie Fitzgerald fought for their lives.

She felt terrible for them ... and for herself.

Her identity seemed to ebb away. *I've used the power of voodoo,* she thought. *Now I must serve its power.*

The irony almost made her laugh, but she knew she must not. The petro loa in her demanded her vigilance. If she let down her guard, even for a moment, it would take over again. And then what little was left of Sara Thomas would vanish.

Completely.

Big Sweet had been right. He had told her that she could not resist the petro loa on her own. If she tried to stand against the spirit, it would make her insane. It would take complete control of her — maybe even kill her.

She remembered other bits of information he had given her after one ceremony.

"Can you heal me of the petro loa?" she had asked hopefully.

Big Sweet had only shaken his head. "No, I cannot do that. But I can teach you how to stay healthy while you learn its ways."

"Learn its ways?" she had asked. "What do you mean?"

"The loa may leave you in time, Sara, but for now, you must learn to live with it. Learn when it is awake and when it sleeps. Learn what it requires of you. Then you will be able to use what is left for yourself."

"You're asking me to let the spirit rule so that it might let me have a little of my life back?" she had asked incredulously.

Big Sweet had nodded. "I know no other way. When my father studied with Marie Leveau, we knew a man who had been a loa cheval for forty years. In the daytime he was a wonderful man. He used to take me fishing. He often brought little candies to us kids. But my father warned us to stay away from him at night. That was when his petro loa came out. He was very violent then. It took five men to hold him down. But his life was not a total loss. He had his days."

Unable to think of this any longer, Sara turned from the hospital and headed down the street. She didn't care where she walked or for how long. She just had to get away.

The streets of Sorrento seemed barren as Sara wandered them. Soon she passed the old church near the library where she worked. Unable to explain her attraction to it, she came to a stop in front of the church, then turned and moved up the stairs. She hesitated before trying the door.

It was open.

It was eerie inside the church at this hour. It was lit only by a small lamp near the front and a few votive candles.

Sara took another step inside and suddenly began to feel very nauseous. Holding her stomach, she turned to go when she was suddenly startled by the presence of an elderly man kneeling in the back pew. He was thin, and his white hair caught the moonlight.

She hoped he wouldn't notice her. But suddenly he looked directly into her eyes.

"Sara?" the elderly man stammered. It was obvious he was as surprised as she was.

For an instant Sara was frozen with shock. Who was this man? How could he know her name? The nausea suddenly increased. She backed away toward the door.

The elderly man rose unsteadily to his feet. "I am Pastor Barchett. Just now I was praying for you. Please, won't you—?"

Sara spun around to the door. The nausea was worse. She had to get out. Still, something inside was crying, begging her to stay. With great effort, she forced herself to turn around and face the pastor.

"Help me ...," she cried. "Please ... help—"

Suddenly her mouth slammed shut. She spun around, then ran for the door.

"Sara, please—"

She could barely hear him over the laughter filling her head—taunting laughter that was not hers. She felt herself moving outside and down the steps. There was no stopping now—the loa was in charge again.

And it was forcing her to return to the ceremony.

❧ ❧

"I say we go back," Scott insisted.

"Scotty ..."

"Listen." Becka's brother was up on his feet, pacing. "We've done everything the Bible said, right?"

"Well, yeah, but—"

"We've prayed and believed, right? Just like Z suggested, just like that pastor guy said."

"I know that, but ..."

"But what?"

"Scotty, she nearly died."

"But she didn't. Come on, Beck, where's your faith?"

"My faith is ..." Becka took a long, deep breath and slowly let it out. Her temperature was up again. She fought off the chills. "I'd like to go, Scotty. But I'm ... I've got nothing left."

Her brother looked at her.

"I'm sorry." She shook her head and pulled in her legs to try to keep herself warm. "I'm wiped out. I'm ... I'm sorry."

Scott looked at her for a long moment. But instead of making her feel guilty, he quietly knelt beside her. "You're right. I don't know what I was thinking. It's been rough on you—way rougher than on me."

"I'm sorry," she repeated. "I feel like a total failure. But I just don't even think I could ..."

"That's okay. You just stay here."

Becka stared at him. "What?"

"You stay here at the hospital and call Mom and Aunt Myrna to pick you up."

"You're not going alone?"

He slowly rose. "Beck, we came here to do a job."

"You saw the power there. You know what can—"

"I know, I know. We've lost a few battles with this one. But the war isn't over. Not yet." He headed for the door.

"Scott—"

"'If you believe, you will receive whatever you ask for in prayer.' Remember, Beck?"

She struggled to her feet. "I know that, but—"

He turned back to her one last time. "Give Mom and Aunt Myrna a call. Have them pick you up. And then the three of you can pray for me."

"Scotty?"

"Pray a lot."

"You can't go there by yoursel—"

But he was already out the door. It slid shut behind him.

Becka fell back in her seat, feeling frustrated and exhausted. She closed her eyes, trying to think what to do. Scott must not go back to the ceremony alone. And yet—

"Excuse me, are you Sara Thomas's friend?"

Becka opened her eyes to see a young doctor standing in front of her. She nodded.

"We'd taken a sample of Sara's blood and were running some tests . . ."

"Yes?"

"Her blood seems to contain trace amounts of a rare poison."

"Poison?"

"Yes—curare. It's from a tree that grows in South America. When you apply it externally like a salve on the skin, it sometimes renders the victim unconscious. It can slow down the heartbeat to where life signs are very hard to detect."

Becka could hardly believe what she heard. "You mean it makes you look like you're dead?"

"Yes. If it's applied externally in small amounts, its effects last less than an hour, which explains Sara's return to consciousness. Unfortunately, if it's taken internally, or if the subject receives too much over a short period of time, well . . ." He hesitated.

"Please, go ahead," Becka insisted.

"I don't know where your friend would have contact with something like this, but she should be careful. If she's exposed to it again too soon, it will kill her."

Becka stood stunned, her mind reeling. The first time, Sara had been lucky. But if she was heading back to the ceremony, and if Big Sweet applied the poison again ...

"Listen, you look a little pale," the doctor said. "Maybe we should take your temperature and—"

Becka started for the door. Of course he was right. She felt terrible. But Sara's life was in danger. And if somebody didn't tell her, if somebody didn't warn Big Sweet and Scott ...

"No, I'm fine," she lied. "Thank you."

"Are you sure?" the doctor called.

But Becka was already out the door. As the doctor's question followed her, she shook her head. She wasn't sure she had the strength to make it back to the ceremony. But she *was* sure of one thing. She had to try.

"Help me," she prayed as she headed down the street. "Please, Lord, give me the strength I need."

9

Doomba-doomba-doom. Doomba-doomba-doom.

The drums echoed through the swamp. Becka was fine as long as she could follow their sound. The moon was three-quarters full and bright enough to allow her to make her way through the thick undergrowth.

She shivered, wondering if the cause was her rising fever, the night air, or the resurgence of her fear. Probably all three.

Doomba-doomba-doom. Doomba-doomba-doom.

Somehow she managed to avoid falling into the water or running face first into branches—both strong possibilities when stumbling through the bayou at night.

Doomba-doomba-doom. Doomba-doomba-doom.

But she still had the drums to direct her. She still had—

Suddenly, they stopped.

Becka hesitated, straining to hear the slightest sound, the slightest clue. None was forthcoming. She had never been in this part of the swamp. Without the drums, she was lost.

Panic gripped her. She wanted to run, to scream for help, to plow through the swamp and its treacherous waters, to keep running and running—running to get out of the swamp, running to help her brother, running to prevent Big Sweet from reapplying his magic balm on Sara.

She struggled with fear—the same fear that had been her enemy throughout the trip. Fear on the plane, the fear of the thresher, and the fear of Sara's curse...

"No!" she shouted to no one in particular. "I am not afraid!"

The fear subsided but only for a moment.

"NO!" she repeated. But the fear left and returned even faster. So she did the only thing she could think of. She began quoting Bible verses—some she had learned as a child and some she had read with Scott earlier that evening.

"'The one who is in you is greater than the one who is in the world... Whatever you ask for in prayer, believe that you have received it, and it will be yours... Perfect love drives out fear...'" As she continued, the fear slowly faded. A peace settled over her. Filling her head with God's truth left no room for fear's lies.

As the peace came, so did a quiet logic. She decided to sit on a nearby log and wait patiently for the drums to resume.

But what if the drums never started again? What if the ceremony was over? What if Sara was already—

Once again Becka thought of the verses. Once again a gentle peace settled over her. Soon she could hear the soft rhythmic chirp of crickets. A thousand tiny insects buzzed. Frogs called from deep within the swamp. The place was a virtual symphony of nature.

Yes, God was good. Very good.

An owl hooted from a distant tree. She soon heard a splash as an animal entered the water, followed by the rattle of a snake...

A snake! Becka froze.

Maybe she was wrong. Maybe it was something else.

No, there it was again. It was a snake's rattle. It was closer than before.

Becka peered at the ground around her feet, looking for some movement.

None came.

The rattle had seemed to come from the left side. She rose, preparing to run to the right.

Then she heard the rattle again.

This time it came from the right.

Ever so slowly, Becka turned. Out of the corner of her eye she saw it. Something slithered along the ground. She turned fast to the left.

Too fast.

Her foot caught on the log. As she toppled forward, she tried to shift but fell backward, arms flailing as she tried to regain her balance.

It did no good.

She landed exactly where she didn't want to be—less than a yard from the snake.

The rattler raised itself up, preparing to strike.

"Please, Jesus," she cried, "make it go away!"

As if in answer, the snake rattled even more menacingly and reared its head back. Becka could see its silver black eyes glaring at her in the moonlight. She closed her eyes, expecting the worst. Then, just as suddenly as it had risen, the snake lowered itself to the ground and slithered off in the opposite direction.

Becka watched, amazed at how loudly her heart was pounding. She realized that the pounding she heard wasn't her heart, but the drums.

She stood up, took a deep breath to steady herself, and headed toward the sound.

❧ ❧

Big Sweet nodded slightly when Scott entered the clearing and found a place in the outside circle. The dancers had already worked themselves into a frenzy as they chanted, whirled, sang, and screamed.

Immediately Scott spotted Sara. She danced with the same jerky movements as before, all the while crying out in a strange language. Her voice was unnaturally deep and husky.

Scott knew the signs.

Sara was possessed.

The time for action had come. He started toward her.

The showdown was about to begin.

Big Sweet also rose from his wicker chair. He wasn't sure what Scott was about to do, but he wasn't taking any chances. The petro loa in Sara Thomas was powerful. If it was cast out of Sara, there was no telling how many of his people it would attack. He would not let them be injured.

Carefully he reached into the leather bag hanging from the back of his chair. He extracted a small tin container. In it was the same potion he had used earlier that night—a potion from the strychnos tree. The tree was originally from South America. Big Sweet's father had transplanted it in the bayou when Big Sweet was a small boy. Its resin was black and brittle. When mixed with certain roots, it turned into a dark brown salve. This was his magic balm.

Scott continued toward Sara. He was ten feet away when she suddenly spun around. She seemed to stare right through him.

Scott had seen that cold, lifeless stare before. He knew that something else looked through Sara's eyes. That something else was what Big Sweet called the petro loa. Scott knew it by another name. Demon.

He came to a stop. Slowly, he raised his right hand. The battle was about to begin.

Sara moved like a puppet. She suddenly snatched a walking stick from a nearby dancer and twirled around, catching Scott off guard. She slammed the stick against Scott's knee, knocking him to the ground.

The demon caused Sara to lunge at him once more, then raised Sara's arm for another blow.

"No!" Big Sweet shouted. He held the open container in his left hand. The fingers of his right hand were covered with a white powder to shield him from the effects of the magic balm. "I speak to the petro loa occupying Sara Thomas. You shall not hurt this boy."

Sara's head nodded in agreement, but the nodding grew more rapid and exaggerated until it was obvious that the spirit mocked Big Sweet.

Scott raised himself to one knee, trying to clear his head. But instantly the petro loa swung the big stick down hard on his shoulder. He cried out in pain.

Big Sweet motioned to his men. Three of them leaped on Sara from behind while Big Sweet dug his hand into the tin of magic balm, preparing to smear it on her.

Sara struggled and almost broke free. A fourth man soon joined the fray. The four managed to hold her down. Big Sweet moved to smear the balm on her arm.

"Stop!" Becka ran into the clearing. "Don't touch her with that! It's poison!"

Big Sweet looked at her. "I must use the magic balm to quiet the petro loa!" he shouted. "It will not kill! It will make the loa sleep! You saw yourself!"

Becka strode quickly toward them. "It *will* kill!"

Big Sweet frowned.

Becka continued. "I spoke to a doctor at the hospital. He said the more you use it, the more dangerous it is. You've already used some to knock her unconscious. He said that if you use more too soon, it will kill her."

"But I must quiet the petro loa before he brings harm to her or to one of my people. Look at your brother."

"I'm okay," Scott said, struggling to his feet. "Nothing's broken."

Sara's body writhed once again. The four men struggled to hold her down.

Big Sweet started toward her once more. "I must quiet the petro loa."

"*I* will quiet the petro loa!" Becka shouted.

All eyes turned to her. She nodded at Scott.

He slowly rose to his feet, returning her nod with a thumbs-up.

She took a deep breath. Turning to face Sara, Becka called out in a loud voice, "In the name of Jesus Christ of Nazareth, I command you to come out of her!"

Nothing happened.

Becka moved closer. "Demon who occupies Sara Thomas, you come out of her now, in the name of Jesus Christ! I order it!"

Suddenly, with superhuman strength, Sara tossed aside the four men who held her. She rose to face Becka. "Who are you?" Sara's mouth moved, but the voice was guttural. "Why do you force your will on others?"

"It doesn't matter who I am," Becka said with confidence. "I am not the one forcing my will. You are! Now, be gone in the name of Jesus Christ—"

"What makes you think—?"

Becka cut the demon's words short with a sharp motion of her hand. She knew all too well how demons argued only to stall or weaken a believer's faith. She would allow neither. She couldn't afford to. "I said go in the name of Jesus Christ! Now!"

Sara's body tensed as if charged by electricity. She let out a loud, ghastly cry before dropping to the ground.

All who watched gasped. Many began to murmur, wondering at the power they had just witnessed.

Becka moved to kneel beside the still girl and tenderly touched her arm. "Sara," she said. "Sara, it's okay now. Sara ..."

Sara's eyes snapped open. Before Becka could move, the girl kicked her with all her might.

Becka cried out, tumbling backward.

"There's more than one of them!" Scott yelled.

Sara leaped to her feet and started for Becka.

"Stop!" Scott shouted. "Enough trickery! I command you to stop in the name of Jesus!"

Sara froze, then slowly faced him with a look of menace.

Faith surged through Scott. He was not about to be intimidated, not when he knew who truly held the power in this situation. "We command you in the name of Jesus Christ to be gone! We cast you into the pit!"

Becka struggled back to her feet and approached from the other side. "Be gone. All of you! We cast all of you out of Sara and into the lake of fire. In the name of Jesus Christ, go!"

Sara's body began to tremble, her face contorting grotesquely. The onlookers backed away. Some turned and ran.

Sara threw her head back and shrieked a long, agonizing wail, more animal than human. It echoed through the trees and across the swamp. Finally, she collapsed on the ground, unconscious.

Becka and Scott looked at each other. They knew she was clean this time. All of the demons had gone. They knelt beside Sara.

"Sara?" Becka said. "Sara?"

A moment later, the girl's eyelids flickered, then opened fully.

"Are you all right?" Becka asked.

Sara nodded. "I think ..." Her voice was hoarse. She licked painfully dry lips. Her eyes looked weary but hopeful. "The spirit's gone, isn't it?"

Becka nodded. "Yes." She started to add, "All of them are" but changed her mind.

Relief crossed Sara's face. For the first time she seemed to relax.

"Is this what you want?" Becka asked. "To be totally free of that kind of spirit forever?"

Sara nodded. "Yes ... yes ... of course." Then her forehead wrinkled. "But what about ... what I did to John and Ronnie?"

"Are you sorry you hurt them?" Scott asked.

"Yes." There was no mistaking the sadness in Sara's voice. "I am very sorry."

Becka smiled warmly. "Then why don't you pray for them with us?"

"Pray? To who?"

"To the very person who gave us the power to cast out the petro loa," Scott answered her.

Sara looked at him. Slowly she nodded.

Becka and Scott bowed their heads. After a moment, Sara followed suit.

"Dear Jesus," Becka began, "we ask your forgiveness for what Sara has done."

"Forgive me," Sara murmured. "And forgive me for what I did to Becka ... by trying to put a curse on her. I'm so sorry for that!"

Becka sighed. "I also forgive her for that, Lord. And we ask that you heal those boys. Make them whole again."

Sara nodded, tears forming in her eyes.

"And, Lord," Becka continued, "please reveal your love to Sara. Help her know your truth."

Sara began to sob.

Becka prayed silently for several moments. When she finished, she looked up at Big Sweet. He seemed astonished by the encounter with the demon and the prayer that followed.

"The magic balm is dangerous," she said.

Big Sweet nodded. "I will not use it again. I only did as my father taught me. The petro loa was bad."

"It was a demon," Scott explained. "Not the spirit of someone who died but a fallen angel. A demon—more than one, actually."

Big Sweet sighed. "Perhaps."

"We believe in one God," Becka explained, "the *Bon Dieu* who rules over everything."

"Bon Dieu." Big Sweet nodded in agreement. "That I understand. But he does not communicate with us."

"He does through his Son," Becka said. "And it was the power of his Son that you saw demonstrated here tonight."

Big Sweet met her eyes. "His Son?"

"That's right," Becka said. "Jesus."

10

Becka and Scott invited Sara back to Aunt Myrna's that night. The three of them talked long into the early hours of the morning.

"I'm really sorry for the way I treated you," Sara said. "I—I was just afraid, after what I did to John and Ronnie, that somebody would try to ..." She dropped off, then shook her head and resumed. "It seems funny now, but this last week it's like all these things happened to someone else. Like it wasn't even me."

"In a way it wasn't," Becka explained. "The more you got involved with voodoo, the more you lost yourself."

Sara shuddered at the thought. "I'm just glad it's finally over."

Becka and Scott exchanged looks.

"Actually—" Scott cleared his throat, "—it isn't over ... at least not yet. But it can be."

Sara looked up concerned. "What do you mean?"

"Those evil spirits—they'll try to come back."

Sara sank deeper into the chair. "Oh no!"

Scott nodded. "The Bible says they will come back if you haven't filled up the vacancy they left."

"Filled the vacancy?" Sara asked.

Becka explained. "The only thing that can protect you from evil spirits is accepting Jesus Christ as your Lord and Savior. Once that happens, once he's in your heart, then when they try to return, you'll have the authority to stop them."

"Are you serious?" Sara asked. "I can have that authority?"

Becka and Scott nodded.

"Well, what do I have to do?"

Carefully Becka and Scott explained how Jesus died on the cross to forgive Sara of her sins. They told her about his being raised from the dead. All she had to do was ask him to forgive her, since he already took the punishment for those sins.

"That's it?" Sara asked.

"That's only half," Scott said. "You also need to let him be your Lord."

"Lord?"

"Yeah, you know—like your boss. The boss of your whole life."

"You mean let him be the boss instead of me?"

Scott nodded. "No offense, but so far things haven't turned out so great with you in charge." He groaned at Becka's quick nudge to his ribs.

Sara nodded, almost smiling. "Then that's what I want to do," she said. "I want to give your Jesus all of my life. I've had lots of trouble. I don't want any more."

"It isn't so much that you won't have trouble," Becka corrected. "It's just that Jesus will always be there to show you the way through any troubles you encounter."

Tears welled up in Sara's eyes. "That's really all I've ever wanted—somebody to show me the way."

And so, after they were sure that Sara understood and was serious about her decision, Becka and Scott led her in prayer. Together they helped her ask Jesus to forgive her of her sins and to come into her heart as the Lord of her life. Soon, before they even knew it, all three were crying and hugging one another. They knew it was just the beginning. Sara would still have a lot to deal with. But she no longer faced the battle on her own.

It was nearly sunrise when Aunt Myrna agreed to drive Sara home. And after several good-byes and a few more hugs, Becka and Scott headed back into the house to get some sleep.

"Can you believe it?" Becka asked. "Everything worked out."

"It sure did," Scott replied. "Not the way we thought it would, but better."

"That's the weird thing about God," Becka said. "He never does things our way."

"Guess he just wants it done right." Scott smirked.

"Guess so."

Becka was asleep before her head hit the pillow. This time, there were no dreams, no tossing and turning—just sleep. Deep, peaceful sleep—something she had needed for days; something she finally enjoyed.

❧   ❧

The next day flew by. Before long, Becka, Scott, and Mom were packed and riding in the car back to the airport.

"Where're you going, Aunt Myrna?" Becka asked as the car pulled onto the main road and turned left instead of right. "This is the way to Sorrento, not the airport."

"Oh, I know, honey, but I wanted to show you something."

Minutes later they passed the library and pulled up in front of Pastor Barchett's church.

"What's going on?" Scott asked.

"Just hold on," Mom said. "You'll see."

They climbed out of the car and headed up the steps to the door.

"Good," Aunt Myrna said, looking inside. "We're just in

time." She opened the door wider. They all slipped into the church.

Only a handful of people occupied the church. But there, standing up front in the baptistry, were Pastor Barchett and Sara Thomas.

Pastor Barchett was in the middle of speaking. "And do you, uh ..."

"Sara," she quietly reminded him.

"Yes, of course." He cleared his throat. "And do you ... Sara, fully understand what you are about to do?"

Sara nodded, looking very solemn.

Becka and Scott watched in silent anticipation.

"Then—" the old man folded her arms in front of her—"I baptize thee in the name of the Father, and of Jesus Christ the Son, and of the Holy Spirit."

He lowered Sara back into the water, then lifted her again. She came out of the water looking radiant. Tears of joy mingled with the water streaming down her face.

Becka and Scott joined the others in applauding. But there was another sound—big, booming laughter, laughter that could only belong to ...

Becka spun around. "Big Sweet! What are you doing here?" She smiled at the two little girls with him.

Big Sweet laughed again. "Why do you say that, Rebecca? I only tried to help Sara. I never wanted her to have such trouble."

Becka nodded. "You're right. I know that now."

He pulled his two daughters closer and continued. "My father taught me voodoo so I could protect myself and my family from bad spirits and curses. Sometimes it works—" he shrugged—"sometimes it doesn't. But this Jesus, this Son of *Bon Dieu*, the God of gods, has much power. I will come by this church now and again to see what I see. What do you think about that?"

"I think that's great," Becka said.

"Me too," Scott agreed.

"I just have one question." It was Aunt Myrna. "What about my goat?"

"I am sorry, Miss Myrna. It wandered onto my place and joined the others. I did not know it was yours. I will give you one of mine. I will give you two."

Everyone applauded that decision.

Outside, the good-byes were brief.

"Come on," Mom fretted, "the plane won't wait."

"Did you hear the news?" Sara asked. "John Noey came out of his coma last night. And they think Ronnie Fitzgerald will be okay too."

"That's great," Becka said.

"Looks like you got your first prayer answered," Scott said to Sara.

She beamed. "And your aunt has hired me to help her out a couple days a week."

"Well ..." Aunt Myrna cleared her throat, a little embarrassed. "I can use a good worker like you around the house. Besides, I could stand a little company, now that my family is going."

"Oh, Aunt Myrna ...," Becka, Mom, and Scott said together.

There was another round of hugs and more than a couple of tears as everyone congratulated Sara and said good-bye.

Then, just before Becka entered the car, Sara whispered something in her ear — something Becka would remember for as long as she lived. "Thank you for showing me the real power," she whispered as she gave her a final hug, "and the real love."

👁 👁

Becka's heart leaped to her throat as she saw Ryan Riordan waiting for them at the airport's baggage claim. He still had that incredible black hair, warm blue eyes, and of course, that killer smile.

"Ryan!" Before she knew it, she had thrown her arms around him.

"I really missed you," he said, pulling her back to look at her. His smile flashed again.

"I missed you too."

"What about me?" Scott broke in. "Anybody miss me?"

Ryan scratched his head. "Dunno, kid. That's a tough one. I'll let you know if I come up with someone."

Scott laughed. "I'll bet Cornelius did." Cornelius was the family's parrot. "That poor bird is probably tired of having only Darryl to squawk at for nearly a week." Darryl was his best friend. "Maybe Darryl's tired of being squawked at too!"

The rest of the group laughed and agreed.

It was just like old times as the good-natured bantering began. But later that evening, when Ryan joined them at home and asked Becka to take a short walk with him, his mood had changed considerably.

"Beck, I've been waiting till we were alone to ask you something."

Becka caught her breath, hoping for some heartfelt words of romance. But when she saw the look in Ryan's eyes, she knew he had something else in mind besides romance.

"I really worried about you while you were away. Is this going to be, like, a regular thing ... you running off to some faraway place whenever that Z guy contacts you?"

"Of course not!" She laughed in relief. "We haven't heard from Z for a while. I'm sure this was just a onetime thing."

The tension left Ryan's face. Once again he broke into his killer smile. "That's good because I—"

"Hey, Beck!" Scott ran out of the house.

Oh, great, Becka thought, not at all pleased with her brother's timing.

"There's a message from Z on the computer. He has another assignment."

Her stomach tightened. "What?"

"Yeah, and here's what's really weird. He wants you to go without me."

"Without you?" Becka asked. "Why? Where?"

Scott paused, purely—Becka was sure—for dramatic effect.

"Where?" she repeated impatiently.

He grinned and waggled his eyebrows. "Transylvania."

"Transylvania?" Becka was shocked. "Isn't that where all those stories take place ... you know about ... well, you know ...?"

"Vampires?" Scott said, grinning.

"But vampires don't ..." Her voice trailed off.

"Exist?" Scott asked.

Becka nodded numbly.

Scott shrugged. "According to Z, something over there has got some actress scared out of her wits. He wants you to check it out."

Becka turned to Ryan, unsure what to say.

But as always, he made it easy. "It's all right, Beck ... I understand."

"Oh, and something else," Scott said.

They both turned back to him.

"He'll send a ticket for Ryan too!"

Becka and Ryan stared at each other. Ryan raised his eyebrows.

"In the mood for a vacation?" Becka asked meekly.

Ryan tried to smile. "Sure, why not?"

But she was sure he was thinking the same thing she was ... Transylvania? *Vampires ...?*

What was Z getting them into now?

Discussion questions for *The Curse:*

1. When Becka and Scott went to the Sorrento library to meet Sara, they wrongly approached the girl dressed in black leather, chains, and purple hair assuming she'd be the one involved in voodoo. They also misjudged what Big Sweet would be like. Have you ever pre-judged someone only to find out that they were completely different than what you thought they'd be like? What happened?

2. John takes Becka on a walking tour to explore the sugar cane fields, swampland, wild vegetation, fragrant flowers, river, and dim, leafy-vaulted chambers. She becomes nearly speechless from its beauty and feels as though she's in a holy place. Have you ever experienced a moment surrounded by nature that made you feel in awe of God's creation? Where was it? Describe what it was like. Were you alone?

3. Sara was sick and tired of being picked on and had enough—to the point she only wanted to get even. She opened herself up to a spirit of revenge and it overtook her. Was her life better or worse after this? What were the dangers?

4. Aunt Myrna's foreman, Big Sweet, turned out to be a hungan, or leader in voodoo practices. Do you think he had bad intentions in the way he lived his life? How can damage be done to others without bad intentions?

5. Sara suddenly realized the extent of the hurt she caused when she overheard John's mother crying in the kitchen, discussing his coma. She just didn't think things through and reacted hatefully. Have you ever made the mistake of reacting before thinking things through and caused more damage than you imagined? How did you end up feeling?

6. Becka gets cursed by Sara and it causes her to wander around in the woods obsessed with flowers. Scotty tells Big Sweet that Becka is a Christian and curses have no control over Christians, but Becka does seem to be under the control of a curse. What could be the explanation for this? How did the curse get broken?

7. In the end, Scotty and Becka help Sara to become free from the evil spirits. What was crucial in the process of freeing her? What might things have been like for Sara if Becka and Scotty hadn't helped?

THE UNDEAD

For God did not give us a spirit of timidity, but a spirit of power, of love and of self-discipline.

2 TIMOTHY 1:7

1

She was seventeen—blonde and beautiful.

At least, she would have been beautiful if her features hadn't been twisted into a mask of terror as she screamed.

She backed up slowly, but there was nowhere to go. She was at the end of a dark alley—a dead end. Her heart beat rapidly, and her eyes were wild as she stared into the darkness. She opened her mouth and screamed again.

Two piercing yellow eyes reflected in the glow of a distant streetlight. Powerful eyes. Eyes that burned with an unearthly gleam. Eyes of hate. Of murder.

The girl stopped abruptly. Backed against the wall, she could go no farther. She pressed against the rough brick, trying to get as flat as possible as the eyes approached. Less than six feet away now, the thing began to move more slowly, as if, now that it knew she was trapped, it enjoyed prolonging her agony. The dim glow of the streetlight held no promise of escape—only one of increasing terror as the evil thing floated into view.

It was hideous.

The girl had been silent for several seconds—either resigned to her fate or too drained by fear to scream anymore—but the screams came alive again when, in the shadowy light before her, that part of the creature that she dreaded most came into view: two long, glistening, white fangs ...

"Cut!"

At the word, yelled from the darkness, Jaimie Baylor relaxed against the stone wall.

"Print that one," the director's voice came again from the darkness. "It's a take."

With that, the alley suddenly came alive. Lights blazed on, crewmen swarmed about, and a dozen voices started talking at once.

Dirk Fallon, the director, could be heard above the others. "That's a wrap, people. Break down. Please don't forget to check your morning call times before you leave. Thank you." Jaimie watched as he walked over to her. Although he wasn't a tall man, Fallon's unfriendly nature was intimidating. She knew what was coming and did her best to meet his stern gaze. "Jaimie? I trust you'll be here on time tomorrow?"

She nodded. "I will."

Fallon stared intently at her, and she tried not to fidget. "No problems then with ... things that go bump in the night. All right?"

"No problems, Dirk," she said, but he was already walking away. She shook her head. He always did that. It was just one of a dozen rude and obnoxious things the man did on a regular basis.

Almost instantly people surrounded Jaimie. A kind-looking, older man from props collected the purse and shopping bag she had been carrying, while a middle-aged woman with brightly dyed red hair took her cape and jewelry. "Just drop the rest off at the costumes trailer before you leave, hon," the woman told her.

"I want to press some of the wrinkles out of this dress before we run it over to makeup to get it bloodied."

"No problem," Jaimie replied, forcing a cheery tone, hoping she didn't sound like someone trying to appear happier than she really was.

"You gonna be okay, kid?" the red-haired woman asked as she folded the cape.

Jaimie smiled at her. "I'm okay, Maureen. Thanks for asking."

Nearby, the actor who portrayed the vampire held his mouth open while a young girl from makeup carefully removed his artificial fangs.

"Better be careful you don't cut yourself there," a man in a bulky sweater said as he walked past the two. Jaimie felt herself relax as she recognized Tim Paxton, the producer of the movie.

"Oh, I'm careful, all right," the makeup girl replied. "These teeth are more expensive than my own!"

Paxton laughed. "Great job today, everyone."

"Producers always say that," the propman joked. "Until you ask for a raise."

Paxton laughed again, and Jaimie smiled as she listened to the banter. The producer had the kind of laugh that made a person feel good.

"Have I ever denied you a raise, Bob?" Paxton asked the propman.

Bob shook his head. "No, Tim, you haven't," he replied. "But then, you've never given me one, either."

They both laughed again, but as Tim walked up to Jaimie, a more serious expression came over his face. "You need an escort back to the hotel? I've got a meeting, but I can get someone."

Jaimie held up her hand. "No, Tim. I'll be fine. I think I was just ... getting into my part too much the other night."

Tim smiled. "Okay. That's good to hear. But let me know if you need anything."

"I will," Jaimie replied.

Tim nodded and moved on, making sure to say hello or to joke a bit with most of the cast and crew before they left the set.

"That Tim Paxton is the nicest guy in the movie industry," Maureen, the red-haired costume lady, said as she watched him disappear into the crowd.

"He sure is." Jaimie nodded. "Not like some others I could mention."

They both cast a glance toward Dirk Fallon, who was busy chewing out his cameraman.

"Yeah," Maureen added. "I'd like to take *him* over to makeup to be bloodied instead of this dress."

Jaimie laughed in spite of herself. "Well, I've got to change. See you at the trailer in five, Maureen."

Maureen nodded, but she didn't glance Jaimie's way. She was still staring at Fallon and shaking her head.

                                           ❧ ❧

Twenty minutes later, Jaimie Baylor walked toward the Golden Krone Hotel, feeling better than she had in nearly a week. It was strange enough being only seventeen and acting in *The Vampire Returns,* a horror movie, but filming in Transylvania put things somewhere out in the zone of weirdness as far as she was concerned.

Everything was geared toward vampires here. Even the hotel. When Bram Stoker wrote his *Dracula* novel a hundred years ago, there wasn't a Golden Krone Hotel in Bistrita, but because he had one in the book they wound up building it decades later. And that wasn't all. Bistrita was full of vampire "landmarks," from the names of the hotels and ruins of nearby castles to the items on the menus in the restaurants. With dishes like "Vampire Steak" and "The Count's Chops," it was no wonder Jaimie had a hard time separating her role in the film from reality.

At least, that's what she told herself tonight as she walked through the dimly lit streets. It was the only explanation that made sense. Sure, since filming began a week ago, she'd twice thought she'd seen a real vampire on the streets at night. But what else could you expect in a place like Bistrita?

She shuddered as she recalled the first "sighting." She'd figured it had to be someone in costume, but the second time ... the second time she was sure whoever — or *whatever* — it was had been stalking her. It had started with echoing footsteps behind her. Every time she had stepped, someone else had stepped. When she stopped, sure enough, she heard footsteps shuffling to a quick stop behind her. That's when she had turned around.

That had been her mistake. That was when she saw yellow eyes and a long black cloak. And that was when she ran back to the set screaming ... making a total fool of herself in front of the crew.

She sighed at the memory. Of course, they had all teased her about taking her role too seriously, but that didn't change anything. She was still sure she had seen something. Something not quite human ...

"Stop it!" Jaimie scolded herself. "Stop thinking about it! It wasn't real." She shook her head, determined to put the whole ridiculous incident out of her mind, when ...

Step.

A chill swept over her. It was the footsteps. Just like before.

She continued walking, her ears straining to hear every sound around her. Most of the time the steps matched hers ... but not always.

She sped up her pace — the footsteps tried to keep up. Her breathing increased. Someone *was* stalking her. There was no doubt about it.

For an instant she thought of turning around and looking. But remembering how horrified she had been the last time, she decided against it. She couldn't bear seeing that face peering at her again.

So she began to run.

The sound of her sneakers on the cobblestones beat out a rhythm in her mind as she raced down the street. There was no mistaking the sound that followed, heavy boots clacking on those same cobblestones.

She reached the top of a small knoll and began to run down the hill. Fog covered the bottom, a ghostly mist patiently waiting to wrap about her.

The gray-and-beige buildings towered above her head. They were centuries old; their stained walls created a patchwork from decades of re-plastering. Above them loomed the moonlit mountains—towering, foreboding.

This was no place to be alone. Not here. Not now.

Jaimie reached the bottom of the hill and entered the fog. The footsteps behind her no longer matched her gait. They were more rapid, trying to catch up ... to close in.

Already she could feel her legs starting to weaken, her lungs starting to burn for more air. She had to slow down. She couldn't keep up this pace. She had to catch her breath.

But the footsteps behind her continued to gain.

She could not, she would not, slow down.

The street snaked its way back up another hill. The incline increased the strain on Jaimie's tortured lungs. Her legs began to lose feeling, as if they were turning to rubber.

And still she forced herself to continue.

Up ahead, glowing through the fog, she saw the lights of the hotel. If she stayed on the winding street, it would be another two or three blocks. If she cut through the approaching alley, she'd shorten the distance by half.

But the alley was dark.

Wouldn't he most likely attack in the dark?

Did it even matter?

She felt her legs start to wobble, and she stumbled. She couldn't go much farther. Her lungs felt like they were about to burst; her heart pounded as if it would explode.

She'd have to chance the alley.

She darted to the left and entered the shadowy passageway. Her mind raced with thoughts, terrible images of throats being ripped open, blood streaming down necks, and piercing yellow eyes.

Jaimie knew such images came more from the skills of modern makeup artists and from seeing too many horror movies than from reality, but at the moment they seemed more like her immediate future than someone's warped fantasy.

She continued gasping for air, unable to get enough. Her legs had lost feeling. She wasn't going to make it.

Her right leg betrayed her. It buckled, and she stumbled and tripped. She started to fall but threw out her hand to catch herself against the wall. She succeeded, but in that moment, leaning against the wall, gasping for breath, she stole a look over her shoulder.

A stupid mistake, and she knew it even as she turned her head—but she had to see.

And there, racing toward her in the shadows, was her worst fear.

A vampire.

As it ran toward her, its great black cape billowed out and above like two giant bat wings beating against the night air.

Blind terror forced a scream from Jaimie's burning lungs. She shoved herself away from the wall and started running again. She could see the lighted end of the alley, but she'd never reach it. Her legs no longer worked.

They gave way, and she fell ... tumbling, sliding. Rolling onto her back, she looked up at the approaching figure and screamed again.

👁 👁

Rebecca Williams walked down the steps of the Golden Krone Hotel, accompanied by Ryan Riordan, her boyfriend. At least, that's what everyone they knew considered him. But neither Rebecca nor Ryan felt totally comfortable with the whole boyfriend-girlfriend label. Maybe it was the sexual pressure such a relationship could put on them. Becka wasn't sure. But she was sure of one thing: There was no one she wanted to hang out with more than Ryan, and for some reason she couldn't figure out, he seemed to feel the same way about her.

She often marveled at how good-looking he was. With his thick black hair and bright blue eyes, he could speed up any girl's heartbeat. And when he flashed that amazing grin of his, any red-blooded female was liable to go into cardiac arrest. Even here, thousands of miles from home, girls stopped and stared at him as he went by. But it wasn't his looks that got to Becka. What really touched her were his feelings for her. Her. Plain old Rebecca Williams, who was too tall and had way-too-thin, mousy brown hair. What did he see in her, anyway?

Her best friend, Julie, had laughed when Becka asked her that question. "He sees *you,* silly. The kind of person you are inside."

Becka didn't feel that she was all that great a person inside, either. But she was grateful for whatever it was Ryan saw in her.

"It's kind of pretty here," Ryan said, pulling Becka from her thoughts. "I mean, in a weird sort of way."

Becka nodded. "It's like someplace in a dream."

It was true. In fact, so far the whole trip seemed like a dream. Maybe it was because Becka never thought about going to Transylvania. To be honest, until a few days ago, she hadn't even been sure the place existed outside of movies and horror novels.

But here they were, less than a week after Z's mysterious email.

Things were like that with Z. When they moved to California, he'd started communicating with Rebecca and her younger brother, Scott, on the Internet. All they knew about him was his screen name. They'd never been able to find out his real name, much less anything about him. But, for whatever reason, he had singled out the two of them. For the last year or so, he'd been carefully guiding and directing them in their faith, equipping them with information and truths from the Bible as they helped people who were caught up in the occult. First there had been that group in their own town that had been playing with Ouija boards, then the hypnosis that had almost destroyed Becka, the satanist group that had tried to curse Becka—and on it had gone, from counterfeit hauntings to demons disguised as angels, to UFOs, to voodoo in Louisiana.

So when Z had sent them tickets to Transylvania last week and asked them to help a young actress there, they'd started packing. Of course, Mom came along too. Rebecca and Scott's father had disappeared in a plane crash in the Brazilian jungle, and the tragedy had brought the three remaining family members even closer. But for some reason, Z had thought Ryan would be better suited for this trip than Scott. And since Z had sent only three tickets and since he'd never been wrong before, Mom agreed that Scott should stay behind with their aunt back in California.

Becka couldn't be happier. Of course, she loved her little brother, but sometimes his sense of humor really got on her nerves. Besides, what could be more romantic than going off to some faraway country with her heartbreaker boyfriend!

Okay, so maybe they weren't officially boyfriend and girlfriend, and maybe it was a pretty weird country, and maybe her mom was tagging along a little too much, but still—

This time Becka's thoughts were interrupted by a man in a bulky blue sweater coming out of the hotel. "Excuse me," he called to them, "are you the people who just arrived from America? I'm Tim Paxton, the producer of the film."

"Hello, Mr. Paxton." Ryan and Becka extended their hands.

The producer continued. "There was a message for me at the desk. You want to see Jaimie Baylor?"

"Yes," Ryan said. "We were wondering where to find her, and the hotel clerk said you would be the best person to ask, Mr. Paxton."

"Please, call me Tim," he said, flashing a smile that made Becka immediately feel at ease. "I'm afraid we're all a bit hard to reach at the moment. Just finished shooting for the day, and everyone's probably gone to eat somewhere. But, if you'd like, I'll take you over to the set. Jaimie was still there when I left a little while ago."

"That would be great," Becka replied. She had never seen a movie set. This would be fun.

Tim led them down the old cobblestone road at a brisk pace. "Sorry to hurry you, but it's been a long day, and I'm sure the gang won't hang around long. You guys friends of Jaimie's from Chicago?"

"Uh, well no, not exactly," Becka said, wondering what the producer would say once he found out they had never even met her. But she didn't have time to worry for long. An ear-piercing scream sliced the air, and they spun around.

"What was that?" Becka cried.

"It came from there!" Ryan said, pointing to a dark alley just behind them. He and Tim Paxton ran toward the alley, with Becka close behind—but as soon as she reached the edge of the alley, she stopped cold, frozen by what she saw.

Thirty feet away, a young blonde girl was lying on the street, holding her hands over her face, screaming. And leaning over her was a large figure in a black cape.

Instantly, Tim and Ryan charged down the alley.

At first the creature hesitated, as if it intended to attack the two men. Then he turned with a great flurry of his cape and sped off, quickly disappearing into the night.

2

It was some time before Jaimie calmed down. In fact, they had been back in her hotel room for almost an hour before she fully realized that Becka and Ryan had come to Transylvania specifically to see her.

"To see me?" she asked, her hazel green eyes wide as she looked at Ryan. "You came all the way here to see me?"

"I guess *we* forgot to tell you in all the excitement," Becka said, careful to emphasize the *we*. It was all too obvious that Jaimie had noticed Ryan's good looks. "But *we* came here to help you."

Jaimie looked at her in surprise. "Help me? How?"

"Do you have a computer?" Ryan asked.

Jaimie nodded. "Sure. My laptop's over there by the phone. Only really talk to a couple of people and—"

"Does one of them call himself 'Z'?" Becka asked.

"Z? Well, yeah," Jaimie said. "Do you know him?"

"In a way," Ryan answered. "Becka and her brother talk to him online all the time."

"He's the one who sent us," Becka added. "He bought us the tickets and told us you needed some help."

Jaimie looked bewildered. "He did?"

Becka and Ryan nodded.

Jaimie thought for a moment. "You know, I told him all about the film and my fears and everything. There wasn't anyone here I could confide in, so I talked to him. I figured, since he didn't really know me, it couldn't hurt. But ..." She frowned.

"But what?" Ryan asked.

"Well, I used the code name Lucy Westenra."

"Who?" Becka asked.

"You know, the girl who was attacked in the original *Dracula* novel. I used her name. I wonder how this Z fellow knew it was me."

"He's pretty clever," Becka said.

"Maybe it's because this is the only movie on vampires being made here," Ryan said. "And since you're the only girl starring in it ..."

"I guess that could tip a person off." Jaimie closed her eyes, and a quiet sob escaped her.

"Hey, you okay?" Ryan asked.

She nodded and tried unsuccessfully to fight back tears. "I just can't believe what's happening," she said in a choked voice.

"Don't cry," Ryan said, moving in to comfort her. "You're making me feel terrible."

"I'm sorry," Jaimie said, looking up at him, "but if it wasn't for you and Tim ... I don't know."

Becka watched Jaimie. For some reason, she didn't entirely believe the girl's tears. Of course, Jaimie had every right to be frightened, but Becka couldn't quite fight off the feeling that this beautiful blonde movie star was using the moment to play up to Ryan. She could be wrong, but still ...

Maybe it was time to address the vampire business. To put what was happening in the light of the truth. "Jaimie —" she cleared her throat — "I don't know why this is happening or who is doing this, but we can't let it cloud our thinking."

Jaimie glanced at her quizzically.

Becka continued. "Vampires aren't real. I mean, we all know that. Someone was just trying to scare you, that's all."

"Easy, Beck," Ryan cautioned. "This poor girl's been through a horrible experience."

Becka blinked in surprise. Why were guys always such suckers for girls in tears?

Jaimie just looked up at him, blinking back the tears as she reached out and patted his hand. "Thanks, Ryan."

He nodded, then looked back at Becka. "I don't think Jaimie needs someone putting her through a hard-boiled reality check just yet, do you?"

The words hit Becka like a slap in the face. She blinked again. Maybe she'd been wrong. It was obvious Jaimie was still struggling with what had happened. And you really couldn't blame her for turning to someone like Ryan for comfort.

Maybe he was right; maybe she shouldn't have brought it up so soon. "I'm sorry," she said softly. "I didn't mean ..." She let the words trail off.

"It's okay," Jaimie replied. "It's just that people on the set have been making fun of me ever since the last time I saw it."

Ryan looked at her, surprised. "This has happened before?"

Jaimie nodded and told them about her previous encounter with the vampire—the footsteps, the billowing black cape, the yellow glowing eyes, and her panicked race to the film set only to be met with the cast and crew's laughter and joking.

"Well, at least no one will be telling me I imagined this one," she said. "No one's going to tell me I'm taking my role too seriously now. Not when other people have seen him too."

Ryan agreed.

"Why would someone want to scare you like that?" Becka asked.

"Scare me?" Jaimie's voice rose. "The vampire was trying to *kill* me."

"Jaimie," Becka remained quietly firm, "there simply isn't such a thing as a vampire. I'm sure he looked very frightening, but that was just some guy trying to scare you."

Jaimie stared hard at Becka. Then she reached up and pulled the collar of her turtleneck sweater down a bit. "If he was just trying to scare me, why did he do this?"

Becka caught her breath.

Two long scratches ran down Jaimie's neck. They were not bites really—they were more the kind of mark that would be made if two huge fangs had suddenly pulled away before they could complete the kill.

❧ ❧

The next day, Ryan, Becka, and Mrs. Williams all went down to watch the filming. Though Jaimie was still unknown as an actress and though *The Vampire Returns* was a fairly low-budget movie, they were all excited about visiting the set.

"Are you sure we won't be in the way?" Mom asked as they left the hotel.

"We'll be okay," Ryan answered. "Besides, Jaimie said she'd feel better if we were there."

"Nobody else connected with the film is even close to her age," Becka explained, "and she's still pretty shaky. She feels like she can relate to us best."

"So what do you kids think really happened to this girl?" Mom asked as they walked down the alley.

"I've read of cases where deranged people actually believed they were vampires," Becka said.

"Really?" Mom asked.

"Even enough to bite people in the neck?" Ryan inquired doubtfully.

"Even enough to kill them and drink their blood," Becka replied. "There was this guy in Germany who was convinced he had a blood disease that required him to drink human blood every so often to stay alive."

"That's a cheery thought," Mom said.

Ryan added, "Well, if some guy's actually attacking her, trying to bite her neck, then it really doesn't matter whether he's a real vampire or not. He's just as dangerous."

"Well, in one sense, yes," Becka agreed, "but in another sense, it matters a lot."

"Why's that?" Ryan asked.

Becka met his look. "A real vampire would be a lot more dangerous to catch."

When they arrived at the set, Jaimie and another actor were preparing to film a scene. Becka was surprised at how much equipment and how many crew members were involved. Even though it was the middle of the day, several big lights glowed from large stands. High overhead and spanning across two rooftops, a gigantic canvas made of some sort of reflective material overlooked the set.

"I thought this was supposed to be a small production," Ryan said.

"Think what a big production must be," Becka answered.

All around people scurried about, doing their jobs to set up the scene. Men were laying some sort of track in front of a large cart that held the camera. Several stagehands were positioning huge blocks to look like a castle wall, the lighting crew was aiming the lights, prop people were placing flags, torches, and weapons at various places on the wall, and the hair and makeup folks were putting the finishing touches on the actors.

Suddenly, the assistant director's voice bellowed, "We're ready, people. Settle in, please. Nice and quiet."

Instantly, all action stopped. No one moved. No one spoke.

Ryan, Becka, and Mom stood on a small knoll overlooking the scene. From this location they could see everything.

Jaimie and an older man stood on the makeshift castle wall, waiting to begin.

The director rose from his canvas chair and walked over to the cameraman. He looked briefly through the lens to confirm the shot and then nodded back to the assistant director.

"Stand by!" the assistant director called. "Roll sound."

"Speed," a man sitting at a tape recorder responded.

"Camera?" the assistant director asked.

"Rolling," the cameraman said.

"Mark it."

A young man with a clapboard stepped between the camera and the actors. "Scene 35, take one." He snapped the board shut and stepped out of the way.

"And ... action!" the director called.

Jaimie and the older man began to walk—Jaimie up on the wall, the man on the castle walkway a few feet below. The camera followed them on the tracks very low to the ground and shooting up so that it looked like they were very high, when in reality they were only a few feet off the ground.

"I tell you, I'm all right, Robert," Jaimie shouted back to the actor as she threaded her way slowly along the top of the wall. "There's no need for you to keep me inside at night anymore."

The man shook his head. He spoke in a thick German accent and crossed his arms when he spoke. "You are not all right, I tell you. You have been bitten by one of the lords of the night, and if you even so much as smell the night air, your very blood will cry out to him. And he will find you and take you and make you his slave for all eternity. Is that what you want?"

From the knoll, Becka and Ryan exchanged glances. The scene was quite convincing.

On the set, Jaimie stared at the man for a long moment while the camera slowly and silently dollied in for a closer shot. "Of course not," she said. "But am I to be a prisoner in this house every night?"

The man nodded firmly. "Yes, until we catch the vampire."

With his thick accent, he pronounced *vampire* as if it were spelled *vampeer.* A long moment of silence passed, during which Jaimie turned and took a few steps away from the man. Then she began to wobble, as if losing her balance on the high wall.

"Stop!" the older man shouted. "Don't move or you might fall. Let me come to you."

He carefully walked toward her.

Jaimie regained her balance and turned back to him to shout, "What if you never catch him?"

"Cut!" The director yelled and then walked over to Jaimie. "Jaimie, Jaimie, Jaimie. Sweetheart, you've got to take more steps away from him before delivering that line. It looks too forced this way. Walk as if you're still planning on escaping down the roof, and then spin around and say it to him. All right?"

Jaimie nodded, and the director was starting to walk back when Maureen, the wardrobe lady, came up to him and said something.

Clearly frustrated, the director shouted, "Break! Five minutes while Maureen does the work she should have done before we started!"

Instantly, the set filled with noise and commotion. Maureen ran over to Steve Delton, the actor playing Van Helsing, and helped take off his waistcoat. Quickly and efficiently, she began stitching a button that had come loose.

Jaimie looked up and spotted Ryan and Becka. "Hi, guys!" she shouted. "I'll be there in a minute, just as soon as I get my hair checked."

Suddenly, the director's voice sounded through his megaphone. "Jaimie, stay here. If you go climbing up that hill, your hair will need to be done again. Your friends can come down here to talk to you."

Becka was embarrassed, but Jaimie's friendly wave encouraged her to come down and talk to her.

"Mom," Becka said, turning to speak to her mother, "are you coming with—" but she stopped.

Her mother was several yards away, talking with a rugged-looking man carrying a video camera.

"Mom," she called, "are you coming?"

"No, I'm fine here, dear," she said. "Tell Jaimie hi for me."

The rugged man leaned toward Mom, saying something to her. She laughed and tossed her hair to the side—a clear sign that she was nervous.

"Who's that guy?" Becka asked as she and Ryan descended the hill.

Ryan shrugged. "Who knows? He seems to like your mother, though."

"That's what I mean."

"It's okay," Ryan said as he picked up his pace to head down the hill. "I'm sure she can take care of herself. Come on, let's hurry."

"Yeah," Becka said. She was still concerned, but not so much over Mom as over the way Ryan was suddenly racing ahead of her to see Jaimie. Was it her imagination, or did he seem just a bit too eager? Actually, he seemed a *lot* too eager. By the time Becka finally caught up to him, Jaimie was already introducing him to her friends on the set.

"You've been holding out on us, Jaimie," Maureen chuckled as Becka approached. "Keeping a cute guy like this stashed away."

Everybody laughed, including Ryan.

What's he *laughing about?* Becka wondered as she carefully positioned herself between Jaimie and Ryan.

"Oh, and this is Becka," Jaimie added. Unfortunately, no one paid much attention as they spotted Dirk Fallon, the director, heading in their direction. Suddenly, they all made themselves scarce.

As Fallon approached, Becka couldn't help noticing that the

guy had a major attitude. "Who does he think he is?" she whispered to Jaimie.

Jaimie shushed her. "He's the director."

"I know," Becka whispered back. "But why does he have to act so—"

"Are we ready to go again, Jaimie?" Fallon interrupted as he approached. Becka could see that the man's very presence made Jaimie nervous.

"Yes, Dirk, I'm ready," Jaimie said. "Oh, by the way, these are my friends from—"

"I'll meet them later, dear," he said, cutting her off. "We've got a picture to make." Then, without waiting for a response, he spun around and nodded to the assistant director.

"Places, everyone," the assistant director shouted. "We're ready."

The activity on the set accelerated dramatically as the actors and the crew resumed their positions for filming.

"Talk to you later," Jaimie whispered to Ryan. She gave Becka a friendly nod and hurried to her place.

Ryan motioned over his shoulder toward the director as he and Becka headed back up to the top of the knoll. "That guy's a real jerk."

Becka nodded. "I don't think I like film people."

"Well, Jaimie's real nice."

Becka met his gaze. "Is she?"

"Sure ... I mean, well, yeah." He eyed her, confused. "What do you mean?"

"Nothing, I guess. She just seems kind of phony, if you ask me."

Ryan studied her for a minute. "Beck, you don't think you're, maybe, a little jealous, do you?"

"Jealous!" Becka said the word so loudly that the nearest crew members looked up at them.

"Easy! You'll get us tossed out of here."

She lowered her voice. "What do you mean, I'm jealous?"

Ryan shrugged. "I just meant that since she's a star and everything—"

"She's not a star. This is only her second film, and nobody saw the first one."

"I know, I know, but she does get treated pretty special."

"So?"

"So, maybe all the attention she gets is bothering you a little."

They had reached the top of the hill, and Becka stared at him dully. "Yeah, I guess it does. I guess all the attention she gets does bother me."

Ryan nodded. "You see. But that's just how these people are. Everybody makes a big deal of the star."

Becka stared at him. "I guess they do," she said in cool tones. He didn't respond, didn't even seem to notice her displeasure. Without another word, she turned and started toward her mother. She could feel Ryan's eyes on her, and she could tell he still didn't get it.

Guys ... they could be so clueless sometimes.

Mom and the rugged man were still talking, and as Becka approached, they started to laugh. "What's so funny?" she asked.

"Oh, nothing," Mom said. "John was just telling me what a hard time he's had adjusting to the customs here in Transylvania. He's a reporter from New York."

"Hi, Becka," the man said. "I'm John Barberini. With *Preview* magazine."

"Hi," Becka said, doing her best to sound pleasant, though she didn't much like him. "So, you're doing a story on the film?"

"I sure am. And it looks like I'm in luck. This vampire business will make for great copy."

"You don't believe it, do you?" Becka asked.

"I didn't say I believed it, just that it makes for a great story."

"John has offered to show us some good places to shop," Mom said. "You can bring Ryan."

"Who wants to?" Becka muttered under her breath, then added out loud, "Ryan and I, we sort of made plans to hang out with Jaimie. Maybe we can do it anoth—"

"Guess we'll have to settle for a duet then," John said, turning to Mom and smiling just a little too broadly.

To Becka's surprise, Mom smiled back.

"Becka…" It was Ryan coming up the hill. "Becka, can I talk to you?"

Becka turned to him, but before she could speak, the assistant director shouted through his megaphone, "Quiet, please! Stand by. Roll sound."

"Speed," came the response.

"Camera?"

"Rolling."

"Marker."

"Scene 35, take two!"

"And … action!" Dirk Fallon shouted.

Once again, Steve Delton, the actor playing Van Helsing, delivered his line. "Yes, until we catch the *vampeer*."

Only this time Jaimie took several steps along the wall before turning around and saying, "What if you never catch him?"

Van Helsing walked toward her. "We will catch him, my dear. I promise you. Please, come down from there. You need your rest. And here, I've brought something for you."

He took out of his pocket a golden chain, from which dangled a large and ornate cross. "Wear this at all times. It is your only protection."

She knelt down so he could reach up and put the necklace over her head.

But as soon as the crucifix touched her skin, Jaimie shrieked in pain. Her knees buckled, her body crumpled, and she half rolled, half fell off the small wall onto the ground.

Ryan and Becka thought it was all part of the script until Fallon shouted, "Cut! Cut! What happened? Is she all right?"

Delton stood helplessly over Jaimie's still form. It was clear from his expression that he was no longer playing a role. "I don't know," he said as crew members quickly circled around Jaimie. "She fainted. Quick, somebody get a doctor. Somebody get a doctor!"

3

It looks like an acid burn to me," the crotchety old doctor said as he carefully examined Jaimie's neck. She lay on the sofa inside her dressing-room trailer. An angry red mark now covered the red scratch she'd had from before.

"Acid?" Tim Paxton exclaimed. "How can that be? Where's that cross?"

Tim was one of several onlookers inside Jaimie's trailer, a group that also included Ryan and Becka. Very carefully, a propman handed Tim Paxton the cross. The producer looked at it closely for a long moment and then pushed up the sleeve of his jacket.

Everyone waited in expectation as he pressed the cross against his own skin.

But nothing happened. No burn, no pain. Nothing.

Tim sighed. He looked back to the red mark on Jaimie's neck and shook his head. "I'm sorry, Jaimie. I don't know what's going on, but I promise you, we'll get to the bottom of this."

Jaimie did her best to put on a brave smile.

A light flashed suddenly, and Becka turned to see John Barberini lowering his camera.

"Who let him in here?" Tim Paxton shouted.

"Take it easy. I'm going, I'm going," Barberini said as he left the trailer.

"You'd better not use that shot!" Tim called after him. Then, looking to the group inside, he added, "I think it might be good if we all leave. Jaimie needs some rest."

The crowd agreed and started to move out.

"We'd better get back to the hotel," Becka whispered to Ryan. "I think it's time we contacted Z."

Ryan nodded, but before they got to the door, Jaimie called out, "Ryan, could you please stay for a while? I don't want to be alone."

Ryan looked to Becka. "Maybe I should stick around. I mean, if you don't mind."

"It would sure be helpful for us," Tim said from behind them. "You always seem to pick up her spirits a little."

Ryan nodded but continued to wait for Becka's response.

Becka bit the inside of her lip. What was wrong with him? Couldn't he see what Jaimie was pulling? But before she could answer, Jaimie interrupted.

"Say, Tim? Remember how we talked about needing someone to go over my lines with me?"

Tim nodded. "A dialogue coach, of course. But I haven't found anyone who—"

"What about Ryan?" she asked. "Couldn't we hire him?"

Becka's eyes darted to Tim.

"Well, yeah," he said, "I guess we could. If he wanted to do something like that. I mean, I can't pay much, but if he wants the job—"

"Are you kidding?" Ryan exclaimed. "A job with a movie? I'd love it!"

Tim chuckled and held out his hand. "Then it looks like we've got ourselves a deal."

An excited Ryan shook the producer's hand.

"Just find out when Jaimie's breaks are each day and read through the upcoming scenes with her," Tim said. "And I'll go ahead and add you to the payroll. How does seventy-five a day sound?"

"Seventy-five ... dollars?" Ryan croaked.

Tim smiled. "And all the food you can eat."

Ryan spun around to Becka, not believing his good luck. "Wow! I'm in showbiz!"

Becka could only stare.

Spotting the look of concern on her face, he asked, "Are you all right? I mean, this is cool with you, right?"

Part of Becka wanted to shout at him or slug him. How could he be so insensitive? So dense? But the other part, the "mature adult" part, knew that this was a great opportunity for him. Besides, it wasn't like they were married or anything.

So, before she could stop herself, Becka said, "Do what you want, Ryan. I mean, if that's what you want, then go for it."

"Are you sure?" he asked.

She just looked at him. He was so thoughtful and sensitive ... and clueless.

"Sure." She shrugged. "Whatever."

Suddenly Dirk Fallon poked his head into the trailer. "So what's the story?"

Tim turned to the doctor. The old man had just finished treating Jaimie's neck with an ointment and answered, "Nothing serious. Just a minor acid burn."

"Acid burn?" Fallon's voice sounded both shocked and skeptical.

The doctor nodded. "I put some salve on it. Let her rest for a while, and she'll be fine."

"How long of a while?" Fallon asked. "We're trying to make a movie here, you know."

"A few hours at least," the doctor said as he put his things into a leather bag and prepared to leave the trailer.

"A few hours?" Fallon turned to his producer, incredulous. "We've lost an hour and a half here already, Tim. We're falling way behind schedule."

"Calm down, Dirk."

"Calm down? Calm down?" the director's voice was rising.

"The girl's had a rough time," Tim said.

Fallon shook his head. "Yeah, well, just don't get upset when we run over schedule and out of money."

Tim was not giving any ground. "If we run out of money—and I do mean *if*—as the producer *I'll* be the one who has to deal with getting more. Correct?"

By way of an answer, Fallon turned from the trailer door, hoisted his megaphone, and shouted, "Two-hour break for principal cast. Crew, set up for the next shot."

Meanwhile, Becka had stepped from the trailer and was angrily making her way toward the hotel.

"Rebecca?" It was Tim Paxton calling. "Becka?"

She slowed her pace as he joined her. "Say, I hope you don't mind about me hiring Ryan."

"Why would I mind?" she lied.

"It's just that he seems to be a real comfort to Jaimie, and I think she needs all the help she can get right now."

"Why are you telling me?" she asked. "Ryan can do what he wants. It's not like he's my boyfriend or anything." As soon as the words came out, she regretted them. Sure, she and Ryan tried not to use the terms *boyfriend* and *girlfriend,* but there had always been an understanding between them. Or at least there had been until Jaimie came into the picture.

"Really?" Tim studied her face curiously. "I just sort of assumed ... well, that's great then, for everyone, I mean." Tim checked his watch. "Well, I'd better go. Gotta get back in there and fight with the director. We'll see you a little later."

Becka forced a smile as he turned and walked away. She headed for the hotel, determined not to focus on the fact that she'd more than likely made a bad situation even worse.

❧ ❧

Back at the hotel, Rebecca was surprised to see John Barberini, the reporter, in the lobby. "Hi there," he said. "Tell your mother I'm here, will you? I'm ready to do some serious shopping."

Becka nodded. "All right."

"Sure you don't want to join us?"

She shook her head. "No, I've got ... something I have to do." Becka started to leave but then felt Barberini's strong hand on her shoulder.

"So what do you think about that crucifix business? Is that girl turning into a vampire or what?"

Becka stared at him. "What do you mean?"

"Well, I may not be up on my vampire lore, but when somebody's been bitten by a vampire and then her skin gets burned by the touch of a crucifix ... sounds to me like she's turning."

"Turning?"

"Yeah, you know. That's how it works, right? If somebody gets bitten by a vampire, that person turns into one too."

Suddenly an image of Jaimie sinking her own fangs into Ryan's neck flashed into Becka's mind. She swallowed and answered coolly, "I don't believe in such things." She turned away, then called back over her shoulder, "I've got to go. I'll tell Mom you're here."

Barberini nodded and smiled a crude sort of smile, which made her like him even less. She crossed to the elevator, went inside, and pressed the button. When the door closed, she leaned against the back wall for support. Everything seemed to swirl so fast now. Ever since she'd arrived here, she'd felt like she was in some sort of crazy dream. And now the dream seemed to be turning into a nightmare.

"Mom," she said as she entered their hotel suite, "that creepy reporter guy's waiting downstairs for you."

Mom looked up from applying her makeup in front of the dresser mirror. "What's bothering you?"

Becka shrugged. "Nothing. I just think that guy is a total jerk."

"You don't even know him," Mom said, her tone a little more firm than before.

"You should've seen him snapping pictures of the doctor examining Jaimie in her trailer."

"Honey, that's his job."

"I just get the feeling he's glad that all this is happening, that's all."

Mom leaned into the mirror for one last check and then stood up. "I doubt he's glad, sweetheart. But it is his job to cover what's happening here."

Becka watched her mother put the finishing touches to her hair. Finally she said what had been rattling in the back of her head. "John's not a Christian, is he?"

Mom paused, then turned to face her. "No, Rebecca, I don't think he is."

"You always say I shouldn't date a non-Christian, so what are you—"

"Rebecca, he just offered to help me do a little shopping."

"Yeah, but—"

"Honey, I know this is hard for you, but you have to trust me. I'm not dating John. We're just going shopping. Now, I have to go. We'll talk later, honey. All right?"

Becka took a deep breath and slowly let it out. Her mom was trying her best to be open and fair. Maybe she should do likewise. "All right," Becka said. "I'll see you when you get back."

Mom smiled. As she picked up her purse and crossed for the door, she gave Becka a gentle peck on the cheek. "Bye, honey."

She opened the door, then turned back one last time. "And don't worry so much. Everything will be just fine."

Becka nodded and cranked up another smile before Mom turned and headed out the door.

Later, as she unpacked the laptop and plugged in the power adapter, Becka felt bad about quizzing Mom. After all, it was just shopping. As a single parent, her mom had been through a lot. Ever since Dad's plane crash, she'd been the one who'd had to hold the family together. And if some guy showed a little interest and offered to be helpful, wasn't she at least entitled to that? Besides, Mom was a big girl. She could take care of herself.

At least, Becka hoped she could.

Carefully, she turned on the laptop and typed in Z's address. She planned to leave a message for him to contact her the next time he was online, but she was in luck. He was already in a chat window, waiting.

Hello, Rebecca. How do you like Transylvania?

As she read his words, Becka felt better. Hearing from Z usually gave her a sense of peace. In some strange way it reminded her of when she used to talk to her father. Maybe it was because he always seemed to have the answers. Or maybe it was because she knew he cared.

For the next few minutes Becka typed away, trying to explain to Z all that had happened since they'd arrived. Every once in a while he'd ask a question, but mostly he just listened.

Finally, she'd told him everything ... well, just about everything. She'd left out the part about when she thought Jaimie was putting the moves on Ryan and how she had been feeling some major jealousy. After all, that didn't have anything to do with vampires.

Needless to say, she was more than a little surprised when Z asked:

How is Ryan doing?

Becka typed one word:

Fine.

She waited, but Z gave no response. That's what he usually did when he knew there was more. Finally, almost reluctantly, she added:

He likes it here.

After a moment, Z asked:

How does he like Jaimie?

Rebecca's mind raced. Had Z known Ryan would fall for Jaimie? Had he arranged it by sending Ryan a ticket? Of course, she realized she was being foolish. This was just Z's way ... He always seemed to know what was happening, whether anybody told him or not. It was one of the many strange things about him, and it always made her feel just a little uneasy. But since he already knew what was going on, she quit beating around the bush and typed:

All right, so I'm jealous.

Z typed back:

Remember why you're there. Jaimie needs your help.

Becka was offended. She'd been *trying* to help Jaimie—hadn't she been the one to remind the girl that vampires weren't real? But it seemed all the pretty actress was interested in was Ryan. Frustrated, she decided to change the subject.

What about the vampire?

The response was almost immediate:

There are no such things as vampires.

Becka scowled. Yeah, well, she knew that, but what about everything that had happened? The attacks on Jaimie, the fang marks, the burning cross? *Something* was going on! Before she could type her questions, Z added the following:

I cannot explain all that is happening, but unexplained circumstances don't change truth. And this is the truth: There is no such thing as a vampire.

There he goes again, Becka thought. Sometimes talking to Z could be very confusing. She reached for the keyboard and typed:

So what are we supposed to do?

Z's answer was typical:

Always remember, "God did not give us a spirit of timidity." Look past the fear.

Quickly she typed:

How?

Let God's love show through you.

Becka answered immediately:

Yeah, but—

She got no further. Z's message cut her words off:

Must go. Keep me posted. Z

Becka let out a short, frustrated sigh. Part of her felt comforted because Z had confirmed that there were no vampires, but another part was frustrated, angry, and confused.

And right now, that part was winning out.

❧   ❧

Becka woke with a start. She had sprawled out on the bed, intending to close her eyes for only a second. A quick glance at the window told her it was already dark outside. She must have slept longer than she'd planned.

As she lay in the darkness, she tried to recall her nightmare. She couldn't remember the details, just the fear and the swirling darkness that twisted throughout the dream like a black, evil snake.

And, of course, the strange tapping sound.

A weird tap-tap-tap had echoed through the dream. It kept coming back, over and over again. She could almost hear it now. In fact ... she held her breath ... she *was* hearing it now.

It seemed to come from the window. At first she thought it was a tree branch. Then she remembered they were on the fourth floor.

No trees here went up that high.

Her heart started pounding. She reached over, switched on the light by her bed, and listened.

Tap-tap-tap.

Tap-tap-tap.

She fought the fear that made her want to crawl under the covers and wait for the sound to go away.

Tap-tap-tap.

Tap-tap-tap.

She had to find out what it was.

Tap-tap-tap.

Tap-tap-tap.

Slowly, mustering all the courage she could find, she eased her feet over the side of the bed.

Tap-tap-tap.

Tap-tap-tap.

Carefully, absolutely silent in her stocking feet, she approached the closed curtain.

Tap-tap-tap.

She swallowed hard. The thought of racing out of the room tantalized her, but she knew she'd be wondering about the noise all night. No, it was better to confront the fear now. Besides, didn't this sort of thing always turn out to be something silly?

Tap-tap-tap.

She carefully reached for the curtain. Her mind swam with a thousand thoughts. Where was Mom? It was dark out, and she still wasn't back from shopping. Where was Ryan? How come he hadn't called? Was he still with Jaimie? Jaimie, who might be turning into a vampire. Jaimie, who may be turning Ryan into —

Tap-tap-tap.

Becka took another deep breath. It was nothing. She was sure of it. Just a silly bird or a lost kite or —

Tap-tap-tap.

Tap-tap-tap.

It was time. She jerked open the curtain and went stone cold. Floating in midair and grinning at her grotesquely, the hideous form of a vampire hovered outside the window. His long sharp fangs gleamed like miniature pearl knives.

But it was the yellow eyes that sent the chill through Becka. They held a lifeless evil. A deadness and depravity that spoke of centuries of horror … centuries of murder.

His death white hand stretched out, and one long fingernail extended toward the window, rapping against the glass.

Tap-tap-tap.

Tap-tap-tap.

Becka could not breathe. Her eyes were riveted to the creature's yellow gaze, yet somehow she managed to back away.

Tap-tap-tap.

Tap-tap-tap.

And then she turned and ran.

4

By the time she reached the lobby of the hotel, Becka realized there was no place to go. She certainly didn't want to go out into the night with the vampire right outside her window ... and she sure wasn't going back up to her room.

She could tell the desk clerk to call security, that a vampire was hanging out in front of her window, but somehow she had her doubts that she'd be taken seriously.

She decided to hide out downstairs on the main floor. She had a Diet Coke at the snack bar but didn't eat anything. For some reason she no longer thought "Dracula Burgers" or "Lady-fingers with Onion Rings" were that amusing.

She browsed the newsstand, but the local papers all showed Jaimie's face on the front page. "He's Baaaaack!" one English headline read, leading readers into the story about Jaimie's alley encounter.

Wonderful. Now her archrival was a local celebrity.

She thought of Z's suggestion to love Jaimie. Well, from what she'd just seen, he was wrong about vampires. Maybe he was wrong about this, as well.

At last she came to the lobby. She sat in one of the big leather chairs facing the desk and waited for Mom or Ryan or somebody to come by.

And then she heard it. Giggling. The voice sounded familiar. Almost like Jaimie's. It was followed by a loud guffaw, which sounded like Ryan's laugh.

Slowly, she turned around and peeked over the top of the big leather chair.

It was Ryan, all right—sitting with Jaimie and laughing his fool head off. For one horrible instant, Becka thought they were laughing at her. Then she realized that, even in his worst moments, Ryan was too good a friend for that.

Still, she resented him for not coming back to the hotel with her. If he'd been there with her, maybe the vampire wouldn't have come to her window. And if it had, at least someone else would've seen it. The last thing in the world she wanted to do was look like she was imitating Jaimie. Or, worse yet, look like a fool by insisting that someone was floating outside her window and having everyone say, "But that's impossible. You were on the fourth floor!"

"Becka? What are you doing here?" It was Ryan. He had spotted her spy routine.

"Uh ... hi, Ryan ... Hi, Jaimie." She was flustered but tried her best to hide it. "I just, uh, came down here because ..."

"Were you looking for me?" Ryan asked.

"No," Becka snapped. "Of course not. I was waiting for Mom. She's out with that reporter guy."

"So why aren't you waiting in your room?" Ryan asked.

There was just no easy way to say it. Finally, Becka blurted, "Because the last time I was there a vampire was tapping on my window."

Ryan looked at her incredulously. "But that's impossible. You're on the fourth floor!"

Even Jaimie looked as if she didn't believe her. "Are you sure, Becka?"

"What's that supposed to mean?"

Jaimie cleared her throat. "Well, it's just that, I mean, so far I'm the only one who's been—"

Becka stood up. "I can't believe you don't believe me. Especially you, Jaimie."

"I'm just suggesting that maybe there's some sort of logical—"

Becka cut her off. "Yeah, right." With that, she stalked toward the elevator. She knew she was overreacting, and by the time she arrived at the elevator doors, she also knew she wasn't about to face her room alone. So she turned around and walked right back to Ryan and Jaimie, who were still watching the performance.

"So," she said, "are you coming up with me to check out the room or what?"

Ryan glanced at Jaimie, then rose to his feet. "Sure. C'mon, Jaimie," he said, "let's go check it out."

Jaimie looked less than excited about the idea but agreed and followed them toward the elevator. As soon as the elevator doors slid shut, Becka felt herself growing tense. Going back to her room to see if a vampire was waiting there to kill her might not be that bright of an idea after all.

Ryan must have been having similar thoughts because he turned to her and asked, "Have you got a crucifix?"

"A crucifix?" Becka said, somewhat confused.

"I've got one," Jaimie said. "It's in my room. Let's go there first."

Two minutes later they were in Jaimie's room, arming themselves with two crucifixes and a small bottle of holy water that a crew member had given the actress.

"Ryan, why are we doing this?" Becka asked as they headed back toward the elevator. "I don't even believe in vampires."

Ryan shrugged. "Do you think you imagined that thing outside your window?"

She shook her head.

"Then we have to fight it, don't we?"

Becka was still confused. "What about spiritual warfare?"

Now Jaimie looked confused. "Spiritual what?"

Ryan's face turned red at Becka's question, and he paused. "She means prayer," he told Jaimie. "And using Scripture."

Jaimie frowned. "Scripture? You mean the Bible?" Her incredulous gaze came back to Becka. "You want to fight a vampire with 'Now I lay me down' and Bible verses?"

Before Becka could respond, Ryan shook his head. "I know I'm still new at this, Beck, but I don't remember anything in the Bible that addresses vampires floating outside your window, do you?"

"Well—"

"Right. So I figure it can't hurt to take this stuff with us just to be safe." He pressed the button.

Becka leaned back against the wall, struggling with the jumble of emotions sweeping over her. Fear. Frustration. Embarrassment. Guilt. Especially guilt. Some spiritual warrior she was. She didn't even know what Scripture to use! And now this business about crosses and holy water. They hardly seemed the right weapons to fight with. And yet . . .

When the elevator doors opened on the fourth floor, Becka felt a cold shiver run through her body. Their suite was just five doors down the hall. Slowly, the three of them made their way toward it. Ryan and Jaimie took the lead, each holding a large crucifix in front of them. Becka followed, carrying the bottle of water.

They arrived at the door. Everything was quiet.

Carefully, Becka inserted her key, but when Ryan reached for the knob she waved for him to stop. "Wait a sec. Let me get ready."

Rebecca's hands trembled as she took the top off the bottle

of water. Part of her felt foolish. In all of their encounters with the powers of darkness, they'd never once resorted to things like holy water and crucifixes. They'd always attacked things through prayer and by checking out the Bible. To her this other way just seemed like, well, like stupid superstitions. Still, Ryan had a point. The Bible didn't say anything about vampires ...

She looked up at Ryan, and all three braced themselves.

Finally, she nodded. He threw open the door, and they charged in.

A large form loomed between them and the desk light.

"Get him!" Ryan shouted.

Ryan and Jaimie shoved the crucifixes at the silhouetted figure while Becka threw the water on him.

"Hey! What do you think you're doing?" John Barberini spun around, his hair and shirt dripping.

"Rebecca!" It was Mom, coming out of the other room. "What are you doing?"

A moment of silence passed as Becka struggled to find her voice. "We, uh ... we thought he was a vampire."

👁 👁

Once again, Becka explained about the vampire outside her window. This so intrigued John that he pretty much forgave her for the soaking. "I guess I should be glad she didn't drive a stake through my heart instead," he tried to joke.

Everyone chuckled, but Becka's ears burned with embarrassment.

John opened the window and carefully checked out the ledge. When he drew his head back inside, Ryan asked, "Did you see anything?"

John shook his head. "There's no way anybody could rig something to hang out there. Either someone's playing an elaborate joke, or ..." He hesitated.

"Or?" Jaimie asked.

He spoke slowly and carefully. "Or we've got a real vampire on our hands."

After Mom had called hotel security and after John, Jaimie, and Ryan had finally left for their own rooms, Mom turned to Becka in quiet concern. "Sweetheart, I don't want you to take this the wrong way, but ..."

"But what, Mom?"

"Well, are you sure none of this has anything to do with John?"

"What?"

"Well, I mean, you seemed sort of sensitive about him taking me shopping."

Becka couldn't believe what she was hearing and let out a groan of exasperation.

"And then you attacked him."

"No, Mother." There was no missing the irritation in her voice.

Mom remained silent as Becka began to pace. "I *saw* what I saw, all right? And if you think I'd attack John because I was jealous or something, well, you're just plain wrong. Besides I didn't *attack* him; I threw water on him. I mean, he's no worse for the wear ... In fact, it probably did him some good."

Mom eyed her patiently. "That's what I mean. Honey, it's obvious you don't care for John and you don't want me spending time with him. But there's really nothing for you to worry about. You certainly don't need to douse him to scare him off."

"Mother!"

"Now, hear me out. Isn't it just possible that you imagined the vampire trying to get in here because, well, because that's kind of how you see John?"

"I don't believe—"

"And maybe that's what made you throw water on him after you saw him."

Becka was speechless. Now her own mother was turning

against her! For the millionth time, Becka wished that her father were still alive. Everything was so out of whack, so off balance, with him gone.

She dropped into a chair and crossed her arms, fixing her mother with a steady gaze. "You're right about one thing. I don't like you being around John."

"You see—"

"I mean, the guy's an obvious sleaze."

"That's exactly what—"

"But I didn't attack him on purpose, Mom. I didn't know it was John when I threw the water. And ..." She swallowed hard. A lump was rising in her throat, and she wasn't sure why. "I did see something outside that window. You've got to believe me. I really did."

Sensing her emotion, Mom crossed over and put her arm around Becka. "I believe you, sweetheart. I believe you."

Becka nodded. The lump was bigger now. And she could feel her eyes start to burn with moisture. The hug helped a little. But not enough.

❧ ❧

If vampires don't exist, who invented them?

Becka sat in front of the computer, waiting for Z's response. If he was so certain vampires didn't exist, then he had better have a pretty good explanation for where the idea first came from.

It was late and she was exhausted. But she'd gotten Z online, and she wasn't about to let him get away.

She waited and watched as his reply came in:

Many believe the legend was invented centuries ago to enforce proper burial procedures. The belief was spread that if bodies were buried in shallow graves they could come back to life as the "undead."

Becka leaned over and typed:

So people started digging deeper graves?

Z answered:

Precisely. Bram Stoker added to the myth when he wrote the horror novel *Dracula,* which was published one hundred years ago.

But why do people still believe in them today?

There are various theories. A very high percentage of those who believe in vampires are abused children and teens who identify strongly with vampire victims. Noted authorities, like J. Gordon Melton, believe the resurgence of vampire folklore comes as a result of AIDS and other interests and concerns related to human blood.

Becka leaned back in the chair and stared at the screen. The history lesson was good, but it didn't solve any problems. Something very frightening was still going on, and she was in the center of it.

Z clearly did not believe in vampires, and he had never been wrong before.

Never.

Then again, he had not seen what she had seen.

She logged off, closed the laptop, then crossed toward her bed. It was doubtful sleep would come, but she had to try. Somehow she figured tomorrow would be an even bigger day ...

❧   ❧

Thanks to John Barberini, stories about the lead actress of a movie being stalked by a vampire had already reached the American press. Gossipy news shows like *Media Tonight* and *Inside Scoop* rushed to send out video crews.

When Becka returned to the set the next morning, everyone seemed a lot more tense. Even the easygoing Tim Paxton seemed on edge. "Hello, Rebecca."

"Hi," she said. She wondered if he'd heard about her own little encounter the night before, but he said nothing. Just as well. The fewer people who thought she was losing her mind, the better.

"Listen," he said, lowering his voice slightly, "I know you're a friend of Jaimie's, so I'd appreciate it if you would try to help keep her calm today."

"What do you mean?"

"Well, she's got a couple of very important interviews to do tonight, and I don't want her to seem ... well, too off the wall, if you know what I mean."

Becka nodded. "Sure, I'll do what I can. Hey, have you seen Ryan?"

"He was with Jaimie by the prop truck the last time I saw him."

"Tim!" It was Fallon, shouting from the set. "Tim? Anybody seen my producer?!"

Tim finished his coffee with a gulp. "Duty calls." With that he turned and strode toward the director, who was obviously having another one of his hissy fits.

Becka shook her head and watched in amusement. Showbiz. What weird people.

Moments later she meandered through the busy set toward the prop trailer. As she approached, she could hear Jaimie's voice from behind the trailer.

"You don't understand," Jaimie was saying. "At night these wounds in my neck throb and ache, and somehow I know that the only way it'll stop is if I go out ... and find him."

"I won't let that happen," Ryan replied. "I won't let anything hurt you. I ... I love you."

Becka stopped in her tracks as if someone had slugged her in the gut. She suddenly felt very weak. She had to lean against the prop trailer for support. So it was true; her worst fears were confirmed.

"But what if I'm turning?" Jaimie's voice continued. "What if I'm becoming one of them?"

"That won't happen," Ryan insisted. "We won't let it happen."

Jaimie's voice trembled now, as if she were holding back her tears. "But what if it already did?"

A long moment of silence passed. Becka felt tears well up in her own eyes.

At last Ryan spoke. "If that happens, I might as well be your first victim ... because I don't want to go on without you."

That was it. Becka could stand no more. "Nooooo!" she shouted as she raced around the trailer to confront the two.

As soon as she saw them, Becka realized her mistake. Ryan was sitting on the back steps of the trailer with a script in one hand and a Pepsi in the other. Jaimie sat in a lawn chair a few feet away, sipping iced tea.

They had been rehearsing her lines.

Both turned and stared at Becka. Ryan was the first to speak. "What's the matter, Beck? You okay?"

She felt less than two feet tall. "I ... I ... I thought ... I mean, I thought ..."

"You thought we were serious?" Jaimie said, already starting to giggle.

"No, of course not," Becka lied. "I-I was just kidding ..."

Of course they knew the truth, and Becka wished she could simply disappear.

Fortunately, a voice came over the loudspeaker. "Attention, cast!" It was the assistant director. "We're almost ready on the set, and Dirk would like everyone here."

"Oh, I've got to go," Jaimie said. "Thanks for going over my lines with me, Ryan." She rose from the chair and straightened her costume. "See you guys later. And don't worry, Becka." She tried to hold back her giggle but didn't quite succeed. "I haven't grown any fangs. Yet."

As Jaimie hurried off toward the set, Becka whispered, "That's a matter of opinion."

Ryan turned to her. "What did you say?"

Becka eyed him coolly. "Nothing. I'm going back to the hotel."

Ryan shrugged. "Suit yourself. But you know, I thought we were supposed to make friends with Jaimie. I mean, I thought that was part of why we were here … to help her."

"Well, you've certainly been doing *your* part," Becka replied.

"What does that mean?"

"It means you should have been there with me last night."

"Why? Do you think this thing, whatever it is, would be afraid of me? I doubt it."

Becka heard her voice beginning to crack. She was feeling more emotions than she had thought possible. "I needed you. Don't you understand? I …"

Hearing her emotion, Ryan rose to his feet. "I do understand, Beck. Believe me. And I would have given anything to have been there to help." Unsure what to do, he started to cross toward her.

But the tears began to come, and Becka had to turn away. "I … I'd better go." With that she started off.

"Becka!" Ryan called after her. "Becka, wait …"

But she kept on walking.

❧   ❧

Ryan sat in one of the cloth chairs near the set. He wasn't sure what to do. It was just after nightfall. The shooting had wrapped, and Becka still hadn't returned to the set. Should he go after her? See how she was doing? But what about his job? Wasn't he being paid to help Jaimie? And what about Z's instructions to look out for her?

Like Becka's, Ryan's own thoughts seemed to be growing more and more muddled.

"Ryan," Jaimie called out as she headed for the costume trailer, "I'm afraid I have to go to wardrobe and be fitted for something we're adding tomorrow. It shouldn't take too long."

Ryan rose to his feet and joined her. "Do you think I have time to run back to the hotel? I want to check ..."

Jaimie smiled as his voice trailed off. "Check on Becka?" she asked.

He nodded.

"Sure, go ahead. I'm afraid I'll only have ten or fifteen minutes to grab dinner before tonight's interviews anyway. I'll meet you after the television taping. How does ten sound?"

"Ten will be great." Ryan turned and started for the hotel. "I'll see you then."

❧ ❧

Jaimie watched Ryan's rapid departure. She sighed, wondering what it would be like to have someone care about you the way he clearly cared about Becka. She recalled the look on the other girl's face when she had come around the trailer earlier and smiled slightly. Obviously, those two needed to talk.

But she didn't have time to worry about their problems. If she didn't get to the wardrobe trailer in a hurry, she'd have no time for dinner at all. Glancing around, she saw that there were still plenty of people milling around the set. With all these people around, she didn't even think twice about cutting across the darkened area between the two production trucks.

❧ ❧

The figure in the shadows watched the young girl's advance

and grew eager with anticipation. This was exactly what it wanted. What it had been waiting for.

Jaimie had only taken a couple of steps into the darkness before she paused. She glanced around uneasily, looking over her shoulder and from side to side. It was as though she sensed the presence waiting for her.

The form drew back into the shadows.

The girl shook her head, as though chiding herself for her silliness. She glanced back at the people around the set and then toward the wardrobe trailer. The one watching her gauged her thoughts from her expression. The trailer was less than a hundred yards away ... She'd just pass through the brief darkness and be there in an instant.

It smiled.

She moved forward again, but her steps grew more cautious by the second. She carefully eyed the darkness around her.

The form waited. The girl continued drawing closer. In just a matter of seconds ...

Again, Jaimie slowed to a stop. "Hello," she called. "Who's there?"

The form remained motionless, not even breathing.

The girl was straining to listen, and the cold smile crept over the watcher's lips again. It knew there was nothing to hear. Nothing but the frightened beating of the girl's heart as her growing fear began to pound in her ears.

Ever so slowly the form crouched, preparing to spring.

The girl drew a breath to steady herself. Then, with resolved determination, she moved forward. Quicker this time, anxious to get out of the dark.

A pity that was not going to happen.

The form attacked.

Jaimie had no time to scream. She saw only the glint of white fangs and the evil of yellow eyes. And the hands. The deathly white hands wrapped around her throat.

She struggled, trying to breathe, trying to scream. But the more she struggled, the tighter the creature's grip grew. She was growing light-headed. Things were spinning. Spots danced in her vision. Everything was turning white.

And, for a brief instant, as she was passing out, Jaimie wondered if she would feel the vampire's teeth enter her neck before she died.

5

Tim Paxton and Dirk Fallon were arguing again.

"If we reshoot the scene now," Tim was saying, "it's going to cost as much as a full setup. That set's been down for days."

"I realize that," Fallon replied, "but if we don't reshoot it, we're going to have a hole in the middle of the film the size of the Grand Canyon. I've seen what we shot last week, Tim, and it's horrible. The girl is terrible."

"Have some compassion," Tim argued. "That was the day this vampire business started."

Fallon began pacing back and forth. "I understand that. But it's you who needs to have the compassion. You're the one who has to give me some slack, get some extra money so I can reshoot."

Tim held up his hands. "All right, all right. Let me talk to Jaimie first. I want her to sit with us and watch the scene. If she can't do any better, then—"

"If she can't do any better," the director's voice rose, "then we all might as well pack up and go home."

"But let's wait until after the interviews tonight," Tim suggested.

Fallon shrugged. "That's your call. But the best time to ask your investors for more money would be right after the thing airs in L.A."

"All right," the producer sighed. "Wait here. I'll go get the girl."

Tim hurried off toward wardrobe. Normally, he would have taken the long way around. He wasn't superstitious, nor was he anything close to a coward, but he'd just as soon avoid the shadows in this crazy country. This time, though, he noticed that the television crews from *Media Tonight* were already gathered in front of one of the trucks. They'd made themselves at home, waiting to set up for their interview later that evening, so he decided to cut behind the trucks rather than work his way through the crowd of media vultures.

He crossed through the shadows and was barely halfway when he saw a form lying off to the side.

A body. Jaimie's body.

He raced to her side and quickly scooped her into his arms. "Somebody help!" he shouted. He rose to his feet, lifting the limp form and stumbling out of the shadows into the light. "Somebody get us some help!"

Pandemonium swept through the set. People shouting. Someone screaming. Others asking, "Is she dead? Is she dead?"

Jaimie was motionless as Tim laid her on a nearby bench. A small trickle of blood ran down her neck. Tim reached out to touch her face, and she moaned softly.

"I need a doctor!" Tim yelled furiously. "Where's that doctor?!"

By the time the doctor arrived, Jaimie had come around. "I don't need to go to the hospital," she insisted.

"I'll be the judge of that," the doctor said. But moments later, after he'd bandaged the wound, he finally agreed with her. "It's just a small cut," he said. "Missed the vein in your neck by a fraction of an inch, thank God."

"Will she be able to do the interviews this evening?" Fallon asked.

Tim turned and gave him a hard look, but the director persisted, this time speaking directly to Jaimie. "We need all the publicity we can get, kid. Lots of exposure in L.A. Should be good for all of us, if you think you can pull it off ..."

Jaimie took the glass of water the doctor offered to her. After a long drink, she nodded. "Sure, Dirk. You're the director. Anything you say."

❧ ❧

When Ryan and Becka arrived later that evening, they saw the television cameras already taping. And there, on the crew monitor, was Jaimie, a bandage on her neck, still wearing her bloodstained dress.

"I can't really tell you much else," she was saying. "After he grabbed my throat, I lost consciousness pretty fast. I just remember his eyes. And those fangs."

"What happened?" Ryan cried, but he was quickly shushed by a crew member, who indicated that they were still taping.

"Thank you, Jaimie Baylor," the pretty host of the show said. Then, turning directly to the camera, the woman began her wrap-up: "And so, live from the set of *The Vampire Returns*, *Media Tonight* is grateful to this courageous young actress for talking with us so soon after her harrowing ordeal. We'll be right back with scenes from tomorrow's show."

"Cut!" the television director shouted.

As the crew began taking down equipment and wrapping cable, Ryan quickly worked his way through the commotion to Jaimie. "Are you all right?" he asked.

Jaimie shrugged. "To tell you the truth, I don't know."

Becka moved to join them. She knew she should feel bad for Jaimie, and she wanted to be concerned about the poor girl ...

but as she watched Ryan fawn over her, she couldn't help feeling resentment.

"You sure you don't need anything?" she could hear Ryan asking Jaimie. "I could run over and get you a glass of water."

"I have a glass of water," Jaimie replied.

"I meant a fresh one, a colder glass of water."

Jaimie smiled. "Ryan, I'm all right. Just stay here with me for a while."

Watching them together made Becka's stomach tighten.

"All right," Ryan answered. "I'll stay right here by your side all night if you need me to."

Ryan's last remark turned the tightness in Becka's stomach into full-blown nausea. And to make matters worse, she felt terrible for feeling the way she did. Hadn't Z said—no, hadn't the *Bible* said, "Love your enemies"?

Jaimie wasn't even her enemy ... or was she? Becka watched the girl lean toward Ryan. The nausea continued to grow, until Becka knew she had to get away. Without a word, she turned and headed off in the opposite direction, feeling both angry and guilty.

As she crossed by the catering truck she spotted Maureen, the wardrobe lady, talking with Tim. She slowed to a stop. She didn't mean to eavesdrop. It just turned out that way.

"They should be interviewing *you* over there, Tim," Maureen was saying. "You saved her life. You're a hero."

"I don't know what I did," Tim replied. "I just saw Jaimie and ran to her."

"Well, you scared him off, then."

"Maybe. It happened so fast. I don't even know if I saw him for sure. It was something. Kind of looked like a man ... but kind of like a ..."

Maureen was all ears. "A what? What'd it look like?"

Tim shrugged. "I don't know. I told you—it happened so

fast. But I caught a glimpse of something... It almost looked like ... a bat."

"Oh, my. Did you tell the TV people?"

Tim shook his head. "No, I did not. And I don't want you babbling anything like that, either. It sounds crazy enough. Besides, as any producer will tell you, if you want your movie to be a hit, let the actress be the one who gets her face on TV, not some ugly mug like me."

Maureen laughed. Tim noticed Becka then. He excused himself and walked over to her. "Hello, Becka."

She swallowed. "Hi. Listen, I didn't mean to eavesdrop, but—"

"That's okay. Did you hear what I was saying?"

Becka nodded.

"Then do me a favor, will you?"

"What's that?"

"Don't say anything to Jaimie about that bat business. She's got enough on her mind already."

Becka looked at him and slowly nodded.

"A bat!" Ryan's face was incredulous. "He said it turned into a bat?"

"That's what he said," Becka insisted. They tried to relax in the living room of her hotel suite later that night. "Of course, Tim said he wasn't sure," she continued. "It happened so fast, but ..."

Ryan paced around the small room.

She could tell he was concerned and tried her best to be sincere. "How was Jaimie?"

Ryan sighed. "Okay, I guess. Tim and two of the stunt guys are camping out in her suite."

"Listen," Becka said, "I'm sorry I walked off the set earlier today. I sort of lost it, and I ... well, I just felt foolish, that's all."

"No problem," Ryan replied, "but I ..." His voice trailed off.
"What?"

Ryan shook his head. "Nothing."

"Tell me," she said.

"All right. It's just that ... I got worried about you and ... I left Jaimie to check on you ... and that's when she was attacked."

"Too bad." Becka couldn't keep the sarcasm out of her voice.

"I don't mean anything by it," Ryan tried to explain. "I just feel kind of bad, that's all."

Becka heard her voice becoming icy. "That's nice. It's just too bad I wasn't the one attacked instead."

"That's not what I meant!" Ryan protested.

An awkward silence passed between them. Becka couldn't help noticing that there had been a lot of those lately.

Finally, Ryan spoke. "I heard half the crew was out looking to buy more crucifixes."

Becka nodded. "I heard worse. Some of them are planning on wearing garlic because it's supposed to ward off vampires."

"This is crazy," Ryan said. He resumed his pacing. "If someone had told me what was happening here, I wouldn't have believed it."

"I know what you mean."

"And talk about crucifixes," Ryan continued. "You should see what Tim and those stunt guys have up in Jaimie's suite. It looks like they bought out the store."

"What are we going to do?" Becka said. "I mean, no one is doing anything that really makes sense. It's like they're just sitting around waiting for the vampire to attack again."

Ryan nodded. "We're always on the defensive. Maybe it's time to start playing offense."

"What do you mean?"

"I'm not sure. Maybe set a trap ... try to catch the vampire."

Becka was intrigued. "How?"

"Well, I was thinking—" Ryan grew more excited as he spoke—"if we could lure him into a dead-end alley or some-place like that, then we could jump out with a bunch of holy water and crucifixes and—"

"And do what?" Becka asked sarcastically. "Drive a stake through his heart?"

"I don't know," Ryan said, completely missing her humor. "I doubt I'm up to that. But at least we could get a better idea of what we're fighting."

Becka let out a long sigh of frustration. She knew Ryan was a fairly new Christian, but it was like he'd forgotten everything they'd learned about spiritual warfare. If this thing was real, and she was growing more and more certain it was, then the way to fight it was the same way they had fought other attacks of the enemy: through prayer and the Word of God.

"Listen," she said sincerely, "I'm not crazy about using cruci-fixes, holy water, and all that folktale stuff to fight this thing."

He paused. "I know."

"Ryan, if we do anything, it should be to pray. If there really is some sort of demonic force involved, then we should be fight-ing it with prayer."

Ryan nodded slowly. "Okay, I'll blast him with holy water while you pray."

Becka protested, "Ryan . . ."

"Listen," he explained. "The thing about folktales is that there's usually some truth to them."

"I know, but—"

"I just want to *do* something," he continued. "I mean, we can pray if you want, but I really don't think this other stuff will hurt, do you?"

Becka shrugged. Maybe he had a point. "Okay," she agreed reluctantly. "If that's what you want. But if we're going to pray, we'd better do it now, 'cause things aren't getting any better."

Ryan agreed and moved to sit beside her. Together the two bowed their heads and began to pray.

Becka loved these times. As a new Christian, Ryan always prayed with freshness and excitement. And he was honest. Very, very honest. Despite his weaknesses and his total cluelessness about Jaimie, his honesty always tugged at and captured Becka's heart.

Together they prayed for several minutes, asking God for wisdom about what to do, confessing their doubts and weaknesses, and asking for God's protection over Jaimie and themselves, regardless of what they were dealing with. But there was one thing Becka would not, *could not,* do. She did not ask for God's help to love Jaimie.

They'd barely finished when Mom opened the door to the suite.

"Becka, sweetheart," she said as she entered the room, "John told me what happened to Jaimie. I came back as quickly as I could. Is she all right?"

"I think so," Becka said.

"How are you?"

Becka stared at her for a moment before answering. How was she? Between her frustration over Jaimie's vampire, her anger over a beautiful Hollywood actress practically throwing herself at Ryan, and her mother hanging around with an obvious creep, Becka definitely felt the stress.

"I'm just fine," she said, doing her best to hide the tension in her voice. But even she could hear how harsh and sarcastic the words sounded.

"Would you like to talk about it?" her mother asked quietly.

"No, Mom. It's okay. Really." She sighed again. "I think I'm just tired." Tired of Jaimie. Tired of Ryan paying more attention to a girl he'd just met than to the one who was supposed to be his closest friend. Tired of feeling angry and jealous and guilty.

"Well," Ryan said after an uneasy silence filled the room,

"it's getting late. Let's get together first thing tomorrow and start working out a plan."

Becka nodded and walked him to the door. But even then a thought came to her mind. "We've still got one major problem with any plan we use to trap the vampire."

Ryan paused at the door. "What's that?"

"We may have everything we need to try to trap the thing, but ..."

"But what?"

Becka took a deep breath and slowly let it out. "Every trap needs bait."

◇ ◇

The next day even Dirk Fallon acknowledged that filming another vampire attack on Jaimie might not be a wise idea. Not after all she had been through the night before. So instead they chose to film the scene in the movie where Van Helsing reveals who the vampire really is.

They were filming in an old mansion not far from the hotel when Rebecca and Ryan arrived. They'd spent several hours that morning carefully hatching a plan and visiting the location where they hoped the capture would take place. They would explain it all to Jaimie when she was done with the scene, but for now, they watched silently as Steve Delton prepared to confront the actor playing the movie's vampire.

"So, gentlemen," Van Helsing said, "I ask you to consider who among this esteemed group of lords and ladies could possibly be such an abomination."

The other three men shrugged their shoulders, clearly at a loss. Jaimie sat in the far corner of the room, listening intently.

Van Helsing was obviously enjoying his moment in the spotlight. "No opinions among such learned men as yourselves? I'm surprised. All right, then. But first, I ask, are you aware of the three tests of being a vampire?"

It was about then that Becka felt as if someone was staring at her. She turned and was surprised to see Dirk Fallon, the director, looking in her direction.

What's he doing watching me instead of the scene? she thought. *Does he know what Ryan and I are up to?*

She figured it was unlikely, but she also knew he made her very nervous, staring like that. In fact, she felt so uncomfortable that if Van Helsing had asked her who the vampire was, she probably would have pointed at the film's director.

She looked back to the scene as Van Helsing explained his three tests. First, the vampire could not endure sunlight. Second, he would feel physical pain if he came in contact with a crucifix or other holy object. And finally, vampires cast no reflections.

Becka turned back toward Fallon.

He kept watching her.

She tried to force a smile and nodded. But as soon as she did, he turned away as if he hadn't been looking.

What was he thinking? What did he know?

"So," Van Helsing was saying, "test one requires the sunlight. It is now night. And since I cannot go among the guests here and spray holy water or touch them with crucifixes, I have done the next best thing. If you will look to your left you will see that I had the large mirror over the mantel rehung this afternoon. It now reflects anyone entering this room from the parlor."

The other characters in the scene mumbled their acknowledgment, and Van Helsing nodded to someone near the door. "I have asked Mr. Scott to call all of the guests into this room to hear an announcement. Watch the mirror carefully, gentlemen."

Why can't it be this easy in real life? Becka thought. *Too bad we couldn't just carry a mirror around until we found who the vampire was.* Obviously it couldn't be anyone in the cast or crew, since they were all out in the daylight. But then, who knew if vampires' fear of daylight was myth or reality? Maybe it was the same about casting reflections. Maybe none of what anyone thought was true. Maybe it was all folklore.

She threw a glance back over to the director. He was now watching the scene. Good.

Steve Delton, the actor playing Van Helsing, continued.

"But one more thing, gentlemen — remember that the vampire is a creature of the night and draws his strength from the dark realm. The only sure way to protect yourself is to stay in the light. Unfortunately — and this is what makes our situation so intriguing — you will never catch him unless you venture into the dark."

All was quiet for a second, and then Fallon yelled, "Cut! Print that one."

The assistant director shouted, "Half hour cast break. Crew, set up Scene 72 in the parlor."

Becka and Ryan exchanged nods. It was time to tell Jaimie their plan. They turned and walked toward her. Up close, the girl looked drawn and pale. In fact, she looked so bad that for a moment Becka had second thoughts about even telling her what they had in mind.

But they had to do something. If the vampire — or whatever it was — was to be stopped, this was the time to stop it.

"Hey, guys," Jaimie called out when she saw them.

"How are you feeling?" Becka asked.

Jaimie smiled. "Worse than I look, if you can believe that."

"You look great," Ryan lied.

"Thank you." Jaimie almost laughed. "I'm grateful for the compliment, even if I don't believe it."

Ryan smiled, obviously caught. "Listen … Becka and I were talking last night, and it seems like it's time to change our tactics on this vampire thing."

"What do you mean?"

"Well, up to now, none of us wanted to believe it was real, so we just kept sitting around, waiting for it to attack. Now ... well, maybe it's time we start fighting back."

Jaimie's eyes widened. "How?"

"By trapping him," Ryan explained. "We could set up some place, like in a dead end, and get all our anti-vampire stuff together there. Then we could lure it in there and spring the trap."

Jaimie looked puzzled. "But how do we get him to go into the alley?"

Becka and Ryan exchanged looks. Ryan cleared his throat. "Well, uh, we have to make him think that something he wants is, well, that it's there. Then when he—"

Jaimie still looked confused. "Something he wants. What does he want?"

After a long pause Ryan finally answered. "You, Jaimie. He wants you."

If Jaimie had been pale before, she was downright white now.

"You wouldn't actually have to stay there," Ryan explained. "We'd set it up so you could get out while he stayed trapped."

"There's a dead-end alley a few blocks from here," Becka added. "If we get him inside the alley and block off the front, the only way out is at the end of the alley through a steel door that leads to a warehouse."

"So," Ryan's voice grew more excited, "the plan is for you to go down the alley. And when the vampire comes, one of us will block the entrance to the alley while the other one opens the door to the warehouse to let you escape. Then we quickly close the door before he can follow, and he's trapped in the alley."

Jaimie looked doubtful. "He'll break through the door."

Becka shook her head. "He can't. It's solid steel with two locks and a crossbar."

"You've checked this out already?" Jaimie asked.

Becka nodded. "It's called Dominski Containers, or something like that."

"It has a steel fire door," Ryan said. "I'm sure the manager will let us use it if Tim or someone from the film company asks."

Jaimie listened as Ryan outlined the rest of the plan. "After the vampire enters the alley, we'll block the entrance with crosses and water—"

"I thought you said Becka didn't believe in that stuff," Jaimie interrupted.

"I don't," Becka said. "That's why we're also throwing in a big production truck to block the alley for good measure."

Jaimie still wasn't convinced. "Where will you get the truck?"

"Tim," Ryan answered. "There's no way we can pull this off without his help."

"I see," Jaimie said. "Okay, but no one except Tim should know about this."

Ryan and Becka agreed.

Slowly, a smile came over Jaimie's face. "I guess it's a pretty foolproof plan, huh?"

Becka nodded. "As far as we can tell."

"That's good, Becka," Jaimie said, looking her straight in the eyes. "Because if it doesn't work, *I'm* the one who will be at a dead end."

6

At first Tim stared at Becka and Ryan like they'd lost their minds when they approached him about using the warehouse entrance and the production truck.

"You're kidding," he said. "A couple of teenage kids want to trap a vampire?"

"We're doing it for Jaimie," Ryan replied. "It's only a matter of time before he gets to her again."

Tim shook his head. "I've got people with Jaimie around the clock. And they're armed with every bit of vampire defense we can find."

"Yes, but those are all defensive measures," Becka said.

"That's right," Ryan said. "We can't just wait. We have to go on the offense."

Tim looked at them a moment, then nodded slowly. "All right, what have we got to lose? Except my leading actress, of course. But listen, I want you kids to keep this quiet. Half of Hollywood thinks I'm nuts already. I'll help you, I'll even drive the truck, but until we catch this thing, let's keep it between us and Jaimie."

"Agreed," Becka said.

"Okay," Ryan added, "but somehow we have to put the word out that Jaimie will be there."

"We've still got another alley scene to shoot. She can be rehearsing for it there. No one will question that. But someone will have to go over the lines with her to make it look good."

"That's perfect," Ryan exclaimed. "Jaimie and I will be rehearsing alone in the alley. Then, when we think the time is right, I'll leave as if I'm going to get us a can of pop or something, and Jaimie will wait there alone."

"I could be standing just inside the warehouse door," Becka said.

"And I'll head down the block like I'm leaving," Ryan continued. "But then I'll double back, and when the vampire goes into the alley, we spring the trap."

Becka nodded. "As soon as the vampire starts toward Jaimie, I'll throw open the door and pull Jaimie inside, where it's safe."

"Meanwhile," Tim said, "I'll be waiting in the truck. And when he goes into the alley, I'll quickly back up and block the entrance."

"Right," Ryan agreed. "As soon as I pour the water, you start the truck. And when I get the crucifixes all laid down, you back it up."

The thought of using superstitious solutions still made Becka uneasy, but Ryan seemed so set on them ...

"I'll put the word out as soon as we fill Jaimie in on the plan," Tim said. "It sounds pretty foolproof. Simple and straightforward."

But even as he finished the sentence, a worried silence settled over the group. What would happen to Jaimie if they failed?

"It's not a bad plan," Ryan offered.

It was Becka who said what they were all feeling: "For Jaimie's sake, it had better be a great one."

"This place gives me the creeps," Rebecca said as the front door to the warehouse creaked open. "I'm glad you're here with me."

"It's not so bad," Tim said, shining his flashlight around the room. "It's just old."

It was a little after seven o'clock, and most of the cast and crew were at dinner. Word had spread that rehearsals for the upcoming alley scene would take place in the alley next to the Dominski warehouse. Tim had worked out an arrangement with the manager and had even sent a couple of electricians over to the alley to rig up some rehearsal lights. Then, while everyone else was eating dinner, he drove one of the production trucks over to the front of the alley. Once it was in position, he and Becka entered the warehouse.

After fumbling for the light switch, Tim finally turned it on. "There. Not so bad, huh?"

Shiny metal rectangles hanging from large wooden pegs on the wall filled the front part of the musty old shop. Some of the rectangles were copper, some were bronze, some polished chrome, but all were about the same size. "Wonder what these are for," Becka said as they walked by.

"They look like handles to me," Tim said. "Yeah, that's what they are. See, this piece here fits over the rectangle, and the other end attaches to the box."

"What box?" Becka asked as they rounded the corner toward the part of the shop that faced the alley. She hesitated a moment. It was dark in there, and she wasn't about to go in first.

"Don't you know?" Tim said as he turned the corner, shining his flashlight. Becka waited as he took a couple more steps into the room. "Didn't you see this place before?"

"Not really," Becka said. "I just talked to the manager about it. When he showed me the door, we were outside in the alley."

"So you don't know what they make here?" Tim said as he reached the wall, searching for the light switch. As he did, his flashlight exposed glimpses of metal boxes stacked about the room.

"I tried to look up the word that comes after Dominski on the sign out front in the hotel bookstore, but the closest I got was some kind of container. I figured it's the Dominski Container Company or something like that."

"Close," Tim said as he found the light switch and turned it on. "It's the Dominski Casket Company."

Becka's mouth dropped open. All around her were stacks and stacks of metal caskets. All sizes and types, waiting to be shipped out.

"Listen," Tim said, "I'd better be going."

"What?" Becka croaked. "Can't you stay, you know ... a little longer?"

There was no missing the amusement in Tim's voice. "You'll be okay, kid. Ryan and Jaimie will be heading into the alley any second. I've got to take my post inside the truck before someone sees me."

Becka forced herself to swallow and tried to nod. As long as the light was on, she didn't feel too bad. Still, she found herself whispering a quiet prayer that the caskets with their long lids wouldn't suddenly start popping open.

"Okay, then." Tim turned and started for the door. "I'll be shutting these lights off now and—"

"Shutting the lights off?" Becka interrupted, her voice cracking even more.

"I have to. You can see the light under the door from the alley. It could scare him off before we even spring the trap."

"I'm not too worried about scaring *him* off," Becka said. "He doesn't seem like he'd be that easily scared."

"True," Tim said. "But a vampire's senses are supposed to be highly attuned, so we'd better be extra careful."

Becka wanted to say something, but at the moment she didn't much trust her voice.

Seeing the expression on her face, Tim reached into his satchel. "Don't worry," he said, "I brought an extra flashlight."

Becka gratefully accepted it, but as Tim turned off the lights and left, she began to shiver. She tried to tell herself it was just the cold, but of course she knew better.

The front door closed with a dull thud. The sound echoed about the caskets.

She was all alone. Everything was silent.

For a moment she thought she heard something. A quiet rustling over in the far corner.

Probably just a rat, she thought. But for some reason, the idea gave her little comfort.

Then there were the coffin lids. What would happen if one or two or a dozen started opening?

Maybe it was her overactive imagination, or maybe it was the rodents she heard scampering around the coffins, but more than once she thought she saw moving shadows.

Of course, when she shined her light in that direction, she saw nothing.

She just hoped it would stay that way.

Carefully, she approached the inside of the alley door, shining her light over every square inch of floor in front of her.

She could see a small slot between the bars on the door and pressed her face against it to peer through and view a small portion of the alley. The lights the crew had rigged up cast a dim glow outside, but the shadows overpowered the light.

Becka took a breath to steady herself and wondered when Ryan and Jaimie would show. Her heart pounded already, and they'd barely begun. She wanted this whole thing to be over as quickly as possible. In fact, she wished she had never even given in to the plan.

There was another noise behind her. Faint scampering.

She spun the flashlight around, but nothing was there. The strange noises worried her the most. And, of course, the caskets.

And, of course, the shadows she kept thinking she saw move atop them.

Then she heard scraping gravel. And voices.

Becka eased closer to the door. Through the slot, she could see Ryan and Jaimie approaching.

Finally.

As they approached, Jaimie rehearsed her lines. Pretending to be the character in the film, she walked through the alley with a slight swirl and sashay. It was easy to imagine her in the long and flowing dress she would wear in the actual filming.

"Why are you so shy, David?" she said, hardly glancing at the script. "Do you no longer desire me because of my wounds?"

For a moment there was silence as Ryan fumbled for his place in the script. "Of course I do," he finally said, slightly overacting his part. "It's just that I ... I don't want to ..."

"Well, come closer, then," Jaimie cooed.

Becka felt herself bristle at the sound of Jaimie's voice. Even now, as they waited for the vampire, it was obvious that the girl was coming on to Ryan.

And she *knew* Becka was watching.

Becka could see Ryan moving next to Jaimie. His voice caught as he spoke. "My feelings haven't changed, but I don't want to take advantage of you. I don't want—"

"You're not taking advantage of me," Jaimie said. And with that she reached up and caressed Ryan's cheek.

As Becka watched the scene, her anger grew. Did Jaimie really have to pick this scene to rehearse? And did she really have to touch Ryan like that?

As if reading her thoughts, Ryan cast a glance toward the door. "I ... uh, I only hope that we can resume our romance the way it was before that terrible attack on you."

Jaimie took a step toward him and reached up to slide her arm around his neck.

Becka couldn't believe her eyes. The girl was about to kiss him!

But at the last second Ryan backed off.

"What are you doing?" Jaimie asked.

Ryan fumbled through his script, looking for the line.

Jaimie shook her head. "Ryan, what are you doing? You're not supposed to pull away. This is where I bite your neck."

"It is?" Ryan looked confused.

"Yes, this is where I start to cross over and become a vampire. You don't pull away until you feel my lips on your neck ... *Then* you pull back."

"Oh yeah, uh, okay." Ryan nodded.

For a brief moment Becka thought about throwing open the alley door, grabbing Ryan, and letting the real vampire attack Jaimie. Her self-control got the better of her, but barely.

"You know what?" Ryan spoke just a little too loudly, as if he wanted to be overheard. "I'm pretty thirsty. Do you mind if I get something to drink?"

He was moving to the next step of the plan. Becka glanced at her watch. It was a few minutes earlier than they had scheduled, but for obvious reasons she was grateful he had decided to move things up.

Jaimie said what she was supposed to say, "All right ... but would you be a dear and bring something back for me? I want to block out the scene a bit on my own. You know, walk it through and decide where I'm going to say what."

"Sure," Ryan said, once again just a little too loudly. "I'll run down to that store in the next block and be right back. You'll be okay ... all alone ... the only one here in the alley."

Becka almost smiled. Ryan was doing his best, but an Oscar winner he wasn't.

"I'll be fine," Jaimie said.

"Okay," Ryan said. "I am leaving now. Don't worry; you will be all right." With that he turned and headed down the alley.

It was time for Becka to make her move. Carefully, and ever so quietly, she unbolted the alley door so she could fling it open and yank Jaimie in when the vampire attacked.

She glanced down at her fingers and noticed they were already trembling.

Outside in the alley, Jaimie pretended to rehearse her lines as she walked and paced out the scene.

Other than her soft tones and the slightest scuff of her shoes in the alley, everything was very quiet.

The trap was set and waiting.

Then Becka heard it. A dragging, shuffling kind of sound. Something moved down the alley in their direction.

She grabbed the door handle and held her breath.

Through the crack, she could see Jaimie's body tense. She'd heard the sound too.

The noise stopped.

Jaimie lowered her voice to a mere whisper as she recited her lines, pretending she hadn't heard.

A full minute passed, and everything remained silent.

Maybe he'd moved on. Maybe he'd sensed it was a trap.

Jaimie turned and stole a look up the alley. Becka heard her gasp, then saw her draw her hand up to her mouth.

He was there!

Jaimie, who was several yards from the warehouse door, began backing up.

"Who are you?" she called out. "What do you want from me?"

Becka could hear nothing in reply. The vampire did not respond. Instead, the scraping of gravel resumed.

It was approaching.

Becka scrunched to the side for a better look but could see nothing.

More scuffing sounded as Jaimie continued backing up toward the warehouse door.

It was obvious the vampire was moving in.

Then through the crack, in the shadowy light, Becka saw him! The same creature she had seen attack Jaimie in the alley their first night in Transylvania. The same creature she had seen suspended in midair outside her hotel window.

Jaimie continued backing toward the door, only eight feet away now.

The vampire appeared to be in no hurry. In fact, he matched her step for step. Every time she took a step backward, he took a step forward.

Jaimie glanced toward the door. It was obvious she was thinking of making a run for it. It was also obvious that at this distance the vampire could overtake her before she made it.

In the dim shadows, Becka could see Jaimie starting to tremble. She wondered if the girl would even have the strength to take the last remaining steps.

"W-why …," Jaimie stuttered. "Why are you doing this? Why me?" Her voice cracked with each syllable.

But the vampire did not answer. He did not even blink his fierce yellow eyes.

He just kept approaching.

She was five steps away now.

Becka's grip tightened on the door. Any second now.

There! There it was. The sound of a truck starting up!

The vampire spun around.

Becka pressed against the door for a better look. In the distance she could see Ryan's form spring into view. He dumped the large pitcher of water across the alley entrance.

The vampire growled, distracted.

This was the moment. Now Jaimie was to break for the door. But she appeared paralyzed, unable to move.

"Come on, Jaimie," Becka whispered. "Move! Get closer. Get closer."

Jaimie stumbled backward another step. Then another.

Good. She was within reaching distance.

It was now or never. Becka slammed against the door to throw it open.

But it was stuck!

She threw her shoulder into it again.

It wouldn't budge.

She pushed harder, banging against it with all of her might.

It didn't move.

"Rebecca!" It was Jaimie. Crying for help. She had arrived at the door and was banging on it. "Let me in!"

Becka panicked. Through the slot she saw the vampire make his move. His cape billowing out behind him like giant wings, he started toward the girl.

"Becka!"

Becka slammed against the door again.

Jaimie continued banging. "Help me!"

Then Becka saw it. One of the bolts was still locked in place. With trembling hands she clumsily pushed it aside and threw open the door.

The vampire was nearly there.

Jaimie screamed as Becka grabbed her and yanked her inside.

She reached for the door to pull it shut, and for a brief second, she stood face-to-face with the vampire. He was three feet away, reaching for her. His eyes glowed with hate. She pulled the door with all of her might.

It slammed shut with a loud thud ... which was immediately followed by another thud as the vampire slammed into the door.

Becka fumbled with the bolts, sliding them into place.

"There!" she cried.

SLAM!

The vampire hit the door again with such force that she thought she saw the steel actually give a little.

Both girls turned and raced toward the front of the ware-house. They flew down the hall, running for their lives as the vampire slammed into the door a third time.

Within seconds, they made it to the other side of the shop and out the front entrance to the street.

Immediately Becka spotted Ryan laying down the last of the dozen crosses. He jumped out of the way just as Tim finished parking the truck, sealing off the alley. Tim climbed out of the truck and yelled, "You girls okay?"

Becka nodded and shouted, "Have you got him?"

"We've got him," Tim shouted as he headed around the front of the truck. "He can't get out."

"Let's take a look," Ryan said.

The alley was completely blocked by the long truck, so they had to crawl over the front bumper to squeeze inside.

"Where is he?" Becka asked. She was more than a little ner-vous as she arrived at Ryan's side.

Their eyes scanned the dim alley. There was no sign of the vampire. Anywhere.

"Look at that door," Ryan said, motioning down the alley to the steel door. "It's really bent up."

"Shine your lights in all the dark areas," Tim ordered. "Make sure he's not hiding."

Both Becka and Ryan pointed their flashlights into all the shadows.

Nothing.

"Wait!" Ryan yelled. "Over to the left. Something's moving!"

Becka moved her beam to join his. He was right. Something was moving in the shadows.

Suddenly their beams caught it in the light.

"It's a bat!" Tim cried.

And it was. Exposed now and in the light. The creature's

wingspan was nearly a yard wide, and the thing flew straight at them.

"Duck!" Becka shouted.

Jaimie screamed as they all hit the pavement.

But the giant bat rose and headed over the truck. They spun around and watched it fly high over their heads and deep into the night.

Everyone was breathing hard, but it was Ryan who finally spoke. "We lost him."

"And he was real," Becka said, shaking her head in amazement. "There's no question about it now. He's a real vampire."

7

The words hung on the screen for what seemed like an endless length of time.

Vampires do not exist.

Rebecca simply stared at them. She couldn't believe Z was so stubborn. It reminded her of the arguments she used to have with her dad. Back when he was alive. Back when he knew he was right and stuck to his guns regardless of what she said.

She had just finished telling Z about their failure at trapping the vampire and how the monster had turned into a bat. Still, despite all of this evidence, Z insisted there were no such things as vampires.

She was more than a little frustrated and wasn't sure what to type next.

Z saved her the trouble.

Did you see him turn into a bat?

I told you he disappeared.

Z remained unimpressed.

Disappeared where?

Becka could feel her ears growing hot with anger. Why was he giving her the third degree? Couldn't he just accept that he was wrong? Furiously, she typed back:

He either disappeared into thin air ... or else he turned into a bat!

There was a long pause. Becka drummed her fingers on the desk, waiting impatiently for Z's response.

Finally, it came:

Look for another explanation.

Becka's fingers flew over the keyboard:

I GAVE you the only explanation!

The reply slowly formed on the screen:

Don't you find it strange that no one has been seriously injured? Vampires are supposed to be violent, vicious creatures. Their lust for blood is unparalleled. As is their strength. Would not a real vampire have killed someone by now?

What's that supposed to mean?

The only true power this enemy has is the power of fear. Doesn't the pattern seem familiar?

Becka stared at the screen, trying to understand. Z went on:

Occult activity—whether real, imagined, or counterfeit—is always based on fear. In every case, it becomes a matter of choice to either trust in God's power and experience his love or to believe in the enemy's power and live in his fear.

Becka read carefully, beginning to understand. Suddenly, Z changed the subject:

How are Jaimie and Ryan doing?

Becka felt anger surge through her. Talk about having your buttons pushed! Almost before she could stop herself she punched back:

We're talking about vampires, not Jaimie and Ryan.

Z's answer returned:

It's the same enemy.

Becka caught her breath. Z *did* know something. But what was he talking about? What did he mean, "It's the same enemy"? Quickly she typed:

Explain.

Your fear is leading you to make wrong conclusions about the "vampire." Your fear of losing Ryan is making you jealous and unable to love Jaimie.

Becka's mouth hung open as she reread the words. But Z wasn't finished:

Remember, "God did not give us a spirit of timidity." As you love and trust God, your fear will vanish, allowing you to think more clearly about this so-called vampire. As you ask God to help you love Jaimie, your jealousy over her will also disappear.

Becka continued to stare, barely breathing. He had done it again. Almost effortlessly, he had cut past all the surface issues and gone straight to the heart of the matter.

More words appeared:

Please check in with me once a day so I won't worry.

Becka frowned. If Z was so sure there was no vampire, then what was he worried about? As if he were reading her mind, the answer appeared on the screen:

Danger comes in many forms. Remember Christ's words, "I am with you always." This you can believe. Z

Rebecca closed the laptop, her mind spinning.

❧ ❧

Media people swarmed the set at nightfall when Becka finally stopped by. By now the major TV stations had caught the buzz and had sent crews to Transylvania. Everywhere Becka looked, she saw a camera or a microphone.

"Excuse me?"

Becka turned. A handsome man in his early thirties approached. "Are you connected with the film?" he asked.

Before she could answer, he continued. "I was hoping I could get a few comments for American television about this vampire business."

Becka shook her head. The last thing in the world she wanted was to be seen by a zillion people. After all, she was Becka Williams, the girl who did her best to blend into the wallpaper whenever she was in a crowd.

When she didn't respond, the reporter moved on without so much as a nod. Clearly Becka was of no use to him, so he acted as if she didn't exist.

Becka only shook her head, marveling at the rudeness.

The crowd was largest near the food wagon, and as Becka made her way to the counter, she discovered why. There, in the center of about twenty reporters, sat Jaimie. Ryan stood right next to her, trying to act as if he really belonged.

Becka bit her lip and closed her eyes. How could she fight off her jealousy when every time she turned around something like this happened?

Finally, she turned to the man behind the counter. "Mike," she asked, "can I have a cheeseburger?"

He shook his head. "Sorry, got nothing left. Media people cleaned me out. It was even worse at lunch. Unless you want a microwaved burrito or a pepperoni stick."

Becka rolled her eyes. "Thanks, but no thanks."

He nodded and chuckled. "I know what you mean."

She threw another look to Ryan, hoping to get his attention, but he was too busy playing Mr. Hollywood to see her — or, as far as she could tell, to even care that she existed anymore.

Trying not to feel sorry for herself but failing miserably, Becka headed over to the set of the old mansion where they were finishing up the scene she'd watched yesterday.

When she arrived, Van Helsing was about to confront the vampire.

"Excuse me, sir," Van Helsing said to the vampire, "but I noticed you made a rather quick exit from the drawing room. Is there something wrong?"

"No, Dr. Van Helsing," the vampire replied. "Everything is fine."

"I am at a disadvantage," Van Helsing countered. "You seem to know my name, but I do not know yours."

"Everyone knows of the great Dr. Van Helsing," the vampire retorted. "Your reputation is well known here in Transylvania. And as for being at a disadvantage, sir, you are more right than you could ever imagine."

With that, the vampire turned and raced for the door.

"After him!" Van Helsing shouted. "He's the one!"

The men bolted after the vampire, and Dirk Fallon yelled, "Cut!"

Everyone relaxed, and the director shouted, "Okay, once again. Places everyone. That was just a little stiff."

"I thought you *wanted* stiff," Steve Delton said.

"I want stiff, Steve," the director called, "but not dead, all right?"

As the actors took their positions, Becka caught a glimpse of Ryan and Jaimie arriving. Apparently they had just finished the interview. Reluctantly, she raised her hand to get their attention. "Ryan, Jaimie ..."

"Quiet on the set!" Fallon shouted, and Becka wondered if he meant it especially for her. Feeling a little embarrassed, she moved around the outside of the group until she met up with Ryan and Jaimie. They stood next to one of the soundmen, who was wearing headphones and watching the meters on the audio recorder.

"Hey, Becka," Ryan whispered. "Where have you been?" He was his usual good-natured self, as if nothing had happened.

"I ... I talked to Z," Becka said, although she didn't really want to discuss it in front of Jaimie.

"What'd he say we should do?" Ryan asked in excitement.

Becka shook her head. "That's just it ... He says there's no such thing as a vampire."

"What?" Ryan seemed surprised. "Didn't you tell him about the bat?"

"I told him about everything," Becka said sharply. "But he said that no one has been seriously hurt, so —"

"What about the attack on Jaimie?" Ryan interrupted. It was obvious that he was upset. "If Tim hadn't come by then, she'd have been a goner."

"I know, I know," Becka said. "You don't have to convince me."

Ryan set his jaw and scowled. "Well ... then we'll have to figure out how to beat this thing without Z's help."

"Quiet, please," the soundman said, motioning to the scene that was about to begin.

As before, Van Helsing confronted the vampire, but this time Dirk Fallon yelled "Cut!" before they even finished the scene.

"I'm not buying the vampire running away like that," Fallon said. "I want him to turn slowly and walk toward the door. Then let's have one of the men, the guy in the blue waistcoat, grab on to the vampire's cape. I want the vampire to swat him away, like you'd swat a bug, and then just walk out into the night."

"Do I still shout out that 'After him!' line?" Steve Delton asked.

Fallon shook his head. "No, tend to your friend instead. After the vampire smacks him, he falls into that big wooden cabinet and onto the floor. Can you do that, Blue Waistcoat?" he asked. "Bang into the cabinet and fall to the floor?"

The extra in the blue waistcoat nodded.

"Okay, then," Fallon said. "When he falls to the ground, everybody crowd around while Van Helsing attends to him. Clear?"

Everyone nodded.

"All right, then, let's go."

"Quiet on the set," the assistant director yelled. "Have we got tape?"

"We've got tape," the soundman replied.

"Okay, roll it!" he shouted to the cameraman.

"Rolling."

The clapboard indicated the scene, and Fallon yelled, "Action!"

As requested, the extra in the blue waistcoat leaped ahead and grabbed the vampire's cape. The vampire turned and grabbed the man's hand. Then, with one great toss, he flung the man backward into the cabinet. Only, instead of slamming against the cabinet and falling to the floor, the extra hit the cabinet too hard, causing it to rock backward. As it did so, one of the doors flew open.

And out toppled a dead man.

Two large bite marks showed on his throat, and he appeared to be totally drained of blood.

8

The crew gasped, and Jaimie screamed as the dead man tumbled out of the cabinet and onto the ground.

"It's Tom Kadow," someone shouted.

"Who's that?" Becka asked.

"He's a key grip ... over the rigging crew."

Jaimie explained in a shaken voice, "He disappeared the first week of shooting, before you came. We thought he just couldn't take the country and quit. Everybody who knew him said he'd never walk off a set, but he didn't have any family to contact, so we never knew ..."

"He didn't walk off the set," Ryan said. "He must've been in that cabinet."

"Please," Jaimie said, "I think I'm going to be sick."

"C'mon, Jaimie." Ryan took her arm. "I'll walk you back to your trailer." As he passed Becka he added, "Guess this blows Z's theory to smithereens."

"What do you mean?"

"Now we've got ourselves a real victim."

Becka nodded slowly, her eyes still riveted to the corpse.

She did not follow Jaimie and Ryan but waited with the others as the doctor arrived to examine the body. Everyone appeared fairly shaken. Everyone but Dirk Fallon.

"Listen, Doctor," the director said. "I know examining the body and so forth can take a while. Would you like me to have someone help you move it to the medical tent or—"

"Disturbing the body might obscure something vital to my examination," the doctor replied.

Fallon nodded impatiently. "Well, I should think the cause of death is somewhat obvious ... The man doesn't have a drop of blood in him."

"That will be up to the officials at the morgue to decide. But it does bring up a curious problem, Mr. Fallon."

"What's that, Doctor?"

"Where's the blood? It's not in the cabinet, it's not on the floor, and it's not in the man."

"If you're asking me if I want to go on record suggesting that a vampire did this, the answer is no, Doc. But then, that is the only explanation, isn't it?"

"I don't have another at this time," the doctor said.

"Then can we get it out of here and go back to making our movie?"

Once again the doctor appeared shocked at the director's lack of compassion. "Mr. Fallon, a man has been murdered."

"And the only way I can stop there being more murders is to get this film finished as fast as I can and get us all out of here," Fallon said.

The doctor obviously did not approve of Fallon's attitude, but he agreed to move the body while he waited for somebody from the morgue to pick it up.

Minutes later, Becka watched as they hauled the body away. She felt a cold, numb knot in the pit of her stomach. In all of her encounters, no one had ever been murdered.

Until now.

"Enjoying your visit with us, Rebecca?" Dirk Fallon said as he walked past her without waiting for a response.

By now the crowd had started to break up, preparing for the next shoot. Since it was getting late, and since she really didn't want to be out here in the dark, Becka decided to go back to the hotel. It would have been nice to have some company, but Ryan obviously had other obligations.

Once again, she thought of Z's suggestion to love Jaimie with God's love. But seeing that corpse and realizing how wrong he'd been about vampires ... well, couldn't he be just as wrong about handling Jaimie?

Then again, Z had never been wrong about anything before.

She wasn't sure if it was her fear of walking home alone or her concern for Jaimie. Maybe it was both. In any case, she decided to swing by Jaimie's trailer to see how she was doing. Besides, maybe Ryan would be ready to go back with her.

Becka navigated her way through the production trailers toward Jaimie's. She was about halfway there when, off in the shadows, she thought she saw movement.

She slowed to a stop and peered into the darkness.

There it was again. A black form moving through the shadows behind the trailers. A black form that looked a lot like a black billowing cape. A black billowing cape that she recognized all too well.

Becka went cold. It was the vampire.

Quickly she ducked for cover behind a truck. Then, ever so slowly, she peeked around the corner.

He was moving away, heading into the darkness.

Becka's first impulse was to scream, to shout out an alarm, to run in the opposite direction. But she knew that that would accomplish nothing. The vampire would simply disappear again and prepare to kill another.

Then, suddenly, a thought struck her. This was a golden opportunity. If she followed the vampire and found out where it lived, maybe they could come back in the daylight when it was asleep and destroy it. After all, vampires were supposed to be powerless in the day.

At least that's what all the legends said.

A wave of fear shuddered through Becka at the thought. Follow him? Was she insane? With a vampire's keen senses, there was a good chance he would spot her. And an even better chance that she would lose sight of him in the darkness.

Then again, when would an opportunity like this recur?

She took a deep breath to try to clear her mind.

"Dear God," she whispered, "I'm really scared. But I know you sent us over here to help Jaimie. I'm not sure what to do now, but you promised to protect us, and you've never let us down before. So ... well, please, just be with me. Oh, and God, I'd sure appreciate it if you wouldn't let me get killed."

With the hesitant prayer—and with just a fraction more confidence—Becka moved away from the trailer and started following the creature.

The dark form moved effortlessly past the remaining trailers and into the nearby village. Becka did her best to keep him in sight. Maintaining a safe distance, she followed him down one, two, three alleys before he made a turn and headed to the edge of the town and out into a nearby field.

Becka nearly quit her pursuit at that point. After all, to hide behind trailers or alley walls was one thing; to be seen out in an open field with no cover was quite another.

But, remembering her prayer and the helpless look of fear she'd seen so often on Jaimie's face, Becka pushed forward. She was no longer doing this for herself. She was doing this for Jaimie. That's what God had wanted. And if that's what God wanted, she'd rely on him for protection.

She moved from the cover of the wall and headed out into the field. Fortunately, there was a full moon and she could see the vampire's shadow, which allowed her to stay back a little bit farther.

He cut toward the right and began moving much faster. Faster than she could keep up.

She began losing ground.

Off in the distance, in the moonlight, she saw some kind of an iron fence. She thought the shadowy form had gone inside, but she was too far away to be sure.

A horrible thought struck. What if he decided to turn into a bat? No way could she keep up with him then. Or worse yet, what if he flew back and spotted her out here in the field? All alone, without any protection.

"I am with you always."

The verse Z had quoted rang in her mind, and she felt a little more peace. Why was she so afraid? She had the best protection anybody could have. And yet ...

Beyond the large iron fence were what looked like short, tiny pillars. She caught a glimpse of the vampire's form moving past those pillars. But, as she squinted into the darkness, she realized that he wasn't moving past pillars. He was moving past tombstones.

He had entered a graveyard.

Surprisingly, the graveyard didn't frighten her. Maybe it was the prayer; maybe it was past experience. In any case, she was not afraid of the dead for the simple reason that she knew they were not there ... just their bodies. And fearing dead bodies was like fearing somebody's old discarded shoes. Nobody was in them. Not anymore. People had used them once, but now they were left behind.

All she'd have to do was wait until daylight and then show up with some wooden stakes to drive through his heart, just like in the movies.

Revulsion shuddered through Becka. What was she thinking? She could never drive a stake through —

A low rumbling interrupted her thoughts. It wasn't loud enough to be thunder, and there was a scraping to it. Instantly she knew the sound—the rubbing of stone against stone. It could only mean one thing. The vampire was going back inside his crypt. If she didn't see where that crypt was now, she would never be able to find him.

She raced across the field toward the cemetery. Once she entered through the black iron gate, she slowed to a walk. The graveyard was old, and many of the tombstones were in disrepair. Some had cracked and broken, with the split halves still lying on the ground. Others had crumbled into piles of rock.

As she moved past, she caught glimpses of dates: 1845 ... 1811 ... 1802.

She strained her ears to listen. Though she could no longer hear the scraping sound, she reasoned that if she had heard him opening his crypt, she would hear the same grating rumble when he climbed inside and closed it.

She spotted another gravestone. A. J. Horn, 1723 – 1768. That was before America's independence!

Suddenly, Becka heard the rumbling and scraping again. It was just as she thought but far closer than she had imagined. She turned in the direction of the sound and silently moved through the grass. She moved by rows of tombstones as she peered intently at the larger crypts for any sign of movement.

Then, out of the corner of her eye, less than ten feet to her right, she saw it. A tall caped figure standing next to a crypt with an open lid.

It was him!

Startled and a little off balance, Becka's foot caught a broken piece of stone. She tried to catch herself but continued falling forward ... headfirst ... directly toward the caped figure and his open crypt.

She hit the ground and quickly rolled over, expecting to see the vampire looming above her, swooping down to sink his fangs into her neck.

But he was gone.

She scrambled to her feet. What was going on? Why hadn't he attacked? Surely he had seen her.

She spun around to the open crypt. The stone top was still ajar!

He was inside; she was certain of it!

A small part of Becka wanted to peer into that open crypt, but a greater part of her wanted to live. She didn't know why the vampire hadn't attacked, but she didn't want to stick around to give him a second chance.

She turned and sprinted out of the graveyard. She didn't stop until she saw the hotel.

👁 👁

When she arrived at the hotel, Becka found Ryan waiting for her in the lobby.

"So where'd you go?" he asked. "I came back to the set, and you were—"

The look on Becka's face stopped him cold.

"You've seen him!" Ryan said.

As they headed back into the hotel suite, Becka filled Ryan in on the details of tracking the vampire back to the cemetery. She also voiced her puzzlement over the thing not attacking her when she fell toward his open crypt.

"You know which grave is his?" Ryan asked.

Becka nodded.

"Then let's head out for the cemetery at dawn with a backpack full of sharp wooden stakes and some strong hammers."

"I don't know if I'm up to that," Becka said, her voice still a little high and unsteady. "Wait—what's that sound?"

They both froze. For the first time they noticed a soft beeping coming from the bedroom.

Becka took a deep breath. "It's just my laptop. I left it on in case Z wrote back."

The two looked at each other and then, like lightning, raced into the room. Becka landed behind the computer, her hands already flying over the keyboard. A moment later she pulled up the message. It contained only nine words:

"God did not give us a spirit of timidity." Z

"Is that it?" Ryan asked. "Is he still online?"

Becka shook her head. "No. But that's what he's been telling us ever since we got here. And this time, this time I think I've got an idea of what he means." Ryan looked at her, and she explained. "I've been letting fear cloud my thinking ... and divide us. Jaimie and me, you and me, even Mom and me."

"And ...?" Ryan asked, not fully understanding.

"Don't you get it?" Becka asked. "Fear divides and builds more fear. But God has given us his power and his love—and the ability to think clearly."

"But Z doesn't even believe in the vampire," Ryan said.

Rebecca nodded. "All I know is that this whole time we've acted like we're in some kind of horror movie. But when I tracked that thing to the graveyard and when I prayed, it was like my fear started to go away. Because, at least for those few minutes, I knew God loved me and wouldn't let anything happen. And just as important, I knew I was doing it for Jaimie, out of *his* love for Jaimie."

Ryan continued to look at her.

"Then when I fell next to his crypt, I realized that my wits and knowledge of horror films and vampire trivia were *not* enough to save me. Only God could get me out of that tight spot. I still don't know what happened, why the thing didn't attack me, but I do know that we've been acting like we're trapped in a scary movie instead of thinking things through clearly. We're not using our minds, and we're certainly not using God's power."

Ryan nodded slowly. "I gotta admit, I really want to believe all that vampire stuff, 'cause it's kind of cool. But you're right; we sure haven't been fighting this thing like the other times."

Becka shook her head. "Wooden stakes, holy water, crucifixes—they're not exactly the tools we've used in the past."

Ryan flushed. "You're right. I guess it was easier to rely on them than on God." He sighed. "Maybe we should do some more praying."

Becka flashed him a grateful smile. "That's exactly what I was thinking."

Then without a word, Ryan reached out to take her hand, and they closed their eyes.

Finally, Becka began. "Lord, first of all, forgive me for all the resentment I've been feeling ... and all the anger toward Jaimie and Ryan. Give me a love for Jaimie, *your* love, and please forgive us all for trying to solve this thing our way. Give us clear minds, Lord. Help us to see your will and not allow ourselves to be so easily frightened and divided."

Ryan picked up where she left off. "And, God, help us to separate ourselves from all the craziness going on here. To do things and see things your way, instead of the way everybody else does."

As the two continued praying, Becka slowly felt a haze being lifted, like a fog being blown away, as she began to more clearly understand what was happening. And, as the fog lifted, a plan began to form.

❧ ❧

Thirty minutes later, they were back at the computer carefully reviewing Z's old messages. Again and again, he had made it clear that vampires did not exist.

There are no such things as vampires ... Look for another explanation.

And then there were his comments about fear. First the Bible verse he kept repeating: "God did not give us a spirit of timidity." Becka knew it was true. When God's love and power were present, the fear was gone.

Ryan pointed at the screen, and Becka read:

> The only true power this enemy has is the power of fear ... Occult activity—whether real, imagined, or counterfeit—is always based on fear.

And finally:

> In every case, it becomes a matter of choice to either trust in God's power and experience his love or to believe in the enemy's power and live in his fear.

Now, at last, she understood. It all came down to faith. They could either believe the stuff they saw and heard all around them or they could believe in God. And his truth. Becka slowly shook her head in wonder, musing over the mistakes she now saw they'd made.

A moment later she grabbed a pencil and paper. Ryan moved over to watch her write; then he nodded. He pulled up a chair, and together they worked out another plan. But this one was different. It was based on God's truth. It was based on his love—and the fact that there are no such things as vampires.

9

First thing in the morning, Rebecca put the plan into action. Before she could really call upon the power of God, she had to start obeying his rules. And one of his first rules was that she had to make things right with those she had offended.

"Mom, can I talk to you for a moment?" she asked.

Mom sat at the small desk in their hotel room writing postcards. "Sure, honey."

Becka pulled up a chair across from her. "First of all, I'm sorry about the way I've been behaving. I mean, with John and all."

"That's all right, sweetheart."

"No, it isn't. I have no right to tell you what to do. I've been acting like I was your mother instead of the other way around and—"

"Listen, honey," Mom cut in. "It's really all right. John and I were never anything but acquaintances—"

Becka held up her hand. "No, Mom, seriously, if you want to see him ..."

Mom smiled. "Becka, I don't want to see him."

Becka looked confused. "You don't?"

Mom shook her head. "I tried to tell you that, remember? As you pointed out, John isn't a Christian. So there really couldn't be anything between us but friendship. And he wasn't really even looking for that."

"He wasn't?"

Mom shrugged. "All he wanted was to spend some time with someone to keep from being bored." She smiled. "So you see? You really didn't need to worry, hon."

Becka sighed. "I guess I've just been feeling like everyone was against me from the first day we got here."

"It's been difficult for all of us."

"Well, if things work out the way I hope, we'll be going home very soon."

"Why's that?" Mom asked.

Becka smiled. "Because this time we're going to do it another way. This time we're going to catch a vampire God's way."

❧ ❧

A few minutes later, Becka and Ryan got to work.

First, Ryan met with Tim and told him about Becka tracking the vampire to his crypt the night before. "We're planning on going back while it's daylight and catching him there. Will you help us?" Technically, it was the truth. They just weren't ready to tell Tim everything. Not yet.

"Of course I will," Tim replied. "But I've got a big conference call with money people this morning. I can't cancel it. After that I need to be on the castle set for a while. How does five o'clock sound?"

Ryan frowned. "That's quite a bit later than we were thinking. It gets dark around seven."

"That still gives us two hours," Tim said. "Unless you want to wait until tomorrow?"

Ryan shook his head. "No, he could move his coffin tonight. He knows we know where it is. Five o'clock will have to do."

👁 👁

Jaimie didn't arrive on the set until noon. The poor girl obviously needed all the rest she could get. When Becka finally found her, she was in the wardrobe truck trying on costumes.

"Hello, Becka," Jaimie said, looking at her in the mirror. "I'm not sure where Ryan is."

Becka smiled. "I was looking for you."

Jaimie tensed slightly. She obviously expected trouble. "All right ..."

"No, it's nothing bad," Becka said. "Of course, I can't blame you if you're a little gun-shy around me. I have gone off on you a couple of times."

Jaimie said nothing, making it clear that she agreed with Becka.

"Anyway, I just came to say I'm sorry."

Jaimie raised an eyebrow in surprise. "You're sorry for going off on me?"

"Yeah. And I'm sorry for other things too. Sorry I couldn't be more understanding, especially after all you've gone through. And ... well ... I'm sorry I was jealous about you and Ryan."

Jaimie looked at her quizzically. "Is this some kind of—"

"No, it's no trick," Becka said.

Jaimie continued to look at her. "All right, Becka," she said cautiously. "I'll accept your apology. As long as you understand that Ryan and I are ... well, we're just friends."

"Oh ...," Becka said, not entirely believing her. "Well, that's between you and Ryan."

"Not that I didn't try," Jaimie said with almost a twinkle in her eye. "I mean, he is one of the cutest guys I've seen ... but, well, last night he made it clear he has his eyes on somebody else."

"He did?" Becka's heart sank. As far as she had known, Jaimie was her only competition. Apparently there was somebody else. "Did he—" she cleared her throat— "tell you who?"

Jaimie broke out laughing. "It's you, Becka."

Becka caught her breath. And then once again she felt that old familiar warmth spread through her chest. She really did love him; there was no getting around it.

"Hey, guys."

She turned to see Ryan approaching. He shook his head, clearly displeased.

"I just talked to Tim on the phone," he said. "He's going to be delayed in town. He can't meet us until at least six o'clock."

"Six o'clock!" Becka protested. "That doesn't give us much time to get there and—"

The look on Ryan's face brought her to a stop. "There's more. The weather report says a big storm's coming in. It's going to get darker even earlier."

"Meaning . . ."

"Meaning we may have to confront the thing in the dark."

Becka took a deep breath and slowly let it out.

👁   👁

The scene that afternoon was to be filmed at Castle of the Arges, an ancient structure just a few miles outside of town. Though much of it was in ruins, people believed it was the actual castle used by Vlad the Impaler, the brutal overlord whose cruelty inspired the earliest vampire tales.

As Ryan and Becka rode to the location in one of the production shuttle vans, they couldn't help appreciating the irony. Here they were, about to watch a scene in which Dr. Van Helsing would drive a stake through the heart of the vampire—all the while wondering what their own vampire confrontation would be like just a few hours later.

When they arrived at the castle, they first looked for Tim, but he was nowhere to be found.

"He called my cell phone," Steve Delton said. "Left a message for you. Said he'd meet you at the hotel around six-thirty."

Becka and Ryan looked at each other with alarm. By six-thirty the sun would nearly be down.

"Thank you," Becka said. "If he calls again, tell him we'll be there."

More worried than ever, Becka and Ryan watched the filming in silence.

In the scene, Van Helsing had worked his way down to the cellar of the great castle in an effort to find the vampire's coffin. The room was large and cavernous, full of shadows and a musty smell.

The director called "Action!" and Van Helsing lit his torch. At first he pretended to be excited over seeing the coffin, but as he approached it, he saw another coffin. Then another and another.

The room was filled with coffins.

Thinking back on the episode in the warehouse, Becka couldn't help whispering, "I know what that's like."

In desperation, Van Helsing ran from one coffin to the other, tipping several over, finding only dried bones.

"Cut!" Dirk Fallon's voice echoed loudly in the great room. "Print that. Excellent. Now we insert a shot of the light fading from the window and pick up with Van Helsing realizing he doesn't have any more time."

"That sounds pretty familiar too," Ryan sighed.

Three crew members rushed out onto the set carrying a large mattress, which they positioned just out of camera range on the floor. Meanwhile, Steve Delton took his position on the set.

"Okay!" Fallon shouted. "Ready, still rolling ... and ... action!"

Steve Delton again became Van Helsing. He stared out a window, a look of horror in his eyes. "The sun!" he cried. "It's going down!"

Then, with renewed frenzy, he charged into more coffins, tipping them over as fast as he could until ...

"Looking for me, Doctor?"

Van Helsing looked up in terror at the chilling sound of the vampire's voice.

"Well," the vampire continued, "it's not very sociable to come to a man's home and make such a mess."

The doctor glared at him. "You're not a man, and this is not a man's home ... It's the lair of ... a monster."

With that, the vampire exploded into fury, racing across the room, grabbing Van Helsing, and flinging him backward.

Even though Becka could see that the actor, Steve Delton, landed safely on the mattress that had been laid down, the powerful scene gave her chills.

"Cut!" Fallon yelled. "Good job, Steve. Print that. Now set up the reverse angle."

The same crew members hauled away the mattress and brought out a small rubber trampoline and some breakaway furniture—a couple of chairs and a coffee table.

Ryan glanced at his watch. Obviously he was getting nervous.

The crew set up the breakaway furniture, and the camera turned in the opposite direction to face the scene. A stuntman, dressed exactly like Steve Delton, came out and jumped up and down on the small trampoline, testing it a few times.

When all was ready, Fallon shouted, "Roll film ... and ... action!"

The stuntman bounced off the trampoline and smashed into the breakaway furniture.

Becka watched a nearby TV monitor, impressed that it looked exactly as if Van Helsing were thrown through the air and crashed into the furniture.

"Cut!" Fallon said. "We have to go again. Try to come off the tramp a little lower. It'll make for a better angle."

Ryan looked at his watch again. He turned to Becka. "It's four-fifteen. We can't wait for Tim any longer."

"All right," Becka said, fighting back the tension growing in her own body. "We'd better head out, then."

Ryan took a deep breath and nodded.

As they took the shuttle van back to the hotel, Becka spoke up. "Ryan, I want to apologize for the way I've been acting. We came here to help Jaimie, and I'm afraid I haven't been very supportive of that. I'm ashamed to say that the reason is ... I was jealous."

"Jealous?" Ryan responded. "Of who? Me? I know I got to do some extra things, being on the crew and all, but it really wasn't that big of a —"

"Not you," Becka cut him off. "I wasn't jealous of you for working in the film. I was jealous of Jaimie being around you all the time."

"Oh," Ryan said, as a somewhat surprised expression lit his face.

Rebecca turned and sighed. *Men!* she thought. Their minds worked so differently from girls' that it was a wonder they worked at all!

"Actually," Ryan said, "I'm the one who should be apologizing to you."

Becka waited, hoping he wasn't about to tell her that he'd fallen for Jaimie.

"I should have been more understanding about how you were feeling," he said. "I just thought you were acting silly, but I never really tried to figure out why. That's not the way a friend should be ... I'm sorry."

Those few words touched Becka so deeply that she had to fight back a tightness in her throat. Just when she had been sure that Ryan was the most insensitive person in the world, he suddenly seemed to care about and understand her deepest feelings.

He looked at her, puzzled. "You okay?"

"I'm okay," she said hoarsely. "Thanks for asking."

The shuttle stopped in front of the hotel, and Becka and Ryan went in. They saw John Barberini then, and Becka added another element to their plan.

👁 👁

"You want me to *what?*" Barberini asked, looking at Becka suspiciously.

"Go with us to the cemetery. And bring your video camera."

Barberini looked at her. Ever since Becka had doused him with the water, he had never seemed too comfortable around her. "You know where the vampire is buried?"

"Yes," she replied. "We're supposed to meet Tim Paxton at six-thirty to go over there."

"But it's barely five o'clock," Barberini said.

"That's part of our plan."

"I don't understand."

"I'll give you the whole scoop if you'll help us out."

Barberini hesitated for a moment and then reached over and picked up his camera bag. "Let's go," he said. "Oh, one more thing. Once we get into that cemetery, how do you know we're going to make it back out? I mean, without turning into zombies or something."

Ryan shrugged. "We don't."

Barberini nodded. "That's what I was afraid of."

👁 👁

Even at five o'clock in the afternoon, the old cemetery seemed eerie. Despite the remaining daylight, the approaching storm cast a spooky darkness over the area.

Becka, Ryan, and John Barberini crouched low behind some bushes next to the large crypt and waited.

Ten minutes later, Steve Delton hurried through the gate carrying an overnight bag. Tim Paxton trailed behind him. The wind of the storm whipped at their clothes.

"Hurry up, Tim!" Delton shouted over the wind. "We haven't got much time."

"I'm coming, I'm coming," Tim called. "It's your fault we're so late."

"It's Fallon's fault, not mine. Little creep wouldn't let me go until he made sure the fall matched. I mean, *I'm* the actor. The stuntman has to match *me*. They must've gone through a thousand dollars of breakaway furniture."

"Who cares?" Tim said as he caught up to Delton. "With all the publicity this film is getting, we could triple the budget and still come out with a winner."

"Right," Delton agreed. "Just don't forget good old Van Helsing's bonus."

"You'll be well paid," Paxton said. "Now get ready."

In the bushes by the crypt, Rebecca and Ryan exchanged glances. This was the moment they'd been waiting for. The little red light on John's video camera glowed as it captured the scene before them. They all watched in silence as the two men continued to approach.

As he walked, Steve Delton opened his overnight bag and pulled out a latex mask. He stopped for a moment and carefully put it on.

In the bushes Ryan whispered, "You were right, Beck! He *is* the vampire."

John Barberini shot a photo of Delton wearing the vampire mask. "How'd you figure this out?" he whispered.

"I realized that we'd all been reacting to fear," Becka whispered. "So I tried doing what Z suggested and looked past the fear. If he was right and vampires don't exist, we had to ask ourselves who would benefit most by making something like this up. The only thing that benefited was the film. And then I realized that Tim, the film's producer, had been in on our plan to trap the vampire in the alley."

"So you set up this plan to capture Tim," Barberini said.

"What about Delton?" Ryan asked.

"I knew someone with the film had to be the vampire. At first I thought it was Fallon, but he's not tall enough. Then I remembered that, when Jaimie got burned by the crucifix, Delton was the one who put it around her neck. He probably put some kind of acid on the back of that cross. He was wearing gloves, so it didn't bother him."

"But what about the bat and the vampire floating outside your window?" Barberini asked.

"I don't know how they did those things," Becka said. "But since I've watched filming this week, I've learned that movie people can fake just about anything if they want to."

"Shhh ...," Ryan said. "They're coming this way."

"You straight on the plan?" Tim Paxton asked as he and Delton finally came to a stop at the crypt.

"Got it," Delton said as he smoothed the mask onto his face. He reached back into his bag, pulled out a bottle of makeup, and began to carefully cover the edges.

"Okay, then you won't mind running it by me," Tim prodded.

Delton sighed. "You and the kids get here about six-thirty. I'm lying in the casket, just like they expect. They lead you here to the crypt. You slide the stone cover over and open the casket. I open my eyes and grab your throat."

"Yeah," Tim agreed. "I'll insist on being the stake driver, and I'll keep the kids back, so I'll be leaning over to make it easy for you."

"Okay," Delton said as he began attaching some long and pointed fingernails.

"Just be careful with those nails, all right?"

Delton nodded. "I've been doing this for a couple of weeks. I know what I'm doing."

Tim checked his watch. "I'll have to leave pretty soon. Okay, what about the rest of it?"

Delton shrugged. "I grab your throat. The girl comes at me with the crucifix—"

"It could be the boy," Tim interrupted. "They'll both have them."

"Okay, whoever comes at me with the cross, I shove you back and then leap out of the grave and run away," Delton said.

"Yeah," Tim corrected, "but not right away. You have to kind of snarl and claw at them a couple of times before you run."

"Of course," Delton replied. "The standard routine."

"All right, then," Tim concluded. "I guess that's about it."

In the bushes by the large crypt, Becka looked at Ryan. He smiled and nodded toward John, who was videotaping the entire conversation.

Suddenly, to their surprise, John Barberini stood up, revealing himself and their hiding place. "No, that's not quite it, Tim."

The producer and the actor spun around, clearly surprised as Barberini continued. "It seems you weren't quite careful enough. Looks like your plan has been figured out."

Becka couldn't believe what Barberini was doing. They had agreed to hide and record everything, not jump out and confront them.

"Be careful, John," Becka said as she rose to his side. But suddenly she was looking down the barrel of a .38 caliber revolver.

"I think *you're* the one who should be careful," Barberini replied as he held his gun on her.

Becka threw a panicked look to Ryan. Barberini was in on the vampire hoax with Tim and Delton! They'd made a terrible mistake.

Maybe even a fatal one.

It started to rain. Big fat drops fell all around them.

"What happened, John?" Tim asked.

"She figured out it was a scam," Barberini said. "Didn't you, bright stuff?"

Becka swallowed and said nothing. The wind blew as rain continued to fall, soaking her hair, dripping down the side of her face.

Without warning, Barberini reached over and smacked her hard across the cheek. Ryan bounded to his feet in her defense, but he froze when Barberini swung the gun in his direction. Turning back to Becka, the reporter grinned. "I've been wanting to do that ever since you doused me with that holy water."

Becka held her cheek. Her face throbbed, and she could feel a welt already rising on the skin.

"You all right?" Ryan asked.

She wiped the rain from her face and nodded.

Ryan turned back to Barberini, furious. But Barberini's revolver kept him in check. "The only thing you kids didn't figure out was the bat at the Dominski warehouse."

Tim sighed. Ryan and Becka turned to him. The rain had plastered down his hair, and the wind blew his coat. He looked the most distressed of the three men. "There was a door just across the alley," he explained. "I made sure it was unlocked so Steve could make his getaway."

"Yeah," Delton said. "But not before leaving me something just inside the door. A large cage holding a nice big bat."

"What about the vampire outside my window?" Becka asked, pulling the wet hair from her face. "It looked so real."

"It *was* real," Delton answered. "My room is one floor up from yours. A little rigging, a little wire, and presto! Easy trick."

"Enough gabbing," Barberini insisted. "What do we do with them?"

Delton shrugged. "More victims for the vampire, I think."

Tim seemed reluctant. "Now wait a minute. Kadow's death was an accident. This would be ... murder."

"An accident?" Ryan exclaimed.

Tim nodded. "That's how all of this started in the first place. Steve, Kadow, and I were looking over the mansion location. We were trying to decide if we needed to run some extra rigging to have the vampire swoop away at the end of the party scene. Kadow was up in the rafters trying to show me how he'd stage it when he slipped and fell. He hit the back of his head on one of the stones." Tim shook his head. He died instantly.

"Kadow didn't have any family or anyone who cared what happened to him. When he was killed, we realized we could capitalize on his death. So we started a few rumors about a real vampire and came up with our whole scheme to scare Jaimie—and before anyone could accuse us of a hoax, we had Kadow's body turn up, drained of blood."

"*That* was messy," Delton added, the rain streaming down his stringy hair and into his face. He grinned at Becka and Ryan. "'Course, now that I've got the hang of it, I shouldn't have any trouble doing it again."

"Stop it, Steve." Tim began pacing, obviously upset. "Up to now we've just been guilty of a scam, but killing innocent kids is another thing entirely."

"I'm not going to jail again," Barberini growled. "When you guys brought me in on this plan to get publicity, I agreed. But I've done time in the pen. I'm not going back there again. I'd kill these kids first. I'd kill both of you too, if I had to."

Becka closed her eyes. Her instincts about John Barberini had been right all along.

"All right," Delton agreed. "But don't shoot them, for crying out loud. Vampires don't shoot people. Let's use the fangs we used on Kadow's neck." He reached into his overnight bag and pulled out a set of steel fangs. "They don't look so pretty, and you have to plunge them in hard with your hands, but they do the job, and they leave good marks."

Ryan and Becka exchanged terrified looks. *God, help us!* Becka prayed. From the look on Ryan's face, she was sure he was praying too.

"You first," Barberini ordered Becka.

"Take her over by the crypt," Steve said. "It'll look better."

Barberini motioned with his gun for Becka to move to the crypt. She looked at Ryan one more time before Barberini gave her a push, and she did as she was told.

Delton pulled on a pair of black leather gloves. Then, crossing to Becka, and with Barberini holding a gun to her back, he brought the steel fangs up to her throat.

"Wait!" Tim shouted over the wind. "There must be another way!"

"There's no other way," Barberini yelled.

"He's right, Tim," Delton agreed. "It'll all be over in a minute."

Both Barberini and Delton focused their attention on Becka as Tim turned around, not wanting to see the killing.

Delton leaned in close to Becka, looking for the artery in her neck. Even in the pouring rain she could feel his hot breath against her skin.

Suddenly Ryan made his move. With all of his might he lunged at Barberini's arm. He hit him hard, sending the man slipping and staggering as the gun flew out of his hand. With a roar of anger, Delton reached for Ryan—who managed to spin around and land a good right hook, breaking the man's nose.

"*Augh!*" Delton cried, grabbing his nose. He looked at his hand and saw the blood. Furious, he lunged for Ryan.

Forgotten by her captors for the moment, Becka spotted the gun in the mud and leaped for it. But she wasn't quick enough.

Barberini slammed into her, knocking her aside, and scooped up the wet pistol. "That's enough!" he shouted.

Ryan and Delton stopped grappling.

Delton reached for the steel fangs again. "I'm killing the punk first!" He sneered as he angrily swiped at the blood streaming from his nose. "And believe me—" he leaned forward, practically spitting into Ryan's face—"it's *not* going to be painless!"

"Stop talking about it and do it!" Barberini shouted.

Becka prayed with all of her might as Delton, grinning maniacally, lifted the fangs up to Ryan's throat. And then, just as he was pressing them against the vein: "Hold it right there!" A voice rang out from nowhere.

Delton spun around.

"Drop the gun," another voice shouted.

"You're outnumbered and outgunned," came a third.

Becka watched as three uniformed police officers approached, followed closely by Mom and Jaimie.

"I said, drop the gun!" the first policeman shouted, leveling his own weapon at Barberini, who let his pistol fall and raised his hands.

"Mom!" Becka ran to her mother.

"It's a good thing Jaimie told me where you were," Mom said.

"I got a message from Z," Jaimie said. "He said you might be in danger."

Becka and Ryan looked at each other in amazement. For once, they didn't care how Z always knew what was happening. They were just very, very glad he did.

10

By noon the next day, the weather had cleared, and Rebecca, Ryan, and Mom were leaving for the airport. Jaimie was to stay on another week to finish the film. The doctor's report verified that Tom Kadow had died from a blow to the head. Since both Tim Paxton and Steve Delton were being held in jail pending their trial for fraud, the studio had sent someone else out to supervise production. The stunt double would film Van Helsing's last scene.

Steve Delton was also being charged with attempted murder, as was John Barberini.

"I'm going to miss you guys an awful lot," Jaimie said in the lobby while they waited for a production shuttle van to take them to the airport. "It won't be the same without you."

"You'll be done and out of here before you know it," Ryan replied.

"And don't forget to call us when you get home," Becka added.

"Yeah, if you ever come to visit, we'll throw a big party in your honor," Ryan said.

"Just don't make it a Halloween party," Jaimie joked. "I've had enough of that stuff for a while."

The shuttle pulled up outside and honked its horn. The group headed out the door and toward the curb.

"Well," Jaimie said as they arrived and the driver loaded their luggage, "you two take care."

Becka and Ryan nodded.

Jaimie reached up and gave Ryan a friendly peck on the cheek. "For luck." She smiled.

Becka could see Ryan's face reddening as Jaimie turned to her. "You've got a good thing there, Rebecca Williams. Don't lose him."

Becka was unsure how to respond. Fortunately, she didn't have to. Almost immediately, Ryan was reaching out and taking her hand. "She doesn't intend to," he said, looking at Becka and smiling. "And neither do I."

Becka returned the smile, once again feeling those little flutters deep inside her stomach.

After another set of good-byes, they turned to climb onboard the van. Once inside, they looked out the window and waved one last time to Jaimie as the vehicle pulled away from the curb and started for the airport.

As they headed down the road, Becka again felt Ryan take her hand. And, as she looked into his deep blue eyes, she completely forgot anything and everything about Jaimie Baylor.

"I tell you," Ryan sighed as he settled back into his seat, "between being in a foreign country, working on a movie, and getting caught up in all this vampire stuff, I feel like we've had enough adventure to last us a long, long time."

"Me too," Becka said. "I just want to get home to good old America. The most adventure I plan to have is relaxing, catching up on some magazines, and finally having a normal teenage life."

"I don't think there's any such thing as a normal teenage life, is there?" Mom teased from the seat behind them. "But even if there were, I'm afraid you're going to be disappointed."

Becka turned to look at her. "Disappointed? Why?"

Mom smiled with her head hung low as she continued to read a text on her cell. "It's from Scotty. I wanted to check my messages before we took off, and it turns out he has some interesting news.

"What's he say?" Ryan asked.

Mom passed the phone to Becka. She read it out loud:

> DEAR MOM.
> RYAN'S MOTHER WILL PICK YOU GUYS UP AT THE AIRPORT. I'LL PROBABLY COME TOO. CAN'T WAIT TO HEAR WHAT HAPPENED AND TO TELL YOU WHAT Z'S GOT PLANNED NEXT.

"What?" Ryan exclaimed. "Z's got something else planned?"

"There's more." Becka returned to the telegram.

> TELL BECKA AND RYAN THAT WE GET TO GO TO LA. WE'RE GOING TO HANG OUT WITH SOME ROCK AND ROLLERS. LOOKS LIKE WE GET TO DUKE IT OUT WITH SOME SORTA SATANIC BAND OR SOMETHING. IS THAT COOL OR WHAT?
> SEE YOU SOON.
> SCOTT

Becka and Ryan looked at each other. They each took a deep breath and slowly let it out. So much for the peace and rest they wanted. It didn't look like it would be coming their way anytime soon. Apparently another battle waited to be fought. One for which Z was already preparing them.

Becka settled back into the seat and leaned her head on Ryan's shoulder. She was grateful to have him by her side. But she was even more grateful to know that God was there, that he would never leave her.

Especially with what was coming ...

Especially when it seemed there was no end to the ways, shapes, and sizes in which darkness attacked ...

Discussion questions for *The Undead:*

1. In theory, Becca and Ryan are boyfriend and girlfriend. However, neither one of them care for the boyfriend-girl-friend label. Becca thinks that's because of the extra pressure that label puts on a relationship. Do you think things change when the boyfriend-girlfriend label enters a relationship? If so, how?

2. After they meet, Becca notices that Jaimie and Ryan seem to hit it off. She senses that Jaimie might even be flirting with him. Eventually, Becca becomes so jealous she's completely torn between slugging Ryan and being mature. Have you ever experienced this type of jealousy? Do you think Becca truly have anything to be jealous about? What's another way she could have handled these feelings?

3. Becca always felt better after talking with Z—it reminded her of talking with her father. He always seemed to have the answers and she knew he cared. Is there someone in your family who's like this for you? How about outside of your family?

4. Occult activity—whether real, imagined, or counterfeit—is always based in fear. What are examples of real, imagined, and counterfeit occult activity?

5. John, the New York reporter, begins to show Becca's mom some attention and then asks her out. Becca is pretty cold toward him and hard on her mom for going out. What

emotions and thoughts do you think Becca was having? Did she handle them well?

6. We always have two choices in any difficult situation: we can trust God's power and experience his love, or believe in the enemy's power and live in fear. Think of a time you were in a difficult situation. Which choice did you make? Can you think of another situation where you made the other choice?

7. Jaimie and Ryan were rehearsing lines, and his character was declaring his love for hers. When Becca overheard them, thinking it was real, she stormed in screaming and was completely embarrassed (along with many other emotions). Have you ever been totally embarrassed by something you said or by the way that you acted? What happened?

8. Awkward silences became a frequent occurrence between Becca and Ryan in this book, mostly because she was so tired of feeling angry, jealous, and guilty. What did she do about it? What could she have done differently that might have been better?

9. Successful spiritual warriors fight the enemy with prayer and the Word of God. Ryan wants to battle the vampire with holy water and crosses. Why do you think Becca was uneasy about Ryan's superstitious approach? Which method proved successful in the end?

10. Ryan was confused about how to use God's Word against the vampire situation, since vampires aren't mentioned the Bible. How could he find guidance from the Bible in this situation?

THE SCREAM

If any of you lacks wisdom, he should ask God, who gives generously to all without finding fault, and it will be given to him.

JAMES 1:5

1

At the Poseidon Arena in San Francisco, the incredibly popular heavy metal band the Scream tore through their last set in front of a packed house. The music was loud and the show was exciting—a combination of the latest high-tech special effects, makeup, and costumes.

The Scream's lead singer, Tommy Doland, had a red pentagram painted across his face. His intense dark eyes peered out from the center. His shoulder-length hair was coal black, except for a great shock of bright blue hair in the front. His outfit was part Roman emperor and part Darth Vader. His long cape billowed out behind while he strutted the length of the stage singing:

I'm riding on wings of fire.
I'm burning the fields of desire.
In touch with the overlord,
He takes me higher ...

On the word *higher* his voice catapulted into a loud shriek, one of the band's trademarks. The audience's response was immediate and frenzied.

The audience itself was something to behold. Dressed in homemade versions of the same costumes and makeup as the band members, the crowd seemed even angrier than the band. They moved constantly, slamming into each other with a fierceness that was somewhere between a wild, uncontrolled dance and an outright riot.

Mike Parşek, the drummer of the Scream, looked toward the angry wave of humanity as he hammered out the driving beat and wondered just how close the crowd was to losing control. Three kids had been hospitalized last week at their concert in Denver. Mike was the first to admit that it could've been a lot worse. Kids had been crushed to death at other bands' concerts. Even so, creating that kind of excitement was the key element of the band's performance. After all, the fans came because they *wanted* a wild ride.

Mike scanned the screaming fans again and frowned. Sometimes he worried how that ride might end.

Tommy Doland never seemed worried about that part of the concert. His method of operation was always the same: Take it higher, drive it harder, push it further.

A highlight of the show was always Mike's drum solo. No matter how much Mike pushed it, Doland always wanted to go a little further. For this tour the drum solo had become a big production number loaded with special effects. The climax of the solo now included the eruption of a giant fire cannon that had been made to look like a fierce dragon. When Mike's solo reached its peak, two huge flamethrowers concealed in the dragon's mechanical throat blasted out twenty-foot streaks of fire over the heads of the audience, making them scream in delight.

It was time for Mike's solo, and he jumped in with a vengeance. As he increased the volume and tempo, he felt the tension build in the audience—who expected something spectacular at this point—and in himself, as he prepared for the coming explosion.

Launching into the final pattern, Mike eyed stage manager Billy Phelps, whose job it was to ignite the cannon. As usual, Billy nodded along with the beat, one finger on the button, ready to fire. Mike steeled himself for the blast and nodded slightly, but the visual cue was unnecessary. Billy knew the timing by heart. He pressed the button.

There was a brief hesitation and then a crackling sound that Mike had never heard before. A puff of smoke came from the dragon's mouth. This was followed by a clinking sound that came off like a groan from the pit of the dragon's stomach, which was then followed by silence.

Something was wrong.

Mike breathed a sigh of relief. Part of him was glad it hadn't worked. Every time the cannon went off, he wondered if the teens in the first row were going to become burnt offerings. Then, out of the corner of his eye, Mike caught a glimpse of Tommy Doland. The lead singer appeared to be laughing.

👁 👁

Later on in the show, the band wailed away as Doland sang the lead to their latest hit, "Army of the Night." Meanwhile, Billy worked on the broken dragon.

"I can't figure out why this thing isn't firing," he muttered to himself as he examined the circuitry of the control panel for the fire cannon. "Everything here looks okay. Must be up in the barrel. Better cut the power."

With that, he switched off the control board and began crawling underneath the cannon. Onstage Doland sang:

Army of the night,
Not afraid to fight;
Marching into danger
Without any light.

As Doland writhed across the stage, the crowd screamed.

Guitarist Jackie Vee ripped into a searing solo. Meanwhile, Billy had worked his way to the end of the cannon's barrel.

Doland continued singing:

Army of the night,
The master's wishes soar;
Risking our life
To fight an unholy war.

At these words, as though an unseen hand moved it, the ignition switch on the cannon's control panel vibrated to the on position. Unaware of this, Billy reached inside the barrel to shine his flashlight down the dragon's mouth. Doland continued to sing:

Army of the night,
Unholy alliance;
Our souls submitted
For your compliance.

Suddenly, the loading mechanism of the fire cannon began to shake, but since Billy was at the opposite end, he didn't notice.

Mike looked up from the drums, sensing a difference in the cannon's vibration. He looked over to the control panel and saw that it had switched on. Then, with horror, he saw the small red light on the loading mechanism also flicker.

The cannon was about to fire!

Mike tried to catch Billy's eye, but the stage manager leaned down so far into the cannon that only his legs could be seen.

"Billy!" Mike shouted. "Get out of there!"

Billy didn't hear him. The loading mechanism vibrated, and the light on the panel shifted from red to green.

Mike knew that he would never reach Billy in time, so he hurled one of his drumsticks at the stage manager's legs. It connected, and a bewildered Billy pulled his head out from the cannon to see what was happening. Spotting the stick on the floor, he looked over to Mike, who waved frantically for him to get out of the way.

But there was no time. The cannon fired.

The flame that shot from the dragon's head was a wall of fire. It shot over Billy's head and out across the stage. Grant Simone, the band's bass player, turned just in time to see his amplifier catch fire. With a yelp, he dived out of the way.

Billy was not so lucky. His clothes were aflame.

The crowd screamed, unsure if this was part of the show or an accident. Mike leaped off his drum riser and ran toward Billy. As he passed Doland, he snatched the lead singer's cape and charged for the burning man. Leaping through the air, Mike landed on top of Billy and knocked him to the ground. Quickly he began to smother the fire with the cape.

After several long, terrifying seconds, it was over.

Thirty minutes later, Billy was carried off in an ambulance. Another fifteen minutes passed before the police had cleared the auditorium completely.

Onstage the road crew began to break down the elaborate set. Mike, still stunned, stood by his drums watching one of the roadies begin to dismantle the huge fire cannon.

"Hey, Mike," the roadie said, "why didn't Billy shut that thing down while he worked on it? Doesn't he know better than that?"

Mike looked at the roadie for a long moment. "He *did* shut it down. I saw him do it. The thing ... kicked on by itself."

The roadie looked at Mike as if he were nuts but didn't say anything.

Mike left the stage and headed for Doland's dressing room. He knocked twice on the door.

"Come in," Doland said.

Mike opened the door to see Doland standing before the mirror, still wearing his stage makeup. "Oh, it's the hero of the hour. Come on in, Mike. What's up?"

"Doland, I know for a fact that Billy shut that cannon down

before he started working on it. I saw him do it. The thing came on by itself like some sort of . . ." He trailed off, not sure what to say.

Doland smiled strangely. "Some sort of what, Mike?"

"Some sort of . . . monster. Like it had a mind of its own."

Doland laughed gruffly. "Come now, Mikey. A church boy like you doesn't buy into that sort of nonsense, does he? Sounds like black magic, doesn't it? You don't believe in black magic now, do you?"

Mike turned away from Doland's sneer. "I've told you before. I don't like you teasing me about my father."

Doland gave a look of mock sympathy. "Oh, you mean the good reverend? I wouldn't dream of it, Mike."

"How can you be joking around like this with Billy in the hospital?"

Doland shrugged. "Billy's going to be all right. You heard the paramedic. He'll be okay, thanks to that quick maneuver you did with my cape—which, by the way, you owe me for."

Mike couldn't believe his ears. "You're worried about the cost of the cape?"

Doland shook his head. "Not really. I know that what happened here tonight is good for business. This little accident will result in a hundred thousand more album downloads for us by the end of the week."

"It's not about money, Doland. It's like I've been saying all along. Things are out of hand. This devil stuff has gone too far."

Doland squinted his eyes and mimicked Mike's voice. "*This devil stuff?* Little church boy's afraid of the big bad devil stuff, eh? Sometimes I think you're in the wrong band, Mikey boy."

Mike knew he was on risky ground since Doland could easily get him kicked out of the band if he wanted to push the issue. "Listen to me for a minute," he continued. "Something has changed. Can't you see that?"

"I see far more than you, Mikey. But don't sweat it. I know what I'm doing."

Mike shook his head. This was getting him nowhere. He started to leave, then paused at the door. "It used to be fun, Tommy, but ... don't you see? We're losing control—"

Doland cut him off with a nasty laugh. "I haven't lost control of anything, Mikey. Everything is just the way I want it."

◈　◈

It had not been one of Scott Williams' better days ...

First the church's youth group camping trip was canceled because they couldn't find enough chaperones.

Then Mom asked him to clean his room. Naturally, he figured that meant piling everything that was on the floor up onto his bed so he could go play baseball with the guys. That part was fine. It was coming home and finding Mom steamed that wasn't so fine. That and the discipline she had in mind for him.

"I still don't see why I have to wash these stupid windows," he complained for the tenth time.

"Because they're dirty," Mom replied.

"Why can't Becka help?"

Mom sighed, tucking a strand of brown hair currently under siege by gray behind her ear. They had had this conversation in one form or another several hundred times. "If you'd cleaned your room the way I asked you to, I wouldn't have given you this extra duty."

"You said you wanted to see the floor of my room. Well?"

"I also wanted to see your bed. Scotty, you're fifteen! You're too old to pull a stunt like that."

"Okay! Okay! I'm sorry," Scott mumbled as he went back to wiping the living room window. Outside he could see his older sister, Rebecca, playing football with her sort-of boyfriend, Ryan Riordan. Scott waited until Ryan lobbed her a pass before rapping on the window to distract her. "Hey, Becka!"

Becka caught the ball before turning toward her brother

in the house. "Yes, Scott?" she called pleasantly. "May I help you?"

Scott grimaced, then called out, "Why don't you guys come in here and give me a hand with these windows!"

Becka laughed. "No way! You earned that job, little bro."

Scott went back to his mumbling. "Might as well clean windows. With the camping trip canceled, it's going to be another boring week. I *never* get to do *anything*."

"What are you complaining about now?" Mom asked as she walked through the room.

"Nothing," Scott answered. "I was just wondering why we never get to do anything fun. It's boring hanging around Crescent Bay all the time."

Mom looked surprised. "How can you say that? You've had quite a few adventures since we moved to Crescent Bay. You've also traveled all over the place. You got to visit Louisiana not long ago. Your sister went to Europe."

"That's different," Scott whined. "We were helping Z."

Z was their friend from the Internet. Although they'd never met him in person, he'd led them into all sorts of intense adventures helping various people.

"Are you telling me that you never have any fun on these trips?" Mom asked.

Scott shrugged. "A little, I suppose. But Z always sends us to strange places. Why can't he send us someplace exciting to do something fun?"

"Let me guess—" Mom pretended to search for an answer—"because Z isn't your personal cruise director?"

Scott frowned but only for a second as he suddenly saw a large FedEx truck stop in front of their house. He raced past Mom and headed outside, even managing to beat his sister to the truck.

The driver laughed and handed him a large envelope. "Sign here, son."

Scott signed the form and quickly opened the envelope.

"What is it?" Becka asked.

Scott examined the contents. "I'm not sure ... some plane tickets, a hotel reservation, a pre-paid debit card, and some other kind of tickets ... *Wow!*"

By now Mom was out the door as well. "Wow, what?"

Scott was so excited he could hardly speak. "It's the concert tickets from Z ... Our trip to L.A.! It's been like a month since he mentioned it. He sent us three free tickets *and* backstage passes to see the Scream in Los Angeles. Awesome!"

"The who?" Mom asked.

"The Scream," he explained. "Remember I told you about them, Mom? They're so awesome! And we're going to get to meet them!"

Mom took the package and read the typed note that accompanied the tickets. "All it says is, 'Look for the drummer. More later. Z.' Well, I can't say I'm happy about Z's wanting to send you on another mysterious trip. But I see there's a ticket for me too," she said. "I suppose I could use a short vacation."

Scott was all smiles. "Then we can go?"

Mom nodded. "All of us can go."

"Great! Just wait'll the guys hear about this!" He turned to his sister. "Is this cool or what?"

Becka looked at him before finally managing a lame, "Yeah ... cool."

But the feeling in her gut told her she was anything but thrilled about this. The Scream was popular with all the kids at school. But from what she'd heard of their stuff, the band was definitely heavy metal—real head-banger stuff. She didn't have a big problem with that. But the fact that they definitely flirted with satanic stuff *was* a problem. That kind of stuff always gave her the creeps. Even now she felt her skin crawl.

What possible reason could Z have for wanting them to meet the Scream?

2

Scott lost no time in telling his friends about his upcoming trip. Already there had been at least four teens at the door, each holding a Scream CD and a photo and asking if Scott could get them autographed. Of course, Scott said it would be no problem. In fact, it seemed to Becka that with each new person he talked to, he made a bigger deal out of the L.A. trip. Before long he had gone from a member of the audience to "a personal friend of the band."

"I never said that," Scott argued after Becka brought it up.

"Sure you did. Something like that."

"I never said I was a personal friend of the band. Darryl asked me how I got the tickets, and I said 'a close personal friend.' *He* said, 'You're friends with the band?' I just didn't say otherwise."

"You nodded as you closed the door," Becka argued. "And you *know* Darryl is out telling everyone that you're pals with the Scream."

Scott's face lit up. "You think so? Cool."

"It's not exactly telling the truth, Scotty. I can't believe you'd lie to your best friend like that. That's not cool with God."

Scott looked defensive. "It's not exactly lying, Becka."

"Mom might have other ideas ... and I know Dad would." Bringing up God and their deceased father didn't seem fair. Becka regretted what she said as soon as she saw the look on Scott's face. She touched his arm. "Forget it. I don't care what your friends think anyway."

Scott nodded. That obviously was fine with him.

Becka changed the subject. "I think we should at least email Z. We should find out why it's so important to him that we see the Scream."

"Why?" Scott asked as Mom entered the room with laundry.

"We need more information," Becka answered. "Right now all we know is that we're supposed to meet their drummer."

"All you knew in Transylvania was that you were supposed to meet Jaimie Baylor," Scott replied. "The rest just happens ... kinda like falling off a log."

"I hope those phony vampire attacks in Transylvania are not your idea of falling off a log." Becka scowled as she headed into the kitchen.

A moment later Mom followed her. "What's the matter, honey?" Mom asked. "You don't want to go to L.A.?"

"It's not really that," Becka answered. "It's just ... the Scream ... I mean, they're popular and all, but they're really into the black-magic stuff—skulls, pentagrams, and stuff like that. I know most of it's just an act ... but it's not an act I really want to see."

Mom nodded. "That's not the kind of group I'd want you listening to, much less associating with."

"Me either," Becka agreed.

"But ..."

"But what?"

"Maybe Z figures that by sending us, we'll help them somehow."

Becka knew Mom was right. That's how it had always been

with Z. He always sent them someplace to help out in some way. And Becka knew something else too. She knew her reluctance to go wasn't about whether or not she liked the music. It was about whether or not she wanted to help the people making that music.

And the truth was, part of her didn't. As far as she could tell, they were too into satanic stuff. Maybe they were nice guys under all that make up and three-foot hair. But they were definitely not her idea of good company.

And yet, if they needed help ...

"I guess we should probably pray about it," Becka said with a sigh.

Mom smiled. "I'm proud of you for suggesting that. One of the reasons Z selected you is because you're cautious. But when it comes to making decisions, you always let God have his way."

❧ ❧

Mike Parsek sat in the back of the limo as it came to a halt. It was one of three stretch limos that pulled up in front of the Regent Beverly Wilshire Hotel. Mike was in no hurry to get out as he watched the Scream's entourage pour out of the cars. The other three members of the band got out of the first limo. Out of the second came two publicists, one road manager, a sound engineer, a light guy, and four roadies. Mike shared the third limo with clothes and guitars.

He was the last to enter the hotel lobby, where the scene was taking on epic proportions. It never ceased to amaze him. Wherever the band went, they were like modern-day kings. Wherever one of the band members turned, there was someone to wait on him. Then, of course, there were the fans—screaming and begging for autographs.

Mike and the others signed a few autographs and exchanged small talk with a segment of their adoring legion. Then Doland nodded slightly to the three burly security men waiting nearby. Instantly the hulks moved into action and smoothly separated the crowd from the band.

The security guys were pros. Their sheer massiveness eased the crowd away as they escorted the band to the elevator. Mike gave a sigh of relief. By now the road manager had secured their rooms, and the publicists and tech guys scrambled for what accommodations were left. The roadies would go on to the auditorium and set up for most of the night. Then they'd sleep in the van.

Twenty minutes later, Mike and the other band members were in one of their rooms eating steak sandwiches and drinking exotic-looking bottles of beer made in the African country of Chad. It was bottled especially for them by a guy in Trenton, New Jersey, whom they paid a thousand dollars a week for the service. Actually, *they* didn't pay it. Their record label did—just like it paid for a hundred other little extras that came under the heading of "touring expenses." Mike couldn't help but smile. Yessir, the rock music industry wasn't a conservative business.

"I think we should start with 'Army of the Night' tomorrow," Tommy Doland said between sips of beer. "It's what they want to hear."

Jackie Vee polished his guitar. It was a 1956 Gibson Les Paul—worth thousands of dollars. It seldom left his side. "We can if you want." He shrugged. "Only don't we usually save it for a grand finale at the end of the night?"

Doland swigged his beer. "I just want to get it over with. Get all the blasted shouting over with up front so we can enjoy the rest of the gig."

Mike knew that it was best for him to stay out of Doland's way during such discussions, but he couldn't resist. "You don't want them to cheer?"

"Of course I want them to cheer!" Doland snapped. "I want them to pass out from screaming their heads off. But I don't want them calling out for 'Army of the Night' all night long and not paying attention to our other songs — especially the new ones, the ones *not* on the CD."

Mike nodded. "But that new stuff hasn't been going over with the audience like some of our older — "

"That's 'cause they don't listen!" Doland interrupted. There was no missing the edge to his voice. "We've got to help them get into these new songs."

"Some say the new songs are way too dark," Mike said so softly that he almost wasn't heard.

But Doland heard. "They're too dark because the idiots don't understand what we're trying to say!" he growled, then paused as a smile crossed his face again. "Like some of you," he went on, his mocking eyes riveted on Mike, "they just don't *get* it." With that, he patted Mike on the head, then headed to his room.

Mike watched him go, then turned to watch Grant Simone while he sanded the frets on his bass guitar with a worn piece of sandpaper. "See what I mean?" Mike said. "That's how he is all the time now."

Grant shrugged. "Whatever ... Say, I'm thinking about redoing these frets again."

Mike shook his head. "If you'd stop sanding them all the time, they'd last longer. Listen, don't you guys think Doland is acting weird?"

"So what?" Jackie piped up. "So the pressure is getting to him a little. I didn't hear you asking to be left out of the limo, Mikey."

Grant nodded. "Or these amazing rooms or the fame or the chicks — "

"Or all that beautiful, cold, hard cash." Jackie grinned.

Mike looked at them both, wanting to respond, to tell them they were wrong ... but he couldn't. They were right.

He looked away and let out a sad, lonely sigh.

Becka still felt unsure about the trip, even on Sunday morning as she packed. The whole family had come to look forward to these "little getaways." The time spent traveling reminded Becka of their missionary days in South America.

But this time something bugged her about the trip. It was way down deep in her stomach. She couldn't seem to ignore it. Earlier, they'd all prayed and felt that the trip was something God wanted them to do. But still ...

She had tried to contact Z earlier on the Internet, but he didn't respond. He hadn't sent them any emails either. For the time being at least, it looked like they were on their own.

"Hurry up, Becka! It's almost nine-thirty!" Mom called from the kitchen. It was nearly time to leave for church. Becka had been dawdling, thinking about what it would be like to be in L.A. with Mom, her goofy brother, and four guys who wore capes, painted symbols on their faces, and had hair longer than hers.

"Hey, Beck, where's my leather jacket?" Scott called from his room.

"You don't have a leather jacket!" Becka answered. "It's mine!"

"Well, where's *yours*, then?"

"In my closet, where it belongs ... And no, you can't borrow it again!"

"Why not?"

Becka sighed. "Because last time you left it outside in the sun with a candy bar in the pocket, remember?"

"Oh yeah. C'mon, Beck! I promise I won't do that. It's too early for candy. Mom doesn't let me eat it in church anyway."

Sometimes Becka couldn't believe her brother. "That's not the point. I told you, you couldn't wear it again if you didn't take care of it."

"I took care of it. I just forgot about the candy bar, that's all."

"You also left it wadded up on the floor."

"So?" Scott clearly did not have a clue what the problem was here.

"So, you were supposed to hang it up."

"I leave *all* my clothes on the floor."

"I'll vouch for that," Mom said, joining in. "You guys better hurry and get dressed. We have to go if we're going to make church and still catch that plane."

Scott tapped on Becka's door. "Beck ... c'mon. I need that jacket."

Becka combed her hair in front of the dresser mirror. "No."

Scott was persistent. "Can I come in?"

With another sigh, she opened the door. "Why? You can't borrow my jacket. And *where* did you get that shirt? Mom's not going to let you wear that to church."

It was the official Scream T-shirt. Four hairy guys scowling and holding skulls in their hands. "It's Darryl's," Scott answered. "And I'm not wearing it to church. Just let me borrow the jacket. You can borrow something of mine."

Becka closed her eyes for a moment. It just wasn't worth the fight. With a shake of her head, she opened up her closet and pulled out the jacket. "Here. I'm surprised you can still fit in it since you're taller than me now." At seventeen, Becka was about five feet six. "Just be nice to me on the plane."

"I always am," Scott said, grabbing the jacket from her. "I can do anything for an hour and twenty-minute trip! ... Thanks, Beck! This trip is gonna be awesome!"

Once again Becka felt a woozy sensation deep in her stomach.

❧ ❧

Half an hour later, Becka felt calmer, now that they were in church. The service helped a little. The worship team led the singing of one of Becka's favorite songs, and the drama team put on a funny skit. Finally, she felt herself relax ... until the pastor began his sermon.

"I want to ask you this morning, why do you suppose that Jesus dined with tax collectors and prostitutes?" he began. "Do you think there was better food in that part of town?"

Several people chuckled as the pastor continued, "Do you think he enjoyed the company of those individuals more than he did the company of priests and scribes? Well, maybe he did, even though many people despised tax collectors, because they collected taxes for Rome. We know that Jesus was not a big fan of hypocrisy. The Pharisees were loaded with it! But I think the real reason why Jesus dined with what was considered a bunch of lowlifes was that he wanted to reach them. He wanted to share the good news of God's kingdom with them. He didn't come just for the priests and scribes. He came for *all* people. How could he expect these people to accept what he was saying if he didn't accept them? They were sinners, to be sure. But aren't we all? Fortunately, Jesus sees beyond that. He sees all of us — social outcasts or not — as people he dearly loves."

Becka's stomach churned like a cement mixer, but her mind remained focused on the pastor's words. She knew that she had heard from God.

"Yes," the pastor continued, "Jesus is also the great Judge. But he didn't come to judge — not then. He came to love those who were trapped in darkness. And love begins with acceptance ... not of the sin, but of the sinner. As those who seek to follow Christ, can we do any less? We're called not only to accept those who are different from us but also to go the extra mile to bond with them, just as the apostle Paul did on his missionary journeys. We need to understand those who are lost so we can speak to their hearts. That doesn't mean that we agree with all of the choices the people we reach have made. It just means that we're willing to share God's love with them. Jesus reached out to prostitutes and tax collectors. Who are the lost *we* are to reach?"

Becka slowly nodded. *Okay, Lord, I get it.* And she did. She was going to L.A. She was going to meet the band. She would talk with them, hang out with them ... even accept them. And when the time came, she would have the courage to speak God's truth to them.

At least, she hoped she would.

3

The main airport in Los Angeles was LAX. That's what the
people called it. No long fancy name after some former city
politician. No warm-fuzzy sounding name with *hills* or *briar* or
crest in it. Just the basic deal.

It was very L.A.

From the plane, Becka and Scott could see mountains, but
they'd seen mountains before—bigger ones than these—back
in South America. They could also see the ocean, but they'd seen
that before too. It really wasn't until they were on the ground in
the airport that they began to see the real sights of L.A.

"Hey, isn't that Suzanne Winters?" Scott piped up as soon as
they reached the baggage-claim area. "You know—the TV star.
Right over there."

"Scott, don't point," Becka whispered in embarrassment.
"People don't like that."

"How would you know?" he retorted. "How many stars have
you seen?"

"C'mon, kids! Let's get our bags!" Mom called.

Out in the parking lot, they caught a shuttle to their hotel. "Why
do they call it a shuttle?" Scott wanted to know. "It's a bus."

"They call it a shuttle because it goes back and forth between the hotel and the airport," Becka explained.

"Yeah, I know," Scott replied. "A bus."

Becka blew her thin, brown hair out of her eyes and heaved her suitcase up into the luggage area. As they headed up the freeway on-ramp, they could see heavy smoke off in the distance.

"What's that?" Becka asked. "Looks like a big fire."

A man sitting across from them said, "There's a brush fire burning out of control in the mountains. It's headed toward Malibu."

"Wow!" Scott replied, in awe of the great pillars of smoke.

Becka's stomach churned. She winced slightly and shifted in her seat.

Mom turned to her. "What's the matter, honey?"

"Oh, it's just my stomach. That sure looks like a huge fire."

"No biggie," Scott said, suddenly sounding very authoritative. "There's some kind of natural disaster going on almost every day in Los Angeles. My geography teacher said the place is like a natural-disaster theme park."

Somehow that didn't help Becka's stomach.

Eventually the shuttle cruised into Beverly Hills.

"Cool!" Scott exclaimed, his face glued to the window. "This is where a lot of the movie stars live. Check out the size of that house." He pointed to a home roughly the size of a museum.

"And look at those shops," Becka added, pointing in a different direction. "Could we do some shopping while we're here, Mom?"

Mom nodded. "A little. But not at those places, honey. That's Rodeo Drive."

She pronounced it *Ro-day-o* Drive, but Scott hadn't heard. He also read the sign. "It says Rodeo Drive," he mused. "You don't want to shop there, Beck. Probably all cowboy clothes and stuff like that."

"Scotty," Becka snickered, "people all over the world know

that stores on Rodeo Drive have the coolest clothes. I thought even *you* would know that."

"And they're *very* expensive," Mom added.

"That's *so* L.A.," Scott quipped. "They expect you to pay a fortune for cowboy clothes."

Before Becka could respond, the shuttle pulled into the hotel parking lot. Just as it did, her breath caught. She quickly exchanged glances with Scott and Mom. The place was huge, as well as beautiful. Bellhops were everywhere, loading baggage onto little golden carts. Rich people in expensive clothes strolled back and forth. And just outside Scott's window was the longest car he'd ever seen.

"Look at that!" he exclaimed. "It's like a double limo!"

"They call that a stretch," the man across the aisle said.

"No wonder," Scott replied. "Must be a stretch to afford it."

They watched as a man with expensive-looking sunglasses and hair a mixture of coal black and bright blue climbed out of the stretch limo and walked toward the hotel. But just before he headed up the steps, he stopped suddenly, then slowly turned and stared at the shuttle bus.

"Hey, isn't that Tommy Doland?" Scott asked as they headed for the door of the bus.

Becka nodded. "Why do you suppose he's looking at us?" she asked, feeling her stomach tighten again.

No one had an answer.

Doland stood there, watching the people get off the shuttle. Becka was the first to reach the exit. As she stepped down the stairs, she glanced up to see the singer still staring. He had taken off his dark sunglasses and looked like he was trying to glare a hole right through her.

She felt a cold shiver run through her body. She clutched her throat, unable to breathe suddenly.

Tommy Doland suddenly snapped his sunglasses back on and hurried up the steps to the hotel.

It took a moment for Becka to start breathing again.

"He was looking right at you!" Scott exclaimed in excitement.

She nodded, feeling numb.

"You should have said something! At least waved. I bet he could have taken us right to Mike Parsek."

"Those are not our instructions," Becka said, finally finding her voice. "We're supposed to see him after the show. Besides..."

"Besides what?" Scott pressed as they headed toward the hotel.

Becka looked at her brother and frowned. She had felt the same sensation she had experienced a couple of months ago when battling some evil spirits that had taken up residence in her best friend, Julie.

Becka swallowed and finally answered, "When he was staring at me, it was like I couldn't speak. Like I was choking—" She met her brother's eyes. "Scotty, I couldn't breathe."

❧   ❧

Mike detected the faint smell of marijuana smoke the moment he knocked on Jackie Vee's hotel-room door. There was no answer, so he knocked again. Then the door opened slowly, and Jackie peered out at him.

"Hey, Jackie. Got a minute?"

"Sure. C'mon in."

As soon as Mike closed the door, Jackie took out a small silver case, about the size of a pack of cigarettes. He opened it and took out a joint. From the looks of him, it wasn't his first. "Want to get high, man?"

Mike shook his head. "No. It throws off my timing. We've got to rehearse in a couple of hours ... I hope tonight's show goes well. I want us to feel really good for that cable broadcast. Forty million viewers, man."

Jackie nodded. "Should be good. Will Billy be back for that?"

"Should be. I talked to him a while ago. He's outta the hospital. Sounds like he's doing pretty well. You should call him."

Jackie took a long hit off the joint and stared blankly into space.

"I said you should call him," Mike repeated.

Jackie looked up, squinting like he was trying to focus. "What?... Oh yeah." He waved his hand dismissively. "I'm too tired to call him now. Maybe after rehearsal."

Mike nodded, but he knew Jackie would never remember to call. He probably wouldn't even remember this conversation. "Listen," he asked, "what are we going to do about Doland? I can hardly talk to him anymore."

"He's off on his own trip, that's for sure," Jackie agreed. "But he gets the crowd going, doesn't he? He plays the audience like I play this guitar."

Mike pressed the issue. "I talked to him about Billy getting hurt. It was like he didn't even care. He just said it would sell more CDs."

Jackie took another hit. "Probably will. Doland knows that stuff."

"Yeah," Mike agreed. "But does he care about anybody?"

Jackie didn't seem to hear. He took another hit, staring at nothing. Mike knew from past experience that the conversation was over. Jackie was too high to listen to anything that required thought. He stood up. "I've gotta go. See you at rehearsal."

He was halfway down the hall before he heard Jackie call after him, "Okay ... See ya, Mike."

He headed for the elevator and pushed the button. A moment later, the door opened to reveal Tommy Doland.

"Doland ... I ..." Doland's sudden appearance startled him. Mike felt guilty, like he'd been "caught" being disloyal.

Doland smiled, but there was something very unpleasant in the way his lips curled. "Hi ya, Mikey. Is your room on this floor? No, that's right. Your room is on the sixth floor. Jackie's room is here ... just down the hall, right?"

"Right." Mike tried to smile. "We were just—" He broke off. Doland's smile had turned to ice.

"I know what you were doing, Mikey. You were trying to turn Jackie against me."

Mike stared at him, stunned—and very uneasy at the look in Doland's eyes. "No, I wasn't ... not really. I'm just worried."

"You should be worried, Mikey. You cross me again and I'll fry you."

Mike was shocked by the threat. "What? *Fry* me? What is *that* supposed to—?"

Doland cut him off. "Fry you? My, my, getting a bit paranoid, aren't we?" He smiled again, his eyes glazing over. "I said I'd *fire* you, Mikey ... from the band." The smile broadened. "You just need to be more careful now, don't you? When you listen to people, I mean." Doland stood there in the elevator, glaring at Mike as the steel door closed, leaving Mike staring blankly at it.

❧ ❧

"This place is unbelievable," Scott muttered as he studied his reflection in the mirrored walls of the elevator. "It's so cool that Z booked us a suite in this huge place!"

Becka shook her head. It didn't take much to entertain some people.

Just then there was a loud ding. As the elevator door opened, she moved to step out. "Our floor, Scott—" She broke off suddenly and stared in surprise. There, right in front of her, was Mike Parsek. In fact, if she hadn't known better, Becka could have sworn he'd been staring at the elevator, waiting for them.

Scott recognized him immediately. "Uh ..." But for the first time in his life he seemed speechless.

Becka grabbed his arm and pulled him from the elevator as

Mike moved past them to enter it. At last Scott found his voice ... well, at least some of it. "Hey, hi ... uh ..."

But as Mike turned and the elevator doors closed, he was not looking at Scott. His gaze was locked on Becka. And he seemed very impressed.

The two stood in stunned silence. Finally, Scott spoke. "Wow! Did you see him check you out?"

Becka was dumbfounded. Most of the boys back at school didn't even know she existed. But clearly this guy did. And he just happened to be a rock star!

"That was Mike Parsek!" Scott exclaimed. "He's the one we're supposed to talk to! Why didn't you say something?"

Becka tried to swallow, but her mouth was as dry as cotton. "Why didn't you?" she finally croaked.

"I did!" Scott insisted. "I asked him how he was."

"Oh, really? 'Cause all I heard was, 'Hey, hi ... uh.'"

Scott turned red. "Yeah, well, at least I said something. You were afraid to even talk to him."

Becka took a deep breath and nodded. "You're right. I was." She slowly turned to her little brother, feeling very uneasy and very concerned. "And maybe ... maybe you should be too."

👁 👁

That evening Becka and Mom got ready for the concert while Scott played with his laptop computer.

"You'd better hurry and get ready, Scotty," Mom called from one of the rooms of the suite. "We're leaving in fifteen minutes."

"I *am* ready," he replied, keeping his voice calm. "Hey, Beck, I'm checking out the Scream's website. You should see it. The whole thing comes out of this huge skull."

"Why am I not surprised?"

"What do you mean you're ready?" Mom yelped as she

stepped into the room and stared at Scott's attire: a worn, torn sweatshirt, dirty jeans, and beat-up sneakers.

"This is what you're *supposed* to wear to the concert," Scott explained in his most patient voice. "This is what *everyone* will be wearing — everyone but you and Becka."

"Really?" Mom asked in surprise. "But you … you look … so … destitute."

" 'Destitute at the Institute.' "

"What?"

"That's a Scream song. You know, 'Destitute at the Institute, but alive in my mind.' "

Mom grimaced. "This is going to be a difficult evening for me, isn't it?"

Scott nodded. "Yes, Mom. I imagine it will be."

She sighed slowly. "All right. You can wear everything but the sweatshirt."

"Mom!" Scott protested.

"It stinks."

"But … it's the coolest thing I've got."

"Well, I want you to take it off."

Becka joined the conversation. "Mom, the sweatshirt is the focus of his entire outfit. It goes with his shoes, right, Scott?"

He tossed her a grateful look. "Yeah … exactly … what she said."

Mom nodded. "I see. And I still say it stinks — literally. It smells, because you haven't washed it in a month. So … change it."

"All right," Scott finally conceded, mostly because he was more interested in what was on his laptop than in continuing the conversation. "It's Z!"

You never knew when you'd hear from him. That was part of the mystery of Z — the person they had never met, but who always seemed to know what was going on in their lives.

"Check it out!" Scott called as he moved in closer.

Becka joined him. Together the two read silently:

Greetings. Hope you enjoy the hotel. I have two pieces
of information. 1) Your mission is Mike Parsek. He is a
pastor's son, but has not communicated with his father
for several years. He knows the truth from his childhood,
but he's in over his head. He has no concept of the
danger he's in. 2) Beware of Tommy Doland.

Becka felt a chill as she read the warning. Her eyes dropped
to the bottom of the screen, where Z had written a brief Scripture. It wasn't long, but it was enough to remind her of the seri-
ousness of their task:

"Be self-controlled and alert. Your enemy the devil
prowls around like a roaring lion looking for someone
to devour. Resist him, standing firm in the faith, because
you know that your brothers throughout the world are
undergoing the same kind of sufferings" (1 Peter 5:8 – 9).

Scott didn't seem to even see the warning or the verse.
Instead, he pointed his finger to the number *1* on the screen.
"See?" He smiled smugly. "I told you, you should've talked to
Parsek."

Becka shrugged. "What makes Z think these people will listen to us anyway?"

"Not 'these people,'" Scott corrected. "Mike Parsek. And I'd
say by the way he scoped you out earlier that he'd be willing to
listen to anything you say."

Becka's face flamed. She turned quickly, grabbed her coat,
and headed for the door. Scott closed the laptop and followed,
smiling. Being a pesky little brother definitely had its advantages
at times.

❦ ❦

The Forum in Los Angeles held about twenty thousand people, and it was jam-packed. But Becka wasn't bothered by the size of the crowd. Instead, she worried about the attitude of the crowd.

Everyone in the place seemed angry—maybe even beyond angry. Most of them seemed ready to explode. Small groups huddled together, scowling at the groups surrounding them. It was the most explosive group of people Becka had ever seen under one roof.

And there are twenty thousand of them. All here.

She glanced at Mom. From the expression on her face, things seemed equally bizarre to Mom. Her mouth gaped open. Becka knew that Scott's comment about torn sweatshirts and faded jeans had been an understatement. Becka hadn't had the heart to tell Mom that.

One guy had three safety pins in his left eyebrow. Another had a stud through his nose and one through his lip. And one girl, all in leather, had four Scream buttons pinned to her lower lip.

This was definitely not Mom's kind of place.

"I had no idea that it'd be this … this … bad!" she shouted as they made their way toward their seats. "Maybe I should have stayed at the hotel."

"You can go back if you want, Mom!" Scott shouted. "We can catch a cab back ourselves."

Mom's response was immediate. "Forget that thought, young man," she said firmly. "Now that I've seen what this concert is like, I'm glad I came here with you." She shook her head. "I'll be glad when this thing is over."

As they took their seats, Becka felt the tension in the air increase. The band was late getting started, which made the crowd even rowdier.

But suddenly—

WHAM! WHAM! BOOOOOOOOM!

The sound of explosions came from the stage. The crowd roared. As the curtain rose, the spotlights came on, bathing a huge skull in reds, blues, and yellows. Doland's voice could be heard.

Army of the night,
Not afraid to fight!

Doland suddenly appeared in the spotlight. He screamed into the microphone as the guitar wailed and the bass and drums pounded the beat. Everyone in the crowd leaped to their feet, screaming.

Everyone but Becka. She couldn't explain it, but she suddenly felt nauseous.

"Becky, what's the matter?!" Mom shouted. She also remained in her seat.

"Nothing!" she replied. "It's just my stomach again! I'll be okay!"

"Maybe it was something you ate!"

Becka nodded, but she knew that wasn't the reason for her stomach trouble. She'd felt this before. She always felt this way when she encountered something demonic. And looking up at the stage, at Doland's blazing eyes as he shrieked the song, Becka knew with sudden certainty that the skulls and other symbols of satanism were far more than props.

There was something very real—and very frightening—going on here.

4

The intensity of the crowd built and subsided in perfect rhythm with the music and pacing of the show. As the band neared the end of their performance, there was one climax after another, with each new one topping the last. By the time Mike launched into his drum solo, the mood of the crowd had been driven to a feverish pitch.

More and more effects were released. Two large fog machines at each end of the stage shot out a mist that quickly enshrouded the bottom three feet of the stage. But Becka's eyes were drawn away from the fog to the huge dragon cannon. So far it had remained a silent yet ominous presence. With firepots and other effects cutting loose all night from unseen places, one couldn't help but wonder what this big machine might do when fired. From her seat in the third row, Becka could see the top of the cannon rising just above the fog.

It began to vibrate.

She felt the urge to pray. *That's silly*, she thought to herself. *I'm not wasting energy worrying about some special effect. It's what the band wants — to freak people out and make them think there's real danger when everything is under control.*

Still, the dragon cannon bothered her. And the harder Mike played, the more it vibrated, as if preparing to fire.

Becka glanced at Scott. He appeared to be watching Doland, plainly enthralled with the show.

Several times during the evening, Becka had exchanged glances with Scott. He also seemed to feel that something strange was going on. She felt good about his silent agreement. But she knew that Scott wouldn't let a weird feeling spoil his good time.

"Scotty—" Becka nudged him—"let me see your binoculars for a minute." She had been about to criticize him for bringing them, since they were in the third row. But now she was glad that he brought them.

She knew he didn't appreciate the interruption, but he handed them to her anyway. She focused on the dragon cannon. It was definitely vibrating. Again she felt the urge to pray but dismissed it as a childish fear.

Then she saw something that made her blood run cold.

One of the large bolts holding the cannon in place had come loose. With every vibration of the cannon, the bolt slipped more and more out of place. Any second now it would fall out completely!

Becka wasn't sure what that meant. She directed the binoculars to the opposite side of the cannon. The other bolt seemed solidly in place. Her stomach knotted as she wondered whether or not she should do something or tell somebody.

The tempo of Mike's drumming increased. Scott reached for his binoculars, but Becka shrugged him off. She stared at the bolt as it shook back and forth. Suddenly, it fell out, disappearing into the fog.

Now, with only one bolt holding the cannon, the great machine shifted slightly with each vibration. The icy fear gripping Becka grew as she watched the cannon turn. *Oh, Jesus,* she prayed, no longer dismissing the urging as childish. *Jesus, protect them!* No one onstage appeared to notice, yet the cannon slowly turned in an entirely different direction.

She felt Scott tapping her on the shoulder, but she wasn't about to give the binoculars back. As the drum solo reached a crescendo, the cannon vibrated even more.

And the more it vibrated, the more it turned, until it was pointing directly at the band. More specifically, it was aimed at Mike Parsek!

God, don't let this happen! Don't let it end like this before we even get a chance to talk with him! Becka's lips moved as she prayed. Through the binoculars she saw a roadie crossing behind the band to some kind of control panel. A spark of hope surged through her.

Please, God, help him see that the cannon is loose.

But the roadie didn't notice. Instead, he flipped some switches on the control panel. The cannon shook even harder, but it could turn no farther.

It was about to fire!

Becka watched the roadie press another button. A deep rumble began, even louder than Mike's drums. The cannon's firing mechanism ignited. She couldn't bear to look, but she couldn't bear to look away.

Mike reached the peak of his solo. He glanced to the side and suddenly saw the barrel pointing directly at him. But it was too late. The cannon ignited ...

But it did not fire.

Something had malfunctioned. Becka saw Mike shouting at the stagehand, frantically motioning for him to shut down the device. The stagehand leaped into action, and the cannon stopped vibrating.

Everyone was safe.

Becka knew why the cannon had failed to fire. Her prayer had been answered! Not exactly in the way she had prayed, but answered nonetheless. And for that she offered up another prayer—this time, a prayer of thanks.

❦ ❦

Before the final note of the show was finished, Scott was already on his feet. He knew what they had to do. "Let's hurry up and get backstage!"

"They just got done, Scotty!" Becka shouted, her ears still ringing from the loud music. "Shouldn't we give them a few minutes?"

"Are you kidding?! In a few minutes there will be a hundred people in front of us trying to squeeze their way in!" He glanced toward the door closest to the stage. Already, scores of kids lined up, hoping for a glimpse of one of the band members.

"But we have passes!" Mom reminded him. She, too, talked loudly, as if trying to talk over the concert noises.

Scott nodded, trying to get them moving even as he talked. "I know, Mom! But you've got to show your pass to the guy at the door before he'll let you through! And before you can show your pass, you've got to get to the guy! And that'll be harder with every second we wait! Come on!!"

"He's right!" Becka nodded. "We'd better go!"

The three of them made their way to the stage door. As they got close, Scott leaned over to Becka and whispered, "What about Mom?"

"What about her?"

"Maybe she shouldn't go back there with us. I mean, she doesn't fit in and ..."

Becka looked at him blankly. It was obvious she wasn't going to help. "And what?"

"Well ... you know." Scott fidgeted. "What are we going to say? 'Hi, Mike, we're Scott and Becka, and this is our mom'? Nobody brings their mom backstage."

Becka shrugged. "I don't think that's our decision, Scott."

"What do you mean?"

"Z is the one who sent the tickets and the passes. He must've wanted her to come along."

"What are you kids talking about?" Mom asked. Finally, her voice had returned to its normal volume. "If it's what I think it is, you needn't bother to discuss it."

For an instant Scott thought Mom was going to be a sport and let them go by themselves. But then she added, "I'm *going* with you. Who knows what might be going on back there?"

Scott sighed. Great. Here he was getting to do practically the coolest thing in the world and his mom had to tag along. He felt like a ten-year-old.

It took a while to get through the horde of kids pressing toward the door — but not as long as Scott had expected. There was one very simple reason for that:

Mom.

"Excuse me, sir!" she called out above the crowd to the burly guard at the stage door. "We have backstage passes! Would you let us through, please?"

Scott knew that would never have worked if he or Becka had shouted it. Either the guard would have thought they were lying or everyone in the crowd would have pounced on them and tried to take the passes.

But with a mother in the lead, it was totally different. Scott watched in amazement as the sea of rough-looking, pierced, and tattooed fans parted to let them through.

The big guy at the door eyed them suspiciously — that was his job — but as soon as he saw the passes, he immediately opened the door for them.

As they stepped inside, they noticed a party going full blast. All kinds of strange and interesting people stood around talking and laughing. None of the band members were around, however.

Scott turned to a tall guy with long blond dreadlocks. "Hey, excuse me. Could you tell me—?" he began, but the guy walked away without giving Scott a glance. Undaunted, Scott turned to a girl who had a fake ruby in her belly button and wore leather pants. "Miss, uh ... could you tell me where to find the band? We're supposed to meet them and—"

But the girl was already laughing. "Don't expect them for a while. It's way uncool for them to show up at their own party any earlier."

With that, she moved off toward a table of refreshments next to a huge bar. Scott shrugged and followed.

In the center of the table was a guitar made of salmon. The strings had been made with cream cheese and the tuning pegs were black olives on toothpicks. It must've been pretty good because several people scooped up crackers full of the stuff and wolfed them down. So, of course, Scott followed suit.

"Yuuuck!" he said loud enough to draw several disapproving looks. "This stuff tastes terrible!"

Now, even that wouldn't have been so bad, but there were a couple of minor additions ...

The first was when Scott tried to spit out the offending bite of salmon. The second was when he tried to get rid of the taste by eating some salsa. The *green* salsa. The *extra-hot* salsa.

He ran to the bar, hand over mouth, gesturing to the bartender for something to drink. The man started to hand him a beer but caught Mom's disapproving look and changed it to a bottled water. It didn't matter to Scott ... as long as it was cool and wet. *Anything* to put out the fire.

After gulping down the water, Scott suddenly noticed at least a dozen people staring at him. He turned to Becka and whispered, "What are they looking at? We're at a backstage party, for cryin' out loud. Everything should be cool here. I mean, *look* at these people! Are you telling me you still have to do things a certain way or people stare?"

Becka sighed. "I think it's called having manners."

Before Scott could fire off a smart comeback, the room broke into applause. He turned to see the band's arrival at the party.

They had on different clothes than the ones they had worn on stage. Some of the band members' outfits were just as outrageous as their stage clothes.

Doland headed straight for the bar, where he ordered a double shot of whiskey, gulped it down, then ordered a beer.

Scott gawked. Tommy Doland, the lead singer of the Scream, was less than five feet away from him! Amazing! And, to top it off, Doland turned and actually looked at him!

He sees me! Scott thought. *He's going to speak to me. We're gonna become friends!*

Doland stared at him a long moment before finally speaking. "Get lost, freak!"

Scott's mouth dropped open even farther. Everyone stared at him as if he had just thrown up in the punch bowl. It was a good thing there wasn't a punch bowl there, or he might have done just that.

And then, to make matters even worse, he saw Mom making a beeline for Doland. *Oh no!* he thought. *She's coming over to defend me!*

Fortunately, Mike intervened by walking up to Scott. "Are you Scott Williams? I'm Mike Parsek."

Scott tried to answer. He knew his mouth moved, but no sound came out of it.

Mike continued, "Z is a friend of mine on the Internet. He told me you'd be coming. How'd you like the show?"

"Uhhh ... I ... uh ... good ... It was good." Scott knew that he sounded like an idiot. He threw a glance at Doland. Fortunately, the guy had already forgotten him and was nuzzling up to a girl wearing an extra-small Scream T-shirt and platforms so high she could hardly walk in them.

Scott turned back to Mike. By that point, the drummer had turned to Becka.

"You must be Rebecca," he said. He sounded a shade friendlier than he had with Scott. "How'd you like the show?"

Caught totally off guard, Becka did a repeat of her brother's stellar performance. "Uhhh … I … uh … good. It was good."

Mike laughed. "I can see a strong resemblance between you two. And this must be your mother," he continued. "Hello, Mrs. Williams. How are you?"

Mom smiled warmly and shook Mike's hand. "Very well, thank you. I'm not used to that sort of show, but I found it … fascinating."

"Thank you," Mike replied with a smile.

"Who're your friends, Mike?" It was Doland, his arm draped over the girl in the too-tight T-shirt. He looked at Scott and smiled. Or was it a sneer?

"Lemme guess — they're from your daddy's church? Or maybe your Sunday school class?"

"Get lost, Doland," Mike replied. He turned back to Becka. "Nice to see you," was all he said before turning and walking away.

Doland snickered and also headed off.

Scott turned to Becka, looking disappointed. "That's it?"

"I guess so," Becka said, sounding as disappointed as he seemed to feel.

Scott shook his head. "So much for the world of heavy metal." How was he going to tell the guys back home about this? What a bust! "I guess we should go."

Becka agreed. "I guess we've done enough damage here for one night."

❧ ❧

"Do you think going to that concert was a bad idea?" Becka

asked Mom. Scott had gone for a late-night swim in the hotel pool, leaving Becka and Mom alone.

"No, honey," Mom answered. "The music was pretty loud though. I thought my ears would never stop ringing!"

"Some of the kids there kinda freaked me out a little," Becka continued. "Most of them seemed really angry. Even the band members seemed angry."

"Some of them were nice."

"*One* of them was," Becka corrected pointedly. "Part of me wants to get away from this place as fast as I can, but another part is saying that I should stop judging the Scream and try to help them. I must be crazy. I mean, these guys have the number one album in the country, and I'm supposed to think they actually need *my* help?"

Mom smiled. "Maybe they do. Money doesn't give you peace. It certainly doesn't get you to heaven." She paused, then said, "That drummer, Mike, came from a decent home. I could tell that just talking to him. But he's mixed up with some pretty rough people. I can see why Z thinks he might get hurt."

"So, what am I supposed to do?" Becka sighed. "Run away from the bad stuff ... or stick around and try to help fix it?"

"I guess that depends on what the Lord is telling you."

"What do you mean?"

"The Bible says we are to flee from evil."

"That's right," Becka agreed.

"But it also says we are to help people, to bring light into the darkness. The trick is to know what God wants you to do and when to do it. If you find your light growing dim because you're getting caught up in what the world's doing, then you should flee. But if your light is shining brightly, then maybe you should stick around for a while and see if you can light up the place with the help of the Holy Spirit."

"And how am I supposed to know the difference?" Becka asked.

Mom took a deep breath and slowly let it out. "I guess that's between you and God, isn't it?"

Becka nodded. As usual, Mom was right.

👁 👁

Twenty minutes later Becka was out on the balcony, all alone, staring out at the twinkling lights around Los Angeles.

She prayed silently. *Dear Lord, things are really weird this time around. I mean, I know you want us to reach out to these guys. I know you love them as much as you love me. But ... how do you do it, Lord? How do you wade through a mud hole to help someone without getting muddy yourself? I really need your wisdom, Lord. I need to know what you would have me do.*

Becka paused for a moment, then continued. *I guess, to be honest, Lord, I really need your heart too. I mean, I'm really tempted to just avoid the guys in the Scream. So help me see them—really see them—with the love you have for them. Thank you, Jesus. Amen.*

She opened her eyes, suddenly aware that she felt better, but not because she had an answer. She was just as clueless as she was before she started praying. But she felt better all the same because she knew that the answer would come at the right time. And that was enough.

👁 👁

The Scream was back onstage before a packed auditorium as Mike blazed through his drum solo. Once again the great cannon began to vibrate as it prepared to fire. Only this time it was not disguised as a dragon. This time it was much bigger and far more ominous.

Becka sat in the audience cheering, when suddenly her expression turned to horror. A gnarled, twisted hand, more animal than human, snaked out from behind the curtain and moved the giant cannon until it was again pointed at Mike.

But he didn't seem to notice it. He just kept playing, getting closer and closer to the climactic moment.

Becka screamed, but he didn't hear her.

No one heard her.

And then it happened. Mike went into his final crashing pattern. Suddenly, flames shot from the huge cannon, engulfing him. He stood up, staggered, and fell to the stage. He was on fire, writhing in agony, rolling this way and that, trying to extinguish the flames. But nothing worked. Finally, his eyes met Becka's. He reached out his burned hands. His charred lips muttered something. She couldn't hear the words, but she knew what he was saying all the same.

"Help ... me. Help ... Please, help ..."

Becka bolted upright, her chest heaving and her face bathed in sweat. She grappled for the light switch and turned it on. She was in bed in the room she shared with her mom. Her mom still slept peacefully in the double bed next to hers.

Becka pressed a trembling hand to her clammy face, trying to slow her pulse rate. The dream had been intense. But at least she had her answer. She would stay. Mike needed her to stay.

It made no sense — not as far as she could see. But as long as there was a chance that she could help, she would remain.

5

When Becka opened her eyes the next morning, the first thing she saw was Scott sitting in a chair at the foot of her bed eating a bowl of cereal. And the first thing she heard was: "You know something, sis, Frosted Flakes taste even better from room service than they do from the box."

Becka looked at him through sleep-swollen eyes. "You woke me up to tell me that?"

"Not just that," Scott said. "I also wanted to tell you about my plan."

Becka sighed. "This better be good."

"No, listen. I've got an idea."

"You always do."

"Let him talk, honey," Mom called out from the bathroom.

"Okay," Becka mumbled, "so talk."

"All right, here's what we do. We check out of this fancy hotel, check into a cheaper hotel, and spend whatever's left on Z's debit card at Disneyland."

Becka rolled her eyes. "That's your plan?"

"It's better than going home. Or staying in this fancy-schmancy place and not being able to do anything else."

"I think we should stay where Z wants us to stay," Mom said, coming into the room. "And I do have a little extra money. Maybe later we could spend a day at Disneyland."

But Scott wasn't satisfied. "A day? I bet there's enough on that card to be there the rest of the week. Besides, Z only wanted us to stay here because this is where the band was staying while they got ready for their big cable show. And now that we're not seeing the band anymore, what's the point? I mean, this place is expensive. And for what ... those little chocolates they leave on your pillow after they make the bed?"

"What chocolates?" Becka and Mom asked in unison.

Scott turned sheepish. "The ones I ate yesterday ... all three of them."

They were interrupted by a knock at the door.

"I'll get it!" Becka said, throwing on her robe. "It's probably the maid with more chocolates. I want to be sure I get some this time."

But it wasn't the maid. When she opened up the door, she found Mike Parsek standing there. And instead of chocolates, he held out a rose. "Hi," he said, smiling at a very shocked Becka. "This is for you."

Becka couldn't say a word. All she could think about was her morning hair ... her morning face ... her morning everything. She tried to smooth down her hair.

Fortunately, Mom came to the rescue. "Mike, how nice to see you. Why don't you come in for a while?" She nudged the dumbfounded Becka aside to let Mike enter the room. Becka flashed off into the bedroom to throw on some clothes. Any clothes would be an improvement over her robe and Crescent Bay T-shirt.

As she hurriedly dressed, all the while wishing that she had time to jump into the shower, she could hear her mom making small talk. "So, how did you find our room number?"

"Oh, Z gave it to me. I found it in my email this morning."

"Cool," Scott chirped.

"Anyway, I just came by to see if Becka would maybe like to go out for lunch."

Becka had chosen that moment to make her entrance in her most flattering jeans and a top that matched her eyes. At first she was astonished by Mike's announcement, then flattered, and finally a little bugged. "I appreciate the invite, Mike, but ..."

"But what?"

Becka shrugged. "I don't know. Could I ask you one question first?"

"Fire away."

"Why did you leave like that? Last night, I mean. As soon as Tommy Doland came over, you walked away without hardly saying a word."

"Ah." He nodded.

"And now you show up here with a rose and everything. I mean, I'm flattered, but ... what's going on?"

"That's a good question," Mike answered, "but not an easy one. Let's just say that Tommy Doland is not someone you want to know."

"You acted like it was you who didn't want to know us," Becka said.

"I know. It's just that ... well, sometimes he likes to make fun of my friends."

"That's pretty lame," Scott muttered from across the room. He suddenly looked embarrassed that he had spoken aloud.

Mike looked at him, then nodded. "You're right, it is. But if you give me another chance by going to lunch with me, maybe I can explain it better."

"Okay," Scott said. "I'm willing to give it a shot."

Becka turned and glared at him. "I think he means *me*."

"Yeah." Mike grinned. "I meant Rebecca."

Scott snorted in disgust.

"Sorry, Scott." Mike shrugged. "But if you're going to be in town, we could sure use some extra help setting up for the cable gig. Nothing too heavy. Just odds and ends. But we'd pay you twenty-five bucks an hour."

"Twenty-five bucks an—" Scott caught his breath and then tried again. Becka smiled as he did his best to respond with some semblance of being cool. "Okay, I'll consider it ... but only if you'll sign some things for my friends that I brought from home."

"Sure. And if you don't mind, maybe I can throw in a signed copy of our latest CD for you."

"You'd do that for—?" Once again Scott's voice cracked, and once again he fought to sound cool. "Yeah, uh, I think that would be all right."

There was no missing the chuckles all around the group.

Becka turned to Mom. "So, is it okay if I go to lunch with Mike?"

"Will you be eating in the hotel?" Mom asked.

Mike shook his head. "The hotel is too ... popular. There's a nice café just down the block. I can give you my cell phone number if you want."

"All right." Mom nodded. "Just don't be gone too long."

Mike wrote down the number. "I'll be back to pick you up around 11:30, Rebecca."

As soon as he left, Becka raced into the shower, trying hard not to grin.

Later as Mike and Becka headed out the door, Mike turned back to Scott. "Listen, if you can be ready to work in a couple of hours, you can ride with me over to the auditorium. They're going to mike the drums for a sound check."

"Great," Scott replied. "But ... what about Doland? He didn't seem to like me very much last night."

"Just act like you've never met him. He was too stoned to remember anything about last night. That's how he always gets."

The Scream

One floor above, Doland's room looked as if it had been trashed the night before. Doland appeared to be passed out on the sofa, as if sleeping off the effects of partying. But Doland wasn't passed out. His eyelids fluttered wildly. Strange noises—more like grunts and growls than words—came out of his mouth. One word formed on his lips again and again. It was a name...

Rebecca.

Becka could hardly believe that she was having lunch with Mike Parsek in a stylish Beverly Hills café. She wondered what her friends back in Crescent Bay would say if they knew.

Her eyes widened when she saw the menu. Four bucks for a Coke?! Get real! But Mike didn't seem to notice. Apparently, he was used to this kind of place.

"So how do you like L.A.?" he asked her as they set the menus aside.

She shrugged. "It's okay, I guess. I really haven't seen much of it yet."

Mike smiled. "Well, if you've got the afternoon free, we can fix that. After the sound check, I'll give you a personal tour, all right?"

Becka caught her breath. She was still having trouble believing that Mike—a celebrity—was so interested in spending time with her. But somehow she forced herself to stay cool. "That'd be nice. 'Course I'll have to check with Mom first, but it sounds like a lot of fun." She almost wished she didn't have to check with her mom.

When the waiter arrived, Becka ordered the shrimp scampi, but Mike ordered a plain old cheeseburger. As soon as the waiter had gone, Becka asked, "Are you sure this place is all right? I mean, we could cancel our order and go somewhere else."

Mike looked surprised. "I thought you liked this place."

"Oh, I do. I just wondered if it might be too expensive."

Mike laughed. It was a nice, easy laugh. Even though she knew he was laughing at what she said, she didn't feel embarrassed. "Don't worry about the price," he said. "I told you I'd take you out to lunch."

"B-but ...," Becka stammered.

"But what?"

"But you only ordered a cheeseburger."

Mike grinned. "What's wrong with that?"

"Nothing. I just thought that maybe you ordered one to save money ... I mean, with all the fancy things on the menu here." She suddenly realized how foolish she sounded. Mike Parsek's band was the hottest in the country. Of course he could afford lunch!

Mike laughed again. "I like cheeseburgers. More than all that fancy stuff. I mean, the other stuff is okay and everything, but once you've tried all the different kinds of food ... well, cheeseburgers still taste the best."

"Oh, good ..." Becka let out a sigh. "I'm glad." She paused for a moment and then continued, "You know, you really seem different from the other guys in the band." She couldn't help noticing the sadness in his eyes, even though he continued to smile. "I mean, the other guys seem so serious ... kind of glum or mad ... especially Tommy Doland. Of course, I don't know any of them, but ..."

"They're okay. Jackie and Grant are pretty good guys. At least they used to be ... To tell you the truth, I don't hang around with them much anymore." He shook his head. "They spend too much time getting wasted. I'm just not into that."

Becka smiled, relieved.

Mike shrugged. "It didn't used to be so bad. Drugs and booze were just a once-in-a-while thing. But lately, it seems like they use them more and more to tune everything out. I'm afraid most of it has to do with Doland."

"What's he like?"

"Doland . . . he's pretty gone. Way over the edge. I think Jackie and Grant know it too, but no one wants to confront him."

"Why not?"

"For one thing, he's the leader of the band. As lead singer, he's the one everybody knows. His voice is a big part of our sound . . . Without him, there would be no band. And also . . . well, he's really hard to talk to these days. He just wants to do what he wants and nothing else."

"Sounds like my brother." Becka grinned.

Mike laughed again, which made her feel glad. Whenever Doland's name was brought up, Mike seemed so troubled. It felt good to see him smile again. "No, Scott's not like Doland," Mike continued. "Believe me."

"I don't know," Becka answered. "He sure wants his way all the time."

"Everyone's like that," Mike said, "especially toward their brother or sister. I know. I've got three sisters, and they all drive me crazy."

Again they both laughed. Becka was beginning to like this guy, and she could tell that he liked her. She shoved aside a momentary thought of Ryan back home. "When did you see them last? Your family, I mean."

Mike looked sad again. "It's been a couple of years, ever since I dropped out of college. I didn't even finish my first year. My sisters live in Arizona with my folks. My dad and I . . . we . . . we don't get along too well."

"What's the problem?"

"Lots of stuff," Mike said. "He wants everything on the straight and narrow, and I'm just not wired that way. I like to experiment, to do different things. He likes everything in a box, nice and neat. His career, his family . . . and especially his son."

"I guess that could be hard," Becka agreed. "But I'm sure he still loves you."

Mike glanced up, clearly surprised at her remark. "Yeah . . . I suppose. But we can't live together, I can tell you that. I never could live up to his expectations."

"Why did Doland ask you if we were from your dad's church?"

Mike sighed. "Before my dad retired, he was a pastor. Doland likes giving me a hard time about it."

Becka frowned. "What's he got against pastors — or churches?"

Mike looked out the window of the café for a moment before answering. "What's Tommy Doland got against pastors and churches? Nothing . . . except that he worships the devil."

👁 👁

In a dimly lit hotel room, Tommy Doland sat at a table, holding hands with three other people. A black candle sat in the middle of the table. A large bald man with a short black beard began to chant softly. "Darkness and shadow hold back the light; darkness and shadow hold back the light."

Doland and the other two people quietly took up the chant: "Darkness and shadow hold back the light; darkness and shadow hold back the light."

The chanting lasted several minutes, growing louder and louder until it filled the room . . . until it filled their minds and bodies. "Darkness and shadow hold back the light; darkness and shadow hold back the light."

Finally, the leader raised his arms. The others fell silent and followed suit. Then the leader called out in a loud voice, "Overlord of the Western Hemisphere, Demon Prince of the city, what do you wish us to do with the intruder? What fate do you decree for the one who dares to challenge your authority over this carefully groomed project? What would you have us do with this person who has come to undermine our brother's efforts? What do you decree for Rebecca Williams?"

There was no response. Only silence. Then an unmistakable chill filled the room.

Suddenly the leader started to shake. The sound coming from him started as a deep rumble but grew into a vicious snarl. Doland's hands broke out into a sweat, but he kept his eyes clenched tight, continuing to concentrate.

Slowly the snarl evolved into a voice—a terrifying, guttural voice. As it spoke, the flame on the candle in the center of the table began to waver. Suddenly, the voice screamed four words that reverberated through the room for a long, long time:

"DEATH TO THE GIRL!"

6

As soon as she returned from lunch, Becka asked Scott if she could use his laptop to contact Z.

"Wait until I get back, and I'll do it," Scott suggested.

"No, you'll be gone for a couple of hours. I need to talk to him now."

Scott hesitated. "I don't know. It isn't mine, you know. It's Darryl's, and he'd be pretty mad if you messed with it."

Becka sighed. "I'm not going to play football with it, goofball! I just want to contact Z and ask him some questions about what Mike told me."

"All right," Scott said, handing her the laptop. "It's still got about an hour left on the charge, so you don't even need to plug it in."

"Thanks," Becka said, already typing on the keyboard.

"Whoa," Scott said, looking at his watch. "I'm supposed to be downstairs meeting Mike. Hope he holds the limo for me. See ya later."

"Bye ... Oh, Scott, stay away from Doland. I'm afraid he might be—"

But Scott was already out the door.

Scott bounded out of the elevator and into the lobby, where he could see the limo waiting. "Cool!" he shouted a little too loudly for the somewhat reserved atmosphere of the Regent Beverly Wilshire Hotel. Running also was frowned upon. Scott forced himself to slow to a fast walk as he headed toward the door.

"Hey! Where's the fire?" a voice called out behind him. Scott turned around to see Mike.

"Didn't think we'd leave without you, did you?" Mike continued.

"Uh, n-no," Scott stammered. "But who is 'we'?"

"Well …" Mike hesitated. "Doland wants to check out the effects unit. They repaired it after last night."

Scott was caught off guard. "Doland? But I thought—"

Mike cut him off. "Hey, Doland! Meet the newest member of our crew."

Scott hadn't noticed Doland sitting near the door. The guy looked like his mind was a thousand miles away as he stood up to meet them.

"Doland," Mike said again as they reached the door, "this is Scott Williams. He's going to help us get ready for the show."

Suddenly Doland's eyes came into focus. His gaze was intense. "Hello, Scott."

Scott swallowed nervously. "Hi … Tommy." He didn't feel right calling Tommy Doland by the more familiar "Doland" like Mike did. He was relieved that Doland didn't seem to recognize him from last night's party.

But as they headed out of the hotel entrance, Doland turned and said, "So where's your hot sister today? Upstairs? In your room … I presume?"

He said the last phrase in a singsong voice, as if it were a rhyme he'd made up especially for the occasion. Scott could only stare, still nervous that Doland might remember him.

Doland said nothing, obviously waiting for an answer.

Finally, Scott said, "Yeah … I guess. She was using my laptop to contact …" He'd almost said Z but figured it was none of Doland's business. Why should he tell Doland anything?

Doland smiled that twisted smile of his. "Using your laptop, huh? Guess that's the story—A to Z."

He emphasized the *Z*. With a cold chill, Scott wondered if it was just a coincidence or if Doland had somehow read his mind.

👁 👁

Becka had no problem getting through to Z via the chat window. She quickly filled Z in on what had happened so far, especially about her conversation with Mike.

What can I do to help Mike?

She waited a few moments. Suddenly, Z's reply popped up.

Get him away from Tommy Doland.

At first Becka figured she'd miscommunicated something. So she tried again.

How can we do that? Doland's the lead singer of the band.

Z's answer was typically honest and straight to the point.

Doland has willingly given himself over to the devil. He will keep Mike from the spiritual truth he needs.

Becka sat there, puzzled. Slowly, she typed:

How can I ask Mike to quit the biggest thing in his life?

The answer returned quickly.

In Matthew 16:26, Jesus said, "What good will it be for a man if he gains the whole world, yet forfeits his soul? Or what can a man give in exchange for his soul?" Without

Christ, there is no life. Everything else will pass away.

Becka nodded. Z was right; she knew it. But his being right didn't make her task any easier. She typed:

The Scream is the hottest band in the country.

Of course she knew there was no comparison between a hot band and the God of the universe, but she didn't know if she could get that across to Mike. For a moment she wondered if Z would even bother replying. But the response soon came.

Better to be the least within the kingdom of God than the greatest without.

Finally, Becka typed out her greatest concern:

If Mike's father, a pastor, couldn't reach him, how can I?

The response was swift.

Maybe you can't, but you should try.

Becka answered:

But how? Maybe after we've known each other for a while, sure. But not yet.

Z's response appeared on the screen, filling Becka with dread.

Mike does not have that much time.

Becka remembered her dream of the fiery cannon and was suddenly terrified for her new friend. But before she could type anything else, Z's final words appeared.

Must go. Do your best. And be careful. The devil knows our weaknesses and uses them against us. Remember that people are praying for you. Z

Becka didn't fully understand the last part. Suddenly, she felt so overwhelmed that she didn't care what Z meant. Instead, she did what she usually did when overwhelmed. She prayed. She guessed that Z had referred to Mike's family when he said that a lot of people were praying. She figured it wouldn't hurt to add one more to that number.

❧ ❧

Scott was amazed at how much bigger the auditorium looked when no one was there. "It's like you could put the whole town of Crescent Bay in here!"

Mike smiled, then turned to a scraggly-looking guy with a bandaged hand and several sores on his face. "Scott, this is Billy Phelps. He's our stage manager. He got hurt at the San Francisco concert. But he's doing better now, right, Billy?"

Billy grinned. "Right."

"He'll show you what you need to do," Mike finished.

"Hey, Scott," Billy drawled with a slight Southern accent, "you ready to rock?"

Scott shrugged. "Yeah ... I guess."

Billy nodded. "All right. You can start with that bucket of empty whiskey bottles over there."

Scott turned to see a large tub filled with empty bottles.

"Take 'em over to that sink back there, and wash 'em out real good."

Scott nodded. "Okay. Then what?"

"Then come see me. I'll be tinkering with the lights somewhere around the stage. Get me when you're done, and we'll fill 'em up."

"Okay," Scott agreed, wondering why they wanted to reuse the bottles. *Oh, well,* he thought. *Guess it doesn't matter. I'm now part of the world of rock. Awesome!*

❧ ❧

Doland watched the boy talking to Billy and Mike, feeling the rage build inside of him. He leaned over the control panel at the edge of the stage. So Rebecca Williams sent her brother into the battle, did she? Well, that was just fine. He could handle them both. And handle them he would.

👁 👁

After setting the sound levels for the drums, Mike quickly returned to the hotel to pick up Becka for a tour of the city. She had wanted to see a bit more of Los Angeles, and he had wanted to spend more time with her.

Now they stood at the famous intersection of Hollywood and Vine and looked up at the Capitol Records tower just down the street. When Becka looked to the left, she could just make out Mann's Chinese Theater, where the handprints of all the great stars — everyone from Clark Gable and Marilyn Monroe to Johnny Depp and Gywenth Paltrow — were encased in cement.

It should've been an exhilarating experience, but it wasn't. The Hollywood of old was long gone. Off to Becka's right were overpriced souvenir shops and topless bars. The street was busy all right, but no movie stars were to be seen. Instead, the sidewalks were filled with drug addicts and prostitutes. There were tourists here and there, but there were far more homeless people present. And it caught Becka off guard to see many kids her age — and some even younger — among them. Young people from around the country had come out to Hollywood thinking they'd escape their boring hometown lives ... only to find themselves caught up in an urban nightmare. For them, the street of dreams was nothing but a street of pain.

She felt a sense of relief when they headed for the limo. Mike had the driver take them past the fancy mansions of Beverly Hills and then out to the Venice Beach boardwalk. The afternoon was growing more perfect by the moment.

They hadn't talked much about the Scream. Becka was anxious to ask more questions after what she'd learned from Z, but she suspected the subject would upset Mike. She didn't want to do that. Everything was too perfect.

Half an hour later they were having ice-cream sundaes at an outdoor shop in the Century City mall. The big office building towered over them. The mall was crowded with busy executives.

"See that guy over there?" Mike nodded to the right.

Becka turned to see a short man dressed in an expensive business suit, Italian sunglasses perched on his nose, walking hurriedly through the mall. Three taller men wearing similar suits and sunglasses tried their best to keep up with him.

"That's Jason Unger, the agent," Mike said. "Some people think he's the most powerful guy in the entertainment business."

"Who are the other three guys?"

"Dunno. Underlings probably. He's got a zillion of them, or so they say."

"Do they all try to dress like he does?"

"Sure," Mike said. "And walk and talk like he does too."

Becka laughed. "That's crazy."

"You got that right," Mike said with a grin. "Now, what do you want to do next?"

"Watch the sunset from the ocean," Becka said before she could catch herself.

Mike smiled. "All right—one sunset coming up. But after that, I need to get you back to the hotel. I told your mom we wouldn't be out too late."

It wasn't until they were back in the limo, heading toward Zuma Beach, that Becka finally worked up the courage to talk about the band. "Mike ... can I ask you something?"

Mike nodded. "Shoot."

"What are you going to do about the band?"

He looked puzzled. "Do? What do you mean?"

"Well, I was thinking about what you said about Doland—about his worshiping the devil and stuff. Doesn't that worry you?"

Mike sighed and looked off into the distance. "Well, I used to think it was an act with Doland ... but not anymore. Sometimes it doesn't bother me at all. Other times ..."

"What?" she prodded.

"Well, sometimes, like when everyone makes a big fuss over us ... sometimes that bothers me."

"Why? I mean, you've worked hard for it."

"Yeah, we're pretty good. But there are lots of good bands. Sometimes I just ... I guess I feel funny about the band's success, because I'm not sure where it came from."

Becka gulped. She had a hunch where this was going.

Mike continued, "In the beginning, the black magic and devil stuff were more of a gimmick than anything we believed in. We even used to make fun of it. But it kept growing somehow. And then ... it just got out of control, especially with Doland. Now it's like the band isn't even in charge anymore."

"What do you mean?"

Mike shrugged, looking uncomfortable as the limo pulled into the beach parking lot. "I don't know. I'm probably just superstitious. All the guys say I am."

"That's just because you believe in something—" Becka stopped in midsentence, not sure if this was the right thing to say—"or ... at least you *did* believe in something ... at one time."

Mike laughed. "Yeah, I guess that's one way of putting it."

Two minutes later, they were sitting on the hood of the limo, watching the sun sink into the ocean. Becka could not have asked for a better day. A great lunch, a tour of L.A. in a limo, and now a perfect sunset beside a great guy.

She took a deep breath and slowly let it out. "This is so

beautiful," she said. "I always try to take time to watch the sunsets at home."

"I bet it's even prettier where you live," Mike said.

"I don't know. It all depends on where you are at the moment."

Mike turned and looked into her eyes. "And who you're seeing it with?"

Becka felt her stomach flip-flop. A warmth rushed to her cheeks. "Yeah ... that too."

He hesitated a moment longer before leaning toward her. She leaned forward too, certain that he wanted to kiss her. Then at the last second she blurted out, "So, are you going to tell me what you meant when you said that the band wasn't in charge anymore?"

Mike stopped and looked at her. "You sure have a strange way of communicating sometimes, Rebecca Williams."

She smiled nervously.

Mike turned to stare at the sunset again. "All I meant was that sometimes things feel so out of control that it's like ... it's as if someone, or some*thing,* else is calling the shots. I don't know ... I think Doland is into some pretty weird stuff and ... somehow that affects all of us."

"Then why don't you quit?"

Mike laughed. "Are you serious?"

Becka nodded. "Sure, if it's the only way you'll be free of Doland."

"Quit the band?!" Mike's voice carried an edge of irritation. "No way! I worked my whole life for this. I'm *never* quitting the band."

Becka felt miserable. "Look, I'm sorry. I didn't mean to upset you. It's just that ... well ... I've seen people fool around with demonic stuff ... and it can get pretty dangerous. I mean, something awful could happen ... and I ..."

He was looking at her again. For a moment she forgot what she was saying. She tried again. " ... I don't want anything ..."

He leaned toward her.

" ... awful to happen to ..."

His lips found hers. For an instant, Becka melted. She kissed him back. Mike's arms came around her, holding her close. Becka knew she should pull away. For an instant, she thought of Ryan back home. How would she feel if he kissed another girl? Then came the thought of a promise she had once made to Mom about never letting herself get into a compromising situation with a boy.

Yet, in spite of all that, she let the kiss continue. It grew in intensity until all she could think of was *Mike, Mike, Mike ...*

Then another thought came to mind: *The devil knows our weaknesses and uses them against us.*

She suddenly stiffened. Mustering all of her will, she pulled away.

Mike looked at her, confused. She could also tell that he seemed a little hurt.

She wanted to explain herself but didn't know if she could. The attraction between them had been surprisingly strong. Was this the weakness Z had warned her about—something the enemy would use against her? Part of her knew that when a person dealt with the supernatural, things were rarely what they seemed.

She let out a small breath of air. "I ... uh ... I need to get back," she finally managed. "Mom will be worrying."

Mike slowly exhaled. "Sure ... I probably need to check in with the guys anyway. We've gotta iron out the final plans for tomorrow's telecast. It's the biggest thing for us yet ... a national broadcast ... It's gonna be a real blast."

Becka nodded. But as they slid off the hood and climbed back into the limo, all she could think about was her dream from the night before—the one with the cannon exploding—and Mike's words: *"It's gonna be a real blast."*

7

The next morning Becka tried to contact Z again. She wanted Scott to join her, but he was too busy listening to the latest Scream CD through his headphones. "If I'm gonna be part of the band, I need to be more familiar with their music!" he shouted.

"You're *not* part of the band!" Becka shouted back. "You're just helping them set up for one show!"

Scott removed the headphones. "That's all *you* know. First of all, when we in showbiz refer to the 'band,' we mean the entire organization that makes the thing happen. The agents, producers, label execs, manager, road manager, and crew. That last part includes me. As for this being my only show, Billy already said that he wished he had someone like me around all the time."

Becka shrugged. "So?"

"So that's exactly the kind of thing they say before they offer you a regular gig."

Becka tried not to laugh. "A regular gig? Don't you think you ought to finish high school first?"

Scott pointed his index finger at Becka and then flipped his hand over in a quick gesture.

"What does that mean?" she said. "Or do I want to know?"

"It means, 'Have it *your* way, burger brain.' It's a band thing. Billy does it whenever the hall manager or the security guys hassle him. I think it's pretty cool."

Becka sighed. "I think it's pretty stupid. You've only been working for them one day, and you're already all caught up in this ... band stuff."

"You're so lame, Becka."

"And you're even more of an idiot than usual."

"I am *not* more of an idiot!" Scott snapped as he put the headphones back on. "I'm just the same as I've always been!"

Becka shook her head in amusement as she turned back to the computer. She wanted to talk with Z, to tell him that he'd been right about the enemy using her weaknesses against her. She was falling for the guy she was supposed to be helping. And instead of making things better, she was afraid she was only making matters worse.

Then there was Scott. He was getting caught up in the glamour of the band's fame—all the glitz and the hype. Yessir, there was definitely a battle going on. It was one they'd never fought before. Instead of in-your-face warfare, everything seemed cool and glamorous. In fact, when she thought about it that way, she realized that the weapons being used against them in this encounter were actually more dangerous than in some of the other fights they had faced. In this encounter, all of the enemy's weapons were things they wanted.

The laptop quietly dinged as a new email came in. Becka was anxious to speak with Z. But then she recognized the address. It wasn't from Z. It was from Ryan.

Hey, Beck! Hope you guys are doing okay. I miss you a lot, but I guess I have to learn to put my needs aside when you're doing important stuff like this. Who knows what good effect this kind of thing can have on others. I guess that's the great thing about being a Christian. All we have to do is say yes to

God, and he does the rest. All you and Scott had to do was be
willing to go to L.A., now God's leading you step-by-step the
rest of the way. I just wanted to let you know that I'm praying
for you guys, and I can't wait until you get back — ESPECIALLY
YOU, BECK. Love, Ryan

It was all Becka could do to swallow the lump in her throat.
Ryan was the closest thing to a boyfriend she had ever had.
And though she still didn't feel comfortable with that term, he
had always treated her wonderfully. Now here he was, trying to
encourage her to let God use her to help others. She had practically dumped him for some guy she hardly even knew! If she had
felt bad about kissing Mike before, she felt terrible about it now.

And it was these exact feelings that helped her decide what to
do next. "Scott," she called, "I want to go to rehearsal with you
today." But Scott was in his own world with the headphones on
and his eyes closed.

"He can't hear you with those things on," Mom said as she
passed by. "You'll have to get his attention."

Becka agreed. Seeing a pencil eraser on the table nearby,
she grabbed it and threw it at him, hitting him square in the
forehead.

Scott's eyes popped open. He glared at her. "Hey! What was
that for?" he demanded, jerking off his headphones.

"I was just trying to get your attention."

"Why didn't you just use a club?"

"I couldn't find one," she countered. "Listen, I want to go to
rehearsal with you today."

"We're not rehearsing. We're recording," Scott replied. "You'll
just get in the way."

Becka shook her head. "I'm going, because I need to talk to
Mike. What time are they sending the car?"

"Two o'clock," Scott replied. "But you'd better not bother
Mike when he's recording."

"He won't get mad at me," Becka said confidently.

"It's not Mike I'm worried about. Doland's the one who'll get upset. He doesn't like distractions."

Becka paused, and for the briefest second she considered not going. Her stomach was already churning. The last thing she wanted was a confrontation with Doland. In fact, she dreaded seeing Doland at all.

But she had to go.

☙ ☙

The band had left earlier, so Scott and Becka were the only ones in the limo that afternoon.

Scott wore his best torn T-shirt and torn jeans. In fact, they were *new* torn jeans.

"Scott, are those your new jeans?" Becka asked incredulously. "Tell me you didn't tear holes in your new jeans."

"Don't tell Mom, okay?"

"I won't have to. She'll figure that out for herself. Don't you think you're taking this band thing a little too far?"

Scott scowled and looked out the window. Even though they teased each other constantly, they had always been close. They had to be after all they'd been through together. But something was happening to Becka's little brother. In the past forty-eight hours he had begun to slip away—growing more and more distant, more and more into himself. She knew that the change in his behavior was because of the band's influence—and the subtle deception he was buying into. She also knew that if she brought it up, he wouldn't listen.

There was, however, Someone who *would* listen.

God, please remind Scotty of your truth, she prayed. *I know he believes in you. But sometimes, others influence him ... And Lord, please protect us. It feels like we're in over our heads with this assignment. I know you told us in the Bible that when we're weak, you're strong. Well, we've sure got plenty of weaknesses this time! Please be there for us. Show us what to do. Amen.*

As soon as they climbed out of the car, the limo drove off, leaving them standing outside a plain-looking brick building. "Are you sure this is the place?" Becka asked. "It looks like a warehouse."

"This is the address Billy gave me," Scott said. "I think they like to keep it low-key on the outside so people won't know about all the expensive equipment inside."

The door was locked, and a small sign said Ring Buzzer. Becka pushed the buzzer. Nothing happened.

"Maybe we should've called first," Scott said after a minute.

Suddenly they heard a whirring sound. Looking up, they saw a small camera tucked away under the awning. As it slowly turned, the lens moved.

"Wow. That's a pretty high-tech security camera," Becka said. "They're checking us out. Wonder who's on the other end."

"Probably some jerk," Scott said.

Then a voice from out of nowhere said, "Watch who you're calling a jerk, jerk!"

Scott blushed. "They can *hear* us!"

The voice spoke again. "Right you are, loser. Lucky I know you're smarter than you look."

"It's Billy!" Scott exclaimed.

"Right again," the voice said. "Come on in."

With that he buzzed the door open. Inside, the place was completely different than it looked from the outside. They entered a large reception area with walls of sleek black marble and a thick, plush black carpet. The walls were covered with silver and platinum records in black metal frames. On them were names like Pearl Jam, Aerosmith, Red Hot Chili Peppers, and Metallica.

"Wow!" Scott said. "Look at this. All these people recorded here!"

Becka was also impressed. "Hey, here's Jars of Clay. I love that band."

In the center of the room was a large black marble reception desk. To the left of the desk, three monitors displayed images from the security cameras at the three entrances to the building. A fancy phone system and a top-of-the-line Mac sat perched on the desk to the right. And behind all of this expensive, high-tech equipment sat the scraggly Billy Phelps.

"Howdy." Billy grinned. "Pretty cool place, eh?"

"I'll say," Scott replied. "Where are the guys?"

Billy pointed down the hallway. "Studio B. They're doing overdubs. But I brought some of your work with me."

"Work?" Scott asked.

Billy pointed toward a large tub of empty whiskey bottles and a couple of plastic jugs full of an amber liquid. Scott nodded.

Becka cleared her throat. "Excuse me ... I came to see Mike."

Billy nodded. "I figured. You're Rebecca, right? They're in the middle of a take right now, but I'll get word to them in a minute that you're here."

Becka thanked him and crossed to where Scott filled the empty bottles. "What are you doing?"

"Yesterday Billy had me wash out these whiskey bottles. Today he wants me to fill them."

"Is that whiskey?" Becka interrupted, pointing to the plastic jugs from which Scott was filling the bottles.

"No," Scott replied. "That's just it. It's iced tea."

"Iced tea? Why would they want ...? Oh, I get it."

Scott waited, but Becka said nothing. Finally, he sighed, "Well, then, explain it to me, will you?"

Becka shook her head in sad amusement. "Don't you get it? They want to strut around onstage, guzzling from these whiskey bottles like it doesn't bother them ... which it doesn't, since the bottles are really just full of iced tea."

"Can't give a good performance when you're drunk," Billy Phelps said, walking up behind them. "You can go in now, Rebecca. Right down the hall. Only make sure you don't enter when the red light is on."

👁 👁

As Becka headed down the hall, Scott turned to Billy. "I still don't get this whiskey thing," he said. "Why do the guys want people to think they're drinking a lot when they're not?"

"Part of the image, kid. The crowd expects that from a heavy-metal band. Part of the whole heavy-metal mystique."

"What about the kids out there who think they should be imitating them by guzzling down booze?"

"Oh, well." Billy grinned.

Scott frowned. He didn't much like the answer.

"This stuff is big business, kid. Too much money on the line to blow something because of a few drinks."

"Doesn't sound very real to me," Scott said.

"It's not about real, Scott," Billy said. "It's about money."

👁 👁

Becka walked down a hall also lined with gold and platinum records. On the left was a large, airtight, wooden door. Becka started to grab the handle, then stopped when she noticed the red light glowing above the door. Several seconds later, it turned off. She quickly entered the dimly lit studio.

Mike, Jackie, and Grant stood near a long recording console just a few feet away. Behind the mixing board sat a bushy-haired guy with glasses. He turned and tweaked various knobs as he listened with the others to the playback of a vocal Doland had just recorded. Through a big picture window she could see Doland, listening to the playback from the vocal booth.

As soon as she entered, Mike smiled and nodded to her. Becka grinned back. She instinctively pulled away from the window to a spot where Doland could not see her.

"You guys are acting like a bunch of wimps about this fire-cannon thing!" Doland shouted at the rest of the band through the monitor speakers. "We're letting the fans down. They come expecting a wild ride. That means the whole ball of wax—fireworks and pushing the envelope."

"Sure," Jackie spoke to him through the intercom. "But we've gotta have this stuff double- and triple-checked. I'm not spending my life in jail because this stupid cannon of yours takes some guy's arm off in the tenth row."

Becka felt her stomach tighten. They were talking about the cannon—the same one that had nearly killed Mike earlier; the same one, only smaller, that she had dreamed about. The image of Mike's burned face and charred lips screaming in agony was so vivid that for a moment Becka actually thought she saw the scene before her. She closed her eyes, and it went away. Unfortunately, the topic of the cannon did not.

"The cannon will be fine. I told you that. Billy looked at it. It'll be fine."

"What was wrong with it?" Mike asked.

"It came loose, all right?" Doland griped. "That stuff happens!"

"What about the night Billy got hurt?" Mike persisted. "What was wrong with it then?"

"I don't know!" Doland was getting more and more angry. "I'm not an expert on cannons. I just don't want to wimp out for the big show, that's all. We're talking national TV here, guys. A forty-million-plus audience. Our biggest show ever!"

"All right, all right!" Jackie raised his hands. "Let's keep the cannon in."

Grant, the bass player, reluctantly nodded. It was clear that Mike didn't agree. What was equally clear was that he had just been outvoted.

That decision settled, they went back to the music.

"That last take was great, Tommy." The bushy-haired producer behind the mixing board spoke into his intercom microphone. "But I'd like to try another one if you can. Try holding back a bit on the second chorus so that it makes more of an impact on the last chorus when you cut loose."

"You want *more* on the last chorus?" Doland's voice through the speakers definitely sounded offended.

"No, no," the producer replied. "I want the same there ... just soften the second chorus so that the last one stands out more."

"That's what I said!" Doland snapped. "You want *more* on the last chorus! Just roll the tape, man."

"Okay," the producer said, doing his best to keep the peace. "We're rolling."

As the song began, Mike took the opportunity to step over to Becka. "Hi," he whispered.

She smiled. "I hope I'm not interrupting anything."

"No, no. Doland just wants to sweeten up some of the vocals."

"Will he mind that I'm here?"

Mike shook his head. "With the bright lighting in his booth and the dim light in here, he can't even see you. Is everything okay?"

Becka took a breath. "Well ... yes and no." *Here goes,* she thought. "Mike, I really have gotten to like you in these past few days, and I hope we stay friends for a long time, but — "

"Whoa!" Mike cut her off. "It's the 'let's just be friends' speech? Already? I didn't expect that for at least another week."

Becka smiled. "Sorry, Mike. It's just that there's this boy back home that I like and ..."

"And what?"

"And ... well, I sort of got carried away last night on the beach with the sunset and all ... and ... you. I was letting my emotions get the better of me."

"Some people call that love, Becka," Mike said.

Even in the dim light, she could see his softened expression. For a moment Becka began to weaken. But Z's message coupled with Ryan's strengthened her. She continued, "I suppose, but I call it ... well, I call it losing control. I mean, I'm flattered and everything, but I know what I want now, and ... this isn't it."

A slight frown crossed Mike's face.

"Don't get me wrong," Becka continued. "It's tempting, but ... I just, I just don't think I'm ready for a serious relationship."

"What do you call what you have with the guy back home?"

"We're friends," Becka answered. "Well, actually, a little more than friends. It's growing, but it's at a slow pace. And that's the way I like it."

"Does this mean you're not coming to the concert tonight?"

"I was hoping to, unless you'd prefer me not to come. I *do* consider you a friend, Mike. I suppose that sounds stupid, but I really do care for you that way. And ..." She hesitated, unsure if she should go on, but knowing she had to. "I've been worrying about you a lot."

"Me?" He looked surprised.

She nodded, but before she could continue, Doland started singing. Everyone suddenly grew very quiet.

The lyrics had barely started before Becka felt that all-too-familiar chill running across her shoulders.

But it was more than just his voice that caused her to react.

As Mike said, because the lights in the control room were much dimmer than in Doland's vocal booth, there was no way that Doland could see her. Yet as he sang, his eyes seemed to focus directly upon her. Gradually they filled with more and more hatred. They bore into her ... and definitely scared her.

The song continued to build. Now Doland seemed to be going into some sort of trance. Becka had seen similar expressions like that before—too many times during encounters with demons. If she had doubted before that Doland had turned the control of his life over to someone or something, she was sure of it now. And whatever that something was, Becka was equally sure it was not good.

A better word would be *evil.*

Soon Becka found herself doing what she always did when she became afraid. She silently prayed. But this time, she didn't utter a prayer for help. Instead, she quietly worshiped as a reminder to herself of God's great power. *Thank you, Lord. Thank you for your love, for your awesome—*

She had barely started, when Doland suddenly screamed. It was a hideous, terrifying sound that was more animal than human—one that hinted of deep rage and pain.

The producer scrambled to stop the tape. "Tommy! What's wrong?"

Even stronger chills ran through Becka as Doland suddenly pointed at her. His voice was low and guttural. *"Get her out of here!"*

"Who?" the producer asked. "Get who out, Tommy?"

Doland glared maniacally. *"Get her out now!"*

Becka looked up at Mike. Her mouth was bone dry. "He means me."

"But he can't even see you! How could he—?"

"Trust me, Mike. He means me. Can we talk somewhere? It's really important that we talk."

"Sure. Let's go into the hall." As soon as they stepped into the hallway, he looked down at her intently. "What happened in there? How'd he know you were there?"

Becka took a deep breath and slowly let it out. "Mike ... I think Doland's under some kind of ... I think the devil has a stronghold inside of him."

"Whoa." Mike held up his hand. "Doland's weird and all, but he's not ... possessed. I mean, I know the guy's a jerk, but—"

"He went nuts just now because I was praying."

Mike looked at her strangely. "Praying?"

Becka nodded. "I was praying when he went crazy."

"Don't be silly," Mike said. "Doland didn't know you were praying. He just doesn't like strangers there."

"But he couldn't see me. You said so yourself."

The reply caught Mike off guard. "Look, I know Doland's weird sometimes, but—"

"Doland is more than weird. You know that better than I do. You said he was into devil worship." She held his gaze, and after swallowing again, said, "It's dangerous for you here, Mike. You know the truth. You know what Doland's about. And if you keep refusing—"

"Look, Rebecca." Mike cut her off. There was no missing the anger in his voice. "If you don't want to go out with me, fine. But don't preach to me."

Suddenly Doland threw open the door to the studio. "What is *she* doing here?!"

"She's ... she's my friend," Mike said.

Doland yelled loud enough for the rest of the band to hear. "I'm out of here until Mike's through messing around with the chicks! I'll be in the bar next door!"

He started toward Becka. She braced herself, but he did not touch her. Still, even as he passed, his glare was so intense that she found herself taking a step back.

Something evil was at work there. She knew it beyond the shadow of a doubt.

8

Doland stormed out of the studio, letting the door slam behind him.

Mike looked at the floor and slowly shook his head. "Well, that about does it for today. I'd say his concentration is definitely blown." He turned to Becka. "Listen, you want a ride back to the hotel?"

"What about Scotty?"

"What about me?" Scott asked as he strolled up with Billy and Jackie.

"We'll take him home," Billy offered.

Becka hesitated. "Okay ... I guess we'll see you back at the hotel, then."

"Sounds good to me," Scott said. Without another word, he turned and followed Billy and Jackie out the door.

As soon as they were in the parking lot, Jackie turned to Scott and asked, "Are you coming to the broadcast party?"

"Sure," Scott said without thinking. "Where is it?"

"House up in the hills," Jackie replied. "Starts in a couple of hours. It'll probably be a little wild."

Scott knew that he shouldn't go. Something felt wrong. He

even thought about praying about that feeling. But the broadcast would begin in just a few hours. After that his job would be over. Tomorrow he would be back on the plane heading home. The band would just be a memory.

Before he could stop himself, he answered, "Sure, I'll be there." He tried to ignore the prickly feeling at the back of his mind that seemed to grow stronger.

👁 👁

In Mike's limo on the way home, Becka said another silent prayer. It was time to bring up the subject of the band again. This time she hoped that Mike would understand. "Mike ... I ... I want you to know something. It's only because I care about you that ... that I think it's important for you to think about leaving the band."

Mike's eyes flashed anger. "You sound just like my father when you say that."

"Don't you think your father cares about you?"

"Sure he cares about me. But he wants to control my every move too."

"Isn't that just because he loves you?"

"You don't know him."

"No, I don't. But I do know that God still loves you."

Mike made a face. "Please ..."

"Mike, don't confuse your feelings about your dad with your feelings about Jesus. Your father may have been a pastor, but he wasn't perfect. Christ's love is perfect. Don't turn your back on him."

Mike sighed. "I suppose now you're going to tell me that Jesus wants me to quit the band too?"

"Do you think Jesus wants you to sing songs that give glory to Satan?"

Mike shook his head. "Becka, that's just part of the show!"

As the car pulled into the hotel's parking lot, she turned and looked him straight in the eyes. "Even you don't believe that."

He glanced away.

"Besides, why *pretend* to like the devil just to sell records? How do you think that affects your fans?"

"Look, Rebecca—" Mike's voice was cool and even—"I used to think you cared about me. Now I'm not so sure. I don't know what the deal is, but—"

"Mike—"

He cut her off with an angry shake of his head. "Hey, if you don't want to go out with me, that's cool with me! That's your business! But I'll live my life my way! I don't need your preaching!"

His words stung Becka. She had tried every argument she knew. Nothing had worked. She was sad, frustrated, and mad. Okay, fine! If he didn't want to listen, if he didn't want her help, that was *his* business. She threw the limo door open and stepped out. "If that's the way you want it, Mike Parsek, then that's the way you'll have it!"

She slammed the door and stalked toward the hotel. She could feel his eyes on her. A moment later she heard the limo squeal off down the driveway.

👁 👁

When Becka returned to the suite, she snapped on the computer. There was a new message in her inbox.

"Mom," she asked, "has Scotty seen this?"

Mom shook her head. "I don't think so, dear. He's been in the shower for quite a while."

Becka nodded and clicked on the email. It was from Z.

Rebecca: Don't throw the baby out with the bathwater. Contact me as soon as possible. Z

Becka frowned. "What does that mean?"

"What does what mean, honey?" Mom asked from across the room.

"'Don't throw the baby out with the bathwater.'"

Mom laughed. "Oh, that's an old expression. Your father used to use it all the time. It means don't lose sight of the big picture."

Becka scowled as if she still didn't understand.

Mom smiled. "Sometimes people get so caught up with a little problem that they lose sight of the overall good. You know, like not seeing the forest for the trees."

Becka felt more confused than ever. "I sort of understood you until you got to the trees part. I think I'll just wait to see what Z says."

Mom nodded. "Sounds like a good idea."

"I have to talk to him anyway," Becka continued. "I've gotten nowhere with Mike. The big concert is tonight, we go home tomorrow, and not a thing has changed."

"What do you mean?"

"It's obvious Mike should quit the band. I mean, Doland is so far gone he's practically growing horns. But Mike just won't see it. I'm afraid we've wasted Z's money and our time. So we might as well—"

She came to a stop as Scott emerged from the bathroom. First, there was the towel on his head, which, frankly, looked kind of stupid. Then, after he took the towel off, there was the shock of red hair sticking straight up from his forehead. Not red like a redhead—red like a fire engine.

"Scotty!" Mom half gasped, half shrieked. "Did you dye your hair?"

Scott fingered the rest of his brown locks. "Uh … yeah."

"Why?"

"I figured it would look cool." Scott tried to say it with a straight face, but Becka could tell that he was pretty mortified himself.

She did her best not to snicker, but it was a losing battle.

"What?!" Scott snapped. "What's wrong with it?"

"Nothing's wrong with it," Becka said, trying to hide her laugh with a cough, "if you're a rooster."

Anger struggled with humor on Scott's face. Humor won out when he glanced at his reflection in a mirror. "I guess not everybody looks good in red," he said with a laugh.

"You march right back into the bathroom and wash that stuff out!" Mom ordered. Suddenly she looked a little scared. "It *does* wash out, doesn't it?"

"It's just Kool-Aid, Mom," he said. "Most of it will come out in one wash ... unless you're a blond."

"Then go wash that Kool-Aid out of your hair this instant."

Scott headed back into the bathroom. This was one experiment that had obviously failed.

Becka said nothing more about Scott's hair until after he washed it and sat drying it vigorously with a towel. "You wanted to look like a rocker, didn't you?"

Scott stopped rubbing for a minute. "I wanted to look ... different. Like somebody else besides plain ol' Scott."

Becka nodded. "I kinda went through that a few years ago."

Scott laughed. "You mean when you got that French haircut?"

"Yeah," Becka said, joining in the chuckle. "It did look pretty weird, didn't it?"

Scott shrugged. "Yeah." After another moment, he continued. "So ... you and Mike are through?"

"We're *friends*. That's the way it should be, don't you think?"

"Yeah." Scott nodded. "I mean, you can't forget about Ryan. He's pretty cool. But it was kinda cool to think I had a sister dating somebody famous."

Becka smiled in spite of herself. She grew serious moments

later. "Scott, I'm worried. I think the band could destroy Mike … By the way, I'm not sure it's doing wonders for you."

Scott shook his head. "You're way off base about the band, Beck. I know Doland's a little weird, but Jackie and Grant are okay. And Mike's cool."

Becka decided not to mince words. "Scott … Doland worships the devil. He's a satanist."

"No way!" Scott almost sounded hurt. "That's just an act! It's just so they can sell CDs!"

Becka shook her head. "It may have started out as an act, but it isn't anymore. And even if it is, think about it. They're pretending to like the devil just to sell more CDs. That's pretty sleazy, don't you think?"

Scott looked at her, then shrugged, as if to say that that was just her opinion. But Becka could tell by the way he clammed up that he was thinking things over.

"Scott!" Mom shouted the instant he stopped drying his hair and let the towel fall around his neck. "Your hair … It's … it's yellow!"

Becka put her hand to her mouth in surprise, but a laugh still escaped. "I'd say it's kind of green too."

Scott groaned. "Oh no!" Apparently the Kool-Aid wasn't as easy to wash out as he had thought.

Mom sprang into action. "Get your shirt on. We're going to the salon in the lobby to ask their advice."

"Mom …," Scott complained. "That salon's for girls!"

"Sorry, Scott," Mom said as she handed him the shirt. "We've got no other choice!"

With another loud groan, Scott slipped on his shirt, resigned to his fate.

As soon as they left, Becka heard the laptop ding. Maybe Z was getting bact to her. She crossed to the keyboard quickly.

9

With fingers flying across the keyboard, Becka carefully explained to Z what had happened with Mike. She then asked him to clarify his last message about the baby and the bathwater.

Z's reply was swift.

Many Christians think that members of a band like the Scream are not worth loving.

Becka quickly typed:

The guys in the band aren't bad. They're just confused. Mike is cool though.

Z's response again was swift.

So why are you throwing him out with the bathwater?

Becka suddenly felt guilty and didn't like it. She quickly shot back:

I told him to quit the band. It's not my fault if he doesn't listen. Besides, he wanted TO GO OUT WITH ME. What about Ryan?

Z replied:

Are you angry at Mike or at yourself?

As Becka thought about that question, the memory of the evening she spent at Zuma Beach with Mike replayed itself in her mind. She slowly typed:

I shouldn't have let my guard down around him. I think I was caught up in how I felt.

Z's next words gave Becka a sense of relief.

Wisdom is often gained at a price. You have learned. Forgive yourself and move on. Just because Mike is not the person who should be your boyfriend doesn't mean he can't be a boy who is also a friend.

Becka nodded as she read Z's reply, before quickly explaining her growing fears for Scott. Z replied:

You and Scott are doing what most Christians do when confronted with a culture or group activity that's new to them. They either want nothing to do with it or the people who participate in it (as in your case) or they get so involved that they get caught up in it (like Scott).

Becka typed:

What do I do about Scotty?

Z replied:

Scott's clothes and hair are not the problem. The question is, is he compromising his beliefs?

Becka quickly typed:

How will I know?

Z answered:

Start by asking him. This evening will be your last chance
to reach Mike. Be careful of Doland. And remember
Ephesians 6:11: "Put on the full armor of God so that you
can take your stand against the devil's schemes." Z

Becka signed off, her mind in a whirl. What could she do
to help Mike? She had already told him that he should quit the
band. What else could she say? She understood why it was hard
for him to leave, but the more she recognized the growing evil,
the more the pluses of leaving outweighed those of staying, no
matter how popular the band was.

And then she heard it — a light scratching or rubbing sound
that seemed to come from the bedroom she shared with Mom.
She went into the room and turned on the light. Just as suddenly,
the sound stopped.

It probably came from the next room, she thought. *I'll bet even
in the best hotels you sometimes hear people laughing or making
noise in the next room.*

Becka waited half a minute before she shut off the light and
returned to the main room of the suite. As she flopped on the
sofa, her mind drifted back to Mike. Maybe he didn't need to be
told that he should give up the band. Instead of hearing what he
should do, maybe he just needed to be reminded of God's great
love for him.

Being a pastor's son didn't always mean having a perfect
understanding of God's love. Sometimes pastors were so busy
meeting other people's needs that their families ended up paying the price. Perhaps Mike did not receive all of the attention he
needed. Maybe Mike had forgotten just how loved he was.

Scratch ... scratch ... scratch.

There it was again. The sound *was* coming from their bedroom. But as soon as Becka switched on the light, the sound
stopped. *This is ridiculous,* she thought. But, ridiculous or not, the
sound was driving her nuts ... and making her a little afraid too.

She decided to play a trick of her own. Once again she shut off the light and walked out of the room. Only this time, she tiptoed back in without turning on the light.

Scratch ... scratch ... scratch. Sure enough, the sound started again. *Scratch ... scratch ... scratch.* As she listened closely, she suddenly realized where the sound was coming from. It came from the door that connected their suite to the next one! Someone in the next room was trying to pick the lock!

Heart pounding, Becka made a dive for the phone to call the manager, then changed her mind and tiptoed toward the door leading out of the room. All she could think about was getting out of there! But before she could leave the room, she heard the lock click open.

Someone was coming inside!

She looked around, then quickly ducked into the closet, keeping the door open a crack. She suddenly wished that she and Mom had packed more clothes for better camouflage.

As she peered through the crack, she could see two men moving about the room. One was thin and scraggly looking with a mean face. The other was big, burly, and bald, with a small black beard. They quickly moved through the bedroom toward the main room of the suite. As they passed the closet, Becka could see that the burly man carried a large potato sack and the scraggly guy had some rope.

A cold wave of fear washed over her as she realized that they searched for her. They were planning to kidnap her!

Jesus, help me! she prayed.

"She ain't here," the scraggly guy called.

"Must have snuck out," the other grunted. "You think she heard us?"

"Maybe. We'd better get out of here in case she ran to get help."

"Let's go," the big man agreed. "We'll come back for her tonight when they're all asleep."

Becka heard the men go back through the connecting door and relock it. She waited for what felt like hours but could only have been minutes, praying and trying to calm herself. Finally, she opened the closet door and stepped out.

A sudden flash of light blinded her, while a deep voice shouted, "Get her!"

They had faked her out!

Becka tried to run, but big, meaty hands grabbed her. Another pair of hands slapped a large piece of tape over her mouth.

"Get that bag over her!" the deep voice commanded.

Becka felt the coarse potato sack burn her face as it dropped over her head. Then she felt ropes tied around her hands and the bag.

"Got her," the second voice said. "Doland said to take her to the warehouse."

"Right," the deep voice agreed. "We'll fry her there the same time Doland fries that drummer onstage."

Please help me, Jesus! Becka prayed frantically.

As rough hands grabbed her, she kicked and wriggled but could only move in short hops. She suddenly felt herself hoisted onto someone's shoulder.

Please, Jesus, please!

Just then, she heard the hall door open. Scott's voice called, "Wait'll you see this, Beck!"

She wanted to shout, but her mouth was sealed tight. She felt herself carried toward the connecting door.

"Beck, where are you?"

Suddenly the light came on in the bedroom. She heard Scott shout and the big man's voice yell, *"Run!"*

The next thing she knew she was dropped like ... well, like a sack of potatoes. She heard the swift pounding of footsteps.

Moments later, a very frightened Scott pulled the bag from her face. "Beck, you all right?"

Becka nodded as Scott carefully removed the tape from her mouth. "We've gotta call the cops!" he exclaimed.

When the tape was gone, she gasped for air. "We've got ... we've got to warn Mike! I heard them say Doland is planning on killing him."

"What? Say you're kidding me, Beck!"

Becka shook her head. As soon as Scott untied her, she tried to call Mike, but there was no answer from his room.

"Wait!" Scott said, looking at his watch. "He wouldn't be in his room now. He's at the broadcast party."

"Do you know where it is? We've gotta warn him!"

"Yeah. Jackie gave me the address ... but ... we'll have to take a cab. Mom's downstairs having her hair done. We need to call the cops too, to get after those guys that left!"

"There's no time to get Mom or the police!" Becka snapped. "Leave her a note and let's get outta here!"

Mike stared at the other band members, trying to block out the sound of the party all around them.

"What about 'Army of the Night'?" Jackie suggested. "Are we doing the rap part or not?"

"We've gotta do the rap part," Doland insisted. "The fans really get into that."

"Yeah," Mike replied. "When we did that in Houston, we almost had a riot on our hands."

"A riot? Come on!" Doland mocked. "A couple of chairs get thrown and you call *that* a riot?"

"Some fans got hurt," Mike replied. "*Our* fans."

Doland threw up his hands. "Nobody got hurt bad—"

"One girl had to get seventeen stitches in her forehead. I'd call that bad enough."

Doland fidgeted, barely able to contain his anger. "Oh, you're such a defender of the people now, aren't you, Mikey? Next thing you know, you'll be running for office, man."

Mike shook his head in disgust. He'd had it. "I'm outta here!" He started to leave but turned back. "I just want to know one thing, Doland."

"What's that?"

"Is there *anyone* or *anything* left in this world that you care about … besides yourself?"

Mike turned and walked away, barely missing Doland's sly smile. As the door closed, Doland turned to the others and grinned. "Now the party *really* begins."

👁 👁

Fifteen minutes later, Scott and Becka's cab arrived at the party site.

"Twenty-two dollars?" Becka gulped.

The cabdriver nodded. "This is L.A., miss. There ain't no place easy to get to."

Becka nodded but didn't completely understand. "Here … I'm sorry, I've only got fifty cents left for a tip."

The cabdriver sneered. "Well, ain't this *my* lucky day."

They headed up the walk and rang the bell. Billy Phelps opened the door. "Hey, guys. C'mon in."

"Do you know where Mike is?" Becka asked.

Billy scratched his head. "He just left. He and Doland had another argument, so he took off. Doland and the guys left right after that."

"Oh no!" Becka said. "We've gotta talk to him!"

Billy shrugged. "Try the hotel."

"I … I don't have enough money for a cab."

"Don't worry about it," Billy said. "The other limo is parked in back. Just tell the driver I said it was okay. He'll take you."

Becka smiled. "Thanks, Billy. Let's go, Scotty!"

Scott hesitated. "I'd kinda like to stay here, if it's okay, Beck."

She turned to him, not believing her ears. "After all that hap-pened—you want to stay here?"

Scott shrugged, not able to fully explain why he wanted to stay. He glanced around and lowered his voice to avoid Billy's hearing. "You don't know for certain that those guys were con-nected with the band."

"I heard them use Doland's name!"

"You probably *thought* you heard them use his name. After all, you were inside that sack getting thrown all around."

"Scotty, who else would've put those guys up to it?!"

"Scott can ride with us to the gig," Billy suddenly said, trying to be helpful. "That way he can help us check everything out."

"C'mon, Beck," Scott pleaded. "This is my last chance to ride with the biggest band in the country ..."

Becka wasn't sure what to do. But she knew she had to get to the hotel as fast as she could. "You say Doland's already left?"

Billy nodded.

That gave her some comfort.

"Don't worry, big sis," Billy said with a grin. "I'll take care of your little bro."

Becka slowly nodded. "Okay ... but be careful." She ran toward the limo.

👁 👁

As soon as Becka was out of sight, Billy turned to Scott. "So, you want a beer?"

"Uh ... yeah, sure." Guilt washed over him the minute the words were out of his mouth, but he just clenched his teeth. So what if he was underage? So what if he hated the taste of beer? What he hated even worse was looking like he didn't fit in. Besides, one little beer couldn't hurt, could it?

A few seconds later, Billy had shoved a brew into his hand and headed off, leaving Scott to wander the party, pretending to sip his beer and trying not to look like a geek. He failed in both departments.

It didn't take long to notice that the people at the party were even stranger than the ones at the party after the concert. Nearly all of them were dressed in black. Several had symbols painted on their faces. As Scott walked around, he realized lots of drugs were being passed around.

Scott managed to avoid the occasional joint that was passed through the crowd, but it became clearer by the second that staying had been a mistake. Seeing the plastic skulls, daggers, and pentagrams all over the place didn't help matters either.

He knew that he was taking a risk even being here. But after all he'd been through in the past year, he still sometimes questioned whether having faith in God was worth it. Sometimes having faith was like asking for trouble.

He tried convincing himself to be more open-minded, to pretend that the skulls and daggers were just decorations — like a perpetual Halloween party. That might have worked too, if he hadn't spotted people in the corner chanting some kind of gobbledygook and others in the kitchen burning black candles and joining hands in a séance.

So much for open-mindedness. He was in way over his head.

Scott searched for Billy to get a ride home. He found him kissing a girl in another room. He felt embarrassed having to interrupt. "Hey, Billy ..."

"Not now, sport," Billy said without looking up. "Come back later."

Scott backed out of the room, unsure of how he was going to get out of there. He decided to see if the limo had returned. But as soon as he stepped into the backyard, he sensed that something else was wrong. His head began to hurt slightly, the way it had in past demonic encounters. He spotted Jackie and Grant standing with about a dozen others near a small bonfire and headed toward them.

As he approached, he nearly ran into Doland, who headed up the driveway carrying a small cat. The rocker turned and glared at him but said nothing. Instead, he continued past him and walked to the center of the small circle of people.

Scott watched, swallowing back his fear as Doland raised the squirming cat over his head and pointed it toward the fire. The poor animal was in a panic. It wriggled wildly, desperately trying to get away.

"So, almighty one," Doland called out, "give to us portions of your power as we offer this sacrifice to you."

Sacrifice! Doland was about to sacrifice that poor cat to the devil. Before he could think about it, Scott shouted, "Stop! What do you think you're doing?!"

The group turned and stared at him. But it was Doland's gaze that frightened him the most. In the glow of the fire, the singer's eyes seemed to shine. As his body began to shake, he looked like a wild man ... like someone losing control of his will ... like someone who had just opened himself up to another spirit.

Realizing he'd used up all of his courage with that first shout, Scott silently prayed, *Dear Jesus, please help me. I've ... I've really been stupid. I'm in way over my head. Forgive me for not praying sooner. Please step in here with your power.*

Doland shook more violently. Moments later, Scott's prayer seemed to have an effect on Doland. He suddenly stopped shaking and took a step toward Scott.

"You want this cat, freak?" Doland yelled, holding the wriggling animal above his head.

Scott nodded. He wanted to speak but didn't trust his voice.

Doland's smile twisted across his face as he suddenly hurled the cat at Scott. He managed to get his hands up to prevent his face from being scratched, but his arms weren't so lucky. The cat's claws tore into him, drawing blood from three deep cuts.

Scott yelped in pain. Even so, he was glad to see the cat land safely on the lawn and bolt into the night. He slowly backed away from Doland.

Doland continued glaring at him but didn't come after him. "That's right!" Doland shouted. "Better get out of here, loser!... Get out while you still can!"

❧ ❧

Becka's limo pulled into the big, circular driveway in front of the hotel. She looked up in time to see Mike getting into a cab that started to pull away. She leaped from the limo and chased the cab down the drive, shouting and waving her hands. "Stop! Wait a minute! Mike! Stop!"

But the cab never stopped.

Frustrated, she turned around only to see the limo she had traveled in pull away as well. Again she ran, shouting and waving. This time she was heard. The limo stopped, and the driver rolled down the window. He was a kindly looking, gray-haired gentleman. "Yes, miss?"

Becka tried to catch her breath. "Can ... can you take me to the auditorium?"

The limo driver looked at his watch. "I suppose so, miss. But we'll have to leave right this moment so I'll have enough time to swing back and pick up the others from the party."

Becka looked back toward the hotel. She wanted to call the suite to have Mom come down. But there just wasn't time!

With a quick prayer, she climbed back into the limo. It sped off into the night.

❧ ❧

Scott held firmly to Billy's jacket as Billy's motorcycle pulled in front of the auditorium.

"Thanks for the ride, Billy!" Scott shouted as he climbed off the bike.

"No problem, man. Listen, I've gotta go in and check some wires ... Here's the money you earned working with the crew. I really don't think it'd be a good idea for Doland to see you after what happened at the party. So, you just stay out front, okay?"

Scott nodded. As he took the money, his eyes widened. "Wow! A hundred and fifty bucks! I didn't work enough hours for that!"

"Don't worry ... Consider it hazard pay for those cat scratches," he chuckled. "Besides, the other guys on the crew drink up that much just in beer. See you around, Scott."

"See ya, Billy."

👁 👁

Back at the hotel, the lights were off. The hotel room was illuminated only by the flickering flame of the black candle in the center of a table. Doland, the large bald man, and three groupies held hands across the table. The chant began, low at first, but then gradually increasing until it became a shout: "All must die! All must die! All must die!"

And with each word, Doland felt the power within him growing stronger. Tonight would be the night.

10

Becka was one of fifty teenagers crowding around the backstage door in the auditorium. A huge man with a green beard and a red-dot tattoo in the center of his forehead blocked the entrance. As far as Becka could tell, he only spoke four words: "Not on the list." That's what he said to the girl in front of her and what he said to a dozen others before that.

Becka had had no problem getting inside the auditorium. But the wait at the backstage door was long as one teen after another tried to persuade the guard to let him or her pass.

Each time, he scanned a tiny piece of paper in his hands and said, "Not on the list." Becka guessed that there couldn't have been very many names on the list, since the piece of paper was no larger than a bubble-gum wrapper.

Finally, her turn had arrived. "Hi," she said. "Remember me? I was here the other night for the concert."

The big man showed no sign of recognition.

"I'm Rebecca Williams. I'm a friend of Mike Parsek's."

"Not on the list," the guard said, barely glancing at the paper.

"No," Becka said. "I'm on the list. I'm sure of it. You didn't look close enough. Rebecca Williams."

The guard looked again. "Not on the list."

Becka shook her head, fighting the panic that threatened to wash over her. "No! That can't be right! It's very important that I see Mike before the show. His life may be in danger. Maybe it's under Becka Williams. Look up that name. He calls me that sometimes."

The guard's eyes glazed over.

Becka suddenly felt the girl behind her press against her. "Hurry up, will you?" she muttered. "The man said you're not on the list. So, go already!"

Becka turned around. "This is not what you think. I *am* a friend of Mike's, and he said—"

The girl made a face. "I heard he dumped you."

Becka was shocked. How would this girl know anything about that? "He did not ... no one dumped anyone. We were just friends and ... if anyone dumped anyone, it was *I* who did the dumping ..."

Again Becka turned back and looked at the guard, hoping that somehow he would remember her.

"Not on the list," he repeated.

❧ ❧

Mike stood behind the curtain. The auditorium looked virtually the same as it had for the previous show, except for the more elaborate lighting. One new piece of equipment had been added—an even larger fire cannon.

As Mike strode onto the stage, Billy came out from behind the control board. "So what do you think of her, Mike?" Billy asked, looking at the cannon.

"It's a monster."

"You should see it fire! I tested it earlier today. The fireball went about forty feet up into the rafters. I thought it was gonna blast right through the roof!"

Mike frowned. "What about the crowd? Are we going to be raining fire on them?"

Billy shook his head. "No, it dissolves into nothing after that initial blast. But I'd sure hate to be in that first forty feet. There'd be nothing left but cinders and ash."

Mike nodded, looking slowly along the length of the huge, shiny black barrel. "You're sure this thing is safe?"

"Sure," Billy said. "It's got a warranty and everything. We're gonna fire it off about three times during your solo at half strength and then at full strength at the end like we usually do."

As Mike stared into the large black hole at the end of the barrel, an uneasy feeling swept over him. He shook it off, feeling frustrated. He'd been listening to Rebecca Williams too much.

👁 👁

By the time the broadcast had begun, Becka had tried the other five backstage entrances with the same results. In fact, she was pretty sure the guards must be related because they all looked alike and said the same thing.

Except for the last guy. Instead of "Not on the list," he chose to say "Beat it, bimbo" to every girl and "Beat it, jerk-boy" to every guy.

Finally, the lights dimmed and the music began. With a resigned sigh, Becka searched for her seat.

The crowd was even larger and rowdier than before—for good reason. There were TV cameras everywhere. It was a big event, all right, and the band rose to the occasion.

As Becka made her way to her seat, Doland was already cutting loose in the first song. He was frantic—a madman with a microphone. The crowd hung on his every word.

"Over here! Becka, over here!"

She turned toward the familiar voice and saw Scott waving at her, pointing to the empty seat. "We're over here!" he shouted.

She moved through the crowd toward him, yelling, "I thought you were backstage!"

Scott shrugged as she finally arrived. "Doland showed up at the party and some weird stuff started happening. I'm kinda fired. But Billy gave me a ride over and paid me a hundred and fifty bucks!"

Becka looked at him, caught by one part of what he'd said. "What kind of weird stuff?"

Over the pounding music, Scott explained the intended animal sacrifice and showed her the scratches. "They don't hurt too bad!" he shouted. "Billy poured hydrogen peroxide on them before we took off."

Becka's stomach churned. Something was going to happen. She was certain of it. "I never got to talk to Mike!" she yelled. "Security wouldn't let me pass!"

By now the concert was in full swing. As the TV cameras rolled, the Scream gave the performance of a lifetime. Doland never let up. Jackie Vee's fingers flew over the strings of his guitar as though he were carving an intricate sculpture out of a wall of sound. But it was the rhythm section that really dominated. Mike Parsek was at his peak, pounding out the beat as Grant Simone tracked him lick for lick on the bass.

They were phenomenal, and everyone in the auditorium knew it.

It wasn't until Mike launched into his solo that Becka noticed the new fire cannon. It was huge. But that wasn't what caused her breath to catch. There was something oddly familiar about it. A chill suddenly washed over her ...

It was the cannon from her dream.

As Mike increased the pace of his solo, Becka's heart pounded. She had to warn him. Suddenly, a terrible blast shot a huge tongue of fire into the air above the crowd. Everyone screamed, including Becka.

"Take it easy!" Scott shouted to her. "It's all part of the show."

Becka's eyes shot to him. "Not this time, Scotty! This time I think Doland is—"

The sentence was cut off by another mighty blast, even bigger than the last. The crowd screamed as never before, and Mike picked up the pace.

Becka caught sight of Doland as he cheered Mike on from the edge of the stage. One by one the other members of the band left the stage just as they had during the other show. Mike was left to carry on with a fury of drum rhythms.

Becka's eyebrows rose as Doland suddenly slipped behind the curtain. *What's he up to?* she thought. A moment later, she caught a glimpse of him all alone at the control panel. Billy had moved from the panel to watch Mike along with everyone else.

"Scott, let me borrow those binoculars!" Becka shouted. She snatched them and quickly focused on Doland. He was quickly turning a knob on the control panel.

Just like my dream! she thought. Only instead of a gnarled and twisted claw touching the control panel, it was Doland.

Becka began to pray. But when she looked up at the barrel of the cannon, she groaned. It slowly turned toward Mike ... just as it had in her dream.

Becka bolted, pushing her way through the crowd. She knew she'd never get close enough to warn Mike, but she had to try. *Jesus, Jesus, help me!* she prayed.

Scott moved behind her, trying to help them both navigate through the crowd. But the crowd was wall to wall. No one moved.

"Excuse me! Excuse me, please!" Becka shouted over and over again.

But no one listened.

"Out of the way!" Scott yelled. "This girl's sick! She's going to puke any second! Let us through!"

The crowd instantly parted. Becka and Scott squeezed toward the stage.

Mike neared the peak of his solo. He was so intent on his playing that he didn't even notice the cannon barrel slowly turning toward him.

"Mike!" Becka shouted. "The cannon! The cannon!"

Scott joined in. "The cannon, Mike! Get out of there!"

But it was no use. They could not be heard.

Becka continued pushing through the crowd. The cannon was aimed directly at Mike as he launched into the height of his solo. In just a few moments, it would fire.

"Please, Lord!" Becka prayed out loud now, not caring who heard her. "Save him! Save him!"

Mike feverishly pounded the drums. Becka was so close she could feel the vibrations coming from the cannon as it prepared to ignite.

There were only seconds left. Becka and Scott pushed through the crowd harder and quicker but were still too far from the stage.

They weren't going to make it. She wouldn't be able to warn Mike.

She felt Scott grab her. "Get on my back!" he shouted. "Hurry!"

Scott boosted Becka up to his shoulders. She frantically waved. "Mike! Mike!"

The cannon began to shake.

"MIKE! MIKE!"

And then, suddenly, he looked up and saw her waving.

She pointed frantically toward the cannon.

He turned and saw the barrel pointed his way.

Suddenly, a colossal explosion rocked the stage. Becka screamed, but Mike was already in the air. He leaped off the drum riser, flying through the flames as they ignited his platform, his drums—everything around him.

The crowd screamed as the curtains caught fire. Panic filled the auditorium as fans stampeded toward the exit.

Becka managed to catch a final glimpse of Mike before she tumbled from Scott's shoulders. He staggered to his feet. He looked a little worn and bruised, but he was unhurt.

"Thank you, dear God," Becka prayed as she was jostled this way and that. "Thank you ..."

❤ ❤

In all of the confusion that followed, Becka and Scott managed to slip by the guard at the backstage door. Once past him, they hurried down the long corridor that ran underneath the stage. When they came out on the other side, they saw Mike helping Billy, Jackie, and Grant clear the instruments and sound equipment away from the charred and smoldering curtain.

"Mike!" Becka shouted as she ran into his waiting arms. They embraced for a long moment.

Finally, Becka pulled away. "I've been trying to warn you for hours!" She swallowed as a sob threatened to choke her voice. "Thank God you're all right." She gave a shaky sigh before continuing, "When two men tried to kidnap me at the hotel, I heard one of them mention Doland's name and something about frying the drummer onstage, and ... and—" her eyes burned as tears cascaded down her cheeks—"I tried so hard to warn you!"

"You *did* warn me," Mike said softly. He looked deeply into her eyes. "You saved my life!"

Again she embraced him, so happy that he was alive.

"Too bad."

The voice made her grow cold. She turned around to see Doland sneering. "You spoiled the show!" He stalked toward them menacingly. "I wanted to burn you onstage, Mikey. It would've been the best publicity stunt ever. Now, I just get to fire you the normal way."

"You can't fire me," Mike said, his voice trembling slightly.

"And why is that?"

"Because I quit. You're one sick freak, man! I want nothing to do with you or your music!"

"Oh, I'm crushed," Doland sneered. "Lucky for me drummers are a dime a dozen. We can find another one anytime we want."

"Not with me, you won't."

Becka turned to see Jackie stepping forward.

"Or me," Grant said, moving up beside him. "I'm quitting too. We're all quitting!"

Jackie Vee nodded. "You've gone too far this time, Doland. I think the cops want a word with you now, for what you tried to do to Mike. You're goin' down this time, man."

For a second Doland seemed lost, but only for a second. He spun back around to Becka and Scott, his features suddenly contorting.

Becka braced herself. She had the feeling that something horrible was coming next.

"This is your fault!" Doland suddenly growled. His voice was guttural, unearthly. *"You are the ones who must pay!"*

The other band members stepped back in alarm as Doland's face contorted until it was unrecognizable.

Becka stood still, watching. This was the hatred she had felt from the moment she first stepped off the shuttle bus at the hotel and caught sight of Doland. Now, waves of hatred bored into her with amazing intensity.

For an instant Doland's face seemed like a grotesque gargoyle mask. She had seen a sudden transformation like that in other encounters.

Doland's face just as suddenly turned back to normal. But she wasn't fooled. She knew the battle was finally out in the open.

As Doland started toward her, she opened her mouth to speak. But nothing came out! Alarm washed over her. She couldn't speak! It wasn't fear—she knew that. She didn't know what it was! Could this be a new power she had never encountered before?

Father, help me! she prayed silently. As she did so, peace washed over her. But still she couldn't speak.

Suddenly, she heard Scott praying softly behind her. "Deliver us from evil, O Lord. Deliver us from evil."

Doland hesitated, shooting Scott an angry glare. He continued toward them. Soon, he was only four feet away.

Becka still was held in silence.

Another voice — Mike Parsek's — suddenly joined Scott's prayer. "Deliver us from evil, O Lord. Deliver us from evil." His voice was barely above a whisper.

At that moment, it was as though a gag were removed. Becka knew that she could talk once more. Swift understanding came to her: God had given Mike the opportunity to step out in faith. And he'd done it! Now she was allowed to move in and help. She took a slow, deep breath and spoke clearly: "In the name of the Lord Jesus Christ, I command you to stop!"

Instantly, Doland stopped moving.

Becka swallowed, then continued, "I speak to the demonic force controlling Tommy Doland." Her voice was stronger now. "In the name of Jesus Christ and by the power of his blood, I command you to leave! Come out from Doland — now! Come out of him and never enter him again!"

For an instant the gargoyle-like mask reappeared. But suddenly, Doland's face returned to normal, as if the demon had settled back inside of him once more.

"What's going on?" Mike whispered.

Doland grinned and took a step toward Becka.

"I said come out of him!" Becka ordered. "Come out in the name of Jesus Christ!"

Doland's features changed rapidly in quick succession.

"He doesn't want it to go," Scott explained, with a note of wonder and sadness in his voice.

Becka continued to hold Doland's glare. Despite his hatred and the hideous sneer, she felt sorry for him. Very, very sorry.

Mike looked on, then quietly spoke. "He's condemned himself."

Slowly, sadly, Becka nodded. But there was more work to be done. Her voice broke through the silence, bold and confident. "In the name of Jesus, I command you to leave! Leave and do no more harm to these people!"

Instantly, Doland staggered back. It was as if he were suddenly afraid to even look at them. He retreated another step or two before turning and slinking across the stage.

"Remember," Becka called, "you are bound from ever harming these people again. We command that in the power and authority of Jesus Christ."

All watched in silence as Tommy Doland exited the stage. The police waited for him near the bottom of the stage.

A couple of crew members started to mumble. They'd obviously seen nothing like this before. And, as the encounter faded, Becka felt the weakness return to her body. It was one thing to speak in faith, to feel the power of the Holy Spirit surging through her. But it was quite another to be plain ol' Rebecca Williams.

👁 👁

The following day Mike drove Becka, Scott, and Mom to the airport. The four of them had spent most of the night together. By the end of the evening, Mike had not only quit the band but had recommitted his life to Jesus Christ. And, thanks to Mom's gentle urgings, he had even agreed to visit his parents.

"No promises," he said, "but I'll give it another shot."

Now, as they stood at the gate ready to board the plane, Mike turned to Becka one last time. "If it's okay with you, I really *do* want to be your friend."

She looked up at him, swallowing back the tightness growing in her throat.

He continued, "You're one of the few people I know who cares about me because I'm me ... and not just because I was a member of the hottest band in the country."

She nodded and looked at the ground. It was important that he not see her tears. Saying good-bye was harder than she had expected.

"Oh, and, Scott—" he turned toward her little brother—"I've got something for you." He reached into a small bag and pulled out a Scream T-shirt. "I'm afraid it got a little singed in the fire, but I think you'll like the way it turned out."

He held it up. The shirt was perfectly fine ... except that one letter was scorched. Where it had once read *Army of the Night*, part of the *N* was burned and smudged. It now read *Army of the Light*.

Scott beamed as he took it. "'Army of the Light.' Now *that's* cool."

A minute later they said their final good-byes. Becka, Scott, and Mom walked down the ramp toward their plane. Becka guessed that Mike would remain to watch their plane take off. Her eyes filled with tears. But they weren't tears of sadness. They were tears of gratitude. She was grateful that they had decided to simply stay friends. But she was even more grateful that once again, Mike Parsek had found, and was getting acquainted with, his very best Friend.

On the plane Becka couldn't help but notice that Scott looked more like his old self. "Hey, Scotty, where are the torn jeans?" she teased. "You look halfway normal."

Scott shrugged. "I don't know. I guess I kind of lost interest in all that stuff. I mean, I used to think it was, like, really being real ... But there was an awful lot about those people that wasn't real at all. They used all that fake booze and stuff just to psych out the audience."

Mom nodded. "It's kind of strange how things turned out. At first the Scream and all of their fans were people I'd want to avoid like the plague. But if we had, then Mike might not have returned to his faith."

Scott agreed. "God really does care about everybody. I guess we can't write anybody off."

"But that doesn't mean we have to be like them," Becka said, giving him a teasing smile.

"Yeah," Scott sighed as he rubbed his hair, which still had a touch of yellow and green in it. "I wonder what the guys on my baseball team are going to say about this."

In less than two hours the family had arrived at another airline ramp. Only this time they were close to home. Becka was the first to see Ryan at the gate. His jet-black hair and sparkling smile made him stand out from the crowd. In one hand he clutched an envelope, in the other a welcome-home bouquet of flowers.

Before she knew it, she found herself running through the waiting area to greet him. As they embraced, she held him tighter than she had ever held him before. She suddenly realized how much she had missed him. When they separated, fresh tears sprang to her eyes.

"Hey," he asked in concern, "are you okay?"

She nodded, unable to speak.

"Are you sure?"

She could only roll her eyes. Men ... would they ever learn?

"Hey, Ryan!" Scott called.

"Hey, Scott. Hi, Mrs. Williams."

"Flowers for me?" Scott joked. "Why, Ryan, you shouldn't have."

"You're right. I shouldn't, and I wouldn't." He faked a punch at Scott and gave the flowers to Becka.

"Ryan ... they're beautiful." Once again tears welled up in her eyes.

Ryan frowned. "Maybe it's allergies," he said. "You should probably have that looked into."

Before Becka could answer, Scott did what he did best ... butt in. "What is that?" he asked, motioning to the manila envelope in Ryan's other hand.

"Four tickets to New Mexico. They came in the mail a few days ago," Ryan said. "They're from Z."

"Z?" Becka asked.

Ryan nodded.

"Cool," Scott quipped. "Sounds like another assignment is about to begin."

Becka let out a low, quiet sigh. At that moment she'd had enough of Z's assignments. She just wanted to go home and get some rest.

She was glad when Ryan took her hand as they headed toward baggage claim to pick up their luggage. She had no idea what awaited them in New Mexico — or what spiritual counterfeit she'd have to face next. But for now she was just grateful to be home.

Discussion questions for *The Scream:*

1. Mike had become uncomfortable with how frenzied and dangerous the Scream's show had gotten—especially after Billy got burned. He'd spoken repeatedly to Tommy about it but was just mocked for being concerned. What do you think Mike should have done next?

2. As Scott continued to share the news of his trip to L.A. to see the Scream, Becka said he went from a member of the audience to "a personal friend of the band." Scott denied that he was lying to his friend Darryl, but clearly didn't set him straight when Darryl got the impression that Scott was friends with the band. Is it lying if Scott didn't correct Darryl's assumption? Discuss a situation when you may have lied by omission.

3. Becka was conflicted about going to L.A. to help the Scream. But the Sunday church service before their flight offered her some clarity when the pastor talked about loving those who are trapped or who are different than us. We're called to reach out and help them, even if we disagree with their actions. Have you tried to show God's love through acceptance of those different than you? How did things turn out?

4. Becka has recurring stomach troubles—something she always feels when she encounters something demonic. Have you ever been in a situation where you felt the presence of evil? Did you have any physical symptoms? If so, what were they?

5. Becka was torn between two biblical principles: flee from evil, and help bring light into the darkness. Her mother explained that it's important to listen to what God is telling

you to do and when to do it. Discuss a situation when you needed to decide whether to stay and flee. What did you do? Did the person/people ever see the light?

6. Becka calls on God in prayer very often throughout this story. She goes to him during moments of feeling uneasy to moments of confronting evil head-on. She always feels better in just knowing the answer would come at the right time. When do you pray to God? Is it when you want or need something, or do you ever pray simply out of gratitude? Do you feel any different after you pray?

7. Mike realized that Doland was pretty over the edge. He felt that Jackie and Grant knew it too, but no one wanted to confront Doland. What are the reasons that prevented them from confronting the lead singer? Have you ever had to confront someone that you knew was spiritually out of control? How did that go?

8. Z warned Becka that the devil knows our weaknesses and uses them against us. She remembered this advice practically in mid-kiss with Mike, realizing that perhaps the devil was using her weakness for cute boys to sidetrack her from the assignment. Scotty was side tracked by his weakness too. What was his and how did he give in? What is your weakness?

9. Mike didn't believe in the dark direction that Doland was taking the band, and how it was affecting their audiences. For a long time, however, he just went along with it. There is a popular saying, "The only thing necessary for the triumph of evil is for good men to do nothing." What does this mean to you? Have you ever seen one person take a stand and make a huge difference? Discuss the potential of how one person can make a difference.

10. Becka confronts Doland after Mike nearly gets blasted by the cannon during the telecast. The evil spirits within Doland are clearly present, and despite Becka's prayers, they remained. Doland condemns himself, but once Becka shines the light of God in her prayer and conviction, Mike, Jackie, and Grant all quit the band. Have you ever witnessed the power of God's light? What happened?

Author's Note

As I developed this series, I had two equal and opposing concerns. First, I didn't want the reader to be too frightened of the devil. Compared to Jesus Christ, Satan is a wimp. The two aren't even in the same league. Although the supernatural evil in these books is based on a certain amount of fact, it's important to understand the awesome protection Jesus Christ offers to those who have committed their lives to him.

This brings me to my second and somewhat opposing concern: Although the powers of darkness are nothing compared to the power of Jesus Christ and the authority he has given his followers, spiritual warfare is not something we casually stroll into. The situations in these novels are extreme to create suspense and drama. But if you should find yourself involved in something even vaguely similar, don't confront it alone. Find an older, more mature Christian (such as a parent, pastor, or youth leader) to talk to. Let him or her check the situation out to see what's happening. Ask him or her to help you deal with it.

Yes, we have the victory through Christ. But we should never send in inexperienced soldiers to fight the battle.

Oh, and one final note. When this series was conceived, there were really no bad guys on the Internet. Unfortunately that has changed. Today there are plenty of people out there trying to draw young folks into dangerous situations through it. Although the characters in this series trust Z, if you should run into a similar situation, be smart. Anyone can *sound* kind and understanding, but their intentions may be entirely different. All that to say, don't take candy from strangers you see ... or trust those you don't.

Bill

Powerful Pastimes

Are you into horror movies with creeping beings? How about films with brooding, pale heroes who need to fight their urge for blood in order to keep the girl of their dreams? And what about dark music with screaming guitars, questionable lyrics, and singers who live dangerously on the edge? In today's culture, *paranormal* often means entertainment, and Christians and non-Christians alike can't seem to get enough.

It's all pretty harmless, right? After all, werewolves and vampires and zombies don't exist, and the singers are just putting on a show. But as Becka, Ryan, and Scott discover on their travels in *Deadly Loyalty Collection*, things we think are imaginary or just for fun can actually have a lot of power.

Not long ago vampires captured our attention. They were everywhere—from books to films to TV shows. Don't get me wrong, they can have a certain attraction—incredibly dangerous, calculating, appearing human but hiding a dark secret that could mean our demise. The new breed of vampire is a tortured soul who makes hearts swoon and can even come across as the perfect boyfriend. In fact, they can be soalluring that some people actually want to be vampires themselves ... and convince themselves they really are members of the living undead.

As Becka experienced on the set of *The Vampire Returns*, over time even rational people can start to wonder if vampires are real. In our world very few individuals actually think they can turn into a bat and live forever. But there are people who think they are different, and over time come to believe they need blood to survive. In fact, if you were to speak to a "vampire," they would most likely tell you they can't define exactly what a vampire is, or how they became one, but that they felt themselves change at some point. To solve the vampires-don't-age issue, they may even say they will simply reincarnate and be reborn over and over.

It sounds silly, but those who think they are vampires can actually be dangerous. As the popularity of vampires rose so did violent crimes committed by people who kill in order to drink human blood. So-called covens appeared, luring in people who wanted to meet a vampire and have their blood drank. Even major news programs have done pieces on the dangers of the vampire world.

You may say, "I don't think I'm a vampire, so what's the problem?" While the Bible doesn't talk specifically about vampires, it does warn us against being sucked too deeply into the ways of the world, and it warns us to protect ourselves from the influences of evil. Romans 12:2 tells us not to let the world shape our thinking, but to let Christ reshape our thinking into ways that are brand-new. So while it isn't *wrong* to read a novel with vampires in it or wear a cape to a party, we need to keep focused on what is good and true. The legends and even modern-day stories of vampires can be very dark and take our minds off what is healthy and good for our souls.. And, since we've only got one mind and one soul, why let someone mess with them?

The same can be true for other elements in our culture. As Mike Parsek learned in *The Scream*, you can get tangled in something you never intended if you aren't careful. He went into the band thinking the Satanist persona was all for fun, and no one was getting hurt. But by the end, things had slowly escalated, until his lead singer was caught up in definite devil stuff.

No one's saying watching a dark movie or listening to heavy metal will turn us into Tommy Doland, but there are things that can gradually pull us in. We've all heard the old saying, "you are what you consume" more times than we can remember, but it doesn't stop it from being true. Think about your favorite band or singer: How do their songs make you feel? How often do you listen to them? And how many times have their songs played over and over in your head? Music is a powerful tool for good or evil. It can literally change the way we think. The question is, are we letting it influence our thinking for the good or the bad?

Scott enjoys the Scream because of the music's appeal. He never really thinks the lyrics will affect him. Of course, it doesn't hurt that the band is also famous, and being associated with it boosts his popularity. As a result, he dismisses Becka's and his mom's concerns, even though it's pretty clear there are some strange things going on. It's not until he sees the truth about Tommy that he realizes how close he was to slipping into a world he never would have entered otherwise.

If something makes you uncomfortable, walk away. There's a good chance that the feeling is God's way of warning you. (He's a big fan of protecting those he loves). Similarly, if a band or song, or anything else you spend your time with, doesn't fit in with God's ways and with what he says, it may be time to reconsider your involvement. In their journey to Louisiana, Becka and Scott run into different characters who try and channel the spirits of the dead hoping to gain power over their own lives. However, these spirits are nothing more than demons in disguise. As we've seen from the siblings' other adventures, giving demonic entities influence in our lives never turns out well.

Things like voodoo have become exciting plot points in TV shows and movies. Though it may seem like a bunch of silly rituals, there is real power behind voodoo, and a number of witch doctors around the world have been reported to possess the power to curse people—including Christians. We are in a spiritual war, but Jesus gave us power to win. In fact, in John 14:12, Jesus says that whoever has faith in him would do the same things that he did ... and even greater. If we study his life, we see that one thing he did over and over again was free people from curses and evil spirits. It's important to remember the enemy does have some power—but if we belong to Christ, we have nothing to fear. This doesn't mean we should go looking for a fight with witch doctors or seek out make-believe vampires. But it does mean that when we are face-to-face with those things, we can rely on Christ's promises that we can overcome anything the devil throws our way. If you're a Christian, then the Holy Spirit, the same power that raised Jesus Christ from the dead, lives inside of you. Demonic powers are nothing compared to that. They know where they stand, so they try and trick us, using fear, superstition, and lies to distract us from what we can really do in Christ's name..

The devil knows he's going down (take a look at John 16:11) and he's trying to take as many people with him as he can. But remember God is in total control, and he has given his children authority over ALL the work of the enemy.

For more information about recognizing occult activity and the power that Jesus has over it, check out **www.Billmyers.com** or read *The Dark Side of the Supernatural* by Bill Myers and Dave Wimbish.

Forbidden Doors

A Four-Volume Series from Bestselling Author Bill Myers!

Join teenager Rebecca "Becka" Williams, her brother, Scott, and her friend Ryan Riordan as they head for mind-bending clashes between the forces of darkness and the kingdom of God.

Dark Power Collection

Contains: *The Society,*
The Deceived, and *The Spell*

Invisible Terror Collection

Contains: *The Haunting,*
The Guardian, and *The Encounter*

Deadly Loyalty Collection

Contains: *The Curse,*
The Undead, and *The Scream*

Ancient Forces Collection

Contains: *The Ancients,*
The Wiccan, and *The Cards*

ZONDERVAN®
.com

The Dark Side of the Supernatural, Revised and Expanded Edition

Uncovering God's Truth

You've seen movies and TV shows or read books that have supernatural ideas. A lot of times, it's entertaining. Boys who are warlocks with magical powers, women who see the future, a girl who sees and talks to dead people—as ideas go, these have great potential to tell a good story. But is it real? And if so, what does that mean?

Bill Myers has spent years researching supernatural phenomenon, and has even made movies on the topic. In this book, he'll share his research, along with interviews and true-life experiences of psychics, Satanists, and people who have been possessed, or even abducted by aliens. His encounters with a variety of supernatural topics will open your eyes to what is real and what is fantasy. You'll learn more about:

- Wicca and witches
- Reincarnation
- UFO's
- Ouija boards
- Angels and demons
- Ghosts and near-death experiences
- Satanism
- Vampires, and more

If you're curious about these issues, or have friends who are caught up in them, *The Dark Side of the Supernatural* will uncover the truth and explain how to help.

Available in stores and online!